CAPTIVE BEAUTY

Edin shrank back against the wall, trying to disappear. But her captor was relentless. He folded his arms
over his chest and glared at her. He commanded, "Take
off your clothes."

When she hesitated, he reminded her, "I could do it
for you." And he thought, *She will obey me, by Thor! She
will obey me or else—*

Edin didn't look at him, but slowly, unsteadily began
to disrobe.

Her arms were raised, her torso taut, her breasts
lifted. Then her lovely face emerged, with her spill of
thigh-length golden hair, and Thoryn felt like he'd been
drinking fire. He wanted this Saxon captive with more
desire than he'd ever wanted a woman before. But the
Viking wanted more than his own satisfaction. He
wanted her will, her responding desire, and he swore
that before the night was through he'd own not only her
body, but her heart as well. . . .

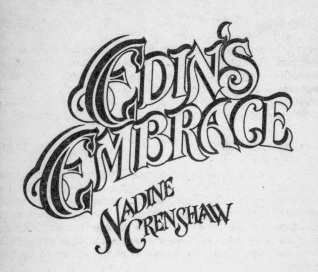

EDIN'S EMBRACE

NADINE CRENSHAW

ZEBRA BOOKS
KENSINGTON PUBLISHING CORP.

ZEBRA BOOKS

are published by

Kensington Publishing Corp.
475 Park Avenue South
New York, NY 10016

First printing: December, 1989
Printed in the United States of America

For Robert,
who is at the heart of all my
aspirations.

Prologue

The world was a colder, darker place then. It was an axe age, a wind age, a wolf age, a time when men didn't dare give mercy, a time when the powerful exacted what they could and the weak granted what they must.

In the bleak northern lands of Scandinavia, lands of long winters, of ice and snows bitter enough to kill, a people were bred to sharpness and suddenness. Dark, fir-covered slopes, skies grey with thick clouds, seas so cold they made men's bones ache—all exacted their blood tax. Those who would survive to breed new generations had to possess a contempt for softness. The generations were bred, however, and each became hardier.

At first these Norse were not joined into kingdoms under monarchs; they remained divided under local chiefs, or jarls. Each jarl enjoyed the rank of a petty king over his local territory—as long as his people deemed his leadership beneficial to them.

Meanwhile they came to know how to make fine sea boats and acquired the skill to navigate them. At the same time, they began to hear that across the sea existed lands filled with desirable goods they couldn't make for themselves. Reports of accessible churches and coastal marts and riverine villages seeped through the Viking world like water through thirsty earth. A few jarls called together their folk to fare forth after these rich pickings. They abandoned their timid coast-hugging habits and pointed their foamy-beaked vessels across the uncharted sea. Braving the perils of the ravaging whale, the devouring whirlpool, the polar storm, they made a few quick raids on island and coastal towns, hit-and-run attacks. Their longships made it easy for them to appear, outrage, and escape.

When these victorious few returned to their homes, word of their successes traveled like sparks on a high wind. Curiosity and greed blew on these sparks till they burned incandescent and set many a mind afire. Soon it was the folk who were clambering at the door of the jarl's longhouse, calling, "Come away! The ship pulls at her anchor, and there is a bright world to gallivant in. Blue water froths to the four edges of the world!"

Even if that particular jarl happened not to be one who wanted to pirate, even if the hay in his home field needed to be cut for the cattle, or the flock needed shearing, and his womenfolk needed to be fed, he had his position of leadership to keep, for his power was always circumscribed; it always depended on the devotion and regard of his subjects. His very title depended on their favorable voice at the assemblies where he presented himself to them. If they wanted to go a'viking, he could not very well refuse to lead them.

And, after all, a journey! At the word, the blood bounded, a wildness rose in the soul. Was there ever a proposed journey that was not a magic casket filed with promises? To the wife or mother who tugged at his sleeve, murmuring in a voice thick from crying, "Go not, there is danger, there is hardship," what answer could a man give but the bluff answer: "What Norseman fears hardship?"

And so these men of the north broke the silence of the seas once and for all. With the driving force of a mast under a bellying sail, the mighty Viking conquests began. The unexpected, swift, savage raid on Lindisfarne in the year 793 was as a bolt from the blue and marked the beginning of what was called the Norse Terror; it went on for 250 years.

Two viewpoints existed concerning the men who reveled in this barbarous age. There was the viewpoint of those who suffered because of them, who thought them cruel, bloodthirsty savages with terrible blazing eyes who left behind nothing but bones and ruin. This was the perspective of the victims, those who knew the Norse as their enemies. They had every reason to fear and hate them, since they saw them at their roughest and worst.

Then there was the viewpoint of the saga makers, who spoke of bold, fearless, heroic men — blond, blue-eyed, tall men; broad-shouldered, rock-ribbed men, honorable men — who sailed out on glorious adventures and brought home treasures beyond imagining.

Both these points of view may stand a little to one side or the other of the truth. But one fact is undeniable: The cruelty of that age was universal and incredible; destinies were decided quickly, thrillingly, cataclysmically — and usually by force. What prizes there were went to the darer.

Now it happened that the longship Blood Wing *strand-hewed on the coast of Wessex, and a notable tale hangs thereon.* . . . .

Chapter 1

On the last day of spring, a soft afternoon when Britain was still bursting with hope, a prowling band of Norwegian predators brought their dragonship in for a beach raid on a convenient flock. The white sheep were tended by a young shepherd who hadn't spied the longship's sail on the horizon because he'd closed his eyes after his midday meal of bread and sheep-milk cheese. Dreaming of anything but a raid from the sea, the first he knew of the Vikings was the feel of the cool, flat surface of an axe blade laid against his sleeping brow, and then, suddenly, came terror.

The invaders bound him and kept him by while they slaughtered the choicest ewe of the flock. The butchered mutton they rubbed with salt to keep the meat fresh. Those who weren't occupied with this enjoyed loud and hearty conversation among themselves, often directing sly comments toward the shepherd. Since he spoke no Norse and had no notion what they were saying, this considerably increased his terror. One big fellow with huge, golden cat eyes jabbed a blue-tipped spear at him. And once, the broad-featured, surly-looking one whose cool-bladed broadaxe had wakened the shepherd came near enough to laugh and capture the young man's nose with two fingers and give it a hard tweak.

When the mutton was secure aboard their ship, the

11

giants stood looking at him as if undecided about what to do with him. The young man was near to gibbering with those light-eyed gazes on him. Whether or not the Norse understood anything he said, he began to babble, trying to save his life: "I can tell you where you'll find plenty of wine and food and-and whatever else you like—gold! Plenty of gold! Enough to make life gorgeous! A wedding. Cedric the thane is taking a wife. A great beauty she is, a yellow rose—she'd glow beneath you."

The Vikings seemed unmoved. A wind blew in from the open sea, flapping their clothes and sending the shepherd's coarse hair backward. He shivered and cringed in his bindings, for everyone knew these rough dealers believed in no such nonsense as fair play.

The tallest among them, a warrior less merry than the others, stepped forward and pulled his sword out of its scabbard. This he passed before the young man slowly, so that the shepherd saw every feature of it: its double-edged blade three feet long, the gold wire that had been beaten into engraved grooves then filed smooth, leaving a golden design in the steel.

The Viking squatted before him, filling all the space in the shepherd's view. The giant was dressed as the others in a tunic that reached to his mid-thighs, trousers, leggings beneath his knees, and shoes of soft leather. And like the others, he wore his yellow hair long enough to cover his neck, kept off his face by a cloth band worked in a pattern of silk threads. His jewelry included a gold arm ring and finger rings, and a big single bead strung about his neck.

Yet, other than the fact that he was the tallest, there was something very different about him. The shepherd seemed to hear a thrumming in the air, like a rush of bird wings. The sound seemed low, and large, too large to be a bird. Was it wind? The shepherd was a Catholic, but behind and beneath the imposing fabric of Christianity, older beliefs lingered, a folk memory of an

12

ancient legend, an image of a huge, gaping creature from deep time, the Monster of the Mist: the dragon. And at that moment it seemed quite possible that that extraordinary creature was intensely alive—and not in some dank cavern, but wandering far more pleasing realms.

The Viking said, in plain Saxon, "Where is this wedding to take place, goose boy?"

The shepherd's voice did seem to honk rather like a wild goose as he replied, "Down the coast, a few miles, Fair Hope Manor." His sentences were disjointed and broken-backed. "Plenty of treasures, down the coast and up the river. An undefended manor house, the great hall of Cedric the thane, and well-stocked farms. You can't miss it, master! A wedding—tomorrow! They'll have food, wine . . . *please don't kill me!*"

The sword point passed beneath his chin again. While looking at him, the big tawny giant spoke to his comrades. They laughed. The shepherd thought his end had come, and closed his eyes and began to whisper his prayers. But then he noticed the quiet and looked to see that the Viking had put away his weapon and turned toward his longship.

It was known that Vikings moved more swiftly than ordinary men, but even so, the shepherd was amazed at how they shoved off and rowed out onto the opal sea, took the breeze in their sail and simply vanished from sight.

He felt so relieved he could have cried, and did cry where he lay bound in the rich late-spring grass. He cried until he felt as if his eyes had been pickled in brine, until his eyelids felt as if they'd been curled back and scraped raw by the glistening edge of that huge damascened sword, the thought of which made him cry some more.

Another shepherd, this one yet a boy, also suffered

13

that afternoon, in his mind at least. The lad Arneld lived on the manor farm of Fair Hope, and today the Lady Edin had him on a stool outside the kitchen of the manor house where she was resolutely shearing his heap of auburn hair.

"Sit still, Arneld, I'm almost finished."

The boy obliged her without complaint. It was Udith, her face glowing from her cooking fire, who complained as she passed by with a little chopping axe to get herself some kindling. "To think you'd make time on this of all days to look out for the likes of him, my lady. You're too kind by far. Surely you've got better things to do than fuss with an orphan boy."

Edin said nothing to the stout, big-jawed, good-hearted woman. She only stood back to examine her work, then smiled secretly at Arneld. "Not a thing better to do," she said gently. "We orphans must stick together, afterall." She was rewarded with an adoring grin.

Her face sobered, for the unmistakable tangy smell of sheep droppings came from her adorer. "You look much better, but you must have a bath, Arneld."

"*Aww,* my lady!"

"No bawling now. Tell Udith I said you need the tub."

"I'd just as soon go down to the river and have a swim."

A shadow passed over Edin's face. She looked beyond the fine-timbered barn with its gabled roof and the modest wooden buildings behind it to the trees that flanked the river. "You'll be careful? You'll take some-one with you, to watch in case—"

"Aw, my lady, I can swim good."

"Let the boy go, Edin." This was a masculine voice, and with it came a new smell, the reek of hot hay. "All the lads can swim, the girls, too. So near the sea, we're children of the water. You're the only marrowless one among us."

"My lord." She curtsied.

Cedric waved his hand in the direction of the boy, who catapulted across the dooryard for the river in a frenzy of obedience. Edin was left alone with her youthful bridegroom, who said softly, "You used to call me Cedric."

"It would not be seemly now."

She hadn't quite looked him in the face since he'd appeared. She felt terribly shy of him of late. Though she'd grown up alongside him, as close as brother and sister, now he was going to be her husband, and that was a different thing altogether.

"Edin." He moved closer and claimed her hands. His figure was slightly made, hardly taller than her own. He had a rather wispy brown beard, and an equally wispy, drooping mustache; and his mouth was a little too sensitive for his new role of thane. He wore a linen tunic to his knees, gathered at the waist by a broad belt from which hung a sword—which Edin had never seen outside its scabbard. His legs were protected by leggings, and his feet by the rugged leather shoes he wore whenever he oversaw work on the sprawling manor farm. Edin wore similar clothing, except her shoes were softer and her dun tunic fell to her ankles.

Abruptly he pulled her into the shadow of the manor house wall. "Edin, kiss me!"

"My lord, not here!"

He drew back his jaw as if riding a blow. "Yes, here! Why not? We're to be married on the morrow."

"I—" She had no chance to say more, for he took her in his arms and pressed his mouth to hers. Wisps of his beard tickled her cheek, and she felt a giddy urge to laugh. When his hands moved to her bosom, however, she strained back in alarm.

"Edin!"

She stopped straining immediately. "I'm sorry, my lord." She was near to tears.

"And will you be sorry tomorrow night?" He cupped her chin with his hand, forcing her to look at him. "Do

15

you realize that I'll make you mine then? Did my mother never speak to you about—"

"Yes! But tomorrow night is not now, not here in the kitchen yard!"

He regarded her. "You don't like my kisses, Edin. You are always so very kind to the people who serve you, yet seem to care so little for me anymore. I would serve you if I could, my dewy rose, to get a little of that sympathy. We were such friends once—until I fell in love with you."

She felt herself wilting under his steady examination.

"Love has made my hands sieves," he went on. "I can't seem to claim your complete attention anymore. And I *want* your attention, Edin. I'm in a constant state of frustration because of you. Do you know that sometimes I *ache* for you?" He took her hand once more and placed it against his groin. "I ache *here*," he whispered quickly, hotly.

She snapped her palm away as if burned, and slipped sideways out of his arms. "I-I have so many things to do, my lord. You must excuse me!"

She tried not to run as she fled through the double line of rose trees she'd nurtured for the last three years, on through the garden where she tended and grew herbs for the healing of the sick and the flavoring of Udith's cooking, to the front door of the manor house and through the splendid oak-raftered hall to the stairs. She was walking so fast, however, that her unbound amber hair flowed behind her.

In the upper hall, she paused. With a rush of guilt, she pulled herself together. She *should* like Cedric's kisses. The next time he wanted to kiss her she must let him, without so much as a flinch.

A voice seemed to speak in her ear: *Tomorrow night he will do more than kiss you. He will bare that weapon he says aches so because of you and bury it in your body.*

Oh! She had things to do, so many things, and no time to think about tomorrow night!

In the chamber that had been her uncle's and aunt's—Cedric's parents'—she went to the big bed and took up the folded linens left on the bare straw mattress. The chamber hadn't been occupied since Edward's and Bertra's deaths last winter, but tomorrow she and Cedric would sleep here.

Tomorrow! Her fears began to crawl back. She poured all her concentration into savoring the smoothing of the linens. The making of order was a delightful thing to her. She was grateful that she had this home to call her own. Grateful to Uncle Edward and Aunt Bertra, who had taken her in when her parents died in a drowning accident. Grateful for the leafy, tranquil decade she'd spent here. And grateful to Cedric for asking her to marry him and thereby letting her stay, but—

Tomorrow!

She stilled the thresh of her emotions and bent her head so that her hair fell forward around her face. She whispered, "Dear Father in Heaven, please help me. I know I'm no mere girl anymore, but a grown woman with a woman's duties before me. If you will but help, I promise I shall try to be a good wife. I shall try to do whatever dear Cedric requires of me—I will! But I do need your help."

She always felt she didn't pray well, though she persisted. There were a great many things she felt she didn't do well or right. For instance, she felt she wasn't very clever, though she longed to be. She knew that she had a certain beauty, but often feared that people overestimated her because of it, and would find her out, and then she would be a cause for disappointment.

She remembered something Uncle Edward, a thick square man, had said to her just before he died. "Edin," he'd whispered, patting her hand, "you're so like your mother; you have the very beauty and flavor of her, her deep-grained habit of kindness."

That often came back to her, because it wasn't true. Her memories of her mother had an ethereal iridescence. She hardly recalled more than a figure that was mysteriously detached, but from what people told her, unkindness had been out of her mother's ken. Edin wished desperately that she could be like that, but she wasn't. Look at how she'd just made Cedric miserable. She'd failed him. She should go back . . . but dared not. Because she was certain that if she did he would want to kiss her again, and then she would disgrace herself and hurt him all the more. She might even cry. She might even whisper, "I'm so afraid."

She heard voices in the hall and went to peek down the stairs. Cedric was making a stranger welcome. The man was saying, ". . . since the great heathen host quartered for the winter in East Anglia and were supplied with horses . . ."

Heathens—that meant Vikings. They'd stayed the winter in East Anglia? That was unusual.

"I see you have no walls or safeguards of any kind," the man was saying. "Have you buried your coins? Nothing's safe that isn't in the ground, neither coins nor folk."

"My father felt we were safe here as we are, and that's good enough for me." Cedric could put on a certain air of command, but he was young and carried his authority a bit anxiously. "You can't see Fair Hope from the sea. No one would know it was here."

The stranger grunted, accepting a silver bowl of ale from the servant girl Juliana. He watched the girl walk away before he said, "The heathens have an unerring nose for likely targets." He tipped the bowl to his mouth, glancing up as he did so, thus spying Edin. Driblets of ale leaked down either side of his beard as he forgot to swallow.

Cedric turned. "Edin, come and meet Ceolwulf. King Alfred has sent him to witness our marriage."

Edin wrenched herself into motion and started down the stairs. The great hall was adorned and decorated as it never had been since her coming. Even the air was fragrant. She'd had the year's old rushes swept out into a fetid heap beside the cow byre, and on the oaken planks a carpeting of new sun-dried rushes had been laid then strewn with crumbled lavender and thyme. The tables were set for tomorrow. Edward had valued beautiful tableware enough to import glass from France and silverware from as far as the Eastern Empire. At the head of the hall was the table for the bride and groom, and there Edin's own gold-adorned wooden goblet sat.

"We're honored, Ceolwulf," she said respectfully, battling the shyness that overcame her when any stranger must be met. She'd become the mistress of the house since Aunt Bertra's death, not a small matter considering the baking, spinning, and weaving to be done, and shy or not it was she who must attend to the requirements of important guests.

The man was not handsome. He had a forehead crossed with wrinkles, great bags of skin lay under his jet eyes, and one corner of his mouth drooped pitifully. At the moment he also seemed beyond speech. "Honor's mine . . . marriage of a scion of a noble Wessex family . . . King Alfred couldn't come. . . ."

She studied him. A stranger was always a curiosity. He smelled of leather, which told her that he'd come by horse along the old Roman roads. He was dressed in a dull-green, belted tunic that stretched to his knees and woolen leggings. His sword was silver-hilted. Over his shoulders lay a four-cornered woolen cloak, brown, held at the front by a large silver brooch.

She felt a hand on her shoulder. Cedric had come near and was touching her in a possessive way, smiling with a new and quiet ferocity as if to say: *Mine*.

Embarrassed, Edin sought to make conversation. "Did I hear you say there were Vikings in East Anglia?"

"Danes." He nodded. "All last winter, my lady."

She was unamazed that Fair Hope had heard nothing of this. They were an out of the way place, and news spread very slowly. Fair Hope always seemed to exist in a state of grace. It was a green and pleasant spot, peaceful in an era of turbulence, and apparently secure. While kings fought and kings went down, Fair Hope prospered; the farmland produced. This news of Danes elsewhere seemed not to have anything to do with Edin.

"And they're still keeping men from their sleep at night with sea raids," Ceolwulf added, eyeing Cedric. "A thane's remiss not to build a wall, or at least post lookouts."

"This is no talk for a bride," Cedric chided. "We've always been safe here. Our nights are quiet."

The man grumbled into his bowl, "It's usually quiet before the storm breaks." He tilted his head back to drink. His prominent Adam's apple bobbed as in three deep draughts he emptied the bowl.

The ale seemed to affect him quickly, for by the time he wiped his mouth, he was grinning. "You're right— no talk for a bride. And this luscious fruit is ripening fast, eh? Do you think she'll keep till the morrow?"

Edin blushed, and as she did so, even then, with awful inevitability, the savagery of the times was reaching its claws toward her.

As the afternoon waned, and the late darkness fell, the dragonship nosed into the mouth of the river. The moon was only a silver crescent in the midnight sky, casting down barely enough light for the Norsemen to navigate by. The only sound, besides the endless sound of the sea, was the slight plop of oar blades as they sliced the water. The ship was beautifully made, high at stem and stern, with low-swept gunwales. As she rode the bore of the tide up the channel, two of her shipmen hauled down her striped sail and folded it carefully. They unstepped her mast as well and laid it on the deck so that it could not be seen from the river's high banks.

They were well practiced in stealth. Already this season they had fallen hungrily upon two monasteries, for that was where the fortune of this land was gathered, in the gold figures of saints, in sapphire-encrusted crosiers and exquisitely wrought caskets—enough wealth to make any Norseman's grasping heart sing. And everything was easily stripped from the submissive monastic communities.

As the ship continued up the river, every man slipped a cloak and hood over his helmet and iron-mesh war shirt, so that the starlight wouldn't glint on the metals. A pair at a time, they wrapped their oar blades in old sheepskins to prevent the water from clapping on the wood.

Like a silent reptile, the dragonship continued up the flood-tiding waters. The never-ending hiss of the sea grew distant and disappeared. The river flowed placidly through a quiet valley between wooded hillocks. The banks stood still and deserted. No smoke plumed over the treetops. Saxon peasants knew better than to put their huts near a river's mouth. They usually built well upstream where they felt less exposed to those who raided from the sea.

The ship rounded a bend; the river narrowed. On for another mile. When she scraped her keel in shoal water, her rudder was lifted by pulling on a rope. Here paths along the banks signaled that a village must be close by.

On the ship's prow platform, beside her dragon's head, stood the giant Viking. Over his fair hair he wore a helmet now, bearing the insignia of a hammer. Thoryn the Hammer, he was called by some. He was known to be an amazingly strong man. He could swim across Dainjerfjord and back without pause; he could wrestle down the best of the best. From his dull iron helmet to the gold jewelry on his arms and fingers and the decorated sword hanging in his scabbard, he looked Olympian. He stood by the dragon's head as still as a runestone, his features never moving. Only his pewter-grey eyes moved, and his hand, which he lifted in a single mute signal.

The longship slithered parallel to the riverbank, where she was quickly tied fore and aft with plaited hide ropes. She tugged at these moorings like a serpent that smells blood, while thirty-two sea warriors eased over her waist.

Now came the small sounds of men drawing swords, feeling for war axes. They were a mixed party, with new-bearded youths on their first sailing, tempered warriors who had fought countless battles, and a hand-ful of older men whose beards and hair were streaked with grey. Each carried a round wooden shield, and they were variously armed with knives, clubs, axes, spears, and broadswords. Silver edges glinted in the starlight. Bearded, leathern faces grinned with antici-pation. Unlit torches appeared, as did horns of strong ale, for the men would drink before climbing to the village.

"All is ready," Thoryn was told as he joined his men. Over his tunic he wore a shirt of mail, and over that, a sweeping cloak of grey, the cowl raised. Most of the men wore round or conical helmets of metal or heavy leather. His had the hammer insignia and a protecting nosepiece that divided his gaze. In his hand was his father's damascened sword, *Raunija,* The Tester. The blade carried a runic inscription: "Let *Raunija* spare no man."

The broad-faced, surly man was the only one who wore no helmet on his big shaggy head. He'd drunk twice as much ale as any of the others, and now, as he spoke, a furious white froth came from his mouth. "My axe sings with thirst!"

Sweyn Elendsson was called the Berserk. In battle he sometimes seemed overcome with a berserk fury, the sudden insanity that legend said gave a double portion of might and took away all sense of pain. He surged

22

into a fight rolling his eyes and howling. He would rush toward his adversaries without apparent thought of danger. He was both feared and greatly looked up to for this. But, berserk or not, he was Thoryn's sworn man, bound to obey his jarl, which he had barely been doing for some time now. Thoryn said to him, "You will let your blade suffer a little thirst, I trust. Dead people bring very little profit in any marketplace."

Thoryn smiled like winter as he looked from Sweyn to the others. "We have come for treasure. Of captives, only the most likely will be taken. We will *not* slaughter those we don't want. And—" he paused, looking particularly at the deeply rutted and weatherbeaten face of Ragnarr— "and there will be no sport with the children." Ragnarr had been known to throw an infant up to see if he could catch it on the point of his spear. Thoryn asked him softly, "Do you hear me, Norseman?"

The river made its liquid sound nearby; then "Aye, *barknakarl*" came Ragnarr's whispered response.

Barknakarl, the children's friend. Ragnarr said it with grudging respect.

He was not sworn to Thoryn. He was the jarl's neighbor at home, a *bondi*, a small landowner and a free man. His allegiance to Thoryn was based on respect, not on an oath such as Sweyn had sworn. Which meant that he wouldn't follow Thoryn blindly to the world's edge, where the mermaids played and the seahorses whinnied on the waters. Still, if Thoryn told him, "No sport with the children," then he more or less obeyed, knowing that if he didn't he would be challenging Thoryn's rule, which would mean personal combat with him.

A jarl had to prove himself over and over. A Norseman never admitted to fear—but there were men they treated with extreme caution. Their jarl had to be one of these. And Thoryn was.

Following his lead now, they said a prayer. A patter-

23

ing of gruff voices rose as each man made his own, it not being the Norse way to pray in harmony like a herd of lowing Christian cattle. They asked Odin for the might of thunderbolts forged in fires, and asked Thor for the stealth of lightning hammered bright.

At last Thoryn said, "The time has come." They set off in a line up through the riverside growth, leaving the dragonship to wait impatiently on the dark glimmering water.

No one spoke. Leaves formed a billowing canopy over their path, through which the late starlight and scant moonlight barely sifted down. The shipload of men surged like a sinuous snake through the dark shadows. When they came upon an outlying hut, a dog started to bark. A pair of small red eyes burned. Ragnarr quickly faded from the group with his war club. There came a *chop* sound, like two jaws snapping together, then all was quiet again. Ragnarr returned, grinning, and the invaders continued.

They stopped on a mound an arrow's flight from the dark village. Before them was a small cluster of cottages, byres, and outbuildings. The shepherd had spoken truthfully in that there were no walls, other than here and there a low stone pen: small fences for Norsemen to leap. In the nearest, sheep bleated quietly and shuffled about.

"Child's play," muttered Beornwold Isleifsson, who wore his yellow hair in four thick plaits bound with copper wire.

Beside him, Fafnir Danrsson — nicknamed Longbeard for his pale silky beard — gave Beornwold a comradely slap on the shoulder — and a warning: "The wise man never praises the night before the coming of the morning."

The largest building was a hall of oak with a steep thatched roof. Sweyn the Berserk lifted his bronze- and silver-inlaid axe and grinned, showing big horse's teeth. A mad light had grown in his ashy blue eyes. "That will

24

be the chief's hall; there the treasure resides, and the fairest women, and there Sweyn will be at the fighting's end!"

Thoryn stared ahead. The cords of his neck straightened and fell, straightened and fell. At last he threw off his cloak and raised his sword. He gripped the silver mount of his wooden shield and cried out as he lunged forward into a battle run. His deep voice was like the fog, like winter wind, like a metal sea on an iron-cold shore.

Those behind him began to bellow likewise:

"Norsemen, would you live forever?"

"May Thunder-Voice bring us victory!"

Other cries of ferocious challenge resonated against the walls of silence. Flint struck iron, and torches flared. Faces went livid, eyes blazed with light, and throats pumped. They advanced in a wedge, Thoryn at the point, his men fanned out behind him. The village dogs clamored into hysterical barking as the Norse ran between the grey huts of the sleeping community, wreaking havoc.

Chapter 2

Edin brought her slow and barefoot pacing to a pause. The flame of small rushlight that lit her chamber was guttering. She replaced it with another and turned, throwing her waist-long hair back over her shoulders. The silence of Fair Hope seemed to be concentrated in her room tonight, a silence so thick it was all but sound. It was long past time for her to be abed, but she feared sleep, feared the swift passage of time that sleep brought. The whole of her future yawned before her, and she felt a need to watch the passing of these last few hours of her girlhood.

She went again to the dress hanging against the wall, her wedding gown, made from treasured lengths of brocade and satin. The dark peacock-blue kirtle fell to the ground and had long sleeves with billowing cuffs; over it, the lighter blue tunic was short-sleeved and knee-length. She was rightly proud of its splendid embroidery, which she and the chore-girl Dessa had produced, working silently, patiently, for hours. Over the tunic went a creamy yellow mantle, to be held by brooches, one on each shoulder. For her feet, elegant slippers of soft yellow leather. She would also wear a necklet, and a diadem to keep her hair neat and in loose waves down her back.

She knew what Cedric was going to wear as well:

grey-blue trousers and a green knee-length tunic held by a belt with richly ornamented clasps and mounts. His red mantle would be fastened by a brooch of beautiful workmanship and great size.

The ceremony was to be held at noon in the small pasture that lay between the hall and the village, where a wooden cross stood. This served as the open church for the people of Fair Hope. Afterward, everyone would feast in the great hall, where the smell of flowers and thyme would rise up from the fresh green rushes. The room could accommodate one hundred people at the trestle tables arranged in a line down each side. And the feast would be splendid. Beef and venison and huge plates of fish from the river. And, of course, lots of thickly scented ale. The fire would leap on the hearth, and candles would throw shadows. No doubt the feasting would be prolonged far into the night. At the single table across the head, where the thane's wife would sit with her husband, they would be served mead and precious imported wine and—

Everything would be perfect if only Cedric hadn't changed so! If only he didn't seem such a stranger suddenly. His proposal hadn't been a surprise; his parents had always voiced the desire to see him wed Edin. But this unbrotherly intensity had been completely unforeseen.

She tried to force a mental picture of lying in the same bed with him, granting him what his affection demanded, but again her mind skipped away. She *must* picture it! She must search inside herself for acceptance. *Imagine,* she ordered herself, *you and Cedric naked beneath the bedclothes, the rushlight blown out, the soft summer darkness.* . . .

"I have to get some rest!" she murmured, pulling open the blankets of her bed. Already undressed down to her shift, she now bent to blow out the little tallowy light. Before she could, however, a terrible noise caused her to straighten. The night's silence cracked with

27

harsh cries, and the noise of wood shrieking, splintering, giving way — the tall double doors of the hall below.
Then came men's voices, screaming like animals. What
. . . who . . . ?

Her stomach filled with a sick sense of disaster: *Vikings!* Her mind caught on the word. To her it meant
man-beasts from the cold and foggy north, hateful,
reeking scavengers. Thieves . . . rapists . . . killers! Giants swinging razor-sharp battle-axes! It couldn't be.
Not here at Fair Hope! Surely not!

But the demonic roar swelled.

Her door had no bar, nothing but a flimsy latch. She
raced to fasten it. Then hurried to the carved cedarwood chest at the foot of her bed to find her dagger, the
pretty jeweled ornament she often wore at her waist.
Then . . . she could think of nothing more to do. She
sensed these minutes were priceless, but one after the
other they escaped her. Frozen with fear, she clutched
her little blade to her breast with both hands. Her fingers clasped around it until her knuckles went white.
Could she use it on an enemy — or should she use it on
herself? She felt a strange gnawing at her insides, as if
she'd swallowed something cold and hungry.

The shouting got nearer, her door was tried — then
abruptly there came a blow to it. She started violently.
Fear moved in more tightly. She flinched as the stout
wood was kicked again and finally flew back on its
hinges.

A huge man lurched through, blood slicking the club
in his hand. He paused to let his eyes search. Edin took
him in all of a piece, his war shirt and leggings, his club
and shield. She could almost see his savage mind working: *No one to fight here. Just this unprotected creature.* His
pale eyes gleamed like lake ice, and he grinned.

She no longer heard the war shouts and death
screams of the battle below. She heard nothing but the
heavy breathing of the barbarian approaching her. She
saw nothing but his sweat-reddened face. He loomed

sinister, malevolent, his eyes brimming with ugly desire.

She retreated, until her back came up against the wall. He tossed down his club and shield and reached for her with arms as big as tree branches. She was too frightened to scream. She saw his hands, big, blood-stained. She knew he hadn't seen the dagger clutched in her fists, or mayhap he'd thought the jeweled hilt was the top of a crucifix. The blade, though slim, would never penetrate the fine iron mesh of his war shirt. Her eyes frantically sought — and found in his bare throat — a place where a blue vein stood swollen. She took the hilt in a new two-handed gasp, raised it, and jabbed it into the soft flesh behind his collar bone. She shoved it down, praying the blade was long enough to pierce his heart.

His eyes fluttered wide. His face went dark and strange, a face from a nightmare, expressionless yet ominous. His arms dropped like dead weights and he took a step back. She saw blood oozing over the jewels studding the dagger's hilt. He stumbled on his own club as he clutched the side of his neck.

Yet, for all that, he still seemed very much alive. Edin thought, as in a dream, *I suppose I couldn't expect to kill him. I hurt him, though; he can't feel very good.* A trembling nausea came over her, a sick terror.

With a bull-like roar, another Viking pitched into the room: a huge body, a hard, steeled iron head above a thick neck, a round shield, and a long, broad, ornate sword. Edin's attacker cautiously turned to face him. The new man rose from his ready crouch. He was larger, even fiercer-looking, and Edin couldn't find a trace of gentleness or kindness anywhere about his partially masked and bearded face. He watched as his fellow monster fingered the hilt of the dagger then yanked it from his throat. Blood spouted immediately, staining the covers of Edin's bed a yard away.

Seeing that bright scarlet spurting, her hands went to

29

her mouth. The man took no notice; he looked at his own blood on the dagger's blade as though he couldn't imagine how it had gotten there. When he tried to speak, nothing came but a gurgling sound. He sagged to his knees. With faithful-dog eyes, he seemed to entreat his companion, but then, to Edin's surprise, he fell face forward, like a huge timber put to the axe.

The newcomer lifted his gaze from his fallen comrade. Caught by the warm light spilling from the rushlight, his face seemed as bitter and cold as the face of a thousand winters. The helmet he wore and the glittering sword in his hand added to his terrifying appearance. Yet as their eyes met, Edin was fascinated. He had a sinister quality as he stared steadily back at her. He seemed sharply intelligent. And exquisitely dangerous.

Squatting, he took the dagger from his axe-brother's lifeless hand and said a few gruff words in Norse.

He looked up at Edin again, and looked her over in a way she'd never experienced before. She lost all sense of where she was. She heard mere blurs of sound from far away, but she and the Viking seemed to exist alone together in isolation. His eyes reminded her of dark grey clouds tumbled low in a sky as cold as pewter. That trembling sensation came again, more violently.

She bent to reach for the dead man's club. It was heavier than she expected, and as she struggled to bring it up, the newcomer stood. With a negligent flick of his sword, he knocked the club away from her. Her fingers burned with numbness: One instant she was gripping the heavy club with all her strength, and the next it was flying from her hands.

He stepped forward, forward again, until he towered over her. She turned her face away a little, as she would turn from the glare of a too-bright, overcast sky.

He put down his shield, and his freed left hand came up to her throat. It seemed nearly to encircle it entirely, so that she could feel his hard fingers beneath her ear.

30

and his raspy palm under the hair at the nape of her neck, his broad thumb barely touching her windpipe. She swallowed convulsively. The hand smoothed down, hooking the wide, round neckline of her shift and pulling it off her shoulder, so that her right breast was bared. Her hands fluttered upward, then fell to her sides again. Her eyes sidled to his, and then away. The indecency seemed to her less ghastly than the coolness of his stare fastened on her breast.

At last he grazed the tip of it with his middle finger. She had the hazed nightmare feeling that this was a check, nothing more, the way a man checks equipment he intends to use. She felt the beginnings of sexual terror. Her stomach pounded like a second heart; panic pounded through her veins.

Just as she felt herself growing weak with the piling up of horror, a further movement came at the door. There Cedric stood, with his sword out of its scabbard at last. He held the weapon awkwardly, with the hilt gripped in both fists. Upon seeing one dead Viking in the room and another looming over Edin, he paused. His eyes met hers.

That intense, large-eyed stare was much too weighty and sustained. Her understanding rebelled for a moment against what she saw in it — no deep cunning thoughts, just his sense of helplessness, his fear. And his desire to simply leave her to whatever fate was in store for her. She saw him as he was then, unmarked by experience, decision, or impact. She had been willing to become his wife, to give herself to him, her body, her heart, her life. From a young age, there had existed in her mind a set of expectations and hopes, an aggregation of conceptions picked up from remarks, descriptions, reveries, all of which sheltered under the word *love,* and now in her bridegroom's eyes she saw that there was . . . fondness, certainly . . . and desire . . . but not love.

Whether he would have quietly stepped back and

fled for his own life she was never to know, for the Viking lifted his eyes from her breast and saw the direction of her gaze. He whirled, his sword coming up reflexively. Everything seemed slowed down as Edin watched. The length of his sword added to the length of his arm gave him such a long, killing reach. Cedric saw the broad, keen blade coming. He moved his own sword with desperate ineptness. He shouted; the Viking made not a sound. The blade sliced horizontally. Cedric's mouth opened wider, though only a gasping sound came from him now. He seemed to fold at the waist, over that damascened blade, then he crumpled to the floor.

Edin screamed. She struggled against the Viking's grip on her arm which kept her where she was. Cedric's face was a terrible thing. Clearly he was in mortal agony. His legs moved, and his mouth still gaped silently, as though there was not enough strength in him to give voice to his pain.

The barbarian muttered something, glanced at Edin with those coolish eyes, then frowned, shook his head, and suddenly plunged his sword into the young thane's heart.

Edin felt something in her slip. Her pulse slowed to half its rate. She swayed on her feet; her vision darkened. She hardly noticed that the Viking had let go of her. She sagged to her knees and crawled to Cedric's side. "My lord?" She reached for the tatters of his blood-soaked shirt and tried to close them over his wounds. "My lord . . . Cedric . . . you've ruined your shirt. I could try to sew it, but . . . oh, Cedric, you should have fled."

She felt a hand on her arm again and looked at it, at the twiglike scars that started at the fingers and went up the wrist until they disappeared beneath the sleeve, scars of innumerable blade cuts. She looked up into those pewter eyes that were divided by the iron nosepiece of the helmet. A Viking. She ought to be terri-

32

fied, she understood that distinctly. His appearance there above her was violent and impossible. For a moment more she was uncomprehending; then anger such as she'd never known flooded her. Everything savage in her surfaced at once. She yanked away from his grip and stood, facing this man who had in the space of minutes stolen her future. Her heart turned bitter inside her. She raised her hands over her head, joined them into one fist, and went for him, went for his bearded face with all her strength.

He merely lifted his free hand and caught her doubled fists in fingers of steel. At the same time he jerked her forward so that she fell against him. It was like falling against a stone wall. There was no give in his stance, no give in his hard chest beneath his metal war shirt. She tried to arch away from the shocking contact, but now his hand was around her waist. Her face lifted beneath his chin. She shook her head to throw the wisps of her hair out of her eyes and saw him staring down the nosepiece of his helmet at her. She felt her will waver, then crumble into fear.

His smile was thin, his voice soft, soft: "Even the dullest thrall knows never to strike her master."

Part of her mind absorbed that he'd spoken this in Saxon, and part of it absorbed what the words meant. She struggled again, now with strength born of terror. Her hand went to his face, really hoping to scratch his eyes out so that she might escape him.

As if impatient with such puny resistance he simply shoved her away. She stumbled back, tripped over the dead Viking's legs, and fell. For a moment she was wrapped in her hair. When she got it out of her eyes, she paused. She dared not look at Cedric, at that open dark hole his mouth made in his dead face. Nor did she dare look at the standing Viking. She felt relieved when he turned his grey, unflinching gaze to the door. He bellowed, "Rolf Kali!"

In a moment, a third Viking entered, big, as evidently were all their breed, showing reddish hair beneath an iron helmet decorated with copper and red rubies. He looked about him, his roving gaze ending with the Viking on the floor. The two spoke; their jaws seemed to chew the unintelligible Norse words like gristle. Then the newcomer looked at Edin. A droll little grin escaped his mouth.

Cedric's murderer approached her. She tried to scramble away, but he caught her arm in a grim grip and pulled her up. She raised her hands over her face, anticipating a blow, but he only spun her around so that her back was to him, and wrapped his arm around her rib cage beneath her breasts. Thus he lifted her right off her feet. She was held with her back to his chest. She struggled again, tore at his arm, kicked. Since her feet were bare, she knew he hardly felt her heels beating against his legging-wrapped shins, yet he growled at her, in Saxon again, "Don't take on so."

She *would* take on. She must. If she surrendered, her vulnerability and helplessness would rush at her.

He gave her ribs a squeeze. "Still you don't learn! A man would be dead and stark already for what you've done."

She gasped for breath—then went on writhing under his forearm. His hold, and her straining, served little by little to draw up her shift, so that the whiteness of her upper legs flashed. She heard his icy voice again, speaking in Norse to the redheaded Viking who stood watching with that grin dancing around his face. The giant seemed to be issuing an order, something severe and unsparing—then he paused, as if listening. The redheaded man turned a little, also listening. Among the garrulous, loud voices coming up from the hall, Edin now heard a terrible battle laugh.

The two men looked at one another. They spoke again, briefly, while Edin went back to twisting in the giant's grip. His arm didn't give a bit, though she was becoming exhausted; her movements were jerky, puppetlike.

Then suddenly her wriggles brought her breast into the palm of his hand. Her heart jumped up into her throat and nearly throttled her. As if he too felt something akin to an uprushing flame, the Viking all but threw her at the man he called Rolf.

Rolf let her put her bare feet on the floor before he pulled her from the room. After the dimness of her chamber, the sudden torchlight was strong. When her sight adjusted, she beheld the ruin of the manor hall.

The place was all alight. The big double doors, thick and ironbound, the manor house's strongest defense, had been broken wide open. Many of the wall tapestries had been pulled down. One tremendously fat man was stuffing all the edibles he could reach into his mouth, and in a corner two men were breaching a cask of the pale yellow wine meant for her wedding feast.

Edin was pushed down the narrow stairs. She saw the king's man, Ceolwulf, lying dead among the thyme- and lavender-scented rushes. His darkly brooding eyes stood open in what seemed great surprise. He'd brought a dark cloud of ominous news to sunny Fair Hope, and now it seemed he'd been caught by an unnatural justice.

Arneld, white-faced, dashed by the foot of the stairs, chased by a terrible-looking savage. The boy dodged this way and that as the savage tried to scoop him up. The scene resembled a gruesome game of tag. When the lad spied Edin, he cried out, as if he thought she could save him. He was mistaken, as the Viking proved by catching him, hooking his squealing body under one huge arm, and starting for the splintered door with him. The wine drinkers in the corner cheered their man — for his courage in taking so fierce a captive? The savage tried to swallow a grin, but it got away and slipped across his face.

What was he going to do with Arneld?

What was this Rolf going to do with her?

A frantic urge to escape stiffened Edin. She stopped. The Viking gave her a push to get her going again, and when that didn't move her, he stepped past her and tugged her wrist. She took him by surprise when she planted her feet and twisted her arm to break his grasp. It was easier than she could have hoped. His fingers slipped; in fact, he nearly fell down the stairs. Heart pounding, not with exertion but at her own audacity, she ran back up the stairs.

The whole manor house had the bizarre air of disaster, of things badly out of kilter. Seeing room after room being looted and no place to hide, Edin zigzagged in a frenzy. But then the redheaded Viking blocked her way. When she tried to dodge by him, he threw his leg out and tripped her. She fell full-length right at the feet of another warrior.

This one wore no helmet; he had a shaggy head of long blond hair that hung over his ashy blue eyes. He started to speak, to crow by the sound of his voice, and dropped his ornately inlaid battle-axe into a loop on his belt. He drew her up off the floor, up onto his chest, placing her breasts at the level of his face, which he rubbed against them.

The redheaded Rolf spoke a warning of some sort. Edin's shaggy-haired captor left off nuzzling her to glance about in an exaggerated, scornful way. His blue eyes sparkled with strange fire.

Edin's arms were caught in his clutch around her hips. He laughed as she tried to squirm free. She reclaimed one of her fists, however, and rapped his eye with her sharp knuckles. He jerked his head to the side. Her courage whetted, she bent and sank her teeth into his ear.

He yelped and threw her backward. She hit the wall, hard. Her head struck it with a dull thud. Stunned, she slid down until she was sitting on the floor.

It seemed someone had thrown a spider-lace black shawl over her eyes. Through it she saw the Viking glaring at her, his face white, going whiter. He smiled, but the smile was unpleasant. A froth appeared on his lips. She was too stunned to move, but her heart clenched as he took his axe from his belt. With a scream, he raised it over his head in both hands . . . only to lower it slowly as he felt the edge of another ornate blade against his neck. Nightmarishly, Edin recognized Cedric's killer once more, recognized those grey eyes and that bloodstained, damascened sword.

"You ill-handle my property, Sweyn." Thoryn looked levelly at his sworn man.

Sweyn laughed. That laugh had struck terror into many hearts this night. He swept his axe, *Death Kiss,* in a round scything motion. Only he could say how many times its biting edge had taken its meal. He said, "I sought only an amber-haired maid to light me to bed."

"Were you not told the woman is mine?"

"I told him, Thoryn," Rolf said, shrugging, "but the Berserk doesn't listen when his battle craze is on him."

The maiden was sitting with her legs sprawled, her short shift riding up above her knees, exposing her silken thighs. Thoryn watched as Rolf gathered her and lifted her to her feet, where he supported her. Thoryn saw her peculiar emotionless stare, the ashen color of her face. But then she blinked, and her hands lifted, like cup handles, to her head. The motion reassured him that she would recover.

He turned back to Sweyn, now with a cold, dry smile. Other Norse were gathering, as though some instinct had told them trouble was brewing. They muttered from one to the other as Sweyn said, "What makes her yours, Jarl?" Trouble indeed. A clear challenge to Thoryn's authority. The Norsemen shifted on their feet as they waited, tense and restless, reckoning to see blood spill and to feel the earth shake to the weapon strokes of their two mightiest warriors: their jarl and the strongest of their jarl's elect.

Thoryn said: "I see the Berserk needs to be reminded

37

why I am called 'jarl.' " He backed away from Sweyn, his face set. He placed himself, left foot forward. His motions were deliberate, and Sweyn recognized that Thoryn had accepted his challenge. His own ashy blue eyes went huge and wild, and he laughed again, laughed as though he owned the skies. Then, abruptly, the laughter faded to an ugly grin, and he lifted his axe. With a yell, he rushed at Thoryn, swinging his great weapon.

Thoryn's shield was made of thick wood with a heavy iron boss in the center. Sweyn's first mighty blow splintered the top right off. Thoryn retreated, discarding the wreck.

Sweyn struck again — swung his axe up then brought it down toward Thoryn's head. Thoryn stood still as a stone as the blow came, then stepped to the side and with a two-handed grip used his sword to catch the axe shaft. His father's blade still carried the old magic; the sharp edge of it penetrated the heavy handle of Sweyn's axe to the depth of half an inch.

Sweyn had to pry the axe free. The cords of his neck stood out; a vein pulsed in his forehead. Once again he attacked, and once more Thoryn thrust out his sword and parried the blow.

Sweyn made to lift his weapon yet again, but now Thoryn sliced, so swiftly that Sweyn had to suck in his stomach and curve his back in order to avoid a slit in his belly. Sweat beaded his brow. Seldom did it take him more than one or two blows to finish a man. But then, seldom did he face Thoryn. He stood uncertain a moment, clearly wondering how best to proceed. Meanwhile, Thoryn gave a bellowing cry and leapt forward. Sweyn lifted up his axe to fend off the sword-sweep, but Thoryn's attack was too shrewd. His sword was raised in two hands, swinging back over his shoulder; his left foot stepped as he braced himself to pull down the blow; his blade crunched right through Sweyn's mesh armor and into the joint of his shoulder.

Had it not been for that armor, his arm would have been severed. A Norse sword could take off a man's arm, or his head, in one smooth blow. As it was, his grip loosened; his axe clunked to the floor. He stooped, disbelieving, tried to regain his weapon, but found his fingers would not close on the handle. He sagged forward onto one knee. Blood spilled down his useless limb to pool on the floor.

The onlookers stood with their weapons lowered, their eyes full of wonder and fear to see Sweyn the Berserk's arm streaming with the hot crimson wine of war. Sweyn lifted his own gaze from the exposed, pulsating veins in his wound, and looked from face to face, ending with Thoryn. "The hour of departure arrives and we go our paths, I to die, and you to live. Which is better only Odin knows." His lips drew upward so that Thoryn could see his yellow teeth clenched in a smile of fatality. "Finish it!"

Thoryn lifted his sword and stepped forward grimly. The Norsemen stood by wordless, their faces showing nothing of what they might feel.

To his credit, Sweyn faced his death with seeming stoicism, with his lips still pulled back from his tarnished teeth.

But into the silence of that moment the maiden spoke: *"Don't, Viking! Please!"* Three words in Saxon which no one but he understood. His head moved imperceptibly. He saw her eyes . . . green, eyes the silvergreen color of sea swirl. A man could willingly wade neck-deep in such threshing froth. He felt an appeal to something inside himself, a knowing somewhere deep, but failed to comprehend it.

He looked back at Sweyn, then moved in on him, leading with his left leg again, ready for the closing blow. His sword, gleaming red in the torchlight, swept around.

But in the last inches he turned it, so that the flat of the weapon, and not its edge, struck Sweyn's neck with a smacking sound.

There was a moment of confusion among the Norse. They had seen their jarl poised for the death blow that would have ended Sweyn.

But Thoryn had heard those faint, foreign, feminine words, and now, to his own surprise, he was stepping back from his victim.

Sweyn's face changed. "Finish it, Jarl! I wish to feast this night with Odin in Valhöll, on benches covered with the corselets of my brothers!"

Thoryn looked at the man unpityingly, then at the maiden. She stood in Rolf's hold, nearly naked except for that thin shift, wrapped in her hair, rampantly feminine, motionless. He felt like a man between two horses, being pulled two ways at once. The feeling made him angry.

He said, "The fair Saxon pleaded for you, Berserk. Mayhap she wants you to live to bed her after all. Come up with enough gold and I'll sell her to you. Then you can smother her beneath you anytime you wish."

Sweyn's face, deathly wan, swiveled to the maiden. "Aye, I would smother her. How much?" he growled.

"Eight half-marks of pure gold." Thoryn knew the price was far beyond anything Sweyn could afford, yet it was close to the price he expected to get for her.

He signaled the others to help the wounded man before he turned away. Sweyn snarled, "*Barknakarl!* You insult your namesake Thor. I broke my oath to you! Deal me my punishment, Jarl! Is Sweyn Elendsson so much your underling you can't stoop to give him the death he deserves? You've crippled me—now do you leave me to endure pity?"

But Thoryn, his eyes hooded against all outsiders, only gave his sundered shield a kick as he stalked off to oversee the looting.

Beware, a voice chimed in his ear, *beware, Thoryn, this maiden with sea eyes and hair like tangled, amber water weed!*

Chapter 3

Redheaded Rolf pulled Edin away from the scene. She didn't resist. Her head throbbed; she still felt dazed — and sick. The blood of too many spectacles had been offered to her undiluted.

On the staircase, where now the air was heavy with the smell of spilled wine, one of the last battles was taking place. An ill-armed housecarl was being backed up the stairs by a great fellow with a barrel chest and four long yellow plaits bound with copper wire. The Viking's bare arms, from fingernails to neck, were tattooed with pictures of trees and other things. The iron of his weapon rang like a bell against the housecarl's shortsword. Edin could hear the young man's raw panting. Then, to her dismay, he was distracted by the sight of her. He turned his head slightly.

That was all his golden-bearded attacker needed. The Viking swept the man's feet out from under him. As he fell, he spat a perfectly comprehensible profanity. At the same time, the Viking threw his battle-axe back over his head, and with uninhibited cruelty the broad blade came down, swiftly, exact as a drawn line — without feeling, without charity — and cleaved the man's skull.

Edin cried out. The surprise drove her backward. The dead man's legs twitched, then he was quite still. A clinging greyness surrounded Edin; a ringing void came rushing into her brain. Rolf's grip on her arm tightened. Just as she felt her knees turn to water, he bent and put his shoulder into her waist. As her upper body fell over his back, he lifted her, head down, hair hanging. She felt him carrying her roughly until she lost her senses once more.

The next time she woke it was to find herself lying in dewy grass. She reached to feel her head and found her wrists were bound with a rope of plaited hide thongs. The lump on her head was almost the size of a man's fist. Wincing, she got to her knees and discovered she was on the ancient mound just outside the village. A bearded Viking wearing a conical battle helmet frowned down at her. She looked past him to what could only be the blazing of Hell.

She moaned. They were burning Fair Hope. Vikings jostled out the splintered doors even as flames licked up from the rushes behind them. Fair Hope, where she was to have fulfilled her womanhood in marriage and maternity. Fair Hope, her future. The manor house seemed to freely, wantonly, yield to the fire. It seemed to long to burn.

"My lady," a young voice came from behind her, "thank the saints! When he brought you, we thought for sure you must be dead."

She twisted on her knees to see first a pair of sheep grazing, tied together as if the Vikings meant to take them, then several of her folk, blessedly alive, but bound like herself; and who knew what that meant? She tried to cudgel her tired wits. The voice had come from Arneld, whom she'd last seen chased down in the hall. Beside him was Juliana, the dark-haired servant girl. And there was plump Udith, the cook, and her husband, Lothere, a lank, knuckly man, his neck stretched and his head turning this way and that. There were two field serfs as well, who had nothing on but their linen underpants and short-sleeved linen shirts. One of these inquired, hesitantly, "Lord Cedric?"

"They—" Her voice broke as memory drenched her. "They murdered him!"

"Don't cry, my lady." It was the boy again; she felt his small warm hands on her arm.

When she saw the tears in his eyes, and saw Udith digging her knuckles into her eyes, Edin stopped herself, realizing she must set the example. If she had her way, these Vikings would never see any of them cry. She looked into the faces that were looking back at her so expectantly. "We must be brave."

Her words brought an exchange of weak, hopeless glances. Then the boy said, "Here they come!"

Edin heard feet thumping the ground and turned. Tears were forgotten as fear took its place. Her folk huddled behind her. She saw the dull gleam of metal mesh armor in the flamelight, and her eye tallied more than a dozen men with blades and axes. So many of them! Three new captives were being herded along. The Vikings towered above these poor Saxons, laughing and swinging their great axes like shepherds' pipes, so that they hissed with every sweep and kept the gentle folk moving in a trot.

As the newcomers were tied like the others, more Vikings came to the mound, all laden with stolen valuables. Two of them staggered past with an iron-strapped chest—Cedric's chest, the great coffer he'd kept in his room as Uncle Edward had kept it before him. The lid was split across and wrecked, and the cups and coins inside glimmered in the flickering light.

Leaving the guard again, the pirates made final forays into the cluster of thatched cottages. By now the sky was all vermillion smoke. In that light, Edin made out two villagers lying lifeless outside their doors, two unfortunates probably caught by the first deadly charge.

The Vikings dashed in and out of the cottages, yowling. Edin cringed to hear their voices, high and reedy and cruel. More of her people were dragged from their hiding places. More cottages were set ablaze, until flames painted the night the color of copper.

When all of value had been garnished, the Vikings reassembled. As the red flamelight rose and dwindled, their faces alternately shone, then shadowed, then shone again. Some of them pranced like war horses, drunk on Edin's wedding wine. One blood-spattered youth stumbled off into the dark with his treasure sack and had to be brought back.

Two others were too wounded to stumble anywhere. The one called Rolf was half-leading, half-carrying the man who had nearly cracked Edin's head open. And the grey-eyed giant's outline was visible against the background of fire as he helped carry someone who hung limp between him and another man. When they put this one down, she recognized him as the man who had murdered the housecarl. He looked nearer death than life, lying on his back with his face to the heavens, his breath hissing through his clenched teeth.

One or two others walked slowly to the mound, like men who had come a long distance and were nigh exhausted. Edin herself was swaying on her knees. All the captives were kneeling, most with their palms together beneath their chins and their lips moving in prayer.

Cedric's murderer shouldered through to them. He nodded to the burly man guarding them. This one, spear in one hand, shield in the other, barked something strange and heathen at the Saxons. Naturally the Norse words made no sense to them, yet a shimmer of apprehension passed through them.

The Viking repeated his order, this time using his spear point to urge Lothere to his feet. They were being told to stand, and they obeyed, Edin included. They bunched together, rubbing against one another like deer that had caught a sudden, pungent whiff of wolf scent. Edin, dressed in nothing but her flimsy under-shift, had no modesty left at this point, and what good would it have done her anyway?

The Viking lined them up, and now the grey-eyed

one, as if resigned to a distasteful job, slid his sword into its scabbard, lifted off his helmet and flung it down. He had a truly magnificent head of yellow hair. His golden arm ring and the one big bead he wore as an amulet winked in the firelight. He started at the far end and made his way along, looking each Saxon over. He examined hands, felt arms and legs, looked into mouths and at the straightness of backs. Many were rejected by him: the dairy woman, who was getting along in years; a field serf who looked as if he'd been pressed for decades between the pages of a heavy book; and many others.

When he got to Edin, he blinked slowly. She saw malice beneath his heavy eyelids. She stared back at him with what she hoped was frigid haughtiness. In return, he gripped her upper arm with a mighty hand, pushed her back and looked her over sharply — not her face, as one person looks at another, but her body. He turned her around, as if turning an inanimate object, presumably to look at her backside. When he turned her to face him again, she didn't resist. He reached for her hands. Her chest gave two sharp heaves. He couldn't help but notice, but there was no change in his expression. He was the tallest man she'd ever beheld, tall and muscular in his mail war shirt, and dangerous. His hard, battle-stained fingers turned her palms up. Unlike the other captives, she had no calluses, and for that she felt suddenly vulnerable. She clenched her fingers shut. His eyes lifted and met hers at last, his expression still grim.

He felt her head. At first she thought he meant to take it between those strong capable hands and crush it, but he only found the place where her skull had met the wall so hard. His fingers measured the size of the lump, drawing a small sound of pain from her. He left off, yet his touch hesitated in her hair an instant longer, finally lifting a few strands and letting them fall from his fingertips.

45

Squatting, he felt under the hem of her shift with one rough palm. There was snickering among the men surrounding them, and Edin realized why: This was not the same examination he'd given the others. He wasn't looking for strength of muscle. His palm was open. He was testing the smoothness of her skin rather than the strength of her limbs. A flood of ugly visions swamped her mind, and as his hand rose and slipped between her thighs, she flinched and tried to step away. He dropped her skirt and caught her hips.

He kept this hold on her as he stood again. She stared into his face, trying to read him in the flame-light, trying to gain some notion of his intent.

He spoke, again in Saxon, again softly: "Silken thighs and a rippling fall of amber hair somehow doesn't make me forget the sight of your pretty dagger in Ragnarr's throat. And there is Sweyn, my best warrior, whom I was forced to cripple in the axe arm. You have caused me a deal of trouble, Saxon."

"I'm surprised you don't blame me for that other man who's hurt, too."

Despite his big frame, his movements could be sudden. He let go of her hips and gripped her arms. Her hands automatically pressed against his chest. He was so close she could feel his great beating heart beneath his mail shirt, and the breath behind his half-whispered threats: "Don't speak imprudently. Think what you are — soft, a maid untouched, with skin like silk — and think what my power over you is. I could see that the man who buys you is old. Not so old his quiver isn't full, not so old he wouldn't be able to enjoy your fine, lovely thighs — but still, a man not young anymore, mayhap rotten-toothed, mayhap not given to bathing."

Though her knees threatened to give way, she defied him. "I am not cowed by a wild dog given over to every mean and filthy vice." She would have said more . . but he had such fearfully pale eyes, eyes the color of ashes from a forge where the fire has gone out.

46

There was an awful quietness, during which she had time to wonder if she'd already said too much. She heard the huge fire writhing and shivering behind her. And then the Viking said, "I will see you cowed. I'll see you on your knees — all the more satisfying since they lack grease for deep bending. But you *will* bend them, like a proper Christian, and clasp your soft palms beneath your chin. Aye. I would see it now, but the tide is turning, and I can't spare the minute it would take. I warn you again, though, you are my thrall, mine as I please. Don't drive me to extremes, Saxon; I can be rough."

He stepped away to finish his inspection of the others. Edin risked a look elsewhere and found pairs and pairs of pale blue eyes staring down at her.

At last the giant gave orders to his men. Six captives were separated with tears and wails from those to be left behind, who were stripped naked while the invaders hooted. The chosen six were driven down the path to the river. They went like beasts to a knacker's shed, fearful yet hurrying, each oddly anxious to keep up with the others.

They came out of the riverside growth onto the bank, and Edin saw what she first thought was a monster risen out of the sea. A grinning dragon bounced on the urgent tide. It struck such fear in her heart she hardly noticed being shoved out of the way while the booty was brought down, while the pair of captured sheep were slaughtered and gutted almost at her feet, while her people clung to her mutely.

The Vikings, their shields slung on their backs, trooped with their pickings down the path, each laden with silver, utensils, and cloth.

Gathering her wits, Edin saw that though the sky was silvering, the darkness of deep night lingered in the riverside growth. She wondered if she might slip into it. She took a sidling step, then another. No one seemed to notice, so she took two more. The woods were near

47

enough that one more step might save her. That was
when the big Viking threw his sword with a swift underhanded heave. It stabbed the earth a hand's-breadth
from the hem of her shift.

He came at her then, so enormous and ferocious.
She felt a compulsion to run, but wisely checked it. He
pulled his weapon out of the soil, wiped it on his trou-
ser-leg, and sheathed it. He said, "Now you have been
warned twice."

The dragonship in the river wrestled with its ropes;
the ebb tide was sucking greedily at the current. The
booty had been loaded, and now it was the captives'
turn. The Viking swung Edin off her feet and waded
with her out into the water. Sounds of panic squeaked
through her closed throat. She clutched the Viking with
her bound hands, hiding her eyes against his shoulder.
When they reached the side of the sinister, dragon-
headed ship, still she clutched at him, fearing the water,
if not more than she feared that monstrous vessel, if not
more than she feared him, then certainly more unreasonably. With an impatient frown, he tore her from his
chest, lifted her over the gunwales, and dropped her
unceremoniously to the deck.

There, another Viking, this one with unusual cop-
per-colored eyes, used his feet to tamp her into a corner
where she and the other captives would be out of the
way.

She kept her head down. As long as she didn't have to
see the water, she could fool herself that she was all
right.

The wounded men were brought aboard. The
shaggy-headed one walked to his place on the arm of a
companion, stumbling only a little, silently bearing his
injury, yet curiously blank-eyed and twitching at the
mouth and muttering. He sat by the shield-gunwales,
unnoticing of the friend who bandaged and braced his
shoulder with rags.

The other injured man was carried aboard white and

groaning, with hardly more blood left in him than a finished flask, it seemed—only the dregs that cleave to the sides.

Suddenly the men on the ship and those still on the riverbank began to clap their hands in rhythm and shout, "Jarl Thoryn! Jarl Thoryn!" Thus the grey-eyed giant came aboard. He made his way among them, indifferent to their tribute, even when they slapped him on the back with the flats of their swords.

When he was near the bow, the dragonship seemed so anxious to get away on the sucking ebb that she snapped her moorings. The last four Vikings had to swim to gain her. The jarl called out something in Norse. Immediately, half the men used their long oars like poles to push the ship away from the river's shoal margin; the other half leaned over the banked shields to give their swimming shipmates a hand.

There was much levering with the oars before they were clear of the clutching mud. At the same time the swimming men were being pulled aboard. With so many on the landward side of the shallow vessel, it listed until Edin felt sure they were all going to slide into the dark water. Her heels dug into the deck planking, and she pressed her back against the side. She closed her eyes and prayed in earnest. "Supreme and holy Grace, save us! Deliver us from the savage Northman who has laid waste our homes!"

The other Saxons took up her prayer: "Save us, oh God, from the fury of the Norseman."

How often had she heard that, Sunday after Sunday, as a regular part of the Mass? *"A furore Normannorum libera nos, Domine."* Deliver us . . . save us . . . from the violence . . . from the fury . . . from the Norseman. The words had meant nothing to her. The swift summertime raids she'd always heard about had meant nothing to her. But now all her senses were acute as they had never been before, and she knew that the fury of the Norseman was very real, and very frightening.

Here was a race inured to violence, men who came down on the innocent as if borne on a tidal wave.

Eventually the Vikings hauled their wet fellows up, all of them dripping and moon-eyed with laughter. The ship entered the stream and lunged along. The leader roared a word—*Oars!* Edin guessed the Norse word meant, for the long, bladed oars were quickly thrust out the rowing ports and the Viking's backs bent to their work.

At the same moment the dawn broke. The river ran silver beneath full-leafed willow branches. Big white sea birds appeared and turned overhead. Edin's heart overflowed with all manner of feelings. She was squeezed into a corner with a stolen coffer chest and several of her folk, who twittered like partridges disturbed from their nests. Arneld murmured, "I heard you defy him, my lady. Have a care."

"He's nothing but a heathen."

"Still, my lady," the char-girl, Dessa, whispered, "have a care. You're all we have between us and them."

All they had? Then they had next to nothing. Still, their faith instilled a need for false bravado in her. "He's a heathen and that's that. A curse on him!"

They reached the mouth of the river, where, with the changing tide and the whim of the river wind, strong waters seemed to come from all directions at once. The ship breasted the countercurrents like a great jointed thing and advanced with slow purpose. Udith hugged her fat arms to her bosom. Edin clung to what handholds she could find—and at the same time twisted to get a last glimpse of her home.

She saw naught of the little village clustered about the manor house, naught of the low, one-room cottages of rough plaster, naught of the animals that had cropped the grass in the pasturelands. She saw nothing but a billow of smoke beyond the tree tops. Fair Hope, where she had thought to unwind the maypole of the years with Cedric. She couldn't see it, which was just as well. She knew that what the torch had not burned the axe had cut down. Little more was left of her home than what these Vikings had stowed here in their longship. Even she was being carried off. Everything else, the fields, the buildings, the golden hay piled to the rafters of the byres — everything! — was gone.

She recalled with bitterness that just last evening she'd felt dissatisfied with her too comfortable future. She hadn't realized that at that very hour she was like a tiny spider floating at the end of a silken thread above a chasm of flame.

Another bitter thought assailed her: All of this had transpired while other women were in their beds dreaming of the pleasant day to come, of wearing their best veils and tunics and richest ornaments, of the wedding of Lord Cedric and his Lady Edin, of the feast, the dancing, the laughter. Bitter, bitter was the thought of those still-innocent dreams.

She took one last look at the land she called home, before it could disappear from her sight forever. Something seemed to reach inside her and wrench, until her face grimaced. In the end she had to turn away from that last sight of England just gilded by the rising sun.

The longship, though heavy with booty, rode the sea like a nutshell. Its serpent-head and tail had, in that first moment in the dark, struck Edin as a grey thing of the sort that squats in the dark. The morning sun now showed both head and tail were richly cased in gold. Gold was beaten into the chiseled grooves of the wood, and rubies big as a man's thumb-knuckle were set in a mask for its eyes; its curling tongue-of-fire was hammered of rosy bronze.

The Viking jarl took the steerboard shaft himself and drove the vessel like a rider spurring a stallion. The ship's interior had impressed Edin at first as nothing but a wooden trough with that terrifying dragon's head on its stem. More study showed it was clinker-built of overlapping black oak planks, with places for sixteen pair of rowers. It was perhaps forty-five paces from stem to stern, and fifteen paces across the beam.

The captives consisted of four women, Udith's husband Lothere, and the boy Arneld. They continued to cry and fret. Udith stuttered out a story she'd heard about Danes: "After a battle, 'tis said they cook their food on spits stuck in the bodies of their victims."

Edin shushed her.

Only a moment later, however, Dessa said, "It's God's fulfillment: 'Out of the north, evil shall break forth upon all the inhabitants of the land.'"

The group seemed bound to start up again and again, like anxious birds lifting and lighting, lifting and lighting. Lothere moved to find a better place for his lank legs, showing a set of knobbly toes beneath his long underpants; then he broke into a horrifying tale describing how Vikings reportedly broke open the backs of male captives and pulled their lungs out through their ribs—something called "carving the blood eagle," alluding to the lungs flopping like wings with the men's last gasps.

"Lothere!" Edin admonished sharply. The shocks she'd received, combined with the sleepless, heart-rent night, had exhausted her and left her with no patience.

But the dark-haired serving girl, Juliana, whispered irrepressibly, "And everyone knows they lust after women."

"Where are they taking us?"

"What will happen to us?"

Edin sighed. Goaded by their tears and terror, by their endlessly murmured fears and questions, she wanted to cry out from the depths of her misery *Stop!* Instead, she rose.

In an instant every Viking aboard turned his head to look at her. Not one spoke, not even as she began to make her way down the middle of the war galley. They let her pass without a single gesture or word. Naturally, rape was her keenest terror, much more horrible than

52

mere abduction. She cringed to think of being served over to this shipful of crazed Vikings.

Yet somehow she kept walking and at last stood only a sword-length away from the jarl on the stern platform. She asked, formally, to hide her fear, "My people would know where we're bound for, Viking."

He took a long time to lower his gaze to her, and then seemed to look right through her.

She was all but trembling, feeling so many eyes on her, and she was intimidated by his indifference. She was afraid, so afraid, yet determined to show no weakness. She said, "I thought you understood Saxon," and added for emphasis, "Jarl of the swine."

He seemed to let that pass, too, almost as if he hadn't heard. But then, calmly, he gestured for another man to take the steerboard. His replacement's eyes shone in the morning light. The man's nose was like an axe blade; there were scars on his face, and his teeth were bared in a savage grin.

The jarl stepped down right in front of Edin, forcing her to back up in her bare feet. His bearing was frightening. Hints of danger blossomed.

He said softly, "I warned you, twice." His pale eyes glared with the light reflected off the water. " 'Jarl of the swine'?" His face was dark with the expression of a man with an unpleasant task before him. He said, in a tone as hard as a clenched fist, "For that you will die."

Her heart pounded up—while he seemed to think. "How shall I do it? Slowly, by cutting off your hands, then your feet, then your arms at the elbows, your legs at the knees?" He raised his blond brows, as if measuring her, calculating. "I must say I prefer not to soil the deck . . . so mayhap I'll simply toss you overboard. Ah, that makes you blanch! You don't swim?"

She answered, eventually, since one of them had to stop the silence, "No."

"I thought not. Well, that is the way, then."

He put his hand out to touch the starboard railing,

casually stroking the smooth oak as a soldier strokes his horse's side. "But not just this minute. I'll let you brood on it. Then, sometime when you aren't watching, when you're looking the other way or you've fallen asleep I'll pick you up and toss you in."

Here was a man as wild as a wolf, a man who indulged in orgies of butchery and destruction. What had she been thinking to bait such as him?

He let out a little contemptuous growl. "You seem surprised. It's a rather simple truth that he who attacks must foresee counterattack."

He thought, pulling the mouth corners of his beard. "If you can stay on the surface at all, we'll row around you, offering you the end of an oar—only to pull it back as you reach for it. That will amuse my axe-brothers, to watch you struggle until you're—" he bent a little nearer, reached down and lifted her face with a touch that was as fearful and thrilling as fire, then spoke almost in her ear—"until you're gone, Saxon. Just *gone*. In a swirl of sea fret."

Her fragile courage cracked. She felt dizzy. She turned her face away and tried to conceal its expression. He had so easily found out her worst fear. She could hardly meet his gaze, that mocking, jeering gaze.

"I would do it right now if any save me had understood what you said. No thrall can speak to her master as you do. But since only I speak your dog's tongue, I can prolong your punishment."

She closed her eyes—which seemed to make him more vicious. His voice got softer still, just audible above the hissing sea: "I suggest you go back to your place and think about your upcoming death, Saxon. Such a pity and a waste to be sure—you would have brought me a good price—but then much of life is pity and waste, is it not?"

She couldn't answer, couldn't speak. Her legs trembled as though she'd run a mile. All she could do was open her eyes. And when she did, on top of the fear he had instilled in her, she felt shame. She felt the drench of humiliation—because she could see his satisfaction in what he'd accomplished in her.

"And you said you couldn't be cowed," he scoffed. "You see how easy it is? How does it feel, Saxon? Do you know how it feels to me? Remember the feel of your little splinter of a blade striking bottom in Ragnarr's throat? Think of that and you'll know how I feel."

Chapter 4

Ever afterward Edin would remember that journey north like a bad black dream. As the sun sailed high behind long banner-like clouds, she dared not take her eyes from the Viking jarl. Others about her fell into exhausted dozes. Her eyelids were heavy, too, and she found herself nodding; but she repeatedly jerked herself awake.

Her body forced its needs, however. The soft voluptuous pleasure of sleep crept over her limbs, through her body, and into her senses, and she drowsed, only for a few minutes, but long enough to dream of a shadow falling over her, two large hands reaching, catching her up, swinging her, and letting her go. She cried out as she dropped into the suffocating sea. The water closed over her head, and she strangled for air. The liquid silence stopped her ears and isolated her from all the world.

She woke with her neck straining upward and her fettered arms reaching for a purchase that was not there. Next to her, Arneld stirred in his sleep but didn't wake. She sat up. She was stiff and cramped, and her head ached from the banging it had received the night before. Her eyes darted frantically to find the man who was going to drown her. She couldn't at first locate him, and with a feeling of having wakened from one nightmare into another, she also realized that the steady

56

stroke of the oars had stopped.

It took her a moment to see that what was going on had nothing to do with her. The Vikings were busy with the ship's walrus-hide cables, hoisting a red-and-white striped sail. Her senses now alert, she scanned their faces. Those who weren't working with the sail were lounging on the wooden chests that also served as their benches when they rowed. They were all gazing upward, watching the sail catch the wind. To her they all looked weatherworn and hard. Then, as the sail bellied and the long-bodied ship seemed to leap forward, Edin found the jarl.

He too had been looking up, but as he brought his eyes down, his gaze came directly to her. It moved on, shifting to inspect the sea. The lines about his eyes deepened into a squint. Without his helmet, the breeze puffed his beard and blew his straight, fair hair back from his shoulders. So indifferent and cold! She mustn't sleep again!

Daring to look away from him for little instants, she saw that they had come far from the land. Under sail, the ship seemed to snake through the water, as if with life of its own. The beast was carrying her away from England, away from the warm ashes of Fair Hope, away from any handhold she could cling to for safety.

Some of the Vikings began to examine the fruits of their brigandage. The one with the high, axe-blade nose turned in his hands a silver-gilt beaker that looked suspiciously to Edin like church plate. She wondered over him. Was he a man like other men? If so, how could he ravage and burn helpless towns, kill people and play jokes on corpses? Or was he, as Dessa said, a direct visitation of divine rage against the sins of England?

Edin watched a burly man curl in a sleeping bag on the deck. Two others got out a chess set. The board's squares had little holes drilled in them, and the game men had small pegs in their bases. They were made so the ship's pitching couldn't upset the game. Arneld had wakened, and being too young and too restless to stay put, he inched over to watch. After a while, one of the men made a move that lit his opponent's face with grins. Arneld smiled at them, the way one smiles at happy people. But when he innocently reached for one of the exquisitely carved, walrus-tusk ivory game pieces, the owner of the set shouted at him and reached for his belt knife. A breath of ice crossed Edin's soul. "Arneld!" She opened her arms to him, and he made a blind, scrambling dash for the shelter she offered. As he quaked with terror, she tried to comfort him, exchanging looks with the owner of the chess set, until the snap of the sail startled her back to her own concerns. Her eyes darted to find the jarl.

Again she concentrated on watching him, hearing only the wind hissing gently across the vast empty sea—until a new, rattling sound drew her weary attention. Her tired gaze slid to the two wounded men.

The housecarl's murderer was lying on his back. The rattle came from him, with each slow rise of his chest. Edin guessed he was not long for this world. The shoulder-injured one, he of the ashy blue eyes whom the jarl had called Sweyn, was sitting up glaring at nothing. As Edin's gaze slid past him, their stares collided. He grimaced, showing big yellow teeth. Even wounded, he was frightening. She saw the white scars of other wounds on his arms and face. He suffered her gaze a moment, then seemed to go purple with rage and shouted something at her, which she interpreted as "What are you looking at!"

Quickly she shifted her attention back to the jarl who gave her no more than a brief frown, a glancing blow of a look, before he went back to studying the sea.

Meanwhile, the two slaughtered sheep were butchered. The two men in charge hung joints of it over the side, letting the meat trail in the water to keep it cool and salted for when it was needed. The rest they sliced with their bone-handled belt knives. The slices they either covered with hot ashes in a smoldering fire lit in a flat, iron pan on the fore-platform, or strung on a spit over the fire. It seemed these Vikings had a systematic way of doing just about everything. They were orderly and efficient as well as bold and reckless.

The crew ate the spit-roasted mutton as it was cooked, and drank from skin bottles of fresh water. Nothing was offered to the captives, most of whom were sleeping anyway.

The day passed. The sun's rays sliced thinly between breaks in the thickening clouds to the west. The ash-baked meat was tested and wrapped in greasy pieces of leather. One of the cooks lifted some deck planks near the mast-stepping and lowered the meat down into the dark over the keel, where the men had earlier stored their axes and spears.

Hunger and thirst began to take nips at Edin. Juliana sat up and gave a great yawn; she reveled in it without bothering to cover her mouth. One by one the others woke and took up their fretful murmuring. Now they were wondering if they were ever to be fed or given water.

Edin felt the burden of the responsibility that they placed on her. They still thought of her as their mistress and looked to her for succor in their distress. Guilt gnawed at her. She should ask for water for them, and food, and some kind of protection against the elements. But the jarl had unerringly found her worst fear; he had stripped her of her courage to do her duty. She hated him for that almost as much as for all the other horrors he had committed against her and hers.

However, hate was not the same thing as courage, and she did nothing as her people grew thirsty and famished.

The terrible surfeit of pain and shock and fear — and now thirst and hunger — by slow degrees benumbed her. She didn't even realize how engrossed she'd become in one Viking's casual slaking of his thirst, how she watched him swallow, and swallowed herself, hard enough to be heard. The man took a bite of meat. Her mouth moved with his as he chewed. Meanwhile she'd forgotten to watch the jarl. Her heart nearly stopped when she realized he'd moved down the ship and was now only a few paces away. Fear hit her right in the stomach like a knife. She leapt to her knees, prepared to make what defense she could.

He stopped, and stood looking at her, his face all iron, stunning in his size, backlighted by the sullen evening. After a moment, he laughed — if one could call that short bark a laugh. Her fear, her preparation to fight him even though her wrists were fettered, even though she was hardly half his size, seemed to amuse the cruelty in him.

He moved another step toward her — just to tease her it seemed — then threw a skin of water and a package of meat on the deck at her knees. She didn't move, didn't even look at it. A gust of wind blew up, tossing her hair wildly about her face and arms. He waited, then said, "Eat, Saxon, and drink deeply. It may be the last time you taste anything but salt and fishes."

He walked away with all the ease and grace that came of great physical strength. To Edin he'd become the sum of evil. She felt ashamed to see her people looking at her, patiently waiting for her to apportion the food among them. So far she had done nothing for them. She wanted to cry with fear and tension and this awful sense of helplessness.

Instead, she shared out the food and ate the meat as daintily as she could with no utensils. Hungry as she was, she soon found she couldn't swallow her meat. Round and round it went in her mouth, the mutton fat getting colder and more congealed.

Though the *Blood Wing* danced easily enough on the

wave tops, she could be contrary to handle, being so broad in the beam, and Thoryn preferred to handle the steerboard as much as he could.

The coast of Britain was just visible. As long as it was in sight, he could steer by the shoreline. On the open sea, he would navigate entirely by the sun and the stars. He'd learned early to recognize the Pole Star and to depend on it. But he always kept an eye out for portentious signs: A strange bird, a bit of floating wood, fish surfacing unaccountably, a cat's-paw of wind on the water—these all had meaning for the seawise.

The sun slipped down between a great slow-rolling cloudbank and the horizon, and stared at them across the open sea. The Vikings lay at their ease in the low-planing light, letting the wind belly the four-square sail and drive them homeward. They were weary from voyaging and sated with looting. Most of them had removed their battle dress and were back to wool trousers and shirts of linsey-woolsey. In most cases, the trousers were brown or grey and the shirts red or blue or green—though Hauk Haakonsson's was a definite mulberry color. Hauk, with his high, axe-blade nose, was fashion conscious. It wasn't cold, so no one had put anything more than a sleeveless leather vest over his shirt. With their helmets put away, they protected their heads with woolen caps. To a man, they stuck to beards and long hair. It took a good growth of hair to protect against the bitter winds and burning sun of the North Sea.

Some napped, sitting up on their sea chests with their arms folded, as motionless as flies in the last sun. Most of their personal property was stored in these chests. Thoryn, as captain and owner, was responsible for "finding" the ship, for furnishing all necessary equipment—lines, spare sails, buckets, etc. Each man brought his own warm sea clothes, his kit of needles and thread, weapons, and so forth, which he stowed in his chest and his allotted section called his "room."

One or two had climbed into their sleeping bags. Ottar Magnusson and Jamsgar Herjulson, called the Copper-eye, were playing chess. A few others watched the game, trading coarse jibes. Several men were seeing to their weapons. Time at sea was often filled with wiping weapons dry against rust, and touching blades to whetstones.

Hauk, Jamsgar, and Ottar were among those in Thoryn's private hire. They lived on Thorynsteading in the longhouse in return for acting as his personal men-of-arms. They were men built to feast on other men, so brisk and strong and well armed that they had no enemies, men made of iron true enough to hold an edge. Sweyn the Berserk had been one of them.

Thoryn sighed. The darkening sky was full of enough high clouds that the breeze should last the night. That would put them nearly a third of the way home.

His ever-shifting gaze moved to the Saxons. He'd waited to feed them until he was sure none of them was going to hang miserably over the gunwales retching up his meal. The boy, lying by the shield-wall making little marks on the deck planks with a wet finger, would make a good shepherd. When he grew, he'd do for a field worker. The three servant women were for Inga, who needed more help in the longhouse as she got older. The man was a thin weedy type, and Thoryn wouldn't have brought him except that he was obviously a carpenter. Thoryn had a notion in his mind that was going to require carpenters.

One spear of rosy light picked out the maiden. Now there was a prize. She was tilting the waterskin to drink and caught his stare with a sideways look—and nearly choked. He averted his face and schooled himself not to scowl.

He'd finally quelled her. One of his strengths was his unerring nose for frailty in others, and at first he'd been amused to see how thoroughly he'd ferreted out hers ut now the joke palled. She was *too* frightened. Her eyes burned for sleep, and her face was as pale as a linen shroud. He resisted the idea, yet felt mayhap he had done wrong.

Don't think about wrong. I have enough troubles without taking on "wrong." I don't even understand "wrong!"

After all, what had he done but show her the reality of her situation—that he had the power of life and death over her, right down to the power to decide what the quality of that life or death might be? She was bound, not harmed in any way except for that lump on her head; she could bear a well-deserved lesson in discipline.

But disciplined or not, with that hair like amber seaweed, and that skin as fresh and soft as a babe's, and those eyes, wide-set—and green!—and that mouth with its lilt at the corners that gave her a seductive expression capable of melting any man's metal, aye, even undisciplined he would get his price for her. He imagined her on the block, her shift stripped from her shoulders. . . .

Blood Wing tugged hard on the steering oar and urged ahead. It was as though the dragonship had spoken aloud: *Keep awake and steer, Northman!* Thoryn felt the overlapped planks of the hull twist. She was like a live beast bucking the waves.

But even the dragonship couldn't keep all his attention right now. He soon fell back to thinking about the woman.

Mayhap it would be a mistake to sell her in Kaupang. It was the closest big mart to Thorynsteading, but he might get a much better price for her in Hedeby, where sometimes Rus traders visited in search of new faces and bodies to take down the Volga for the Arabian harems. The Arabs were said to crave fair women, and this one was certainly fair.

"You gloat, Thoryn?" Rolf Kali clapped him on the back as he joined him on the steering platform. The evening was cooling, and Rolf had his grey cloak on, held to his chest by twin gilt-bronze brooches.

Thoryn raised his brows in question, though he knew exactly what Rolf thought he was gloating about.

Besides that rusty-red hair and beard, Rolf sported a widespread, unrefined nose and the scar of an old gouge wound on his cheek. He was somewhat older, and a different kind of man from Thoryn altogether. He was, for one thing, much less serious-minded. Friendship, to Thoryn, was a matter of expedience, but if he possessed such a thing as a true friend, he supposed Rolf was it.

Right now the man's complexion was high, whipped by the wind. He said, "Whatever you told the woman seems to have scared her badly enough. She sits there like a hazelgrouse in the woods on hunting day. You've shown her who's boss."

Thoryn preserved his silence for a moment, then said, "Whatever I told her she well deserved. She need to learn she's but a thrall."

"And at her master's mercy."

"Aye."

"And you are her master."

Thoryn's eyes grazed the soft curve of her shoulders. She looked tired and defeated. He said, "Aye, I am — for the time being. I was just considering whether I could get a better price for her in Hedeby."

Hedeby lay on the east coast of Jutland at the head of Schleifjord on the shores of the lagoon of Haddeby Noor — far from Dainjerfjord in Norway. Thoryn saw Rolf considering this. "We couldn't make that voyage until spring," he said. "Were you planning to keep her maiden that long? Over the winter at Thorynsteading? With the men?"

"The men will leave her alone."

At just that moment Jamsgar Copper-eye squatted before the captives and pulled on the bare foot of the one with dark short curls. The girl woke with a start.

He smiled broadly, pointed to himself, and said, "Jamsgar. Jamsgar Copper-eye."

The girl giggled and pointed to herself, saying, "Juli—"

The maiden sat up straighter, threw her arms around the dark-haired wench, as if she were the girl's protector, and said, "Juliana, don't speak to him!"

Thoryn bellowed, "Jamsgar!"

The Copper-eye looked at his jarl and shrugged. With a grin, he went back to his room.

"The men will leave her alone?" Rolf said. "If you say so. But she's a tempting bit, axe-friend. Those lips, and that hair, and . . . have you ever seen a woman with green eyes before?" He sighed hugely. "She'll cause trouble. Winter is long, and there are days when the longhall feels like a corral and the men start acting like stallions."

Thoryn shrugged. "The profit I'd turn on her would justify a little trouble."

"Most likely; but truth be told, she would get you a good price even if she weren't *quite* a maiden."

"The men will leave her alone—or else."

"During the day when you have your eye on them, aye. But what about at night when you go to your own chamber and nothing but a curtain keeps the wolves from invading her good and fragrant pasture? If I were her master, I think I would see she was safely locked up at night. Preferably with me."

Thoryn saw the twinkle in his eye.

"Come, Thoryn, this talk of selling her! As if I'm not a man who knows men—more important, a man who knows you. The lass is beautiful—and she's yours! Since when were you so monkish? No one sells a thrall like that. The best a man keeps for himself. Take her to your bed and be happy. Then, when you've had enough of her, we'll talk of markets."

Thoryn exhaled through his nose. "You talk nonsense. She won't command eight half-marks if she isn't

65

a maiden."

Rolf shrugged. "Mayhap you'll lose a few half-marks. It depends on how sorely you use her. And mayhap, after a time, you'll decide not to sell her at all. Think of it, brother!" He pretended to consider the woman. "Having her in your chamber, alone. She would probably be reluctant at first, being a maid. She would need training—much training—many a pleasant night's work, that. You would want to take her slowly the first time or two, so as not to frighten her. I know there are those who prefer a good scuffle, but this one—no doubt she's been brought up cautiously on a diet of piglet and lamb and fresh milk straight from the goat's udder. I don't think you would want to frighten her. No, take her slowly and teach her to shudder with—"

"You give me much helpful counsel, friend, none of it worth a horse's cast shoe." He glanced pointedly at Rolf's crotch. "I see your body has outgrown your brain again."

Rolf laughed. "When a man has been as long from a woman as I have, even a hole in a water keg seems inviting. I've been eyeing the younger men aboard for the past week. Now I have something better to eye."

Thoryn snorted and looked away, out to the sea. "The woman doesn't tempt me half as much as does the idea of eight half-marks of pure gold. Besides, my father took a Saxon thrall to his bed, and later regretted it, as I recall."

Rolf was wise enough to let that pass. A moment slipped by. He stepped away to pull on a line of the striped sail, then came back and placed a hand on Thoryn's shoulder. "Beornwold is nearly gone. Hark to his gasping; he can hardly put one breath after another."

Thoryn nodded, keeping his eyes from where the dying Viking lay sprawled. Instead, he looked up at the bellying sail. "And what of my berserk?"

"That one will live—and live to cause you grief."

Thoryn lowered his eyes to the sea again, avoiding any glance at Sweyn, who was muttering from the corner of his spittle-flecked mouth. Thoryn should have killed him rather than condemned him to a life of uselessness.

That woman!

He said, "It must be in Odin's heart for Sweyn to cause me grief, for he has certainly done so often enough. Him with his berserk ways, stamping himself into fury, biting his shield rim, going around bellowing in the coldest air without a stitch on. He's made many a virtuoso performance of speed and brawn and complete brainlessness."

"He's fought for you without fear."

"He's fought for a leader of rank and means in return for good pieces of gold and the promise of meat in his belly all the winter long. True, he has no fear, but he has no care, either. Mayhap, when we reach home, I'll give him enough blood-money to buy a small steading and a few cattle, and be rid of him."

Mayhap, he thought privately, being his own steading master would give a cripple enough self-respect to make his life as worthwhile as it had been when he was a proper-shaped man. Thoryn felt he owed him that much, having made him useless as a warrior.

Rolf again moved to adjust one of the intricate system of clue lines that enabled them to reef the large sail. When he was finished he said, in a considering tone, "I would ask you a question, Thoryn Kirkynsson."

"Ask on, Rolf Kali, provided you don't want to know where the winds come from, or where the tides start, or what makes the moon round. I don't know those things."

"Why did you do it; why did you spare him? Beornwold will die only once, but you've condemned the Berserk to die daily. What did the woman say to you?"

A cold serpent twisted in Thoryn's vitals. He cast a

glance at the Saxon—

—and met her eyes. They emptied his lungs. They were enough to fell a forest, to move a field, to drain a lake. The whole world could be dismantled and dropped into those green eyes, to sink without a trace.

By Odin, she was a woman to tempt a man!

Don't think of that.

He struggled to find his wits again, to achieve a semblance of solemnity. "Sweyn broke his oath to me; he disobeyed my order."

"I didn't ask why you challenged him—"

So easily did Rolf put that aside! He had no conception of the will Thoryn must summon up to get himself through such fierce and bloody tests of dominance.

"—I asked why, when once you bested him, you didn't finish it?"

"She said 'please,' " he answered shortly.

Rolf frowned, unsatisfied.

"What's that look now? Say what's in your mind, without fear or favor."

"It makes no sense, Thoryn. She pleaded because she's a woman and can never understand that a lame fighting man is worthless to himself and everyone else. Or that giving and taking death well are two of the things a proud man does. Sweyn Elendsson lived by the axe and reckoned to die by it."

Thoryn grew irritated. "Call me a madman and pelt me with bones if you like, but I'm afraid you must take my unseemly answer anyway."

Rolf eyed him with a look that eased into affection. "Then . . . did you hope to gain her favor by it?"

"Aye, right after killing her bridegroom before her eyes and right *before* someone dropped his torch and so set her home afire. Considering how much was taken from her at one blow, I'm sure my sparing of Sweyn created a real lust of gratitude in her."

"If not her favor—"

Thoryn clicked his tongue. "This conversation tires

me. Can you speak of naught but the thrall? By Odin, I swear you yourself would like to get into her secrets."

Rolf's look turned sly. "I won't answer that, Oh Hammer of Dainjerfjord. I prefer to keep my sword arm intact."

Rolf left, and Thoryn fell to thinking about how he had killed the maiden's groom. He recalled how she'd crooned over the body, speaking senselessly about mending the boy's shirt. And he had been just a boy, hardly a man yet. Thoryn recalled a thinnish beard and a drooping mustache. But when Thoryn had seen in the maiden's eyes that there was someone behind him, it had been pure reflex to turn and swing his sword. Then, seeing the boy sliced open and in agony, he knew it only merciful to pierce the boy's heart so that his end would be swift.

He could still feel the iron going in, and how he'd leaned on it to drive it farther, and pushed his weight after it. *I think I felt the boy's last heartbeat.*

Chapter 5

"They're talking about you."

Juliana whispered what Edin knew well enough already. By their glances, she knew the two men beneath the curled tip of the stern were discussing her. Now and then she caught snatches of the jarl's deep, compelling voice. Was he telling the redheaded Rolf that soon he was going to throw her overboard? Oh, why hadn't she used her dagger on herself when she had the chance? Better that than. . . .

She looked at the darkening water and shuddered, then looked at the Viking once more. She saw no signs of clemency in his face.

Juilana whispered again: "The big one wants you."

Edin could have laughed. *Wanted* her! He only wanted to kill her.

"It's no shame on you, my lady. With your looks—"

"Juliana, please!"

The girl shrank back behind Arneld to sulk. The boy went on scribbling on the planks, using his finger as a pen and drops of sea water as paint. Edin was left to herself once more, left to consider her situation.

She had no defense; she felt dwarfed and helpless among these immense men, awed by their masculinity. She'd lived in a gentle, pleasant household. Cedric had been manly in the way of a young gentleman, not in the harsh way of these warriors. Comparing him to these

70

was like comparing the barnyard rooster to the hawk soaring overhead.

Cedric! She pressed her fettered wrists to her forehead, trying to block out the image. The dragon had thrust out its tongue, and poor Cedric was pierced through. Edin was caught anew by the horror of it.

Her eyes didn't tear, however; in fact, they were too dry. She blinked them hard. They burned. She was so weary. The food had only increased her craving for sleep.

Both Vikings were staring at her now. Their expressions made her feel naked. She had to look away.

Yet everywhere she looked she saw Vikings, some of them very near, near enough for her to hear the rustle of their clothes and see the gleam of their golden arm bracelets. One was sitting just above her on his sea chest. The dying light cast him in bronze. She could make out the individual hairs on his head and in his long, pale, silky beard which was flapping in the sea wind. He was wiping his sword, a gold-hilted malignancy with a calfskin scabbard.

Vikings! She was a captive of Vikings!

But not for long. What would happen to her people when she was drowned—Arneld and Udith and the others? Who would speak for them among these ruthless, wrathful, purely heathen barbarians? Who would advise them and buoy them up?

Oh, I don't want to die, not at the sea's hands! A dream, let this all be a dream, just a horrible dream!

For the hundredth time Edin jarred herself awake, a cry of terror poised in her throat. Her breath came hard and fast. Unable to sleep, unable to stay awake, she was near madness. The longship lay becalmed in a fog. The Vikings had put up roof-slats, then stretched a canvas over them to make a tent against the night. All up and down the deck they slept in their warm bags of

71

unshorn sheepskin. They seemed not to mind living like ants in a dish, practically on top of one another, without room to move.

The captives had been given a few unsewn sheepskins as well. They were doing their best to sleep, and most were succeeding. Only Edin sat goading herself to wakefulness, not daring to sink into the oblivion her body begged for.

The night seemed endless, timeless. Minute after minute fell dead, never adding up to a passing hour, never bringing a change. It felt as though her eyelids were weighted with iron, and her head felt as if one of these warrior-monsters had buried his axe in it. How long had it been since she'd slept. Two days and two nights? The worst two days and nights of her life. She felt dizzy and disoriented and increasingly crazed.

Finally she came to a decision, and with it came relief, sharp and sweet. She rose and picked her way over the sleeping form of Udith. She took careful steps toward the prow, giving attention to where and how she put her feet. Slowly she made her way over the Vikings' sleeping bags and stooped out from beneath the tent.

Because of the mist, it took her a moment to spy her enemy on the prow platform by the head of his dragon. She paused. Remembered pain and panic rippled across her skin. Nonetheless, she went toward him, wobbly, but without hesitation. She almost felt herself drawn forward, as if by some formidable magnetic force.

She stopped at his feet and reached to tug the hem of his cloak with her bound hands. She was smiling, feeling euphorically pleased that soon her horror would be over.

He half-turned, saw her, and turned to look down at her fully. Her gaze lifted from his legs to his harshly hewn features. She flinched and swayed on her heels as if she'd been physically struck, for even in her mad euphoria, she felt uneasy under the relentless gaze of those cool eyes.

He said softly, so as not to wake the others, "What have you come to ask me this time, Saxon?"

"Two things."

His heavy-lidded gaze slid to her lips. "Speak out, in clear words; I'm unafraid—mayhap because I can't recall a time when a kitten leapt at my throat and I couldn't save myself."

He wasn't afraid of anything, not even God. But of course, of God in the Christian sense, these Vikings would have no conception. She'd heard that they worshipped many gods. Who? And what did they demand of these warriors?

He was waiting, and she remembered what she'd come to say: "They shouted 'Jarl Thoryn'—is that your name?"

"Why do you ask?"

"I've watched your face for so many hours, I know I'll never forget it; but I want to make sure I have your name right as well, so that I'll always be sure to know you."

"Why should you need to know me? Are you to bring my end upon me, little bedraggled woman-slave that you are?"

"Yes," she said evenly, "if I can."

The corners of his mouth crisped—the nearest thing to a smile he seemed to own. "Many a time I've heard of doomsters—we call them shieldmaidens—but never have I seen one before. According to what they say, a true shieldmaiden has a voice like splintering icicles, or like the swish a gannet makes when it falls out of a cold sky. She wears a winged helmet and carries a shield." His gaze skimmed down her. "You don't fit the description. Isn't that your underwear you're shivering in? And your voice—well, it's not like splintering icicles, not at all."

She lost patience with his game. She was giddy and having trouble keeping her stance, even though the

73

ship was barely rocking. "I asked you, is your name Jarl Thoryn?"

"I am a jarl and my name is Thoryn. Thoryn Kirkynsson."

She nodded, satisfied. "If I can, I will seek you from beyond, Thoryn Kirkynsson. You will live to regret all you have done to me and mine, but too late."

He squatted down to her level, as if to see her better through the grey mist. She felt his presence, restless, dynamic, surging with energy. She also felt his anger, but somehow kept herself from stepping back from it.

"What is your second question?" he snapped.

She faltered, then said, "I ask you to do it now."

What followed was a ghastly silence. She dared not look at the black water. Her heart pounded as he stepped down before her. Now he positively radiated crude power. She was more afraid in that moment than ever before.

"Now?" he said. His expression became darker and more ominous as each second passed.

"Yes!" she hissed. She dared not look into his face anymore; she knew there was no smile there, and no mercy.

He took her waist in his hands. She didn't resist. As his grip tightened and he lifted her off her toes, she only closed her eyes. His fingers bit into her waist so hard she thought he would pulverize her. In the darkness behind her eyelids she saw butterflies in brilliant profusion . . . yet she was quiet. She could feel that splendid chest flexing—then felt his beard brush her cheek and heard his voice in her ear: "Now doesn't suit me, Saxon. You're weak, so weary you can hardly stand, too weary to afford me the pleasure of watching you struggle."

She opened her eyes. His face was a mere inch from her own. Even in the dark she could see the tiny lines at the corners of his eyes, those shuttered grey eyes that could no doubt simply congeal an enemy in mid-attack.

I wish it were a dream.

He said, "Go back to your place and sleep without anymore jolting up. I grant you my word that I'll not grab you this night."

She couldn't keep the sob out of her voice. "No! I can't bear this waiting anymore! Do it *now!*"

He gave her a shake. "Don't be so thrallish-minded! I'm offering you rest, Saxon. And in the morning I'll see you have a good breakfast set before you, so you can make your journey to the bottom of the sea on a full stomach."

"No!" She writhed half out of his hands, twisting toward the gunwales. He caught her and tightened his hold again. She squirmed futilely in his iron embrace. "Jarl of the sties! Jarl of the pigs! Jarl of the midden—do it now! *Do it now!*"

She was hysterical, and only half-understood what he meant when he said, "Little joy lies in ending this sweet spectacle in such a way, but what is a chieftan to do if he wants the respect of his shipmen?"

She was vaguely aware that she'd awakened them, of the lifting of large male faces with heavy beards and staring eyes. "Do it now!" she cried piteously, plucking at his hard arms. "I can't bear it—the waiting—I can't bear it!"

He said, not harshly, "I understand, Shieldmaiden, and mean to put an end to this foolishness, with all generosity."

She saw his fist and knew he going to hit her with it, and she had only an instant to be grateful: She would drown without knowing. She felt the blow to her cheekbone like a hammer striking from across the sea—and then felt and saw and knew no more.

Until she woke under the canvas shelter at dawn. She sat up bonelessly. The motion of the ship made her head nod on her neck like an unopened lily bud on its stem. Her sleep had been deep and dreamless, and now her headache was gone. But in its place, the side of her face felt sore. She lifted her bound hands and found her cheekbone swollen.

She also discovered that she had a fine cloak wrapped about her, and beneath it, she was wearing a huge woolen jerkin, a man's garment. She considered these sleepily, as if they were all there was in the world for her to consider just now. She wondered without urgency how she could have come to be wearing them. Her hands would have to be untied to be put through the armholes—but her hands were tied now. So someone had untied her, dressed her in the jerkin, tied her again, then wrapped her in the cloak.

"She's awake!"

Edin looked at Juliana's glossy black hair and blue eyes, still a little dumbly, still disorganized, still mostly self-absorbed. The girl said, "*He* gave his cloak to you, my lady. He carried you in his arms and laid you down here like a lover wrapped in his own cloak!"

A sharp, delicate chill soaked through the pores of Edin's skin.

"I told you he wanted you." The girl giggled.

"*Hist!*" whispered Udith.

But Juliana could not be repressed. "Did he ravish you, my lady?"

Ravish. The girl said it as if she thought it a delicious word.

"Did he?"

Edin was fully awake now. "None such as him shall ever abuse me that way!" She paused, bestowing thought to the jerkin, the cloak. "At least, I don't think he did." She turned to Udith. "Would I know—if I were knocked senseless, I mean?" Her hands went to her cheek again. "He hit me, and I don't remember anything after that."

The two servant women exchanged glances. Juliana giggled again and said, "You feel no soreness?"

"It's very sore. I'm sure he blacked my eye." She fingered the swelling gingerly, trying to recall. . . .

She'd been hysterical. And he'd hit her. But the bruise didn't seem overlarge, considering her memory of the size of that fist coming at her. It seemed he'd hit her just hard enough, and no more.

"No soreness *elsewhere?*" Udith asked.

Edin realized what they meant, and lowered her eyelashes. "No."

Udith sighed deeply and crossed herself, while Juliana seemed a little disappointed. Edin took a new look at her. She was a plump creature of sixteen with a wide, inviting mouth and broad hips made for childbearing. It came home to Edin why the Vikings had decided to bring her, when they'd rejected others who were more skilled.

At that moment the Vikings were lifting the topcover, and Edin saw that the morning had broken as clear and as cool as a crystal. A flurry of birds swept about the longship's mast, and a gentle breeze just wrinkled the tops of the long green swells. She searched for the jarl, and her eyes found a large form in a sleeping bag near the prow. Evidently he'd finally given in to a need for rest himself.

He didn't wake till noon. By then the day was much different. Dark clouds had built a fortress on the starboard side, and a grim wind had come up, whipping salt spume into any face lifted above the level of the gunwales. Though the sky was still blue directly overhead, the huge banks of black and threatening clouds moved along the horizon.

As the jarl took command, the wind began to whip the sea into a froth. Terrified, Edin took young Arneld into the Viking's commodious cloak with her. Nonetheless, after another hour, she and the boy were both weeping. The water got more turbulent by the minute.

With astonishing swiftness, a squall of rain closed down. As well as she could, Edin kept her eyes on the jarl. She watched him go aft and give some order to an older, very fair-haired man who was struggling at the steerboard. The jarl shouted to make himself understood against the wind. He took the steering oar himself and heaved on it with all his vast brawn while the other man lashed it to the ship's side.

When the bulk of the dark clouds reached them and lowered down, it was as if the whole world had plunged into darkness. The full force of the storm hit, tossing the longship like a straw. The wind shrieked through the rigging and blew white spray off the tops of the waves. The jarl shouted orders, and men shuttered the oarports that pierced the sides of the ship below the rails and lashed the two wounded Vikings to their places. As the waves continued to rise, every man was in a frenzy to lash and stow his gear and plunder. The jarl moved among them, lending a hand here and there.

The wind rose to gale force. Clouds flew low across the heaving ocean. The atmosphere was one of roaring water and blinding rain.

Night came, and still the wind rose. The Vikings couldn't put up their tent; the dragonship remained completely open, offering no shelter for the shivering crew and petrified passengers.

For Edin, time became a haze of screaming wind and pounding waves. She huddled with her teeth set and her eyes wild. In her worst nightmares she'd never dreamed the sea could assume such proportions. Sometimes the deep green towered as high as the mast, reared above them and hung over them before it toppled down, smashing everyone to the boards, smiting the longship like a stick of wood in a tide, swirling it around and around. She lost her sense of direction, her sense of the world, her sense of herself.

The low sides of the dragonship admitted great sloshes of water. There were small drain holes at the level of the deck, but since the deck was loose, made up of planks set over a skeleton of supports, before the sea

78

water could rain out the holes, it poured between these planks into the shallow hold. This called for constant bailing. Men had to crawl down into the bilge and pass up buckets for dumping. It was slow, exhausting work, bailing by bucket and muscle, and it went on for three days and three nights, until the Vikings began to swear in voices that were exhausted threads, and to kick at any captive who happened to get in their way. The two injured men lay on the boards, groaning and begging their friends to slip a knife into their ribs so they might not have to endure another day of torment. The jarl's eyes grew as chill as the sea.

The captives, a man, a child, and four women, who had all thought to live and die within walking distance of their birth places, prayed and moaned through it all. What were they doing on this vast expanse of unknown water? Once Juliana cried out a Biblical text: " 'It is a fearful thing to fall into the hands of the living God!' "

No, Edin told herself, what was fearful was to be *cast out* of the hands of the living God, which was what she truly believed had happened to her. Her God had forsaken her. Somehow she had offended him, and now she was on her own.

Arneld's eyes were sunken. Dessa's elfin-shaped face was pale. They had been snatching food and drink whenever it came within reach—usually nothing but salted fish and cold meat—and they were all long past fatigue. There was a queer apartness about each one. Edin sensed their spirits were almost gone.

Wet to the bone, rubbing her bare feet together against the cold, she had a dull premonition that they would all drown, mayhap even all be thrown overboard by the increasingly surly Vikings—unless they did something in their own behalf.

The jarl stood on the prow platform, his head level with the bottom of the dragon's head. With one arm hooked around the serpent's neck to keep himself from being tossed overboard, he stared forward into the

world of barreling, thunderous clouds and mountain-
ous waves, looking exactly what he was: a man full of
cruelty, appetite, and death lust. As protection against
the wind and spray, he wore oiled-skin garments now.
He seemed miles away from where Edin now got to her
feet, determined to make her way to him.

She'd seen men fall while trying to move around on
the washed deck, and as a rolling wave caught the keel,
she too slipped. The way the wind blew the rain, it was
like a sandstorm, stinging her flesh, burning her lips,
and blinding her vision. She stumbled several times
more before she at last stood behind the jarl.

"Thoryn Kirkynsson!" The wind sucked her voice
away before it could reach his ears. As best she could,
she scrambled up onto the unprotected, windswept
platform. There she paused, chilled by the presence of
a primal force and instinct too potent for her understanding: a Viking. Then she shouted again, "Thoryn
Kirkynsson!"

He swiveled. His features above his drenched golden
beard were set in a look as black as thunder. He took in
the sight of her still wearing his cloak which drug the
deck, then abruptly threw his free arm around her and
pulled her against him. Stabbed by fear, she felt his
hand clutch her bottom, bracing her against his thigh.
At the same time he shouted, "By Odin, what do you
want now!" The ropey veins in his neck stood out.

She shuddered like an eel feeling the touch of the
skinning knife, but lifted her wrists between them.
"Unfetter us!"

He seemed disbelieving. "You little . . . go back to
your place before you're swept overboard, robbing me
of the pleasure of tossing you in myself!"

She looked up at him, and if it weren't for his arm
fast about her, she would have stepped back, appalled
by the naked malignity in his face. Nonetheless, she
shouted, "If you unfetter us, we can help."

"Help? You could help by serving as sacrifices to the

Great Bearer of Life. Kol Thurik—" he nodded over his shoulder—"the one who fell this morning and sits there chewing his broken tooth—he claims Freya has shown her back to us."

She looked over his restraining arm, down at a powerful middle-aged man who was hanging on to his lashed sea chest as he rolled against the violent motion of the ship. His lip was bloody, and Edin could imagine the pain of the broken tooth behind it.

She looked back. The wind was seething around her, roaring, ripping the green waters on all sides. With the rush under the keel, the rise and fall against the grey world, she couldn't help but lay her hands on the jarl's chest for balance. She felt the deep throbbing of his heart—while her own pattered out a frightened cross-beat. He'd used the word sacrifice. These were heathens. There was every chance he was completely serious. She said, "If you throw us over, Viking, we will only feed the fishes—and the only life we'll bear forth is that of herrings."

The wind surrounded her, whipping her words away, and for a moment she thought he hadn't heard her. But then she felt his chest move with what might have been a huff of grim humor. She said again, "Unfetter us. We can help bail."

Another shower of spray blew her voice back in her face. He'd heard her this time, she knew, but he only tugged the hood of the sodden grey cloak better around her long hair. His face was changed; for an instant the malignity was replaced by lines of sheer exhaustion.

Finally he nodded. He turned and pressed her between him and the tall prow-stem, so that he could let go of the dragon's neck and use his belt knife to cut her bonds. The sea heaved; he grabbed for the stem-post while Edin grabbed for him. She found him so deep of chest that her arms would not meet around his back.

For hours she bailed, until she was in a daze, fighting against the sea that washed again and again over the sides. Her uncallused hands were chafed raw, her back felt nigh to breaking, and the blood sang in her temples. Suddenly she heard Arneld's childish voice explode with horror. She turned her head and whispered, "God help us."

Less than a thousand paces away, hanging like a toothed crag, was a massive cliff of water. From its dark green base, it towered a hundred feet or more to its wind-scourged crest. As Edin watched with drenched face and open mouth, it slid closer, rumbling.

And then it stood directly over them. It cut off the wind; there was silence. It was a moment to freeze the blood. There wasn't an eye aboard not fastened on that green mountainside of water.

The blow fell. The dragonship was buried beneath hundreds of tons of violent water. An instant before the wave hit, Edin threw herself over Arneld—just before she herself was squashed by another body. Her lungs nearly burst. Now she would die. She felt the sea opening its wide foamy mouth—but by some miracle the ship broke the surface. Water poured out the deck-level drain holes, but the ship was wallowing and stumbling like a dragon with an arrow through its heart.

"Quickly!" The jarl was on his knees beside Edin. Had it been him who had thrown himself on her as she'd instinctively thrown herself on Arneld, to protect him? The question hung unasked on her lips as the Viking shouted, "Bale! Or the next wave will surely bury us all."

Saxons and Vikings alike tipped out the storm wrack, using any vessel that came to hand. The jarl used his own helmet. Gradually, the ship floated more freely, until at last she rolled with the great waves again.

After the mammoth wave, yet another day and night of violent weather tossed them. It began to seem to Edin that drowning might be better than such voyaging.

Then, the morning of the fifty day, the gale let up,

hushed . . . gentled . . . stopped. The sky cleared, and the tall seas and wild waves smoothed to glass, a sheet of glass as broad as the ocean, as muscular as a sleeping giant's back.

As the wind had quieted, Thoryn could hear again the slap of water against the planking and the liquid gurgle of the sea as it was cut by the stern. He commanded Leif the Tremendous to fetch up a keg of stiff barley beer from the forehold. The storm had abated, and miraculously, all aboard were still alive. That called for a drink.

The beer was passed around in helmets for all to swill, even the new thralls. "Thank you, Jarl!" came several shouts. The maiden, who had never tasted Norse barley beer before, sampled it before she drank. Watching her, Thoryn seemed to taste its sweet, honey flavor anew.

He cast his eyes over the *Blood Wing*, looking for signs of damage. The vessel was a shambles of men and tumbled plunder — cups, swords, money chests and streams of cloth and skins.

But the mast still stood, the sail still filled, and the steering oar still answered to his pressure. Thank Odin for his compassion.

Fafnir Longbeard and Rolf were seeing to the two battle-injured men, who also had somehow come through the storm alive. Sweyn's color was high; he probably had a fever. Thoryn heard him shout, "Lie off me lest I ram you, Longbeard!" Where did he get the energy? Thoryn felt nearly dead with exhaustion. But before he could rest, Rolf called him to Beornwold's side. He went reluctantly, for he knew what the summons meant.

He knelt by the dying man. In a voice flat and dead, Beornwold said, "Thoryn Kirkynsson?"

"Aye, it is Thoryn. How goes it, Norseman?"

Beornwold was long in answering. "Could be better, lad." He tried a smile, but his lips stopped midway. "I'm tired."

"Then rest, ship-brother."

"Aye . . . and if I do not stir from this sleep, go you to my wife and son beside the fjord and give them my regards."

"I will do that. And I will give them your share of our profits, and a goodly share of mine." The blood-payment for a husband, a father . . . how to measure the loss in terms of silver? "I will tell Hrut that his father met the three basics of a good warrior: courage, skill, and grace before the presence of death."

Beornwold whispered, "Hrut . . . a man must abide by the worst of his acts, and I will stick by mine: Hrut has been spoiled. He has a native cunning and a wild heart. Guide him . . . tell him that man is but a little creature, with a life hardly longer than a fly's."

"Lie easy, brother, don't talk."

"Aye."

It was his last word. His jaw dropped open; his eyes became dazzled and unseeing. Thoryn touched his shoulder. "Go easy, neighbor; you have nothing to fear. You were a man. The gods know that and wait for you."

He stood and stepped back, chaffing in his skin, very angry, though he couldn't show it. Sometimes being jarl put him in an isolation so profound it was painful.

Others moved in to wrap a blanket around the dead man, shrouding him for his burial. All stood silent as the corpse was heaved over the side of the ship.

The body lay quietly for a moment on the breast of the sea. Thoryn caught sight of the Saxon maiden watching this with eyes that dared not blink, with a face as white as a snow maid's. What was she thinking—that he had vowed to throw her overboard in the same way? The body of Beornwold sank, showing first man-sized and then small, and then miniscule as he went to his sea bed. The sight seemed to fascinate the maiden. Thoryn felt disgust for himself. She was beautiful and noble and knew no fear of anything—except drowning. And he had used that one fear against her.

Surely it was wrong.

Chapter 6

Thoryn settled himself to steer the *Blood Wing*. The wind had fallen to the smallest whisper. It was getting late in the day, and he saw nothing but sea. They were far off their course and had a deal of sailing to do before they reached home now. The wind changed direction, he felt it and altered his course.

The maiden was looking at him now. Her head on her slender neck swayed gently with the ship, like a field flower in a gentle summer wind. Her look hurt him. Suddenly he shouted, to no one in particular and everyone in general, "It ill-becomes a Northman to sail with his decks uncleared! We have cleaning up to do."

The *Vikingar* began to straighten the deck. The maiden helped in her own portion of the ship. Soon everything was heaped in a sort of order. But then, unaccountably, the Saxon boy began to weep. Reaction had set in, Thoryn supposed. The three servant women also started to sniffle and wipe their noses on their sleeves.

The maiden took the exhausted boy's head in her lap and murmured to the others, and after a moment she began to sing. Gently patting the boy's shoulder with one white hand, she marked the time of her melody. Thoryn stared at that small hand, fascinated. He glanced at his own hands gripping the steerboard and noted the difference with a pang. He knew he was a man of some height and powerfully built, while she was but a little maiden and all alone.

The bustle stilled all up and down the longship. Freemen and slaves alike settled and sat enthralled by the woman's ballad. Of the Norsemen, only Thoryn understood the words — something about green sleeves — yet everyone was caught by her high, sweet voice.

He saw when she grew aware of the fact that she'd become the center of attention, saw her face blanche, then color. She paused at the half-song, and he feared she would stop; yet she didn't begrudge the *Vikingar* their pleasure. She sang on, in that clear, high voice, with the barley ale warm in her head and the sea wind cold on her cheek, till the end was reached.

The hush held when she stopped. For a long moment there was only the sound of the sea lapping the ship. A scent of spells seemed to cling to the air. A little at a time, normal noises resumed. Thoryn saw that his men were satisfied somehow. The sad tune had seemed a respectful way to bid farewell to Beornwold. Occasionally, one or another of them glanced at her, their faces blank and impassive, expressing regard in the subtlest of ways.

Thoryn gave the steerboard to Kol Thurik and strode down the deck. The maiden shrank back to see his legs stop before her. He started to reach for her arm, but saw the way she cringed, so he straightened again and simply gestured for her to follow him.

She rose slowly. And followed slowly. He was at the stern platform several breaths before her. He knew she thought that he'd made his decision and her time had come.

Sensing she was behind him, but not looking to see, he spoke as if to the dragon's head. "Shieldmaiden, as you know I've more than once thought of tossing you to the fishes; but since you helped save all our lives with your bailing, and since that song of yours, well, you

87

entertained me, and I'm at the edge of changing my mind and letting you stay aboard."

He turned to see her face gone blank.

Eyes so green you need to look again to feel sure—

He cut into the thought, saying roughly, "How would that suit you?"

It pleased him to see her recover enough to answer him as plainly as ever: "It would suit me well enough, Viking."

He didn't smile, only nodded and gestured her back to her place.

Suddenly, as if some doom the Norsemen hadn't even been aware of had now passed, there was a burst of easy-going merry-making aboard the longship, even a little horsing. Jamsgar Copper-eye told Kol Thurit that the loss of his front tooth would be no great handicap, ". . . since I hear you're a man who likes a woman merely for what she has in common with a man, and when you take her from behind like that, she can't see your teeth anyway."

Kol muttered from his sore mouth, "At least I *do* like women, Copper-eye, unlike you, who I hear is seduced by any available behind straining to pull a cart."

"Not any," said the irrepressible Jamsgar. "I honor only those who aren't slow to lift their tails, being in much demand as I am."

Leif the Tremendous leapt in with "Was that why my horse nipped you last winter? Was that a coy invitation, Copper-eye?"

This chiding didn't last long. The men were too tired. Soon Thoryn was the only person aboard still awake. The breeze was steady. It had backed a little farther into the southwest, and that meant it wouldn't fall off before night. He peered ahead. They were on the high seas, out of sight of land. They'd been blown far off course. Throughout the storm, they'd been pushed away from the land as though Loki had been pushing at their stern. Now it was up to Thoryn to ge them home. The men slept, assuming their jarl would stay awake a little longer and not steer them off the edge of the Great Void.

In the pre-dawn three days later, the ocean was absolutely calm, like pale greenish-blue satin. The clouds took on a rosy blush, and the sea became pink; then the sun appeared, flaunting its rays across the sky like banners. Thoryn leaned his back against the stern. *We can't be too far out now,* he thought. *I hope no one at home has been worried. There's only Inga to worry about me, of course, but many of the men have wives who might fret. Many have sons and daughters, too.*

As the sky lightened, a lone sea bird suddenly appeared and whirled and cried over the creaking, leaking, battered dragonship. The sight of shore birds meant just one thing. "Land," Thoryn said aloud, "I smell it." He strained to see, and after an hour a storm came up in his veins. There! That was what he'd been praying for: Jutting over the aquamarine horizon was a hazy outline of darker blue. It could only be the tall, grizzled shoreline of Norway. The wind seemed to freshen at just that moment, as if to drive the *Blood Wing* toward her harbor.

By noon, everyone aboard could see the landfall, could see even the little waves ruffling the edge of the myriad outer islands. Now a cloud of birds flew over the *Blood Wing.* Thoryn knew where they were now, and it was nothing to get home.

Near sunset, he put the helm hard over, and they passed the promontory called Outer Rock. The lean-lined longship entered Dainjerfjord.

Inga Thorsdaughter stood on the summit of the headland above Thorynsteading, where she had a clear view of the mouth of the fjord. Only the sound of the water lapping the gravel shore far below broke the evening silence. The sun had no more than an hour left before its setting. Already the sheer sides of the fjord had shadowed themselves.

For the past week Inga had climbed to this cliff-edge lookout several times a day, hoping to see the dragonship's swollen sail. So far she'd been disappointed and, after an hour, went back to supervise the day's sewing and fish-salting and care of the goats, or the evening meal and the bedding down of the steadying folk on their various pallets. This was the fate of a Viking woman: While her men lived like heroes, she had to wait. *Would they come back?* The same painful question was asked in a hundred homes. *Would they winter away? Would she see them ever again?* Stalwart, dry-eyed, proud by necessity, and controlled unto death—these were the qualities of a Viking mother, wife, daughter. Ever prepared to receive the news that her loved ones were lost forever. The sea was her master, her enemy. The sea made her strong so that she might wait for months, years, caring for the farmstead, the harvest, managing the thralls, and coping with her neighbors.

Inga clutched her red cape about her. In the distance, the white sea sparkled and breathed. She thought, *The great sea may be our enemy, but the wind is our friend. The wind brings our men home.*

Sometimes.

She squinted, looking toward the place she knew the dragonship would first appear—and there it was! She spotted the huge sail first, almost lost in the sea dazzle. The red-striped splotch grew larger and larger, and then a dark shape appeared low in the waves. The *Blood Wing!*

Several emotions coursed through her at once: gladness, relief, nervousness. She was glad she'd worn her best dress today, the blue one that was the color of the high summer sky, the same color her eyes had been once. Her hair, thick and heavy like Thoryn's, was arranged in a knot atop her head, signifying her position as a matron. It was a source of pride to her that it was still blond, not as lustrous as in her youth, but not grizzled with age, either. She patted it girlishly, tucking a stray tendril into place. She wanted to look her best for her son.

She was relieved because being in charge of the steadying while Thoryn was away was a big responsibility. This was not a small farm on which the half-grown children and a hired hand could do all the work. There was a large staff of workers indoors and out, men of Viking birth and thralls captured in raids. Their labor had to be directed, their ailments treated, their disputes settled, and the welfare of the whole considered.

Inside the house, she oversaw the cooking, the cleaning, the spinning and weaving of the flax and wool, the provision of food and the care of the furnishings. Outside, there was the sheep-shearing in the early summer, and the flax harvest, then the washing and carding of the wool and the preparations of the flax stems for spinning. The dairy work was a daily round. The steadying had a blacksmith shop where Eric No-breeches had to be kept busy forging tools, shoeing horses, and repairing equipment. There was the tar pit where the tar for daubing ships and treating ropes had to be distilled from resinous woods, and the tannery where the hides had to be cured into furs. There was always the lumbering and carpentry as well as the wood to be chopped for the fires. Inga even had to supervise the saltworks; they used a great deal of salt in food preparation and at the table.

She had to know what was being done everywhere, and had to judge if all was going well. And always without a man to lay his tall body over her and kiss her leisurely.

She sighed. The sea sighed.

Last but not least of the several emotions that surged through her was an incredible nervousness. Thoryn had grown into a severe man in the fifteen years he had been jarl. Few dared stand against him in his wrath. In many ways he was like his father.

Kirkyn. His memory followed Inga always. She could suppress it but never really destroy it; eventually it returned, with slow repeated hammering. Kirkyn, her blond, bright-cheeked husband. She'd loved him recklessly. The world had shimmered with her love. She would have given her right hand for one of his huge enfolding smiles. Then he'd gone to the faraway isles of England to gather gold and silver, riches and thralls. It was just an evening as this when he returned, his eyes unwilling to meet hers anymore. Everything had changed after that, everything was ruined. He'd come in from the ever-winking sea filled with deceptions.

For he'd brought home a thrall-woman. He hadn't needed to say a thing; all Inga had to do was see how he looked at her. The woman had bewitched him, and Inga didn't know how to break the spell. To see him thus had choked her with hate. What was so surprising about that? Nothing. What surprised them all was the end to which it had finally come.

As the sun slipped a little farther down the side of the blue sky, the dragonship drew close enough that Inga could see its oars digging deeply into the fjord water. The *Vikingar* were eager to be back to the windy sheep runs and butter-laden grass of Norway. At least for a while. The sun caught the edges of the sail and glinted from the long, flashing oar blades; the ferocious dragonhead rose with glowing ruby eyes above the elegant hull; points of light mirrored from polished helmets, spear tips, and axe blades. The warriors' round shields hung in a row along the outside of the ship in a fine display. Suddenly one man—was that Magnus Fair-hair's son, Ottar?—leapt outside the gunwales and commenced to "walk" around the outside of the ship by jumping from one moving oar to another. Those aboard cheered him on, and those on shore who had spotted them and were running down the path to the dock shouted.

And there! There in his smoothly polished helmet —
Thoryn! Inga drank him in with her eyes as her hands
plucked nervously at her skirt. She could hardly wait to
touch his cheek, smooth his hair, to reassure herself he
was really back and that the great love between them
lay intact.

Her excitement grew to such heights she could
hardly breathe. And she got a strange taste in her
mouth, that coppery, sweet taste. *No, not now!* She was
apprehensive for a moment. But then it went away. It
passed. It was gone. Shaken, she nevertheless put an
expression of absolute tranquility on her face and set off
down the path. Her beloved son was home.

Norway! Edin knew little about it save that it was
vastly barbaric, an unknown realm on the upper edge
of the world from which swift Viking ships swept down
to make terrible raids. She'd never considered what
kinds of homes the warriors returned to, what garments they changed into out of their ship and battle
dress, what foods they ate, what games they played, or
what else they might spend their time at between jour-
neys. She'd never thought of Vikings as men, as
people, with the needs and feelings and interests and
habits everyone else had.

She gazed over the gunwales at the rugged and precipitous shore the longship was approaching. Already
they'd passed a sort of girdling shield of thousands of
islands, most of them smooth, bare rock. The sea
around those had been comparatively shallow. Nearer
the mainland it seemed to get deeper again, affording,
as even she could see, an exceptionally sheltered ship-
ping lane.

From a distance the mainland itself had seemed
nothing more than mountain ranges tumbling into the
sea. Waterfalls dropped off sheer cliffs, sparkling from
rock to rock as they descended. Deep inlets cut into

shoreline, many only a hundred feet or so wide, others very wide, with steep bluffs rising on each side.

Her heart beat harder when they finally entered one of these many inlets. She heard the Vikings say a word over and over: *fjord*. It seemed to be a long, narrow arm of water betwixt towering mountains whose sides sloped down abruptly from comparatively flat tops hundreds of feet above, over which poured more great falls. The water from one especially high gorge cascaded hundreds of feet down a sheer rockface. Simply looking at it made Edin feel dizzy.

Farther along, several trim farms presented oddly idyllic pictures. One was sited right on the sill of a tributary valley. She glimpsed a field of soft green grass — but she felt a bleak distrust; she doubted that picturesque quality could be genuine.

The dragonships rounded a headland, and there was a trace of flat land with a long stone jetty built out into the water. There was no valley here, and no farm to be seen, yet there were people coming down a path and others who had already gathered under the beetling headland. Almost all of these were as fair as the sun. The women were mostly beautiful, with long golden hair, clear blue eyes, and lovely fair skin. They waved and cheered as the rowing Norsemen eased the ship around the jetty. Two of the warriors were busy unstepping the longship's mast, and another two had furled the sail and were tying it. The ship nosed to a gentle bump against a wooden dock made of boards silvern with age and gleaming with damp. The oars were shipped.

It seemed a renewal of sweet life itself to Edin to step onto that dock and then onto that curve of firm land beneath the cliff; yet it was then that she knew the extent of her weariness. She felt distracted, battered. Her legs felt liquid; even on solid ground she seemed to continue to sway with the sea.

She stayed with her little cluster of people, all of

94

whom were trying to be invisible as they watched the homecoming of the warriors. She was surprised to find that Vikings had wives and children and parents and friends, all seemingly jubilant to have them back.

Several people stopped to speak to the jarl. These greetings took place with a more cautious exuberance, as between people of traditional detachment and reserve. Only one woman truly welcomed him. An older woman. He was preoccupied with overseeing the unloading of the ship, but he turned quickly upon hearing the woman's voice and feeling her tug at his sleeve. She owned an elegant beauty and an apparent gentleness of spirit. Edin saw how his eyes lightened to silver—though they did not really warm—as he looked down at her. He allowed her to touch his cheek. Searing images of terror and ruination passed through Edin's mind, contrasting so starkly with this one sentimental gesture.

Who was this woman who touched the dragon-king so gently? His mother? Could even such as he have been born of woman? Everywhere the warriors were enjoying bursting smiles and embraces and exchanges of happy chatter. Between the woman and the jarl, however, was silence. Even that one instant when she touched him he kept his face hard, his expression guarded.

Edin had no time to deduct what this meant, for she and her people were herded up the path by a man with callused, earth-stained hands who kept saying, "*Velkommen! Velkommen!*" But he said it in a gloating, insincere way. He had wild black hair and grinned at them the way worms must grin at newly interred corpses.

As Edin passed the jarl, though she didn't look into his bearded face, she was fully aware of his male force, worn like a crackling cloak about him. She imagined his eyes turned that threatening, turbulent grey again.

Though not fettered, the climb was hard for the captives, weakened as they were after so long and fearful a voyage. At the top, Edin stood bent, catching her breath. Tendrils of her hair clung damply to her brow. For the moment all she was aware of was relief at being out of sight of that great, golden-haired Viking for the first time in seven days. But then she put her hand to the small of her back and levered herself upright — and found herself looking down into a barriered but secure landscape, a lovely bowl-shaped valley, sheltered and warm.

Scents greeted her in a rush, the sensual scents of good loam and lush, dew-damp, green pastures and the smoke of wood fires. To the west sat three large buildings forming three sides of a rectangle. The two end buildings were about thirty-by-ten feet. One looked to be a dairy and cow byre; the other must serve as a stable. The longer third building had to be the Vikings' ale-hall. It was low, over eighty feet long, and built of logs. One great tree shaded the U-shaped grassy area before these buildings.

Behind the hall was the midden, the rubbish pit. Scattered in the distance were a few cottages, their thatched roofs plush with vivid green moss. The low slant of the last sliver of sunlight cast long shadows before each of them. Fertile, well-watered fields sloped gently down to the valley floor. Edin watched a black sheepdog fly across one field at a gallop, tidily collecting a flock.

Behind the valley, fells climbed up to a forest of birches, and higher to a forest of pines, and still higher to mountains steeper than Edin had ever seen before, mountains that were clothed in snow even in this midsummer season.

She'd just spotted a herdsman bringing his goats down through a quiet and empty stretch of meadowland dotted with birch trees and juniper when she and the others were urged down into the vale toward the longhall. They rounded the byre, and Edin saw a stone dung channel cut down the middle, and neat stalls to accommodate twelve dairy cows. As they passed under the huge shade tree, larks rose up into the bright evening, singing as though they actually adored this place, as if it were a place of fruitful harvests and peace and not of water-borne warriors.

They had to step down to enter the low hall, for the floor had been dug out. Edin paused on the threshold, feeling too young and too weak and too forsaken for whatever lay ahead now. She put her hand on the door, which was covered with designs of great imagination. Blackhair, the man escorting them, gave her a nudge. Unsteady as she was after having been pitched and rolled between wind and wave, she stumbled down into the interior.

She was blinded by the sudden dimness, especially after the glare of the open sky and sea. She looked around, feeling frightened and vulnerable. She was, after all, a female captive in a land full of foreign men.

She took in a deep, trial breath of the strange air. It was air and that was all. It inhaled easily and held no associations — until the smell of hot food hit her. She'd known many more mealtimes than meals since her capture, and had gotten so sick of salt-fish and smoke-dried meat that she hadn't eaten much of what was given to her. The smell of an onion-flavored stew caught her attention now, however, and her very pores flew wide open, thirsting for more.

She blinked and became more used to the light. The interior was one large room of lofty height and great length. The floor consisted of stamped clay and sand on a flagstone base, over which were the usual rushes. The structure appeared to be thick-walled and was warm as a burrow. The roof was supported on rows of posts, and everywhere she looked, elegant animal ornaments were carved into the wood — artwork that was breathtaking with its flamboyant magnificence.

Two lines of tables ranged down the length of the room. In the very center was a long, sunken, stone-lined ember pit, in the near end of which a single, sweet-smelling pine log was burning. A hole in the ceiling allowed the smoke to ascend. Over this fire hung the bubbling stew. Nearby, the kitchen area was well supplied with iron pots, pottery bowls, stone jugs, wooden ladles and the like.

One long side of the room was sectioned off into small compartments. These were open to the hall now, but Edin saw that they could be made private for sleeping by pulling simple cloth curtains. A raised earthen platform along the opposite wall afforded places for the household to sit at their work or for guests to sleep. Two chambers, one at the head of the hall and another at the very end, were fully walled and had doors. Beside the one near the door was a warp-weighted loom.

A few tapestries hung from the ceiling beams; the walls were hung here and there with shields crusted with gold and silver, which glinted in the light of the fire, but the building as a whole had a coarse feel about it. Edin couldn't forget that it was the home of a race that pillaged at will.

Blackhair was going around lighting several huge torches in sconces set in distant posts. When he finished, he lined the captives up to be fed. A thin, pale-faced girl began to dish out stew into wooden bowls.

The Saxons sat at the end of a long table that could have seated forty more. As Edin ate, her glance was drawn to a huge chair which stood directly opposite the longfire. This plainly was the high-seat of the lord of the house. It stood on a low dais which raised it a foot higher than the rude benches bordering the tables. It was flanked by two tall posts completely covered with intricate carvings of sea monsters of some sort, with round heads and hooklike mouths opened to flaunt jagged teeth. It reminded her of the dragon-prowed ship — and of the Viking who had sailed into her life with no mercy or quarter.

She was reaching for a second oatcake when the older woman who had greeted the jarl appeared in the open door. Something about her made Edin feel wary.

The girl who had served them was now bringing each a cup of ale. A change came over her when she detected the presence of her mistress. The woman gave her a cold, intimidating, splinter of a glance. She didn't seem the same sweet-faced woman who had touched the jarl's cheek so tenderly. Obviously she was not a person with just one face for every occasion.

She walked toward the Saxons, who stopped eating. Unlike the others, Edin refused to hunch her shoulders or bow her head in awkward humility. The woman stopped behind her. Edin's hair was still completely free, and she felt the woman was studying it. She turned. The woman was staring at her all right, but she seemed to be looking at the cloak Edin was still wearing. She made a gesture that told Edin to take it off. Edin stood and did so. Then the woman stared at the woolen jerkin.

If this is the jarl's mother, Edin reasoned, *then she must recognize these garments; she may very well have made them.* Without being told, Edin removed the jerkin.

But the woman's gaze stayed on her. Her mouth moved slightly. Edin returned her look, until at last the woman grabbed the garments from her and hurried from the hall.

Chapter 7

The nested sun still veined the sky with gold and rushes of crimson. The deepening purple water of the fjord mirrored the rosy-gold of the sunset as Thoryn stood alone on the dock listening — to the seawater slapping the shoreline, the more distant drop and splash of the waterfalls, and the even farther off murmurous hurry of the streams.

He supposed the voyage had been a success — except for the loss of Ragnarr and Beornwold. The gods distinguished between the dead, between warriors killed in battle who were sent to Valhöll as Odin's chosen host, and the unworthy who died in bed and were consigned to Hel. But how was a mere jarl to measure the gain of gold over the loss of life? Or losses of a different sort, such as in the case of Sweyn?

The last of the loot had been carried up to the hall, and Thoryn had seen the *Blood Wing* taken out and moored by a cable around a boulder in deeper water. He now shouldered his sea chest and started up the path. The chest was heavy, and once he started the climb he didn't want to stop, but Inga intercepted him. When he saw the bundle in her arms, he felt an odd regret.

"I would speak with you." Her eyes smoldered.

He set the chest down beside the path.

"Why did you bring her?"

"I take it you speak of the maiden."

"Is she that? Still?" She lifted his cloak and jerkin as if they proved otherwise.

"Aye, she is, and will command a good price."

Inga's voice trembled. "As a bed-thrall."

Thoryn moved uneasily. He stared down at the fjord, at the *Blood Wing* which from up here looked like just a little thimble of a boat. His mother could be fawning in her affection, and altogether too possessive. He never knew what to do with her excessive emotions.

"She looks like . . . like . . . surely you can see!" Her voice scaled upward in pitch. "I don't want her in my home!"

"*Your* home?" He said it quietly, and then was ashamed. Where had he learned this power of frost and silence? "The woman doesn't really look like Mar—"

"Don't say her name to me!"

He hated it when she got wrought up. Speaking soothingly, he said, "The woman is valuable." That open, beautiful, young face, that glorious hair, the gestures and the poise, the voluptuousness beneath the undershift that covered but concealed so little.

Inga had seen all that, too, or she wouldn't have been here accusing him. She said, "Valuable! You didn't bring her home to sell her; you want her for yourself! You'll—" From her throat came the sounds of a little girl locked in a chest, trying to comfort herself. "Don't trust her! She's a demon. She'll tempt you. You'll betray me!"

"I am *not* my father; but I *am* master here. I *am* the jarl. And if I take a woman for myself—any woman—it is my business, and no betrayal of my mother."

He pulled his helmet off and held it stiffly at his side. The breeze lifted his hair and cooled the sweat on his nape. "The thrall will stay here until I can make a voyage to Hedeby next spring. I'll sell her there for considerable profit, more profit than I can afford to ignore. If that distresses you . . . you must simply make the best

101

of it."

Inga stared up at him but didn't seem to see him. Her face had gone doll-like, expressionless. It was a common enough occurrence. He knew it was his father her eyes beheld. Her memories of Kirkyn were always just under the surface of her mind, ready to rise.

She muttered, "Hedeby is it? Next spring? Not Kaupang? No, because the thrall sparks your lust, and even if she spells your death, you will have her."

Have her. The words sent vipers of flame crawling up his loins. He pushed the sensation away. "Mother!"

No, try a softer tone, coax her out of this.

"Mother, you make too much of it." He laid his hand on her shoulder. She blinked, seeming to wake out of a dream. He said, "Come see the treasure we bring. Two monasteries we sacked, besides a manor house. I have a bolt of cloth for you, woolen cloth embroidered in silver."

Her eyes cleared; she was herself again. "Thoryn . . . oh, Thoryn, I'm sorry."

"No need." He shouldered his chest and started up the path once more. Now she would be fawning. He tried to excuse her; but this had been going on for so long, and he was so sick of the contrary feelings in himself concerning her.

Well, what could he expect? She was a woman. He'd learned to place no great trust in anyone, whether friend or enemy, and least of all in women.

"I'm so, so sorry," she continued behind him. "I don't know what comes over me."

"You work too hard," he said gruffly, puffing under his load and the steepness of the climb. "We had little room for captives, but I brought three women to help you in the longhouse. I trust you'll train them. I'm depending on you to teach them mannerliness and the general rules."

"Her, too?"

He was at the top of the path now and stopped to

look down into the valley that was his home. He inhaled slowly and let it out slowly. The sky had lost its color; a rind of white moon hung there now.

"Her, too, Thoryn?" Inga persisted, the fawning tone gone. "Is she to work for her keep through the winter? Is she to learn her place?" Frost clung to the question.

"Aye, especially her. She's spoiled, not used to taking orders. You must be firm with her. Firmness in the beginning is a kindness, especially when a thrall is overly proud and—"

He stopped. A spear of insight warned him he'd said enough. No need for more words on the subject. More and Inga would start looking at him in that half-demented way again. He adjusted his load on his shoulder, creating a little business to smooth his awkwardness. "Is it agreed?" He made his look level and serious, as if the decision were really hers.

An immense fire glamourized the air of the longhall. The Vikings had been eating for a long time, feasting on a thin pork stew and copious quantities of the dark ale. The pale serving-thrall, Olga, rushed to and fro, trying to keep the men's drinking horns brimming. Edin and her people sat close together along the wall platform. They each had a bowl of ale, thick, brown, and foaming darkly. Edin sipped hers less than eagerly. Her curiosity struggled with her intense weariness. She was trying to make herself realize that she was truly *in* this place; wherever it was, whatever it might mean, she was *here*. In the dim light she saw things that were strange to her: Vikings in their lair, big, bluff, and boisterous, gargantuan in appetite and apparently not overburdened with mental ability.

They sat up expectantly as the jarl, sitting in his thronelike chair, wearing rich garments and drinking only wine, began to preside over the division of the plunder.

Dispute after dispute arose over the profusion of golden crucifixes and pyxes and ciboria, the ivory reliquaries, the tapestries of woven silk and books of illuminated vellum set with precious stones. The jarl claimed and got the lion's share of everything, though the others seemed unwilling to give up anything without an argument. Sometimes he made an airy gesture of giving in; more often his voice rasped of iron, and it was the disputer who made the gesture. At length, Edin grumbled to Udith, "Never were there such quarrelsome men. I swear, these Vikings would sit on the beach with the sea rising about them and quibble about who was going to stand first and give the other a hand up—until they both drowned."

Though the arguments could seem bitter, the men toasted the jarl again and again. She realized that from their point of view he'd led them on a spectacularly heroic adventure, one that would never be forgotten; he was a mighty Wreaker of Deeds. It made no difference that from their victims' point of view it was an exercise in thievery and murder that had brought untold misery.

As the quarreling continued, Edin's eyes felt both staring and weighted. She vaguely noted that now it was the middle-aged Kol Thurik speaking around his broken tooth in disagreement with the jarl. Her eyelids were as heavy as lead. But she sat up as Kol strode toward her. It was not her he took by the arm, however, but Lothere. Udith immediately tried to take her husband's other arm, but Edin stayed her.

The carpenter was pulled before the jarl, where the wrangling continued. Finally the jarl, with a frown, nodded, and Kol grinned. The Viking gestured for Lothere to pick up his battered sea chest. It was apparent that he meant to leave and to take Lothere with him.

The carpenter's thin angular face turned to his wife, fearfully, hopelessly, and Udith, who'd been standing with Edin's staying hand on her arm, broke and ran forward. She ran right across the hall and threw her arms about her husband. Lothere put the Viking's chest down to embrace her.

Kol, clearly annoyed, separated the two so forcefully that Udith tripped and fell to the rushes. When Lothere would have helped her, Kol stepped before him. The big Viking moved like a lynx and stood with a look for the smaller Saxon that was nothing if not threatening. Lothere raised his woody hands in a beseeching way and whimpered like a beaten dog.

Edin's heart leapt and took fire inside her. Without thinking of the possible danger, she went directly to the jarl. "Where is he taking Lothere?"

The jarl's gaze narrowed and darkened like a closed-in pewter-grey sky.

"They're married. You can't separate them!"

"Can I not?"

There is a silence that is not really silent but more a chilling diminuendo of all sound. Such settled over the hall now, like a gigantic raven folding its wings. Every eye was on Edin. She felt her half-nakedness; she felt the fire flaring behind her, no doubt outlining her body in its thin shift; she felt herself hopelessly revealed. She also knew that the smoothing of the jarl's expression was no indication of understanding on his part. Indeed, whenever he was most dangerous he also became his most smooth.

Nonetheless, she said, "You must know they will pine for one another. Lothere will try to get back to Udith; Udith will try to reach Lothere. No good will come from it."

The jarl seemed to consider her, his face a mask that could not be read. At last he gestured her aside — saying, however, in an almost caressing tone, "Stay near, Saxon. I'm not finished with you." Then he called in a voice of iron, "Kol Thurik!"

The two spoke in Norse again. Kol shook his head,

then looked at Udith, who had gotten to her feet and stood leaning forward, straining toward her husband as if pulled by an invisible leash. In turn, Lothere's mouth was pitifully drawn. The jarl kept talking, Kol kept shaking his head; then the jarl said something in a tone of exasperation. Now Kol nodded, his grin bigger than ever.

The jarl's expression was not nearly so pleased. He turned to Udith and spoke in Saxon: "Your husband belongs to Kol Thurik—and you are to go with him, too."

She rushed forward to Lothere. They embraced with muffled cries, until Lothere remembered their benefactor. He bowed low to the jarl. "Thank you, master!"

"Yes, thank you, master!" Udith echoed—then added to Edin, "and thank you, my lady!"

Kol managed to get them away and soon the ornately carved door closed after them. Edin belatedly realized she'd just seen the last of the only person in the world she might call a friend.

When she turned, she found the jarl's attention on her again. If her heart had been warmed by his benevolence, it was chilled now by his stare. He stared at her until she wanted to scream, "*What?*" All up and down the hall, only eyes moved, darting like excited fish as they followed the development of what looked to be a fearful—and extremely entertaining—confrontation.

In his own time, the jarl said, "I wanted that carpenter, but Kol would have him and nothing but him. It was bad enough to lose him . . . but also the cook I brought to help my mother?"

He sat leaning on one arm, his bearded cheek in his hand, his hard, impassive face totally indifferent, looking at Edin, looking and looking at her. "What disturbs me even more, however, is your insolence. No man disobeys when I command. If I say dance, he dances. Yet you, a mere woman, and a thrall-woman at that, you dare to interrupt when I'm dealing with another Vi-

106

king. How do you explain that?"

She stood stiff and erect and prideful. "I have a duty to do what I can for my people."

"*Your* people? If you mean those thralls"—he nodded toward the platform—"they're *my* people—as you are mine."

She squared her chin. "I am nobly born. And *free*-born. You may have stolen me, but the say-so of a barbarian does not make me a slave."

She felt giddy with her own temerity. Whatever was she saying? She was getting beyond her depth. But she wouldn't retreat now. Now that she'd started, she wouldn't give this Viking another victory. Of course, he would take it anyway, but she would make him work for it.

He seemed to consider this in silence. Then, in a quiet voice that nonetheless rang with blood and power, he said, "Come forward, Saxon."

Now she regretted her little speech. She took a few barefoot paces over the rush-covered floor toward his chair. The grins around her were more than coarse; they were positively bloodthirsty.

"Closer."

She complied, full of dread, wondering what was behind his indifferent expression.

"You remind me of a bird, always cranking out nonsense. But . . ." He spoke in Norse to his friend Rolf, who was sitting on the nearest bench. The red-haired man left his seat and brought the jarl his sword. Caution entered Edin as he examined the blade. He touched the edges, felt their sharpness, and seemed to note a tiny flaw, a chip. The drawn steel glittered in the flickering firelight.

There was now a vein of threat in his casual tone as he said, "Aye, you chatter without thought. But you aren't a bird. You are nobly born—*free*born, you say. And no slave. Let us test this claim of yours, Saxon."

He stood and stepped down from the dais of his

chair, and lifted his longsword suddenly, so that it's lethal point touched her left breast exactly over her heart. She gasped, shivered, but did not move. He kept the point against her breast, and he pushed — just enough to make the tip penetrate her undershift and dent her flesh.

There he held her. She felt the sword point keenly. She became aware of her ribs beneath it, of how delicate the bones were, how easily they could be pierced.

He said, "I'm waiting, thrall! What say you now?"

She whispered, "I-I am free, a nobleman's daughter."

Why was she doing this? He had no scruples against murder — he'd already murdered Cedric before her very eyes!

"You suffer from an unnatural belief in your own immortality," he answered softly.

He spoke to Rolf again, without looking at him. Quickly another sword appeared. Rolf's face behind his red whiskers seemed to offer Edin a warning. She looked from him to the sword he held out to her.

"Take it!" The jarl stepped back a half-pace, removing his sword point from her breast yet not lowering it.

Rolf's red brows beetled as she took the sword from him with both hands. Even so, as soon as he released it, its point fell almost to the floor. She struggled to bring it up again, but couldn't raise it even to the height of her waist. It felt as if the weapon had unseen roots anchoring it to the floor. Possibly the same roots that anchored mountains. She heard murmurs and felt the Vikings amusement.

"Lift it!" the jarl said. He waved his own weapon as if it were a twig. "All it takes is a good arm." She saw the sinews in his forearm, the muscles rippling. "It's Rolf's own sword, that," he said, "a good killing blade. Its name is *Tickler*. If you aren't my thrall, you'll lift it and defend your claim. I say you're mine, my property to dispose of as I see fit. Prove to me I'm wrong."

She stood as she was, her arms and shoulders and

back trembling in the effort of keeping the heavy sword point from falling to the floor completely. She couldn't look at him now, but gazed unseeing at his steady damascened blade.

"*Well?*" He was like a dragon in his fury, rending and unreasonable. Those who resisted, he would always mercilessly overcome, if not with his muscles then with the tremendous strength of his mind and purpose.

"You know I can't fight you."

"Because the weapon is too unwomanly," he said crisply. "Very well." He spoke in Norse, and again Rolf appeared, this time with a dagger. He took his sword back and held the knife out to her, but she shook her head.

"Come," the jarl said dryly, lowering his sword, "take it; charge me with it. I know you can kill if you want to."

"I can't."

"You killed Ragnarr."

"I can't."

He made a sound of contempt. "You are a race of slaves, you Saxons."

Her gaze dropped to somewhere near his feet. She wanted to cry, but somehow kept her sobs held in.

"I'm challenging you — fight me, *my lady!*"

"I can't fight you, Viking, as well you know."

"Aye," he said slowly, lowering his weapon at last, "as well I know."

Her gaze lifted again, all the way to his face. "But I will never be a slave," she said stubbornly.

This time he reacted with immediate anger, the most parlous kind of anger, the kind born of frustration. The jerk of his head told her of his ire, and her breath froze at the cold flare of temper in his eyes. In an instant he became fearsome, furious, *mad*. His mighty sword swung up again, and he closed in. There was an ice storm rampaging in his eyes. The flat of his sword lifted her chin, until she was looking at him down its long, gilt-and-silver length. All he said now was "Slave or sword point?"

The flames snapped in the firepit behind her. The cold, steel point pricking her throat never moved the slightest. For an immeasurable extent of time she stood perfectly still, living in a state of strain. She searched for some answer. And impaled on his gaze, feeling all those wild and hungry eyes on her, something of her pride broke inside her. In the end she could only whisper: "Slave."

It seemed an eternity before she felt the metal leave her skin. He slowly dropped his weapon and stepped back onto the dais, lowering himself into his chair. The storm in his eyes had settled to rime-ice. At last he said, "My mother will teach you and the others what you need to know. The first thing she will teach *you* is that you are to be silent—or I shall see you can't be anything else."

Then, more quiet than ever before: "Saxon, for your own sake, don't struggle against your destiny. There is no mercy for the subjugated. I warn you I shall not put my anger aside again. Next time . . .

"Next time I will fall on you like an avalanche."

Banished back to her corner, all Edin wanted to do was pour out her terror in an orgy of tears; but she found she couldn't think of herself and her great humiliation yet, for she discovered Arneld was to be separated from them. Another thrall, a shepherd by the looks of him, had come to take the boy outside. He made gestures that it was going to be all right, yet Arneld cried.

"He probably means for you to sleep in the byre, just like at home," Edin soothed.

"I'm afraid!"

I'm afraid, too! "I'm sorry, Arneld, but . . . there's nothing I can do about it." The bitterness of those words.

The Vikings who didn't live in the hall gathered their

110

possessions to go, and those who did live there headed for their beds. The Saxons were given fur sleeping bags. The fire was banked, leaving the torches alone to cast flickering shadows. In the mill of the closing evening, Edin was subjected to several kinds of quick and shocking touches. Juliana was treated even worse. One man claimed a hearty kiss of her, insistently shaping and fitting her young lips to his own and even plunging his tongue into her soft mouth—until he was stopped by the jarl's mother. Snapping, she showed the women where to bed down in one of the cubbies along the wall.

Juliana was put in with Olga, and Edin and Dessa were given a tiny "room" to share. This was furnished only with a wide wall-bench covered with a layer of straw. It was separated from the hall by nothing but a thin curtain, through which any Viking might walk at any time. Even so, Edin fell quickly into an exhausted sleep.

She dreamed, however, and woke with a gasp in the middle of the night. In the next hour she hit the very bottom of the matter: She was a slave in this strange cold place; she was caught in bondage to heathens. Forever. There in her bed, alone, she entered her soul's night.

Memories rose like a tide, higher, higher, swamping her now that she wasn't distracted by anything else, now that she was completely vulnerable to every loss. In her mind, Cedric died once more, and once more she regretted that she hadn't had the courage to die with him. In her mind she saw her home, saw it all as a dream, composed and calm, full of beauty, a place where honeysuckle grew in lush drifts calling the somnolent bees in the summer afternoons. Her heart had been so innocent, so unaware.

. . . *my property which I can dispose of as I please.*

The Viking's words rang in her head. Again she felt all those men's eyes on her, intent on her degradation.

111

Cold crept into the hollows of her bones. She didn't want to be their victim. She didn't want to be here. But what she wanted was no longer of any importance to anyone.

It seemed only minutes after she'd finally fallen asleep again that she was roughly wakened. The Viking woman was giving her a good shaking. If the jarl was a dragon, then his mother was a dragonette. She struck Edin as a fierce, bitter, violent person.

Dessa was already up, but evidently had been afraid to wake Edin, whom she still thought of as "my lady." She seemed embarrassed to see Edin treated so rudely — yet her simple mind didn't fail to take in that Inga was now the one to be obeyed.

In the hall, Juliana waited. She muttered to Dessa, "Her ladyship has to get up like the rest of us now, despite her airs and graces." Edin's pride ached like an open wound.

Although Inga spoke no Saxon, she managed to show each woman what her duties were. Edin saw that she was a careful manager — a little too careful. Edin who was light-fingered in the preparations of such delicacies as partridges and doves, helped cook a heavy, grainy barley porridge. She set the table with loaves of rye and oatbread. Then, at the first of the two meals of the day, she was given the task of keeping the men's mugs full of buttermilk.

They drank a great deal of buttermilk as they sat on their benches and let the women serve them. Edin, still in her undershift and nothing else, was mortified when early on Ottar Magnusson pointed out to his table mates that the little points of her breasts could be seen beneath the thin linen fabric. After that, they drank twice as much buttermilk, drank it hard, threw it back and placed their empty mugs where she had to reach to fill them, causing her shift to draw tightly over her breasts. The jarl refrained from this sport, but the others — not a hand touched her, yet their taunting was

112

remorseless.

It confused her. If her body was desirable, she'd never known it. She'd been respected by the men in her life, and consequently had preserved the sweetness, the innocence of a sheltered girl. She had an unhardened mind and an open heart and no defense against this kind of male coarseness. She suffered their stares, but they sickened her. The sound of their chuckling cut her.

Nor had she ever been criticized or reviled, but it seemed she was reviled now. The Viking woman, Inga, hated her, and for what reason? Edin couldn't say. But whatever she did was not done quickly enough, or well enough, or in the right way. This was like an injury, a new wound made in the old, this feeling of being utterly despised.

When at last she and the other thralls were allowed to eat, she had no appetite. She had to force herself to drink her own buttermilk.

An hour later she learned that milk does not appear from nowhere, and that a dairy is always in need of extra hands. Inga instructed her in unfamiliar words and a voice like cracking ice.

While carrying buckets of milk from the dairy to the longhouse, she came upon Juliana and the young copper-eyed Jamsgar. The man had taken the girl into his arms, and even Edin could see that she was making no more than a sham protest. He kissed her and held her tightly around the waist. And then he slid his hand up her skirt — with scarcely any resistance. Edin slipped away, more troubled than ever.

Chapter 8

The Viking household regularly consisted of twenty to thirty people, and the work was endless. By late afternoon, Edin was filled with hopeless, unshed tears. That was when Inga led her into her own sleeping chamber near the entrance to the hall. The room was the size of a lockable closet, but at least it was private. Inga reached under her ornately carved bed to pull out a chest. Rummaging, she cast gauging eyes on Edin, and finally tossed her a doubtful-looking, formless garment of faded grey-purple material.

The sack was suitable only for a cowherd—and a much stouter woman at that. If Edin weren't ashamed of being half-naked, she would have refused to put it on. Or so she told herself. As it was, she threw the thing over her head, over her filthy undershift, and fastened it. It had long loose sleeves and no belt. When she looked down, she was struck again by her position. In this gross garment, she seemed to have nothing in common with that young bride-to-be of Fair Hope Manor, the one who had looked forward to being a mistress of servants, a revered wife and mother, a gentlewoman of grace and generosity.

Inga seemed satisfied. She said something in her barbaric language, her voice as tart, as stone-chilled, as the buttermilk the Vikings liked so well. Edin said nothing, could have said nothing with her throat burning as it was, making it so difficult to swallow. She exited the chamber just as the jarl was passing on his way outside. She tried to fasten him with her gaze, but her stare slid off. He in turn took one look at her, then lowered his head and strode on.

She found later that Inga had unwittingly done her a kindness. At the evening meal the Vikings seemed to notice her much less. The ugly dress had its advantages. At least now she wasn't a target for every male eye in the hall.

The evening passed. And so did the night, which at that time of year in the north was so short Edin didn't think a person could cook a joint of meat in it. Verily it seemed the minute she lay down she was awakened. Yet there was enough time for her to dream, and awaken with a start, enough time for that sense of horror to come to her, that absolute, sickening terror that rose from her stomach, and that feeling of total desolation.

Her heart put up a struggle inside her, but gradually the heaped shocks settled onto her and seemed to separate her from everyone around her. When she burned her fingers while cooking, she wondered, *Why don't I feel pain?* When Juliana continued to treat her with contempt and encourage the other thralls to do the same, she thought, *My life is destroyed, everything is lost, and I don't feel anything.* There was too much to bear, and gradually her mind stopped paying attention, and her heart stopped fumbling; everything around her blurred. . . .

For the hundredth time, Edin threw her hair back out of her way. The longhall was quiet. Olga was midway between the clean-up of breakfast and the starting of dinner, Dessa was working at the standing loom, and Juliana was busy with a set of wooden pressing irons. Edin had been set to the lowest job, plucking a brace of wild ducks that long-bearded Fafnir Danrsson had left hanging in the kitchen. She was in that daze, that dullness bordering on despair which had sealed her off from her surroundings. Only now and then did anything break through to fix itself in her consciousness anymore, some distinctive scene, or the occasional pang of some real, physical pain.

The pain was usually caused by Inga's wooden spoon, used whenever Edin stopped her work to go into a moment's trance. Then Inga would poke or rap her, and Edin would obediently return to what she was supposed to be doing.

She was ankle-deep in feathers when she heard Inga's word for her, a Norse word that seemed to be the Saxon equivalent of "You!" She looked up to see the woman in the door, her expression full of cold effrontery. No wonder, since Dessa and Juliana were already there, evidently having been summoned without Edin even being aware that they'd left their work. Dessa beckoned her timidly.

Edin stood and brushed the feathers from her hands as she followed them out into the light of the fine, luculent late-summer noon, a truly golden noon, though to Edin there seemed to be an undertone of grief in the sunlight. Two thrall-men met them. One was Blackhair, he of the wormy smile. Inga spoke to the other one, and he in turn spoke to the women: "I'm Snorri. I'm from England, too—twenty-five winters ago." He was a well-muscled fellow, though only a few inches taller than Edin. He seemed not to know what to do with his hands without a spade or barrow or pitchfork.

Blackhair stood grinning at the women. Edin didn't care; she didn't even wonder why they'd been called outside. She watched passively while Blackhair and Snorri took tools from their belts, the kind used to shear sheep. Dessa and Juliana, following some order, went to their knees before the men, who started to trim their hair. Edin had noticed that the thralls wore their hair short here. Olga's, for instance, barely reached the tips of her ears.

Juliana's hair hadn't been long to begin with, and as Blackhair snipped blithely, only short dark curls

116

dropped to the ground around her. Dessa's longer, soft brown locks fell and fell. Snorri's face held an expression of pained concentration. Edin lost interest.

She looked at Inga, who was intent on the "shearing." The older woman had her own hair bound in its usual knot. She was without a cape today. Her dress was pleated, a dress of light blue with touches of black and four rows of yellow beads across the chest. It was wrapped and pinned in some exotic Viking style.

Edin's attention wandered. Under the nearby shade tree, Hauk Haakonsson, the one with the high, hooked nose, was sitting on the grass, plaiting leashes for some hounds lying about him. He'd pulled his tunic off in the heat, and Edin saw the great snake etched on his long back. Several of the Vikings had tattoos: wolves, bears, dragons. . . .

In the corral, Laag, the stable-thrall, was trimming the mane of a horse. He was a tall, always slightly frowning man with an absent manner. The dark glossy horse hair dropped and dropped.

Edin looked out at the fields visible between the dairy byre and the longhouse, stubble fields from which the barley had already been cut. There were three cots in the distance, the houses of married thralls and their families. From one of the chimneys smoke rose into the still air.

Farther up, the heat of the day had gathered the moisture out of the land to make a faint haze around the heights.

When Dessa and Juliana stood, their hands to their heads, they looked . . . different, Edin thought from where she had escaped to, a safe place a thousand miles or more from Norway. She was slow to realize that everyone was looking at her. "Your turn, lass," Snorri said. Blackhair again broke into that really cruel grin.

Her turn? Looking at the sheers in Blackhair's hand, the situation finally penetrated her understanding. Her hands went to the thick, wavy, amber hair hanging down her back and over her shoulders. Not this, too. She'd never realized she had a vanity until now. They wouldn't take even this from her . . . would they?

They would. She woke, with a punched, gasping feeling. They meant to cut her hair. She came back to awareness with a lurch. And she was appalled.

She took a step back.

"Come on, lass," Snorri said, not unkindly. The look on Blackhair's face was gleeful. His eyes were small and stony and full of evil. Inga looked smug. Snorri said, "It could be worse. In some districts thralls are branded."

Edin took another step backward. "Not my hair. It's rather pretty when I can comb it. If I had a comb —" she looked about her as if hoping to find one hidden nearby. "I have no comb," she said again, distractedly. "Mayhap I could just put it up?"

Snorri gave her a sad look. She glanced at Inga, whose look said Edin was beneath contempt. She uttered something sharp and impatient.

"Sorry, lass," Snorri said, "we have to cut it. We do what we're told, whether or not we like the doing."

Edin, suddenly awake and aware of just how close to the edge of everything she was, felt she had to make a stand. Snorri sighed. Then, as she'd expected, Blackhair made a grab for her. She side-stepped him, turned, picked up her ugly skirts, and fled.

Having surprised them, she got something of a head start. Her hair, judged too ornamental for a common slave, streamed and rippled behind her. She hadn't been allowed to look about the steading, and she had no idea where she would be led by the path she chose. It wasn't the dead-end path that went to the dock, she knew, though it went up over the lip of the valley and started down toward the fjord just as that other did. From the top, she saw the longship at anchor a bowshot out in the water, its sail furled, its timbers dry. Halfway along, the path turned around a bluff, beyond which she couldn't see.

118

Seagulls mewed; heavy footsteps beat the hard earth behind her. Her heart slugged up in her throat. *What are you doing?* It was unlikely she'd find a hiding place, and when caught, that ice-hearted Inga would have her shorn bald.

And when the jarl heard she'd been disobedient again. . . !

A little whimper escaped her as she plunged headlong around the blind turn in the path.

The shipyard was redolent with wood shavings and pitch. Like the dock area, it occupied a shelf of land just above the water. Much of the available space was taken up by stocks, which could hold a longship being repaired or a fishing boat being built. Thoryn was telling young Starkad Herjulson about a type of ship he'd seen out of Kaupang. "It's called a *knorr*, broader and larger than the *Blood Wing*, with higher gunwales to hold back the waves, and the mast fixed solidly in the hull."

Starkad was several years younger than his brother Jamsgar, but he was one of those who had the genius. When he built even a little fishing boat, he paid complete attention to each plank he cut, its breadth, its thickness. Like Jamsgar, his face was broad and brown as leather, and his eyes were as blue as the summer sky; but where Jamsgar had two handsome blond plaits of hair, Starkad's hair was a rust color, and his square-trimmed beard jutted as stiffly as though carved from rust-red whalebone.

Thoryn heard a commotion coming down the path and lost his concentration. "What now?" he muttered, stalking out of the yard. Just as he set foot on the path, the Saxon maiden rounded the bluff. Running headlong downhill, she didn't see him until it was too late to avoid a collision. She crashed into him with enough impact to force a deep *"Huh!"* from him. His arms automatically closed about her — and with the same surge of muscles, he lifted her and swung her around, presenting his back to Blackhair, who was no more than two paces behind her, a pair of sheep shears in his hand. He ran into Thoryn's back. Thoryn bent forward a little, bearing this second collision, which brought his head down into the maiden's fragrant hair.

He straightened as Blackhair ricocheted off him and fell in a sprawl. He felt the maiden fighting for breath in his arms, yet continued to hold her tightly.

Snorri arrived just then. He paused, panted, then reached to help Blackhair to his feet. Thoryn's first thought was that they'd been attempting to molest the maiden, and his stomach clenched with ready anger. He turned to face them, still keeping her in his arms. "What fool trick is this? Speak or, by Odin, I'll skewer you both!"

Snorri tried to answer, but could only speak in infrequent words: "Master . . . she . . . we. . . ." He was too winded.

Inga now appeared on the path, her face flushed with exertion and fury. The maiden began to squirm in his arms, seeking her freedom. But he wasn't ready to let her go, not yet. He had no purpose; but he did have a good hold on her, and he decided to keep it, at least until he found out what was going on.

"Peace be with you, Master," Blackhair wheezed, "but the mistress told us to clip this thrall's hair, and we were going to — except she ran away. She doesn't know her place yet, but she will. She —"

"Mother!"

" — thinks she's too good to do what she'd told like the rest of us —" Blackhair continued in a bullying voice.

"Mother, what's going on?"

The maiden managed to twist her head back enough to say to Blackhair in her native Saxon, "You disgusting worm!"

Thoryn let her slide down his chest, still keeping one

arm around her and now clamping his free hand over her mouth. "Silence!" he said, prevailing over everyone at once. He turned to Inga. "You told this . . . *worm* to sheer her head?"

Inga met his glare with a defensive stiffening. "You told me to supervise her. For five days I've watched her flinging that hair about. It's in the way of her work."

"But it will *not* be in the way of her work with the man who buys her."

Inga snapped her mouth shut on whatever she'd been about to say.

"When a man gives eight half-marks of gold for a bed-thrall, he doesn't want a bald woman."

"Hair grows. By spring—"

"By spring she *might* have as much hair as *I* do." He was having to use some strength to hold her now, which increased his irritation, and without thinking, he caught his fist in her mane to emphasize his point. He gave her head a firm shake. "A man buys a *woman* for his bed, not a shorn ewe."

Inga retreated into the refuge of silence. Her eyes could have iced over the fjord. Without another word she turned and started up the path. The two thrall-men, heads down, promptly followed her.

Thoryn watched them go, fuming. It wasn't until he heard a strained and feminine voice speaking in Saxon—"Please!"—that he looked down to see he still had the maiden gripped against his chest. His hand in her hair was pulling her head back so far that her throat was taut, her chin pointed skyward. The sight of her face tilted so vulnerably up to his hit him like a fist blow. Her beauty was more poignant than spring, a beauty to humble the world. . . .

He heard a chuckle and realized that Starkad had witnessed the whole scene, and the sensations which had struck him as a thunderbolt were immediately twisted into chagrin. It must have shown on his face, for Starkad made a great show of turning back to his own business.

Thoryn partially released the maiden. Keeping her arm, he said in her language, "Come with me!"

He started along the path with her, stopping only when they were hidden from both the shipyard and the steading above. Inga had tacked up the path like a sailboat before the wind, and she and the thralls were just disappearing over the lip of the valley. For the first time Thoryn was completely alone with the lovely thrall.

He released her arm. She faced him, as she always did, squarely, though she could hardly know what to expect from him. He hardly knew what to expect from himself. He stared for a long moment at her heavy, handsome hair. Ripples of water frisked around the banks of the fjord almost at their feet, but he didn't notice that. She was the most beautiful woman he'd ever seen. Hers was a pure beauty. Her eyes were true sea-maiden eyes. He felt an edgy thrill, like being at the brink of a cliff and gripped by the irrational, wanton urge to *jump!*

He had to break this silence! He said, "Tell me—" His voice came out two tones deeper than he'd expected. He tried again: "Tell me why I pander to you and protect you and give you special consideration, Saxon, when you're never anything but trouble to me!"

"I-I don't know. I wish you wouldn't." A gust of emotion seemed to unsettle her. "I wish you'd *never* concerned yourself with me!"

"If it hadn't been for me, you'd have been raped and gutted and left to burn—"

"If it hadn't been for you, Viking—"

"Do you dare talk back to me? Are you *stupid?* Do you truly not understand your position yet? Or mine? Whether you acknowledge it or not, I have the right— and the strength—to do whatever I like with you. I could have you whipped. I could take your head off. I could strangle you with that hair I just told them to let you keep!"

He stopped raging and steadied himself, fighting against feelings that seemed as powerful and mysterious as the tides.

When he spoke again, he was more sober: "Why do you bring yourself to my attention?"

"I don't!"

"What was it you just did then, running straight to me?"

"I had no idea you were down here! I-I just didn't want to lose my hair, too."

Too. He noted the word and all it meant. He said, self-righteously, "I don't know why not—it sticks out like hay in a rick. In truth, Saxon, keep that hair, for if such a prize were lost, Norway might never see its like again."

"I shall try, Viking!"

But despite her attempt to appear brave, she was gripping her hands together, staring steadfastly at his tunic buttons and visibly trembling. In a smaller, almost tearful voice, her head half-hanging, she said, "It wouldn't look like hay if I had a comb."

His nostrils dilated as he breathed in hugely. "Are you saying you are ill-cared for?"

She wouldn't look at him; her hands gripped one another.

"Answer me!"

She said at last, "No."

And he knew that for the first time she had just told him a thing she believed to be patently untrue. Of course she was being ill-cared for—tormented! She was being singled out by Inga, and clearly some of the thralls disliked her—simply because she was what she was, a gentlewoman pulled down to their own level. His men taunted her with their coarse badinage and loutish jokes. He himself had neglected—avoided—her these past days. Oh, he'd been watchful and protective in ways she couldn't know, yet he'd heartlessly left her to accustom herself as best she could to her new condition.

And he would have to be blind not to notice how poorly she was doing: her dazed service at the meals, her lack of expression, her growing despondency.

I did this. I put a seal of midnight on her morning. It's wrong.

How small she was, how vulnerable. And how beautiful, even in that sack. He remembered holding her folded against him—he knew something of what was beneath the gross drapes of that garment. And he had a sudden strong sense of what it might be like to slide up inside her small body. It made him shudder. His eyes focused on the strange lilt of her mouth, and he found himself irresistibly drawn. Before he could stop himself, he reached out and took her arms.

The gentleness of his touch seemed to surprise her, enough so that she allowed him to pull her toward him. When she looked up into his face to see what he was up to, he lowered his mouth surely.

He took her completely by surprise. "Oh!" she said at the touch of his lips on hers, giving him the opportunity to invade her opened mouth and taste her inner sweetness. He was blind and deaf to all but her, could smell nothing but the scent of her, knew nothing but the warm round litheness of her.

Then she jerked her head aside. He buried his face in her throat, and she pressed her hands against his chest.

When he lifted his head, she looked at him as if she saw something primitive and terrifying in his eyes. Though she strained to be released, evidently she didn't really expect to succeed, for she stumbled back when he abruptly let go. She would have fallen if he hadn't caught her waist. She slid her hands up his arms, trying to cling to the very object that was destroying her balance.

For an instant he was strongly tempted to take her to the ground, to force open her legs, not simply to rob her of the only thing she had left for him to take, but to conquer her.

He felt her body's recoiling response to this unspoken thought, and he steeled himself and set her firmly on her feet. His hands dropped from her waist. "You see what a thrall-woman can expect from her master when she brings herself to his attention too often?" He went on, rather stiffly, trying to rein in his galloping emotions. "If you tempt me sorely enough, you may find I am but a man."

He felt he wasn't being very convincing—so often she seemed beyond his authority!—so he turned to action. He unfastened the silver buckle of his tunic belt and whipped it off. Before she could know what he was up to, he wrapped it around her—it took two turns around her waist—then gathered her hair and stuffed it under the leather at the small of her back.

"There! That should keep the hay out of the soup pot! Now be off before I change my mind and shorten your hair myself—or shorten *you* by a head's-worth!"

Keeping her gaze on him, she backed up the path. Not until she was safely out of the range of his arms did she utter the smallest cry and turn and flee.

Yet the feel of her in his arms stayed with him. An impression seemed dented upon his chest, his thighs, hollows that only her body could fill. Like a man in a dream, he started after her—and came face to face with Rolf. He felt his face heat.

"What's been going on?"

"The thrall . . ."

"Aye, she passed me like Odin himself was after her—but I see it was only the Hammer of Dainjerfjord." He laughed. "I can almost see the smoke of your chimney curling out from under your tunic, brother. What have you been up to?"

"I . . . she needed a lesson."

"She needs many lessons, and you're just the man to teach her."

Thoryn swung slowly and drunkenly around. The fjord winked in the sunlight; now he heard the patient, lapping water. He said, "As my father taught his Saxon?"

"Kirkyn has been in Valhöll these fifteen years," Rolf answered gruffly.

Thoryn turned a hard face to him. "Not Valhöll. A man murdered contemptibly by his thrall goes to Hel."

"Bah! That's Inga talking. Her and her tales! I sometimes think she deliberately takes her revenge on the son of the man who spurned her. She sets you to gnawing at yourself until you remind me of a fox caught in a trap and obliged to bite off his own leg. I tell you, part of her mind is rotten, Thoryn—"

"It is my mother you speak of," he said quietly.

"Aye, your mother." Rolf heaved a sigh. "Listen to her, brother, and you'll die with blue loins and many regrets. I've seen you eyeing that girl when you think nobody is looking. You want her, and you're afraid that in a shaky moment you'll—"

"That's enough!"

"You want her."

He wanted . . . a woman to fill his arms in bed and banish the emptiness within him.

He wanted . . . a woman with amber hair and sea-green eyes.

He wanted . . . her.

The only people Sweyn Elendsson saw while he recovered from his wound were Inga, Olga, and sometimes Hagna, the medicine woman. Hagna was a great hand with herbs. Some she mashed in a little copper caldron and then packed around Sweyn's wounded shoulder. Others she boiled with water and told him to drink this "broth." If he'd swilled brewed dragon's brains it couldn't taste worse. However, the swelling in his shoulder went down, and the flesh lost its redness, as the old woman promised.

He wasn't grateful to her, though, for it was Hagna

126

who told him bluntly that he would never have the use of his right arm again, that he'd never go a-viking again, never forage about the world's seas and rivers anymore; and looking up from his wall-bed at the woman's wrinkled and age-spotted neck, he knew he would never be able to get both his hands around it to throttle her.

Sweyn had no visitors. He was a cripple now, and he understood that no whole man knew what to say to him. He was an oath-breaker. He'd ignored an edict from his jarl to whom he'd sworn obedience. He'd dishonored himself. In his mind, it had been just as dishonorable for the jarl to leave him crippled instead of dead, however. Over and over he heard those little pleading, foreign words from the woman, words he hadn't understood—but the jarl had. Those words had robbed him of his rightful death.

Today, thin, pale-faced, slit-lipped, he stumbled outside to sit in the sun and mayhap begin to regain some of his strength. He emerged from the dark longhouse amazed, dizzy, awed by the light. The most brilliant summer weather had ruled lately. Above the lance-shaped fir trees on the heights, the sky shone the deepest blue, without even a dappling of clouds, and the air was filled with that pensive sound of cowbells coming from the cattle that wandered the slopes cropping the short meadow grass.

Sweyn dozed with his back against the longhouse. When he woke, he saw Edin and Dessa hanging laundry on bushes to whiten and dry. Dessa was sporting a new haircut, but not Edin. He'd heard the gossip, of course, laying in his wall-bed with only a cloth curtain separating him from the talk in the hall. Yesterday, Jarl Thoryn had forbade the cutting of the Saxon's hair.

Was the woman a witch? Had she thrown a spell over the jarl? If it hadn't been for her, Sweyn would be a whole man yet—or drinking to Odin's health in Valhöll right now.

That night he joined the men at dinner. Everyone pretended not to see him. No one spoke to him, or mentioned his limp and useless arm. They were all seated by the time he made his slow way to the tables. He found that his former place near the jarl was filled. There was nowhere for him to sit but at the end of a bench, the place where people of the least importance sat.

When Edin passed by him, he saw that her long amber hair was tucked into a man's belt. That silver buckle was the jarl's. The thrall had been given a present, while Sweyn had been left to live a cripple's life. It was biting. He sat staring at her, his good left hand rubbing at his wound.

Chapter 9

Edin had gone about for days unaware of the depth of feeling she stirred up all around her, the feelings of the jarl, Inga, Sweyn, the Vikings in the longhouse, even her fellow thralls. She hadn't even realized. Part of her had declined to live through the passing days, had kept distant, had retreated to a sanctuary of denial.

As it turned out, preserving her heart contributed to her downfall. It meant she'd made no friends and was more sequestered than she ought to have been. The loneliness was crushing. Her separation of part of herself from the reality of the thralls' shared circumstances was noticed immediately—and in return she was shunned and disliked. When they sat to eat together that night, she found she was excluded. She was shunted to a bench-end, the seat farthest away from the light and heat of the fire, farthest way from whatever conversation and laughter there was among them.

Meanwhile, the Vikings, sensing her weakness, had subtly begun to seduce her. Though she'd tried to stay out of their way, she saw now that they seemed to idle in places where they knew the could catch her alone. They didn't touch her or kiss her, they didn't leer or lunge; yet their apparently wayward paths crossed hers constantly, and being something more than ordinary men, they frightened and bewildered her.

Sweyn, who was now able to get about a little, often

watched her and, while he did, rubbed his shoulder.

The day after the jarl kissed her, she was left alone in the hall with the task of making a batch of the flat, tasteless bread the Vikings were so fond of. Sweyn came to sit at the table where she was working. He was wearing a soiled tunic of rough blue cloth. He had his right arm bound against his body, probably to keep it from swinging against things. A panting, slat-sided, tawny dog wandered over and sprawled at his feet. He ignored it and went on watching Edin in silence. Her awareness newly awakened, she sensed his enmity and continued to work the dough in the wooden kneading bowl—but after a while she realized she was trembling. He got up and came so near that she raised her shoulder toward him, to protect herself. He saw this, and gave her a smile that didn't quite reach his eyes, then murmured something in Norse.

The other Vikings tried to talk with her sometimes, but she hadn't learned enough Norse to understand. Even when they spoke slowly, even when they grew impatient and spoke very slowly, clipping each word, she didn't understand. Most of the time she had to resort to gestures—and felt impenetrably stupid.

She looked up into Sweyn's grey invalid's face and shook her head. "I don't understand," she said.

His blond hair hung lank. He was not the man who had raised his deadly broad-axe over her head. But near as he stood, he was still very large. His shoulders were as wide as a byre-beam. His smile remained, and now he raised his good left hand. Before her face he clenched it into a fist. She understood that. That much Norse she'd learned.

After a moment, he turned away and wobbled outside. The tawny dog followed him, as did Edin's eyes.

Thoryn lounged in his high-seat, drinking another cup with his men. Though it had been a bonny summer day, the late evening was chill now, with rag ends of mist wafting and wrapping about the longhouse. His shieldmen stayed near the fire, leisurely shelling and eating boiled shrimp, washing them down with ale, and playing chess or checkers. Try as he might to concentrate on the games, Thoryn couldn't dismiss the distraction of the maiden. The sheer intensity of his want had grown by degrees until it seemed unbearably huge.

Her shining hair had come free of the belt around her waist and fell over her shoulders, gloriously untidy, framing her breathtakingly beautiful face. He already regretted letting her keep that mane of hair. He could spot it too easily, and when his eyes found her, a feeling so strong as to be painful gripped him. It was sexual, yes, but not simply a feeling of the body. It seemed his whole being lusted for the woman. He sensed that she might touch him, fulfill him, satisfy him in some way he'd never been satisfied before. He sensed the potential power she could have over him.

Inga had sent the other thralls to their beds before going off to her own, leaving the maiden with the trying task of serving the late-drinking men. The men she passed followed her with their eyes. Jamsgar Coppereye sniffed the air after her and got a laugh from his brother Starkad. Nothing they did could be specifically objected to, yet Thoryn grew more and more irritated.

He was also irritated to discover Rolf had been watching him watch her.

"Oath-brother, will you sleep alone again tonight? You've abstained so long, I wager you're stiff enough for anything, even a solid-gold maidenhead."

At that moment, the Saxon passed by carrying yet another pitcher of ale. Rolf reached out and patted her behind with a huge callused paw, his grin downright wolfish. Her rabbitlike scamper made everyone laugh. They had all wanted to do that, yet none had dared. The reaction was now immediate. Rolf exchanged looks with some of them. Something unspoken was decided upon. The men grinned at Thoryn, their faces positively lit with merriment—and suddenly the maiden was kept busier than ever. As soon as she filled a cup at the table to Thoryn's left, a man at the far side of the table to his right called for her to fill his. Back and forth she went, back and forth before Thoryn's chair, back and forth, looking so lost and vulnerable, so lonely and in need of a protector.

The talk turned bawdy. It was of conquests and whores and orgies. Every man had a tale he seemed eager to share with Thoryn, and every tale seemed meant to inflame. Stares began to go from the maiden to him and back again.

He saw that she felt the looks and the laughter. He sensed her bafflement. Now Hauk Haakonsson dared to reach out and pat her behind. "Here is fine treasure, Jarl!" he said with his lazy white smile.

She stepped back, away from Hauk, away from the tables. She raked her hair back with one hand, and found Thoryn. Silent and brooding, he met the winking arrows of firelight in her eyes. She didn't understand why, yet she knew she was being used.

The smith, Eric No-breeches, called out, "Here, pussy, pussy!" The others began to mew like cats. She stood aghast in the din, a rabbit hemmed round by wolves. Her face was pale, her shoulders so stiff and straight that Thoryn could almost feel her painful effort to hold herself erect, to try to hold on to her dignity.

The entire household crackled with tension. So forceful was the aura, Thoryn could no longer resist it. He spoke.

He went unheard; but several had seen his lips move, and a bolt of expectation shot through the hall, breaking off conversations and choking down laughter.

Edin had seen his lips move, but with all the noise in the pent hall. . . . Now everyone fell abruptly silent, and from his high-seat he spoke again: "My cup is empty." He said it in Saxon, with a calmness that was

132

frightening. He raised his cup slightly, without taking his eyes from her.

She started for his chair, questions splintering in her mind, her heart pounding in her ears. She felt the eyes watching her — but then she was always watched; rarely was she allowed any freedom from those male eyes that marked her out and unsettled her. Still, this was the worst it had ever been. Someone she passed jeered at her in Norse. She tried hard to understand the words, did understand a few of them, but not enough to catch the sense of what he'd said. Someone else gave her a little shove, so that she stumbled. Her cheeks felt hot. *I am the Lady Edin, the Lady Edin of Fairhope Manor . . . . . . reduced to serving Vikings their ale.*

The jarl's shadowed image seemed to flicker in the firelight. His face was set, his eyes flinty. He looked as if he hated her more than ever, as if he had every intention of hurting her. And no one would stop him. He owned her and could do with her as he liked.

The distance across the hall was easily four miles. Her whole body was trembling by the time she drew near the virulent force of him. *What have I done? What does this mean?* He didn't move as she began to fill his cup, and the menace of his immobility made her tremble more. She slopped a few drops on his hand. He still didn't move. Feeling ridiculously clumsy, she tried to brush away the drops with her fingertips.

Her touch seemed to galvanize him. He stood slowly and stepped off his dais. Someone — Rolf, she thought it was — reached to take her pitcher from her. Freed of it, she stepped backward. But not soon enough. The jarl reached for her and got her by one arm, slowly pulling her forward again. His grip was painful, but she didn't dare struggle. He was too big, too forbidding, too strangely compelling.

The men stood as a group and began to shout in their awful language, which sounded like something they'd learned from seals and walruses and gulls, she thought wildly. All the jarl said was "Aye." There was no translation for that; it was just a noise a man made, involuntarily, as he suffered some pain that couldn't be helped.

She tried to move her arm, to loosen his hold so that she might slip free, but his fingers remained iron steady. Her mind was a blur. Only small details, useless details, seemed to come to her with any kind of clarity: She noticed that his eyebrows were light, so sandy-light who could see them unless she got close, very close, *too* close?

Suddenly he moved, with such speed she didn't have time to react. He bent and placed his shoulder to her waist. Then, with the quickness and determination of a man utterly resolved, he stood—lifting her right off her feet. One of his arms held her legs to his chest, the other pressed her bottom against his shoulder. She toppled forward, face first into his back; her hair came completely free of her belt and streamed down, nearly brushing the rushes on the floor. The Vikings roared.

She felt the blood rush to her head. The man's shoulder was broad and well-padded with muscle, yet the position was uncomfortable in the extreme, especially with that oversized belt buckle digging into her stomach. The pain intensified when he began to walk. She drew a ragged breath.

Yet truly the physical pain was the least of it.

She couldn't see where he was taking her. Kicking was uselss—he had her legs pinned. She slapped at his back once, then gave up to use her forearm to pull her hair away from her eyes.

He turned around the end of a table, and the hall spun—upside-down. Faces bobbed, upside-down. She felt giddy; her eyes filled with bright, bouncing specks. His shoulder continued to grind into her stomach and she let go of her hair to brace herself against his back.

She saw a doorframe. They were leaving the hall.

She was swung dizzily as he turned to slam the door behind him.

And then the noise of the cheering was distant, and she was alone with the Viking.

Another reeling turn—she whimpered—then he bent forward and pulled her off his shoulder. She fell onto her back, into something feather-soft.

It was completely dark, except for a few coals glowing in a small brazier. She sat up. She surmised she was in his bedchamber, on his bed. She heard him fumbling elsewhere, and she slipped her bare feet to the floor. Tiny cracks of light indicated the door, and she crossed to it. The rushes rustled beneath her feet.

By feel she discovered the door was made of thick wood with hide strapping holding the planks together. She also found that it was secured with a heavy crossbar. Her hands felt in the darkness to find how to lift it.

"Think, Saxon."

His voice came so suddenly, she spun, placing her back to the wood.

He continued, in that same matter-of-fact tone, "It would do you no good to go out there. There are eight men out there, all of them eager for me—or someone—to bed you. You wouldn't get a dozen paces before you were caught, and then you might be hurt."

A flame kindled; he was bent over the bronze brazier, holding a coal with tongs against the end of a rush. When the straw was well lit, he touched the flame to a wick immersed in a dish of oil. The lamp flickered, throwing a dim and unstable light up into his face. He set it down; its faint and smokey glow grew and spread.

The room now illuminated was not at all what Edin had expected. He seemed to read her thoughts. "Welcome to the dragon's den, Saxon." His voice dripped fire.

She'd known this was his sleeping chamber, of course, but she'd never so much as peeked into it; so she was shocked to find that not only was it larger than

135

Inga's but more opulent, stiflingly rich, fitted to he point of luxury. Everything—the clothing chest at the foot of the bed, the small wooden stand supporting a washbowl and pitcher, the bed itself with its dragon-head posts—was richly carved. Her eyes skimmed over details: a carved whale-bone hair comb, an ornate drinking cup, a fleecy sheepskin thrown over the floor, down cushions on the bed, a bearskin tossed across the footboard. The bed was huge, meant for a huge man . . . with room for one other.

Her fingernails pressed into her palms. She looked back at him and, in the urgency of her terror, said, "You plan to sell me!"

His face was fierce. "Aye, I do. But since you won't be a virgin, I'll have to bring my price down."

When he started toward her, she turned for the door again, her hands seeking the crossbar. He took hold of her arm and spun her around so hard she clattered against the wall. She flattened herself, ready to leap in whichever direction seemed most prudent. When she saw his face, saw how furious he was— *Why?*—her heart plummeted. "Please . . ."

His face changed, closed down to ferocity. He hissed, "No more of your 'pleases'! If I hear 'please' from you again, I may well run berserk myself!"

She was stung by the sharp accusation in his voice. He seemed a giant looming over her, angry with her— *For what?*—and she felt all her femininity and fragility.

Thoryn was angry, enraged. She'd tempted him until he'd made a fool of himself. Now the regular, established order of his life was shattered. He wanted to strike out, to break something—or someone.

Luckily for her, she didn't move. She shrank into the tapestry that covered the wall, her amber hair all tousled around her face and her eyes staring through it, like a green-eyed rabbit staring out of tangled grass. He slowly backed away, giving them both space to breathe.

She continued to look at him as if he were a savage,

136

however, and that made him *feel* savage. He folded his arms over his chest and glared at her. He said loudly, almost violently, "Take off your clothes."

That at least made her avert her eyes.

"I could do it for you," he said when she didn't obey him. She *would* obey him, by Thor! In this savage mood, he thought, *She will obey me or—*

She didn't look at him, but began to unbuckle her belt—his belt. Her hands were unsteady, but she got it off, then took the hems of her dress and undershift together and pulled them off in one motion. Briefly her arms were raised, and he saw her body completely uncovered, her waist stretched, her torso taut, her breasts lifted. His chest was rudely shaken by the rapacity of his heart. Then her face emerged; she brought her arms down and stood with her clothes clutched before her. Her hair fell around her like a cloak.

She'd obeyed; she'd made herself accessible to him. But it had been done so guilelessly, so modestly, that his temper was softened. And further softened by the way she stood trembling—no, shaking hard—as if she were near to freezing, though the night was not that cool. He'd seen her as she'd removed her clothes, however, and it'd had the effect on him of drinking fire. His jaw was still clenched.

He gathered his control. Holding his breath, still shocked, he approached her, the way he might approach a wild creature, cautious in case she startled. He allowed himself only the touch of one fingertip; he traced it down from her shoulder to the upper slope of her breast. "Where did you get this bruise?"

She said nothing.

"I know about my mother's wooden spoon. She did this?"

Again, nothing.

Yet there must have been something conciliatory in his tone, because her head turned—in short jerks because of her great fear—and her eyes lifted, to his chest, his beard, his mouth, nose, finally to his eyes.

Such terror! It crashed against him with the force of a storm-lifted wave. He remembered well why he'd brought her in here against all the arguments of his reason: because he *wanted* her. Norsemen were never ashamed about their needs. For a man with a need to take a woman without a protector was as natural as a hungry man slaying a stray sheep. And he had a *huge* need. His body's almost uncontrollable passion amazed him, unnerved him — and thoroughly galled him. He wanted her — yes! But not like this. He found he was disgusted with the idea of forcing her, frightening her more. Surely she would just die; her heart would just stop. He remembered capturing a bird once, as a boy, and feeling its heart throb in his hand . . . throb . . . and then just stop. It had died of fright.

Fear so terrible must be put out of the way; there was nothing else for it. With a great gust of emotion, he turned from her. His eyes were wild to find some way out of what he'd begun. He saw the sheepskin rug, and lifted it and flung it into the corner farthest from the door. Then, quickly, he stripped a quilt off his own bed and turned back to her.

Everything about her drew his gaze and held it. Girding himself, he swirled the quilt around her, encasing her, covering her nakedness. She seemed startled. He pointed to the sheepskin. "You'll sleep there."

She didn't move.

"Do as I say!"

She sidled away from him, clutching the quilt closed with the same fingers that were clutching her pathetic clothes. Her face was full of questions as she stepped onto the sheepskin. There she stood, with the veering yellow lamplight scattering over her hair, her small body trembling beneath that bright formless quilt.

"Lay yourself down."

She went to her knees — so doubtful! — half-reclined. He turned away and went about his own undressing,

138

fumbling unnaturally with the silver buttons of his tunic. Was she watching him? He'd never felt such a thing as shyness in a woman's presence before and refused to feel it now. Firm and unflinching, he stripped off his tunic, his shirt, his boots, and long pants. He went about it quickly, his back to her, tossing each item haphazardly into the chair.

But then he had to turn to blow out the lamp. Her eyes stared directly at his erection, and went round as plates. His hand moved involuntarily to his turgid manhood, to shield it from her awed gaze. At the same time her head jerked sideways, as if she'd been struck. Then the lamp flame was out. He found his bed in the dark.

It took him a moment to regain his attitude. He said, "I sleep with my ears open and my hand on my knife handle, Saxon. Don't so much as move in the night or I may gut you by reflex alone."

There was no answer from her corner.

"Do you hear me?"

"Yes." A watery whisper, laden with unshed tears.

Minutes crept by, accumulated, formed an hour. He knew exactly when she believed he was safely asleep, for that was when he heard a sound, buried into her hair and covered by her quilt, a sound like the cracked, forlorn cry of a seagull.

Her stifled sobs went on for a long time, but eventually her breathing grew steadier, rounder, deeper. Her rest was still occasionally sob-broken, but she was asleep. Her mind had simply had enough. She didn't rest deeply at first; her sleep was fitful, and she started up out of it often. It wasn't until the darkest hours that exhaustion finally pulled her down into a truly unguarded repose.

The room became stone-quiet then. Thoryn lay sunk in his big feather bed. He didn't think about the steading, or about hunting or fishing or tool-making; he didn't think about building ships or repairing buildings or raising sheep or cattle or goats. He thought about the fact, the tantalizing, troublous, inescapable fact, that this piece of womanhood was his, that he could do with her whatever he liked.

Her face flashed up in his mind's eyes; he abhorred its beauty.

Whatever you like!

He'd thought the decision was made: He would sell her and earn eight half-marks of pure gold. But now he saw that he'd never made a decision at all, never really considered the two sides of the scales. He'd simply pointed to the side weighted with gold and totally ignored the possibilities of the side weighted with her. Now the choice had to be made all over again. He could have eight half-marks of gold in his money chest . . . or he could have her beside him in this bed, beneath him, to do with as he liked.

Everywhere on the steadying, sleep was giving way to waking, dreams to being. In the longhouse, in the jarl's chamber, a voice whispered to Edin, a pleasant, velvety voice. She resisted waking, however. Waking had become too hard. The ultimate disappointment. Still, she opened her eyes — to find the giant Viking leaning over her.

She looked blankly into his face, studying his beard and the bulging muscles of his bare shoulders. She wasn't sure this was real; his features seemed to drift through opaque swathes of dream-mist. She was still warmly encased in her sleeping sack. How could she be lying beside him?

She moved her head just enough to see that she was not in her wall cubby. It was early morning in this place. A small window hole in the outer wall was open to the fresh sea air, to the first pale-silver wash of light. The shepherds would be going out. In a moment she would have to wake up and start her weary workday.

She was tired, tired in a deep, dull way that had nothing to do with physical weariness.

Her eyes returned to the Viking and met his eyes. Eyes like the grey water on an overcast day. At last his features coalesced from the morning mists. He was there; she was awake—not in her sleeping sack but wrapped in his quilt—and he was really there above her. She was staring up into his eyes while he rested on his elbow and looked down into hers. She felt a stab like a blade in her heart.

She remembered everything, and guessed the rest— that he'd carried her here to his feathered bed while she was still asleep. Now he meant to rape her. Tired, dazed, she resolved to bear it, to let it happen rather than fight it and be hurt all the more.

Because she found she was determined to somehow live through it.

Because, as she'd discovered belatedly, her love of life remained.

With an effort he could never have fathomed, she looked up at him with level calm eyes and said, "All right, Viking."

"All right?" he said. His face changed. Before, it had held no expression at all that she could discern, but now—what was he thinking? "All right?" he repeated.

She didn't answer; how could she? She wondered if he could hear her heart pounding.

She jerked when a frantic knock started at the door. He rolled away from her and leaned up on his other elbow, so that she was faced with his broad, bare, muscled back and buttocks. He roared something in Norse, in a voice that frightened her.

Inga's voice came back through the thick wooden planks, a spew of Norse like breakers of sea bursting into white blossoms of rocky cliffs.

Edin saw the Viking's back heave with a breath of patience, but his answer was as fierce as before.

"Thoryn!" Inga called, pleadingly.

His answer was two words that even Edin understood: *Leave us!*

She sat up, holding to her quilt tightly. He rolled back, swinging his arm around to catch her. She flinched; he was so enormous. For an instant, with his anger still on his face, she perceived his resemblance to his mother, only, as always, he seemed infinitely colder. There was about Inga's mouth a feminine curve that might once have been called sweetness. There was no such thing about his.

"Where do you go, Shieldmaiden?" he asked, in an altogether different voice than the one he'd used to frighten Inga off. He seemed different, relaxed. They were both sitting up. She steadfastly kept her sight lifted above his alarming lap. She needed to hear him speak again. Silent, he was completely alien. She firmed up her shoulders and asked, "What did she say?"

"She called you the doxy of demons and the scourge of men." He seemed to consider her. "Are you?"

He began to toy with her hair. He pulled it out from her quilt, freeing it to flow loosely down her back. Meanwhile, the fine, clear morning light rained over his body. His arm around her pushed her back down into the feather mattress, where he could lean over her once more. "What did you mean when you said a moment ago, 'All right, Viking'?"

Again she refused to answer.

He regarded her for a moment. And then—he smiled. It didn't last long, but the man had a smile like a sunset!

"Come. What does 'all right' mean?"

Her mouth was dry; she needed a drink of water badly. Beneath his gaze, his wide shoulders, his massive chest, she felt completely defenseless. "I have work to do, as your mother knows." Her voice sounded thin and reedy. And never did she think she would yield to the posture of servant so eagerly! She made an attempt to rise.

His arm over her tensed. "Wait—before I let you go—"

Was he going to let her go, then?

"—it means that you won't fight me, doesn't it? You won't answer that, nor can I blame you. Yet it satisfies me that you realize I can take you—now, or an hour from now, or the next time the moon rises full—and that you'll be better off not to resist me."

"Please . . ."

His face grew sterner. He was once again an arrogant giant of a Viking. " 'Please,' again?"

"I promise I'll never bring myself to your attention again."

"It's too late for that—if ever it were possible. I've spent this night thinking—oh, yes, and listening to your weeping, as lonely as winter wind—and I've come to the conclusion that I have no choice but to take you as my bed-thrall. You'll come here to me each night—or whenever else I require you, early or late—"

"No." It was wrenched out of her.

"—and you will open your arms and attend me as your master. During the day, you'll perform whatever domestic services are assigned to you, unless I want you—"

"No!"

"Aye. It will be to your benefit as much as mine, because now that my men believe you're no longer a maiden, I can't guarantee that any one of them might not take it into his mind to sample you. Only if I cast my claim over you completely, will they leave you be."

"No!"

His voice sharpened with irritation. "I don't like it when a thrall says no to me. You must not battle against some things in life, Saxon. You can't battle against me, take my word for it. Nothing is more pitiful than to see a brave female struggling against a man twice her size and strength. I've seen it, and it's pathetic."

143

He paused, mayhap to see if she would make the same mistake—say not to him—yet again. She didn't. His hand went to the quilt. She clutched it tighter. "Let go," he said.

Chapter 10

The Viking said, "You think I mean to take you now? Fear not. I have things to see to this morning — and I want to take my time with you. For now I just want to examine my plunder. Let go of the quilt."

He sighed when she still refused. "A bargain then: Let me see you, and you have my word I won't take you this morning."

Did he think she would trust him?

"I may be many things, but I'm a man of my word."

She considered that, and thought it true to the best of her knowledge. She also thought it best not to anger him again. She loosened her hold on the quilt.

Then she let silence gather around her like a secret protector as he folded back one side, and then the other, laying her breasts bare to the cool morning. She felt her nipples tighten. His eyes seemed to devour the sight; but he didn't touch her, not yet. Instead, he opened the quilt more, uncovering her belly, her thighs.

Now, his open palm — it was cool and rough with calluses — cupped her waist. His hand slid down the curve of her hips; his thumb stretched to the curls bracketed by her thighs. Then his hand came up quickly to take a breast. The touch was like a cool flame and made her wince.

He gathered the breast, shaping it so it stood up in

his hand. She watched his face with mixed anguish and fear, biting her lower lip to keep from crying out at this intimate handling, this manipulation.

The movement of her mouth was not missed. He lowered his head to kiss her. She jerked her head aside.

"Saxon," he said to her, in a gentle and somehow thrilling tone.

Her face was to the wall. He still had her breast.

"Saxon," he repeated softly, without impatience, his voice husky, "a bargain."

His hand left her breast, took her face, and turned it. She glared at him, accusing, "You said you wouldn't!"

"I'm only going to kiss you."

She bore it. Somehow she bore it. His lips were warm and surprisingly soft. And his beard and mustache were fleecy against her cheek and chin. Nonetheless, her hands stole to his chest and pushed at him.

He lifted his head—how slumberous his eyes were now!—and he caught her right wrist. When she tried to free it with her left hand, he also caught that wrist, both in his one huge hand, and he pulled them over her head, pinning them amid the nest of silk cushions there. Then he leaned into her mouth again.

Nothing separated her breasts from his bare chest. His matted hair rubbed her nipples while his mouth nudged her lips open. And then he touched her tongue with his own.

He murmured against her opened mouth, "It's as I expected; you're brimful of sweetness and spirit."

He deepened his next kiss. Though she pulled her tongue far back in her mouth, he tracked it, until her mouth was filled with him. Overwhelmed, she arched to get away—and felt a shock of sensation as her breasts were flattened against his hard, hard chest.

Another shock hit her as he threw his leg over hers and she felt his hot flesh hard against her thigh.

Panic rose. He had her pinned. She should never have trusted him! Just when she was sure of her doom, he lifted his head. His eyes were hooded, his breath a little quicker and heavier. "I want you, Shieldmaiden."

"We have a bargain!"

"Aye, for now. But tonight . . ." He lifted himself up, to bare her breasts to his gaze again. He pondered her, caressing her again. "Tonight there will be no one hammering on my door, and you will be reconciled, having had the day to think through the alternatives." His fingers were toying at the bottom of her belly. "Tonight, I will finger these yellow parsley-curls at my leisure — and when I tire of that, I will have you."

She looked at him; she felt confused by his masculinity. She whispered, "Have I no choice at all?"

"One — to struggle or not. Since I'd prefer not to see any more bruises on you, if you struggle, I might feel it necessary to bind you. Will you make me do that? . . . Ah, you feel you have to consider your response." It seemed he was trying not to smile again. It seemed there was a big smile wanting to break out of him, and then . . . it did! She got the impression he wanted to do more, to laugh outright. That he didn't do. But he said, "Well, take the day to make your decision; should you attempt to extend your time beyond that, however, the choice will become mine." She thought he was teasing. Could he be? Did he know what teasing meant?

The amusement she'd glimpsed vanished. His expression went stern and smokey again. "Don't look so solemn and frightened. I want you unafraid — leastways in this bed. Look at me," he said in that low, velvety, unfamiliar voice. He paused, as if he had something hard to say. "I will do you no harm here, Saxon. Surrender yourself to me and I swear you this: I will do you no harm."

He left the bed, unmindful of his nudity. Or was it his plan to make her used to the sight of him? Whatever, he walked boldly to the washstand. Seeing him still aroused, she thought, *He's going to invade my body with that! How can he not hurt me, rend me?*

147

She pulled her quilt back about her and slid to the edge of the bed. She found her clothes still lying where she'd slept last night. He picked up his trousers and stepped into them. She felt somewhat more at ease with his manhood tucked out of sight. Now her eyes caught on the matted blond hair on his chest, an expanse of chest so deep and so broad — surely his weight would crush the breath out of her!

"Get yourself dressed," he said.

She stood in the quilt, pleading in her eyes.

"I've seen you naked, and you've seen me. There is no use in modesty between us."

His eyes were the color of a gentle dusk, which reassured her a little. Still encased in the quilt, she shook the garments in her hand. Bits of rush-straw fell out. She tossed the sacklike dress onto the bed and in jerky, shy movements dropped the quilt and slipped on her undershift, then the dress. Without looking at him, she immediately began a search for her belt.

He went ahead with his own dressing, though she had the feeling he was aware of everything she was doing. Proof came when she raked at her hair with her fingers. He said, "There's a comb," gesturing to the washstand.

She hesitated, then crossed to it. As she began to comb her long hair, swishing it over one shoulder and then over the other, he said, "I'll see that you get some footwear — and better clothing."

"Truly, I don't mind this. It serves me well."

"As protection?"

She was surprised that he would grasp that, and reminded herself never to take him for a fool.

"From now on you'll need no other protection from my shieldmen than my claim. And I intend to speak to my mother. If I see any more bruises on you, I'll . . ."

She frowned thoughtfully. "You'll what?"

"It would depend on the offense — and on the provocation. If you don't do what you're told, you're welcome to the beating you get. You're still just a thrall."

She made her face go blank.

He finished tying his legging lacings and stood. Stepping past her, he said, "I have to visit the smithy about an anchor, and then see to an ox. Straighten the bed before you leave."

She didn't turn. She heard the door open. From the hall came a *thunk-thunk-thunk*. That was Inga, encased in disapproval, knocking her wooden spoon against the rim of the porridge pot — *Wishing it were me,* Edin thought.

When the sun was well up and the first chores of the day had been seen to, the men filed into the longhall for their breakfast. Edin was kept busy among the iron cauldrons and grills. The other female thralls chittered together as they spooned out parched barley porridge, excluding Edin. Rolf ambled to his place next to Thoryn's high-seat. Thoryn met his gaze with a stony stare, and Rolf was wise enough to lower his head to his meal.

The men were somewhat sobered, sensing that their jarl was not pleased with how they'd goaded him last night. They spoke quietly and looked from the Saxon to him. He said nothing, but simply let the questions and speculations buzz.

The maiden went about her work in an anguished distraction. Inga reprimanded her again and again — for offenses real or imagined — yet her spoon didn't strike, however much she glared with sparks and embers at the girl.

Thoryn ate slowly, forcing the porridge, the cheese, and the herring down. Only an iron will kept his eyes from lingering on the woman. Others conversed in quiet tones, trying not to disturb him or catch his attention. Only Rolf had the nerve to ease closer and ask, "How does the day go?" He was casual, picking his teeth with his knife blade.

Thoryn nodded perfunctorily.

149

"Something troubling you, friend?"

"Nothing I can't take care of."

Rolf's eyes sprayed enjoyment, waterfalling his pleasure. "The matters you can't take care of are few, Oh Hammer of Dainjerfjord. Just as you took care of that small matter last night."

Thoryn looked at him for a long while. "Soft, friend. You've had your way; now you'd best not remind me of how I was prodded to it. Even Rolf Kali must have a caution now and again."

"Mayhap I'm too stupid to be cautious."

"Mayhap," Thoryn agreed dryly.

But Rolf's curiosity was too irrepressible. "Was your performance magnificent?"

Thoryn made a sound in his throat. "Indeed."

"Ah, to be a brisk lad again. Yet the lass has left you uneasy. Does she weave spells on a man?"

"Spells or curses, I can't decide which."

She'd studiously refused to look at him all through the meal. Her head snapped up now, however, when he suddenly yelled, "Saxon!"

She froze in the middle of pouring a man a cup of buttermilk. Slowly she straightened and turned—still without actually looking at him. She stood there like a small statue, waiting.

The murmur of conversation died away. Thoryn felt himself break out in a sweat. "Well?" he said. "Come to me!"

She came slowly, reluctance in her every step, which made more than one man smile and nudge his bench mate. They thought he'd ravished her thoroughly. Ottar, laughing in his throat, murmured to Rolf, "Looks like she can't scamper so fast today."

At last she was before him and stood in the common stillness.

"Put your pitcher down and come sit on my knee."

Now her eyes met his. He had to harden his heart to do this to her. *Was* he spellbound? Or was he as she saw him: a fire- and brimstone-breathing monster, with scales and claws?

"Come!"

She put the buttermilk on the table and stepped up onto the dais of his chair. His hands went to her hips, pulling her in between his legs. "Sit," he urged quietly.

She tried to keep her legs stiff, but his arms conquered her. Her joints gave all at once, and she fell onto his thigh. Immediately his arms gathered her, then his hand lifted her chin. He felt passionate and distant at the same time. When she saw that he meant to kiss her — here, before one and all — she began to struggle.

But it was no use. She mewed as his mouth took hers. The sound was lost in the cheer that went up in the hall. He held her hard, grinding her bones together between his arms and his chest. He knew he was hurting her, yet his purpose demanded it. He wanted there to be no question in any man's mind: He was claiming her as his own.

He wanted *her* to feel his claim as well. He kissed her deeply, holding her in bondage to that fierce, hot delight she'd kindled.

When finally he lifted his head, he caught sight of Inga, pale and stiff, her eyes closed against what was happening. Not letting the maiden go, he said in Norse, "All of you in hearing of my voice behold: This woman is mine — and mine alone! Is it understood?"

The rugged men, with their fair mustaches and beards, shouted as one: "Aye!"

He whispered to her, "Don't look so frightened, Saxon. Dragons are monsters of the dark, and it's full light outside yet. Save your fear for the night." He clutched her to his chest again and kissed her again, burning with a desire that seemed fiercer than any flame.

When he looked up at last, he saw Inga again. A blank shadow had fallen over her face, and he knew she was seeing things again that no one else could see.

Thoryn went out with the others, and Edin was left to try to gather her wits. She ached for someone to confide in. He seemed more dangerous now, more terrible more. . . . She couldn't define her feelings with any degree of precision. But the things he'd done to her! And what he intended to do to her tonight! Everytime she thought of his huge, muscular body, his awful, silky voice, she felt a painful fear like a rake of claws through her insides. If only he weren't so horribly unapproachable, so forbidding. She swallowed repeatedly, an involuntary reflex, and her situation ran dark down her throat.

Her mind searched frantically for some way out of this nightmare. There was only one answer forthcoming: Her panicked mind screamed, *Run! Hurry! Get out of here before it's too late!*

Inga worked her hard in the kitchen all morning. In the afternoon she was set to shoveling the ashes from the fire pit. Even a second's pause caught Inga's blue-crystal eyes and brought her wrath down. She kept her wooden spoon in her hand, and though she didn't use it, Edin expected to feel it on her shoulder bones constantly.

Her ash buckets were full for the third time. As she started for the door, she saw Inga heading for the dairy. A numbing calm stole over her.

She left the hall. At the midden, she dumped the ashes. Then, apparently casual, she looked about at the quiet bare fields. The only people she saw were the shepherds up on the fell, Arneld among them, and around them the pleasant mill of sheep and goats, the jangle of one or two bells, and the light bark of a dog as it urged a wanderer back into the group. No one was watching her.

She was barefooted, with noting but the clothes on her back, wholly unprepared and unarmed — but what choice did she have? She put the buckets down and walked toward the southern rim of the valley. No one stopped her. Once she was safely over the lip and out of sight of the steadying, her urge to flee overpowered every other instinct.

The first hour was the worst, not knowing when her absence would be discovered, wondering what searches would be begun, what punishment would be meted out if she were caught. The jarl was no sleepy dragon; he would come after her himself. Fear of his vengeance jarred her and spurred her on. She thought of the times she'd seen him angry, the leashed violence in his eyes, his awesome, predatory control. What had he said about seeing a woman battle unsuccessfully against a man of twice her size and strength? He was a man who had seen and done all sorts of terrible, grim things. She imagined him following her with silent sureness, the muscles of his iron arms swelling as they reached out, grasped, and closed around her with astounding force, the straps of his neck muscles distending as he felled her and— Her mind would go no farther than that, but with every instinct she possessed, she ran on.

She thought to gain sanctuary in the woods above the fjord. She'd given no thought to where else she might go, there in that strange land, with no provisions, not even any shoes.

After the sunset, she heard horses' hooves. She whimpered in the back of her throat and ran faster. A bush caught her dress. Her hands worked intently, but before she got the material pulled free, it was caught again in a different place. Finally, trembling all over, she stood free, but only for a moment. Panic drove her into a shallow stream, where she stumbled on a slick rock and splashed full-length. The water was like ice; she cried out in a voice raw with fear, gained her feet, and pushed her body into motion again. Leaf litter covered the ground here, which made running easier on her feet, but her hair was caught a dozen times in the lower branches of the trees. She kept going at that breakneck speed until she had to stop to catch her breath.

The sound of the horses was gone. She sank onto her knees, quite out of wind, nearly blinded with colored sparks before her eyes, her pulse racing.

The birch trees here were never still, trembling and swaying, their branches creaking, murmuring in the dusk. After a brief rest, Edin forced herself to go on, keeping her pace brisk. She willed herself to make it up a particularly steep, forested slope. At the top she found a flat stretch with another brook flowing in its shallow bed, pouring itself over the stones lying in its path—another cold brook to wade across. Her lungs sucked in the damp forest air. On and on she went.

Eventually her footsteps began to drag. She couldn't see where she was going anymore. Her lungs ached, her legs felt wooden, and her feet were beyond sore. A vine caught her ankle, and she fell heavily into the duff beneath a somber fir tree. She struggled to her knees, but then sat with her head hanging, her mouth gaping, her labored lungs pumping.

Not a sound came to her, except the motion of the trees. Occasionally a dead needle-covered-bough fell, quietly. She felt as dead as a chunk of wood. She curled her body and closed her eyes. Almost immediately she was asleep.

She lay there under that bleak tree all through the quiet night, through the starlight and the leaf scuffle. She lay curled, nose to knees, in fitful sleep, cold and hungry, her teeth chattering. The mosquitos troubled her, and often a breath of wind whispering among the branches woke her to the thought that someone was out there watching her.

The next morning she found a handful of red berries to eat and, with water from the cold, clear streams, kept herself going. She traveled upward into the evergreen forest, carrying out a half-formed plan to battle a rough way southward over the soaring heights above the steadying. She was quite high up the mountainslopes her second night, when, as she curled her miseries around herself, she heard the wolves in the distance.

In the morning she caught sight of a pack of six or seven of them racing across a rock slope above her. They looked more churlish than dogs, more ragged, and with their ribs showing through their shabby coats, they looked hungry.

I should go back.

A traitorous thought—yet traitorous to whom? Did the Holy Virgin intend for her to wander in this wilderness and die from the attack of hungry wolves, or of starvation? Would it be so wrong to take what comforts had been offered her? The Viking had offered the warmth and softness of his bed, the comparative privacy of his chamber, the protection of his claim—which wouldn't protect her against him, yet would keep others from abusing her. Reason told her she was a fool not to go back.

But her heart couldn't agree. To simply surrender herself—it was too incompatible with everything she'd been taught as a child. She couldn't just walk into those metal-thewed arms, couldn't give the Viking any satisfaction he wasn't able to take. She knew that all she was doing was fleeing. She had no place to go, no purpose, no promise of a solution to any of her problems. She was simply running, to keep from being used like a thrall and then sold to another to use, and mayhap to another. . . . She'd had to try to flee that fate, didn't she? But now that she had her freedom, how to survive it?

Well, she didn't care to die by being torn to pieces by wolf fangs; so she changed her direction and traveled parallel with the heights of the mountains, going east, she believed toward the upper end of the fjord.

By that evening, leaden clouds lowered threateningly. No warm summer night stars came out as darkness fell. Instead, it rained.

On the fourth morning, the overcast sky was pale, unwarmed. Drizzle now and then drenched the green trees she was traveling through, turning them even greener. Today her hunger was no mere whim of appetite; she was miserable with it. Gradually she convinced herself that if she went down to the fjord's edge she might find food.

With the sky so grey, she wasn't sure of her direction anymore; she didn't know how far away Thorynsteading was, though she felt certain — hoped desperately — that she was safely out of the Viking's range.

When she came down out of the woods into the open, she found a small farm with a turf-roofed cot and out-buildings standing between her and the fjord. Lightheadedness tiptoed up and whispered: *Just walk down to the door of the cot and ask to be admitted.* Her head felt hollow, like the great emptiness of a church. *You could sit by the fire, mayhap sip a saucer of sheep broth, and offer yourself as a servant.* She knew she couldn't do that. How could she know how she would be received, or if the master of this place was any better than the Viking? Yet the temptation of a roof and warmth and food battered her heart.

She also knew that she didn't have the strength to go back up into the woods, either.

She settled for circling around the farm, keeping behind a dry-stone wall. She came upon half a dozen sheep and stopped. Bleats of panic from them could easily give her away. They made no sign of alarm, but as she started on, one ewe lifted her head. Edin stared right into her eyes. The sheepy face showed no alarm, and Edin kept low and was soon out of sight of the cot. She traveled down a long, grassy, wet defile that gave way to a high, rocky drop to the water.

Her bare feet were scratched and bruised, and the rocks were dog-toothed. Sea birds evidently perched here, for dead-white smudges of bird droppings capped and spotted the spikey rocks. Edin was too desperate to

156

care that many of these were fresh, too desperate to be fastidious about where she placed her feet. She was quivering with hunger; her mouth watered at the thought of food; food was the only thing she could think about.

The gloom of the day was heavy. The damp air held an almost tangible curtain of moisture to be brushed aside as she moved. Near the strand, she came upon a small flock of nesting sea birds. Disturbed, they flapped up off the dirty pebbles by the water's edge and swung out over the deep, jade-grey colored water, screaming loudly. She ignored them.

For another hour she scrambled over rocks and across short shelves of strand, traveling seaward again, though she hardly noticed. Her head felt light, swollen to pumpkin-size. Food; she must have food.

She came to a stretch of rock basins where heaps of slimy grey-purple seaweed and bladder wrack had been trapped. Tender product of a sheltered life that she was, Edin stuffed some of the seaweed in her mouth — then spit it out quickly. It was definitely not for eating.

Rain began to stipple the sullen water; great drops pattered down slowly, then faster. A ripple out in the water marked a fish roused by the rain. Above it, a cormorant circled heavily, watching, then dove like a plummeting arrow. There was a burst of spray, then the bird reappeared with a silver fish glistening in its beak. Edin stopped and stared; her mouth filled with saliva.

She followed the bird's flight to its nesting place, an idea dawning to steal the fish. She climbed up toward the place where the bird landed. So single-minded was she that she was taken by surprise when wings suddenly exploded all around her. Screams of outrage echoed off the tall sides of the fjord. Feathers floated. She flung her arms over her head. Birds flew directly at her in their fear. There must have been a thousand of them nesting there at the edge of the water. She went to her knees, her hands over her head.

When she could, she scrambled back down to the strand. Abrupt serenity settled over the birds behind her. Soon their fluttering and screaming stopped altogether, and she went on.

She was so wet and weary, so cold with the rain and the cunning wind which now wound about the corners of the headlands, so tired of slipping and sliding over the grey pebbles that pained her sore feet, that she began to think that nothing could be worse than this, not even surrendering herself to the Viking.

The rain stopped again, yet she felt no warmer. She wanted to cry. It seemed she'd been forever on the edge of crying. Her chest ached from holding her tears back. Her heart ached. What was going to happen to her? At this rate, she would be dead within days.

She skirted a covey of gulls that stood shaking their red beaks at each other as though passing judgement on her, and then came upon a large rock pool that cast back the morning light with a dull silver-grey sheen. She caught a glimpse of her own ripple-broken reflection, then looked beneath that image which was so white with fear and desperation—those great martyr-like eyes!—to see that the basin was full of mussels. They lay perhaps three feet below the surface bluish grey, left by the tide, just waiting to be picked up and eaten.

She slipped and slithered down the rocks that formed the bowl, stopping once she was thigh-deep in the pool, immersing her hands in the ice-cold water, getting herself soaked, yet already tasting the shellfish even before she had one broken open.

The first salty mussel slid into her mouth and rolled down her throat like ambrosia. She had the second on her tongue when she heard a rustling above her, a step. She looked up.

Chapter 11

The Viking stood there as stark as a column of rock standing against the pounding seas. He had a long oaken stick clenched in his right hand. On one hip was his longsword, heavy enough to behead a bull; in his belt was a battle dagger, called a *scramasax*. He was glaring down at Edin in the rock pool, poised, motionless against the sky. An emotion of extraordinary volume banged in her chest, goosebumps rose up all over her body, and cold panic swelled in her stomach. With the lapping of the water, and the screaming of her hunger, she hadn't heard him climbing down. He stood there now like a butcher come for the lamb, the bronze of an armband gleaming where his cloak was thrown back over his wide shoulder.

"Eat well, little run-away. You'll need something in your belly to make up for the beating you're going to get."

She could hardly swallow the mussel on her tongue. It stuck in her throat, and she coughed and spluttered. Her hands made unconscious warding-off gestures. She wasn't aware of being starved anymore, only of being afraid. He was enormous on that rock, backlit by the grey sky.

She glanced from side to side to see if there was a chance of scrambling out of the pool.

He laughed sourly. "Don't even consider it. I'll meet

you whichever direction you turn. I cut this stick three days ago, just to use on your back. I'm going to teach you a lesson with it. You'll scream and beg, but this time I intend to beat out every thought in your head that isn't obedient."

His eyes were so cold that she had to steady herself. The slippery, grey-purple sides of the rock pool didn't give her a chance, not when the previous days of hunger had sapped so much energy from her body.

"Come up here."

She made a faint attempt; but she was afraid, and weakened, and her feet slipped. At once casual and intent, he stepped down closer to her. Squatting at the lip of a rock, he reached his stick so that she could grab for it. She was shaking so much she could hardly take a firm grip.

Yet she saw that the rock he'd stepped onto was strewn with slimy purple seaweed. She grasped his staff as solidly as her numbed fingers could and, without warning, gave a great tug.

A savage noise leapt from his throat as his feet slithered out from under him. He came hurtling down. She leapt aside just in time. As he landed with a splash, she was already scrambling out of the pool, terrified lest her feet slip again and she tumble down beside him.

She drew herself up to the rock he'd fallen from. Behind her, he was floundering, trying to get his cloak back from his arms and his legs under him. She was frightened at what she'd done. He would follow her the length and breadth of the land now. She wished she'd simply taken the beating. She wished she'd never run away, that she'd gone to his bed. At least then she'd already know the worst and could be getting used to it. For a flash, she even thought of waiting for him to climb up to her, of yielding to his iron temper, just so she wouldn't have to be afraid anymore.

But then, all at once, he surged to his feet. His

entire titanic body vibrated with rage, communicating fury like a shout, even before the bellow of his voice: "*Spraeling!* When I'm finished with you even the shore birds won't want what's left."

She saw him drag his stick to the surface of the water, saw the cold glitter in his eye, and knew he meant every single syllable. She started to climb.

She gained the top of the headland and started across it, but then saw his horse, its reins loosely looped over an upright rock. The stallion was nuzzling the turf with its nose. She started toward it, ready to swing up on its back and ride away to safety; but the horse saw her coming and skittered sideways. Its look held a warning, and it snorted in a way Edin didn't like at all. She dropped the idea and went on; the stallion went back to pulling at the grass.

She heard noises from the cliff behind her even as she raced toward the opposite drop. She had a good lead until she knocked her toes against a keen edge of upthrusting rock. She cried out with the pain and hopped on one foot—then she saw the Viking, big and brawny and drenched, as he came up over the cliff behind her. Violence glittered in his face. His eyes were slitted, and there was a terrible fury about his mouth. She had to go on.

The far cliff-edge seemed an eternity away. Every stone seemed to twist under her feet. Behind her the Viking's strides got closer. Even in shoes, she could never have run like he could; almost at once he'd begun to catch up with her. She glanced over her shoulder, past her billowing hair: He was coming, his wet cloak swirling behind him.

She had no idea what was over the crest of the far edge of the headland. Mayhap there would be a narrow beach she could run along. Mayhap there would be rocks she could hide among. Mayhap there would be *something* that would save her!

She glanced back again. How close he was! How

frightening he looked, a tall, gigantic, bearded man with an awful purpose! When she looked forward again, the cliff-edge loomed like the edge of the world. Suddenly she was looking down it. Her hope plunged. It was a sheer, shale-covered slope, a sheer cascade of scree simply waiting for an excuse to charge into perilous motion. But she had no choice. She started down.

The loose shale slid away before her feet. She didn't go more than two paces before she fell sideways and started to slide, then to roll. On the first turn, she saw the Viking only three lengths above her and coming down fast. He didn't fall—he had leather boots on, and his feet were digging into the shale because he weighed so much more than she.

He made a grab for her—she actually felt his fingertips on her back!—but she was sliding and rolling too fast. She heard an ear-splitting curse erupt from his chest. It seemed to bounce against the low sky as she tumbled down to where the water—there was no strand!—lapped with deadly patience at the foot of the sheer drop.

And then she was in that water. She dropped into it like a rock, and it closed right over her entirely. The shock of it, the cold! A scream tore at her lungs. She flailed with her arms, but had rolled so much she was dizzy and couldn't tell whether she was straining upward or going deeper. She had no breath. There was only a liquid ringing silence. The cold water seemed to harden its hold on her, slowing her movements, paralyzing her. She sank like a stone down into the half-lights of the bottomless fjord.

Thoryn watched the sea drink her down greedily. The water swirled for an instant, then closed over her. He cursed again and threw his stick aside. It skittered into the water and disappeared. The maiden was also disappearing. He could still just see her, her arms moving, her white hands groping up, a shimmering,

162

amber goddess luring him, then she seemed to vanish, without leaving so much as a bubble behind her to brighten the world.

He somehow got his dragging cloak and weapons belt off, but there was no time for further undressing. He dove in headfirst, directly over where he'd last glimpsed her.

The shock of the cold crisped his flesh as he pulled powerfully downward with his arms. At first he couldn't see anything. He threw his hands blindly forward with each stroke, but found nothing. At last he saw her hair, flowing upward like rippling amber seaweed, and he noticed her breath bubble pass him. *Don't breathe in Saxon!* Then he saw her face; she was looking up at him. Her hair, like undulating seagrass, made so large a corola about her head that her face looked small. Her arms moved slowly, clumsily. *Please,* her expression called, *please.* His heart was captured, and he swam deeper, deeper after her.

His lungs burned; his muscles chanted. His mind sang with the intricate metaphors and kennings of skaldic poetry as she enticed him deeper than any living man should go.

He reached for her hand, touched her fingers, then lost them. *Swim, swim!* In dirtying waters, her hair brushed his wrist. Her amber beauty flashed. He swam as never before, his whole body surging with the effort. Her eyes shone, and her face gleamed like beacons.

He tangled his fingers in her hair, got a hold of it, twisted it around his fist, and pulled. He had her! Bringing his feet beneath him, he saw the daylight far above. His legs kicked, but he didn't seem to move. Her sodden garments weighted her like stones, and he was wearing even more than she was, including knee-laced boots. He kicked again, but the light seemed to get no closer. He kicked and kicked, towing her like a dead weight. His lungs were scalding. It was the worst pain he'd felt in his life. He fought it, and fought the water, and kept pulling toward the daylight with his free hand.

Let her go. She's just a thrall, not worth dying for.

I just have to get her to the light. . . .

That was his sole thought, to kick to the light, to get closer to the light, to reach . . . life!

As soon as he broke the surface and brought her head up, she wrapped herself around him. She was making startling noises, attempting to drag breaths into her water-filled lungs. She clutched even his arms, making his work of keeping both their heads above the surface a close-clenched performance. His mouth filled with the green, salty sea as he sputtered, "No, let go! I have you!" But her will to live was stronger than he would have guessed, and finally he had to let himself sink again. She let go and paddled frantically. He swam up on her from behind, got her around her shoulders, and towed her to a small shelf of rock.

She was coughing hard, straining to breathe, unable to do anything to help herself. With a surge, he gathered her and kicked and flung her up onto the small stony terrace. She landed like a meal sack, wet and limp. Water streamed from her hair. He came up dripping behind her, his arms and beard streaming. He bent over her rounded back and locked his hands together beneath her breasts and squeezed.

Seawater gushed out of her. She retched and coughed and finally sucked in a rasping breath. He squeezed again. More water spewed. He kept it up until she seemed empty, until her breathing seemed clear. Then, his arms still around her, he bowed over her prostrate form and closed his eyes. He had her back.

Now she began to cry, silently. He felt her body shuddering. He turned her, swept the streaming rack of her hair away from her face, and gave her a shake.

"You're alive!" He shook her again. "Do you hear me, Shieldmaiden? You're not drowned."

She quieted. Good. Now he could turn his attention to getting her home before she caught a chill. He went for his cloak and weapons, stepping gingerly along the edge of the scree-slope, using his hands as well as his feet lest he take another dip in the fjord water. He came back wearing his sword and *scramasax* and carrying his wrung-out cloak rolled under his arm.

Casting a gauging eye upward, he saw it would be difficult, if not impossible, to carry her to the top. "Come," he said sharply, "you're going to have to use your own legs."

Her face turned up to his. Her white skin was so marbled from the water that he muttered another oath, but for once she seemed willing to heed his advice. He said, less sharply, "Get your feet beneath you. Now hang on to my belt—can you hang on?"

Her skin was blue, her hair still dribbling salt water, but she nodded.

"Good. Then we go."

He crunched halfway up the scree, then paused to let her catch her breath. "Too bad I lost my stick," he said. "I could use it to help us up this slide." He looked back at her and added in squared-off Saxon, "Not to mention the fact that now I have nothing to beat you with."

She gave him only one peek of fear, biting her lower lip. Her obedience of the moment, this utter surrender and dependence, sent a thrill through him—and also turned over that ember of shame she had from the first sparked in him, which blushed hot and constantly threatened to kindle if he didn't watch it. In fact, she made him fear that there might be a whole flood of desperate feelings locked in the cold, dark rock that was his heart.

At the top of the cliff, he stopped and felt her sway

into his back, breathing hard. All his desire to hurt her had long-since withered. He pulled her around in front of him and took her into his arms. She let him. He murmured, "You're the laziest thrall between here and Byzantium." Yet for a long moment he held her folded against him, the top of her head notched between his throat and his shoulder, a place that seemed made for it. The small waves lapped whisperingly on the rock shore below.

Had he ever held a woman in just this way? He couldn't remember it. The feeling was exactly right, a feeling as rare to him as wild flowers in January.

He shouldn't kiss her, not now, but he sensed that she would let him — and an opportunity wasted was an opportunity regretted. He bent his head and nuzzled with his chin until her face came up. He took her moist lips once, working them until she opened them for him. That was what he wanted, and as she gave in, he praised her. "Very good, Shieldmaiden, aye." He took her mouth and this time drank the sweet and heady mead of her deeply. Time ran away. His sea-shriveled manhood grew stiff in his trousers. Before he lifted his mouth a long while later, his whole being seemed to glitter like embers.

Her head remained where it was, fallen back over his upper arm. Her eyes were closed; her lips trembled and were a little swollen. He enjoyed the deliciousness of the sight; her perilous sweetness almost overwhelmed his good sense. He could take her now — but if he did, it might be the only time, for unless he got her home quickly she might easily sicken and die.

His decision made, he remembered to praise her again for this show of surrender. "That's better," he murmured, "that's exactly as I want." Then he chuckled wearily. "I hope it won't always take near-drowning to make you pliant.

"But come, wake up. You're as cold as snow and

166

soaking wet, and the sky to the west glowers. We have to get home." He didn't notice that he was cold as well, and just as wet. His only thought was to get her warm and fed and rested so that he could plunder the innermost recesses of her mouth again—and make his first brilliant, brutal foray into her richer pastures.

By the time he hoisted her up onto Dawnfire, his horse, she'd started to shiver, from shock as well as cold, he supposed, and her days and nights of hunger and fear and exposure. Indeed, he was beginning to feel the freshly sharpened wind himself. No sunny breeze that, but sneaking, cold fingers that seemed determined to tease beneath their wet clothing and tickled their bare ribs. Great black cumulus puffs formed in the sky to the north, and the sea was getting choppy. He nudged Dawnfire to a trot.

Edin couldn't have stayed on the horse without the Viking's help. He'd put her before him in his beautiful and foreign saddle, and kept his arms around her as the big horse went from a trot into an easy gallop. Her shivering became more and more violent as they rode along. It was difficult to believe she'd ever been dry or comfortable in her entire life. The wind pried viciously at her dripping clothes. She mindlessly huddled against the Viking's broad chest, welcoming his arms, and the sharing of his damp cloak.

Occasionally she slipped back into a moment of tearful sobbing. She was so miserable, and death had seemed so near. The iron-like water of the fjord was in sight all along their way, its surface moving with mesmerizing undercurrents beneath the murky sky.

The Viking didn't shake her and tell her to stop crying. He only held her closer, and sometimes made a noise in his throat that didn't seem at all cruel.

She'd supposed the journey would be long and was surprised when they started down into the steading valley before nightfall. Her whole body was jerking hard with cold, however, by the time the snorting horse came to a stop on the tree-shaded green before the longhouse. Laag ran out from the stable to take the stallion's reins. The Viking slid down, turned, and held his arms up for Edin. Every one of her muscles was in a spasm; her teeth clicked uncontrollably. She felt numb and stupid. There the Viking stood, his hands up to her, waiting . . . and all she could manage was to lean forward and simply fall toward him.

He caught her waist. Her toes touched the ground briefly; then he swept one arm beneath her legs and the other around her back and lifted her to his chest as if her weight were nothing to him. Thus he bore her into the longhouse.

The warmth of the hall didn't penetrate her sodden garments at all. She looked toward the longfire, but the Viking carried her right past it. Her jaw was clenched tight and clicking or she would have protested.

The women, who had been busy among their pots and preparations for the evening meal, stopped their work and gawked. Inga pressed through them and stood scowling. Sweyn came out of his wall cubby and leaned his wounded right shoulder against one of the throne posts of the jarl's chair. The fire threw his shadow huge on the wall behind him.

The jarl ignored them all, except Dessa, to whom he called in Saxon: "Bring fuel for the brazier in my chamber! And then meat broth! See that it's hot!"

The girl lurched into movement, not so much because he'd shouted at her, Edin thought, but because the man was *power.*

Inside his chamber, he asked, "Can you stand?"

She couldn't form a word, but managed a strangled sound of assent. He let her slide to her feet — where she found she really couldn't stand after all, not without leaning against him. But he allowed that.

He was fumbling between them to unfasten her silver-buckled belt when Dessa scurried in with an arm-

168

load of small pieces of wood. She went directly to the bronze brazier and began to build up a little blaze that would very soon warm the thick-walled room. The Viking didn't wait for her to withdraw before, with a single violent movement, he drew off Edin's long, dripping dress and undershift. Dessa took one round-mouthed look, then scurried for the door. The Viking called after her, "Don't forget the broth!"

At the same time he reached for the toweling cloth on his washstand and gathered Edin's hair in it, deftly wrapping it around her head so that only a few neck curls and a few limp and damp tendrils at her temples were left free.

She looked down at herself; she was naked—pale everywhere. Her damp flesh looked as pallid as wax. He lifted her again and thrust her beneath the blankets of his big feather bed.

Dessa returned as he was pulling off his own sodden trousers, the last of his clothing. She squeaked at the sight of his bare buttocks, and hastily put down the two large bowls of broth she'd brought.

As she disappeared out the door, he laughed, in that sharp, barking, humorless way he had. Then he shivered, grabbed a bowl of the broth and a spoon, and climbed into the bed beside Edin.

He propped her head with pillows, and said, "Open your mouth." His voice wasn't gentle, yet he wasn't being unkind.

Still, it was all she could do to obey; her jaws seemed frozen into rigidity. As he spooned the steaming liquid into her, the joints melted, little by little. Soon they worked as well as ever, though the rest of her was still convulsed. Her hunger pangs faded as the broth filled her empty stomach.

Through all this she hardly had time to consider the import of this tall bearded barbarian, this Viking, spoon-feeding her.

When she'd taken every last drop from the bowl, he

got up to claim the other, which Dessa had left by the fire. "More?" he asked, turning with the second bowl. He was not aroused and so looked much less threatening than the other times she'd seen him naked. Nonetheless, he was strong-muscled and potent with power.

She answered his question with a shake of her head. She was too exhausted to eat any more. He tipped the broth into his mouth, drinking it down in long swallows. Then he was beside her in the bed again, taking her between his oversized arms and hard legs. She was so numb she could hardly feel, but then warmth seemed to focus wherever his skin touched hers—which was nearly everywhere, considering how tall he was, how brawny and broad-chested. The chill was slowly sucked from her marrow as she lay naked in his naked embrace.

Her eyes fell closed. Her face was pressed into his warm matted chest. She asked drowsily, "How did you find me?"

His voice rumbled. "Gunnhild, the widow of the man who died aboard the *Blood Wing*, saw flocks of sea birds rise suspiciously and sent her son, Hrut, to peek over the cliffs near their steadying. He saw you, and they sent word to me."

"I thought I was farther away." She must have zigzagged and traveled in circles in her wanderings.

"It would have made no difference; I'd have found you."

He would have stalked her with the patience and lack of emotion that marked him as a true predator. She would liked to have looked at his face just then, but she was too tired to move her head. Her eyelids seemed weighted. She heard him murmur, "You've been captured twice now. You fought well, Saxon— honor can ask nothing more from you in that—but it's time to admit defeat."

His voice was low. He wasn't threatening her for once. And she hadn't the least desire to argue with him. She was defeated. She had no chance of escaping him. He was too able and strong and intelligent.

Nor would she escape those who would own her after him.

Complete surrender to his use of her, however, would come in acts forced upon her long before it would come from her mind. He seemed to know this and, with that as his purpose, shifted her in his hold. Edin felt his lips against the unguarded skin of her shoulder, just above her left breast, which his vast right hand now gathered. She couldn't seem to lift her own hands to defend herself. She could no more move than she could open her eyes. She felt overcome, already ravished, and in want of comfort from . . . anyone.

Thoryn's mouth traveled down, enclosed the tip of her breast and drew on it. She felt a sensation, a pulling, as if his lips and tongue were pulling threads that led from her breast to the deepest nerves in her belly and thighs. He made her shamefully conscious of her body, and softly bewildered.

When he finished suckling, he licked her nipple, as if to soothe the flesh in case he'd drawn too hard. "You," he sighed, "with your green-gold morning eyes—you've become a great trial to me." He continued to hold her breast with his great hand. "Listen to me, Saxon, before you fall asleep. I want this to be well known to you: In this land there are laws, and the laws concerning thralls say that when one runs away he or she is punished with death."

Her eyelids fluttered open.

"You didn't know?" He was looking down at her, his expression very serious.

She shook her head, feeling her heart chugging up.

"You knew you weren't to leave the longhouse. No thrall—"

"I knew you would come after me; I knew you would be angry and if you caught me would probably

171

. . . hurt me, but . . ."

"But not that I would deal you your death? No one told you that?"

She shook her head.

"My mother should have told you."

"I . . . mayhap she did, but I don't understand Norse, and . . . I have let many things pass me by."

He grunted. "I should have seen to it myself. But it's as well that I didn't, because I think you would have run off anyway, and then I couldn't have used your ignorance as a reason to show you mercy," he explained in a calm, even way, which made the fury showing behind the calm that much more frightening. "I *am* going to show you mercy. But should you ever think of running away from me again. . . ."

She'd begun to shiver all over once more, and he gathered her and held her until it diminished and finally stopped. He embraced her until she fell asleep, a sleep full of sound and intensity and rushing event, all of which was distanced by a curious, ringing, liquid silence.

Inga still felt struck as if by lightning at the sight of Thoryn carrying the thrall into his chamber. She felt bewildered and afraid and all alone. She feared for her son and his passion for that woman.

Inga had good reason to dread passion. Passion could devour. Thoryn's passion for this Saxon was a threat to him, if only he knew. And a threat to Inga, because she understood too well the treacheries of passion.

Ah, yes, passion—that sumptuous love that made a person drunk. She'd longed for it, and believed in it while she had it, and envied it when it was lost to her. She'd *loved* Kirkyn; but Kirkyn's love for her had ended, just disappeared, and she'd had to go on with her passion alone. She'd had to bear a passion with

172

the heart cut out of it.

Edin came to the surface of sleep many times, only to sink down again. Once she opened her eyes and saw that the light around her was faint and new. Morning light. She wished to turn onto her side, but found the effort too much trouble. It really wasn't worthwhile. She felt herself pulled under again. The undertow was so seductive she couldn't resist it.

The next time the currents threw her up, the light was quite bright. Noon. How she enjoyed this utter passivity! Nothing to disturb her floating. No need for her to fight the currents. Sleep, sleep, all she need do was sleep.

When at long last she surfaced completely, the light was dusky. She heard the birds' evening songs through the open window hole, and behind her half-closed eyelids she imagined their swift, planing flights.

She knew where she was—in the Viking's big ornate bed. She was alone in it and realized dimly that she'd been alone in it for some time. He'd been in it with her . . . when? It didn't matter, as long as he was gone now. She moved, stretched out a little—and found that her feet were wrapped with something.

"My lady?"

She turned her head on the pillow drowsily and saw a figure sitting forward in the Viking's carved chair. "Dessa?" she murmured.

"Yes, my lady." The girl got up and crossed the room. "You've slept the night and the day through. I must tell the master. He said to let him know right away when—"

"Dessa, wait!" Edin was wide awake at last.

The girl paused anxiously.

"I . . ." Edin searched for some way to detain her. "It seems just today I was brought back."

"It was yesterday, my lady."

"Did the Viking . . . stay with me last night?"

The girl blushed. "You don't remember?"

"No, nothing."

"The mistress brought him a trencher of food at dinnertime. He took it from her at the door. Then this morning he called me. He'd found blood on his legs"—another miserable blush—"and lifted the bed-clothes to show me how your feet were cut. He bade me bathe and salve them and tie them up with cloth strips. Do they pain you, my lady?"

"No . . . no." It amazed Edin that she could have slept through so much. "You must have been very gentle, Dessa. Thank you."

The girl bowed her head over a pleased smile. "Well, they were mostly just scratches."

Edin suddenly felt a catch of hunger in her stomach, sharper than a thorn. "Has the dinner hour passed again?"

"They're just eating now."

"They're uncommonly quiet." She looked toward the door, straining to hear the usual braying male voices.

"They're listening to someone they call a *skald,* who wanders from place to place. He's come to tell stories at the feast."

"Feast?"

"Oh—you wouldn't know since you've been . . . away. There's a feast planned for the morrow. We've all been worked to the bone by the mistress these past three days preparing for it."

Speaking of Inga seemed to remind her of the Viking, and her anxiety to do what she'd been bidden returned. "I really must go and tell the master you're awake, my lady."

Edin saw the apprehension in her round, brown, childlike eyes. No doubt the girl would by punished if she didn't do what she was told. "Yes," Edin said, "you'd better go."

Chapter 12

Edin waited with gnawing anxiety for the outcome of Dessa's message. Would the Viking have cut another stick to beat her with?

Would he ravish her now?

She sat up, holding the blankets to her breasts. Her hair fell around her as she looked about for her clothes in the darkening room. But there wasn't time. She heard a step in the rushes outside the door, then—there he was, framed in the doorway, a horn of ale in his hand. Briefly she heared the subdued clatter of dinner being served, and an unfamiliar voice speaking in Norse—the story-teller, no doubt.

The Viking closed the door; she was alone with him again. She didn't know what to say, and he didn't help. He just stood there and looked at her, his hooded grey eyes appraising. He was so massive! Not only in height and weight, but in impact. His heavy square shoulders, his vastly muscled arms, that deep chest. He sampled his drink, drew a large mouthful, held it a moment as he continued to look at her, then swallowed it in several installments.

She said, "I don't see my clothes anywhere."

He moved then, and went to light the lamp, saying, "Because I had them thrown on the midden."

She considered that, and as he set the lamp down,

she said in a small voice, "But I have nothing else to wear."

He moved toward the bed. His hand took her shoulder. "Lie back." When she resisted, he added in a low, intense voice, "Must I fetch a switch? Is that what it will take to drive it in that you must obey me? I *own* you, Saxon."

She did as he wanted, and the movement made her empty stomach growl.

"What was that?" he said; and added without so much as a grin, "A bear? Do you have a bear in bed with you, woman?"

Before she could answer, he went back to the door and shouted, "Girl! A trencher of that stew! And ale — no, milk — a pitcher full!"

He said no more, only went to his chair and sat down. In a few minutes Dessa came hurrying in with the food. At a gesture from the Viking, she helped Edin sit up, and held the trencher while Edin ate from it. From time to time she passed Edin a goblet of milk or a slice of bread covered with a huge crumbly slab of cheese. At last Edin lay back against her pillows, saying, "No more."

The Viking got up silently to see exactly how much she'd put away. He leaned against the wall by the head of the bed, folded his arms, and nodded to Dessa, dismissing her.

As the girl gathered the pitcher, cup, and trencher, Edin said, "Thank you, Dessa."

The girl gave a little bob, and said in a sweet, soft voice, "Welcome, my lady." Then she was gone.

The Viking stood looking down at Edin. "My lady?" He blew down through his nostrils in contempt.

Edin felt too vulnerable to quarrel. "It's merely what she's used to calling me. You mustn't blame her for —"

"Aye, the minds of thralls are deeper than the wa-

176

ters of the Jimjefjord, which, as all Norsemen know, has no bottom."

He turned away, using his back to dispose of the subject. He went to stand over the little brazier. His hair, yellow and loose to his shoulders, gleamed in the light. His back to her, he asked, "Are you better?"

There was no sense in lying; he was as shrewd and intelligent as he was bold and brawny. She answered, "I could get up and help with the serving."

He half-turned to look at her. "With no clothes? I'm the only one you'll serve naked, Saxon."

She swallowed, mortified to the very core.

He seemed ill at ease. "I've waited patiently for you to wake. Remember that I didn't beat you for running away. Instead, I've seen to your care and your rest. Now I want to be repaid for my lenience. Will you yield to me?"

Panic throbbed in her throat.

He came back to the bedside, reaching to finger a strand of her hair. "I'm asking you, Saxon, when I have no need to ask. And I will have an answer: Will you yield to me?"

How could she deny him? She couldn't fight a man his size. And the brutal lesson her brief bid for freedom had taught her was that she needed him. Though she feared his coldness, he was strong, and if she acquiesced to his desires, and pleased him, he would keep her safe. It was time, finally, for fear to give way to the more demanding need to survive.

"Really," she said at last, "what choice do I have?"

He dropped the strand of hair and folded his arms over his chest again. "You have the same choices you had before: You can yield or you can struggle. If you choose to struggle, I can't promise to show you consideration."

If she chose to resist him, he would merely overpower her with his superior size and strength and

177

cunning. He would do whatever he must to gain his victory.

He would hurt her.

"You —" she swallowed — "you will show me consideration if I yield?"

"I will," he said formally, staring down at her over his folded arms.

"You won't hurt me?"

"There is one wound I must deal you, for it cannot be helped; but you will suffer less if you lie easy beneath me."

For a moment more she sat iron-locked by her chastity and caution. He was demanding her willful assent, her expressed concession to surrender herself in advance of all he meant to subject her to. She looked down at her hands which played nervously on the quilt — and in the end said the only thing she could say with a Viking standing over her, dragon-sized, and with no hesitation in his purpose. "I will yield to you, Thoryn Kirkynsson."

He turned away and began to undress directly. Her heart thumped up; she felt herself suddenly grow weak. What had she agreed to? She stared as he pulled off his tunic. He was built on such a large scale! He looked so powerful, so aloof, so entirely self-assured. His footwear came off next, after which she slid down in the bed and closed her eyes, so she wouldn't have to see him take off his trousers.

She felt the blankets lift, felt a draught of cool air, and then felt his hands on her, his legs. Immediately she knew that his desire was hard.

He lifted her chin and kissed her throat. At least his beard was soft and the scent of him was pleasant. His kiss trailed up the line of her jaw, until he opened her mouth with his lips.

She made a sound. He lifted his head and said with stinging impatience, "You're not to be frightened."

Not to be frightened! So said this man muscled in iron, his mind hard with his determination, his desire so strong it was impossible to ignore! "That's easy enough for you to say, Viking," she whispered.

"Hm!" He abruptly threw back the blanket, exposing her. Her hands went ineffectually to her breasts, her sex. "Put your hands down," he scolded, but his voice was less demanding this time.

He couldn't know what he was asking! She felt her nakedness and her weakness too fully.

But she felt it more fully as he forced her hands to her sides. Her heart hammered at her ribs.

"You fear what you don't know. You find this new and difficult to accept, and so I will teach it to you unmistakably from the beginning." His eyes were hooded and uncompromising, and suddenly he pushed his hand between her legs. She let out a little gasp.

"This is part of what you're afraid of, is it not? Knowing that sooner or later I will touch you here. Now it's already done; now you can stop being afraid of that much." His tone was not exactly soothing, yet was as soothing as she could imagine from him. She took scant comfort in it, however, not with his hand pressed firmly where no hand had ever touched her before. She made no sound, but if a person could keen silently, she keened.

He leaned to take her bottom lip into his mouth, sucked it — how strange the things men wanted to do to women! — and then nipped her upper lip with his teeth. She didn't dare close her eyes again, and evidently their expression didn't please him. He said, "I could be old and deformed."

"With rotten teeth and not given to bathing much," she whispered, remembering that once he'd threatened to sell her to such a man.

He smiled thinly, drawing her even closer. His right hand was still between her clenched legs. Her thighs held his wrist tightly. "Loosen your legs," he said.

Oh, dear God, help me!

Her god either didn't hear, or didn't care.

"Loosen your legs."

She obeyed shyly, miserably. Her hands struggled to keep from pushing at him.

"You may as well relax; I've only started. I mean to touch every part of you. The strangeness of it will pass." As he said this, his left arm beneath her shoulders lifted her up a little so that he could gather her mouth to his. This brought her breasts into contact with his hard chest. In a reflex, she wedged her hands up between them.

And yet there was nothing to separate his callused palm from her sex. The pressure was so intimate, so agonizing.

His kiss was thorough. By the time he finally lifted his head, she felt dazed and fiery. He laid her back and removed his hand from between her legs. He took her hands, one at a time, from his chest and this time pushed them beneath her. Now he was free to fondle her breasts and carefully examine them. She looked up at him beseechingly. Again and again she almost pulled her hands out to stop him, but remembering his threat to bind her, she didn't.

He lifted her chin and kissed her again; then cradled a breast in his hand and kissed that. Then, with his left arm still under her shoulders, his right hand delved between her legs again.

She turned her naked body into him with a little cry. Her left hand went to his upper arm before she could stop herself, but then just lay there, limp. With his thumb atop her pubis, he simply held her, cupped her, for a long moment.

Then he went back to her breasts. He pulled his left arm out from beneath her shoulders and half lay over her, holding himself on his elbows so that he could cup both her breasts at once and suckle them gently, first one and then the other. The sensation was curiously soothing. And she was stunned to realize what he was doing: He was easing her into accepting his touch, approaching her and then retreating, so that her fear would be overcome. This was the consideration he'd promised. This Viking, this barbarian, this savage, was keeping his word.

He bit at her nipples and moved her breasts as if to feel their weight, then said suddenly, "Kiss me."

It meant lifting her head a few scant inches, yet seemed the hardest thing she'd ever contemplated.

"I-I can't! I'm so afraid of you!"

"Yet you're finding me less bloodthirsty than you believed, aren't you?"

It was true, she'd expected to be humilaited at the very least. The very least.

"Kiss me."

She did it, timidly. Her obedience seemed to inflame him. He deepened what she'd begun so innocently, and plundered her mouth with his tongue. She was making little whimpering cries in her throat—yet struggling not to make them too loud. Tears welled up and spilled out her eyes. Did he know what a battle she was fighting to keep from kicking at him, from trying to push him away?

When he finished kissing her, she lay still, her mouth tasting of him. Her eyes were closed, and she was breathing deeply as her tears continued to flow silently.

"Stop."

She opened her eyes. He was leaning up on his elbow, looking down at her.

He stroked her hair and lowered his head to touch his lips to the tip of her nose. "Stop crying. I haven't dealt you any injury yet. I'll hurt you only when I have to."

He massaged her breasts again lightly, and then

stroked her underarms. She sobbed softly, but wrestled with these sobs. She struggled not to writhe away, not even as his hand drifted down to her waist, to her stomach, and again cupped that full-feeling, moist place between her legs. He began to press in firmly with the flats of his fingers, rhythmically, making her recoil at first, and then tremble. He took another kiss from her mouth, a soft kiss, which filled her with a softening distress.

"You see?" he whispered. "You won't find me such a hard master. Only a very thorough one."

A feeling built in her such as she'd never experienced before. Her legs moved restlessly. Her hips moved slightly up, against him, pressing the heat and dampness of her sex against his fingers.

As if he'd been waiting for this signal, his fingers burrowed and made her shudder with terrible sensation.

His touch left her yet again, left her feeling that odd restlessness as he gathered her in his arms, pulled her onto her side and felt her back and her buttocks, then pushed her back into the mattress so he might see the mounds of her breasts again. Possessiveness and pride of ownership were evident in his gaze. He bent over her and bit at them playfully, not hurting her. He lapped them with his tongue — then, as she suffered and moaned beneath him, he suddenly reached between her thighs again.

He opened her once more, and his fingertips fondled. As he touched one place, she sucked in breath. He paused, then gave that place a soft pinch with his thumb and forefinger, which made her gasp again. He continued, as if curious, touching her nowhere but there, until she was swept by a craze — to have him hold her hard, hard enough to hurt her.

She begged for mercy. "Please . . . stop!" Surprisingly, he did, but only to ease a finger inside her. "Oh, God!" She felt it was an outrage, an invasion that had to be endured because it couldn't be escaped. She rolled her head, wondering how long she could bear it—but then, as his finger eased deeper and moved within her, there came an acute sensation of anticipation. She made a wordless sound and placed her hand on his chest not to push, but to tangle her fingers in the wiry blond curls.

His finger settled into a circular motion. Her hand slid to his shoulder, then clutched. She didn't understand it. It was like a sudden loud chant of voices that wouldn't stop, that grew louder and more purposeful. The chanting had no beat, no rhythm, nothing but movement and sensation and fire.

Suddenly he withdrew his hand and rose up, spreading her thighs wide enough to give him clear access. Down between her pinked nipples lying erect on her heaving breasts, between the fork of her thighs, she saw his weapon. As he leaned forward, she whimpered at the first nudge of that hardness.

Panicked, she tried to roll away. But he had her by her shoulders. "I won't hurt you needlessly." He lay more of his weight atop her to still her writhing—and at the same time pushed into her an inch. She cried out. He said, "The worst will soon be over." She was so afraid. She was using her wrapped feet to try to move up in the bed, away from that threat of invasion.

Finally, reaching down to clasp her bottom in one big hand, he simply thrust into her. She felt a frightful stab and went rigid as it coursed through her. Butterflies, bouquets of light, fluttered behind her eyelids. He thrust again, hard, and something within her gave way. He'd broken through her maiden's gate, through her innocence. The stretching and distension! She felt him withdraw his weapon with vast relief—but he drove into her again.

There was some pain with this second thrust, but there was something else as well. She inhaled violently with unwilling sensation.

Yet another driving thrust. And another. A sensitivity bloomed in her. She arched her back to bring herself against him — her breasts were suffused with a need to be flattened against his chest. Her movement was not missed. His mouth angled over hers, and she opened her lips for his tongue. Her next cry was muffled in her throat.

He kept his hold on her bottom and pulled her into each of his thrusts — until suddenly his muscled body went rigid over her. He stopped moving, burying his face into her shoulder, and she heard a muffled "*Huh!*" as his seed exploded into her. She felt him throb, and throb . . . and throb.

His hold on her relaxed; he lay heavily on her, then withdrew himself. He rolled to lie beside her, rested, nuzzled. His gaze touched her face like a gentle caress. She felt . . . spent, and could only look up at him with vacant eyes and a half-opened mouth.

"Still in the battle trance are you, Shieldmaiden?"

Her hair was wound around her breasts, and after a while he got up on his elbow to brush it away from his playthings. Eventually he parted her legs again. She whimpered softly. He entered her cautiously, watching her face as he did. "Good," he praised her, "you do well, Shieldmaiden, better than I expected."

He gathered her in his arms as his hips began to move, slowly and mindfully. She had no words nor the strength to get him off. He was big and determined and well-practiced in the art of taking. Each stroke threw lightning through her — yet it never quite seemed to strike. He took her slowly that second time, with less urgency, thrusting into her until she began to move with him, and to moan.

Inga Thorsdaughter had a sudden fit of uneasiness, a rush of anxiety that gripped her chest till she could hardly breathe. She rose from her bed and rushed for the door of her chamber. All was still in the hall. With that strange anxiety driving at her, she stole along past the tables, past the high-seat, the fire pit, until she stopped before Thoryn's door.

What was that faint noise? What?

She drew closer, placed her ear to the wood, then stood arrested, listening.

It was a strange, breathy, not loud noise. Her blood stood still. It had an almost soundless rhythm, yet was rushing and powerful, as if something large was in violent, hushed motion. What was it? In Odin's name, what was it?

She needn't ask. She knew that noise, though she refused to name it to herself, refused to put it into words, not even silent, private words. On and on it went.

Passion! The word came to her unbidden, and at the same instant her mouth filled with a coppery taste.

"Thoryn . . ." she whispered. But then a strange, distant nostalgia took hold of her, and Thoryn's name was replaced: "Beloved Kirkyn, my beloved. . . ." With all her tortured, rejected love flooding within her, she turned away.

The steadying was awake. Edin heard the cattle lowing, the sheep and goats bleating, the thralls moving about their morning tasks. From the open window she heard the birds' bright squabblings high up in the tree outside the longhouse.

She opened her eyes to see the four monsters guarding her in the big bed—the dragon on each of the four bedposts. The Viking was seated in his chair finishing the lacing of his leggings. She sat up. Her hair was atangle, and she felt rosy from sleep. And a little sore and sensitive everywhere. She held the blankets to her so that they covered all but the upper-most slopes of her breasts.

The Viking was dressed particularly well in a tunic of green silk. He looked up at her—and something strange happened. For an instant they seemed to be caught by one another's eyes. For an instant they were coupled in a mystic bondage as surely as if he were crushing her into the bed yet again.

Without greeting her, he said, "No doubt my mother could use your help today if your feet are healed enough."

Edin thought of Inga, that overbearing, watchful woman, her glower, her eyes that were like blue peb-bles. She said, "Of course," but her voice came out as delicate as her body felt after the Viking's handling throughout the night.

"We're hosting a feast. There will be a sacrifice in thanksgiving for our profitable summer, and prayers for a mild winter, and—"

"You pray?"

He gave her a look. "You'd best get up."

"I have nothing to wear."

He frowned, remembering. "I'll tell my mother—no, I'd better see to it myself. I don't want you drag-ging around in another sack, disgracing me."

Her eyes snapped at that, but she said nothing.

He crossed the floor and stooped over her, catching her face between his hands before she could elude him. The touch electrified her; the air all about her churned.

"You served me well last night, Shieldmaiden," he said gruffly, placing a kiss on her closed lips. "Would that I could while away this morning with you, too, but there is much I must do."

"Don't let me keep you, then," she said in a fruity, impudent voice.

Far from insulting him, she saw the corners of his mouth struggle against a smile. "Let me kiss your breasts at least before I go."

She hugged the bed clothes tighter. "You have so much to do; you'd best not tarry."

Now he did smile. It was as if he didn't want to but couldn't stop himself. Yet he wouldn't let her have the last word. "You seemed to grow to like my kisses last night."

She dropped her gaze.

"Aye, they stiffened to little peaks in my mouth; the tips rolled like little cranberries between my lips."

She turned from him, but not so soon that he missed the tears gathering in her eyes. He frowned, then sat down on the bedside. "Why do you cry now?"

"Because I'm ashamed, Viking!" she lashed out at him. "Do you have any conception of the word 'shame' in your barbarous head?"

That sobered him, and more. "You're ashamed because your master took you?"

"Ashamed because I *gave* myself to you," she said miserably.

His face hardened. "You gave nothing that wasn't mine already."

His words washed over her. She continued to hang her head in remorse. He couldn't possibly understand.

"Show me your breasts," he said again suddenly. Both the command and the tone startled her. She gathered the blankets tightly under her arms. He sat straight, not touching her, and put an even more dangerous undertone in his voice: "Show me your breasts, Saxon. *Now.*"

The Viking moved not a muscle, only glared at her and waited. She'd seen fighting men reduced by that particular voice and that particular glare. And she was but a woman. Slowly she loosened her hold on the blankets and lowered them to her waist, leaving nothing but her hair to shield her nakedness. But not even that was going to be allowed.

"Put your hair back."

She did it and felt her breasts lift with the motion of her arms.

He reached for her casually, with both hands, covered her with his palms—and abruptly pushed her back into the mattress. Leaning close over her, he said, "You possess too much pride for a woman. You make the mistake of thinking that because you didn't fight me—a thing that proves laughable whenever you try it—you *gave* yourself. But are you giving me your breasts this minute—or am I taking them?"

"Oh!"

"Aye, you see now. If you want to weep out of frustration, which women are known to do, or out of anger, or even out of sadness for all you've lost to me, then go ahead, wear your tears like jewels—but you infringe on *my* pride when you claim you *gave* yourself to me. All you did was yield, which is another matter altogether, and even that was tedious for me to enforce."

He allowed just a little relenting back into his voice. "Not that I'll ever refuse anything you do care to yield. Mayhap you'll yield me another kiss now? No?" His mesmerizing, thoughtful eyes dwelt on her. "But you are aware that I could take one? Then I've made my point."

He seemed extremely reluctant to leave her lying there, his for the taking. But he did rise. She was too bullied to cover herself again.

He took up his sword and drew it out of its scabbard to check its edge. Its gold inlays glinted. He returned it to its sheathe and belted it to his waist. He clasped a fine cloak trimmed with squirrelskin to his shoulders with two large golden brooches. Then, looking magnificent, he said, "I'm going to see about finding you clothing. While I'm gone, rise and bathe your face and comb your hair."

Her eyes flashed again, which she knew suited him. The whole incident, she saw now, had been enacted to erase her tears and replace them with anger.

And he was right; anger was better than tears. Better for her — and certainly better for him! How she hated him. He was nothing but a hunk of chaos that had taken on shape, sulky and so evil!

Chapter 13

Fair weather had returned, and while streaks of sunlight were still dancing off the morning dew, guests started to arrive from every nearby steading and *hof*. Some walked, some rowed from the far ends of the fjord, and still others rode horses or came by cart. They weren't all strangers with strange faces; Edin recognized many from her capture and terror aboard the *Blood Wing*.

It was a shock to see those fierce and frightening warriors now dressed in finery, wearing jewels and ornate weapons. They'd abandoned their sensible and comfortable work clothes for tunics encrusted with embroidery. Fafnir Longbeard made his appearance in a bronze helmet bearing a griffin's head. Vain Hauk Haakonsson, he with the nose like an eagle's, had on a pair of high boots sewn with colored threads and ornamented with gold. Many others wore gold bracelets and gold straps around their foreheads.

Every man, even the old and bent-kneed, came well armed and carrying a round shield. Of particular interest was the arrival of Kol Thurick, the man who had lost his front tooth during the storm at sea. He and his sons walked into the hall, each with a hawk on his shoulder, an extraordinary sight: four proud, golden-headed warriors with four imperious falcons staring unwinking from their mail-clad shoulders.

There was an abundance of sturdy young men like these, all intent on carving out a position in life for themselves. To England's sorrow, this race was clearly in no danger of dwindling, not with so many powerful and ambitious youths ready for any chance to increase their wealth by means fair or foul.

The Viking women were stately in their sleeveless dresses. They were like ice and snow, Edin thought, laughing and yet somewhat distant. They seemed very proud of their white arms and shoulders, and it seemed they loved richness and splendor as much as their men. Their gorgeous wrap-around gowns were made of luxurious Chinese silk, heavy gold brocade, satin, and soft velvet. Matrons wore their hair piled and fastened with twinkling combs or diadems; the unmarried wore it down like yellow floss on their shoulders. Edin was dazed by their loveliness—and overcome by her own position of dishonor and vulnerability.

She was thankful that these ladies never quite looked at her—and then felt worse because they didn't. She was nothing to these women who were free. The faint disapproval she sensed was no doubt because, as an abject slave, she was nothing but a strong temptation for such predatory men as were their Viking husbands and swains.

Even the little children who ran through the crowd, swooping and laughing, were dressed in garments exquisitely ornamented with gold, silver, bright silk tassels, and lace. Edin loved children, and when one tiny staggerer came rocking into her path, stopped, and suddenly sat down with a plop and commenced to cry, she naturally picked him up and bounced him until his mother, like a young hen, raced scolding to his rescue. She yanked the child away as if Edin's very touch were objectionable. Edin briefly wondered if she'd broken some rule—or was there an undercurrent here she couldn't comprehend?

The cacophony of greetings and conversations gradually filled the hall to the high log rafters. The men invariably came through the doors first, tall and fair, with their long Nordic heads, their long narrow jaws, and blue or grey eyes; their women, tall, stiff, dignified—also of Viking stuff—followed behind them. The jarl met each group and offered them refreshment. He smiled like a conqueror, betraying nothing of the man Edin was beginning to know.

Earlier, he'd outfitted her for the occasion in a twofold gown that hung from loops caught by brooches at her shoulders. This twin garment was two separate lengths of light-blue wool wrapped around her body beneath her arms, the first from left to right, the second from right to left. He'd also provided a shawl of fine lavender wool, which a third brooch held pinned in place over her breastbone. She finally had shoes again, too, soft leather ankle boots, fur-lined. Besides the three brooches, she wore one other piece of jewelry—a silver-gilt torque, a wide choker engraved with the image of a Valkyrie offering a horn of mead to a Viking warrior. The jarl explained while clasping it around her neck, "Valkyries are Odin's shield-maidens; they select the champions for Valhöll and service their needs there."

"Are they warriors then, or whores?"

"Both."

"I see."

"And so do I see—that you're less than grateful for these gifts."

She looked down at herself. She was dressed far above the standard of the average thrall, yet she said, "Gifts? By your own reasoning, you still own this gown and this . . . this *slave* collar. If everything of mine is yours to take—"

His swift response swept her thoughts away before

192

she could finish voicing them. Suddenly he was again the fire-breathing dragon, determined and ruthless. His hands on her waist lifted her to the edge of the bed. He threw her new skirts up, opened his trousers, and sank into her. She failed to hold in her moan. His voice seemed to come to her from a great distance: "You begin to understand. You are my plaything, my pleasure-thrall, whom I can take at will." Into her again! Again! Until he throbbed sensuously.

When he withdrew from her and stepped back, her legs were dangling, her feet not touching the floor, the comb she'd been using dropped noiselessly from her limp hand to the sheepskin rug, and her face was flooded. She lay motionless, her loins still aflame — and curiously wanting. Their eyes met; something flashed between them, something of the unsettled sensations in her loins and a small frown of bafflement on his brow. Then, as with an effort, their eyes wrenched away from each other.

Edin thrust that memory away, and with it the anguish, the shame — and the mysterious and harrowing half-pleasure she felt with his rough takings.

The first order of business was the religious matter of which the Viking had spoken. As the local chieftain, it seemed he was also the community's religious head. To this end he donned a horned helmet that must have been used only for ritual purposes, for it would have been an encumbrance in battle. He also wore a hammer in his belt — Thor's sacred hammer, Edin was told. Freeborn and thralls alike followed him outdoors and up the slope away from the long-house to where a flat-topped stone stood up out of the ground. The Stone of Thor. Edin could see old traces of blood on it. She located Dessa, who knew more Norse and so could help her understand what was taking place.

The assembled Vikings made both an elegant and

a daunting presence. The jarl seemed to wrap silence around him before he ritualistically put his sword to the throat of a sheep, a goat, and finally a bull — sacrifices to placate the myriad gods they worshipped. Edin stayed carefully on the outskirts of the crowd. She didn't like to be close to him when he had his sword drawn. She watched with deep interest, however. It seemed these people held a less deferential attitude toward their deities than the lowered knee and humility that Christians were taught. Having been forced to bend her knee too often, their uncowering worship intrigued Edin.

A toast to Odin was drunk, for victory and for the jarl's health; then came a toast to Njord and Frey for fruitful harvests and — of all things! — peace. A "chief toast" was drunk to the late jarl, Kirkyn Atlason. A few men also drank "remembrance" toasts in recollection of certain of their kinsmen: "I drink to Ketil Ivarsson, who was awful in his might. . . ."

Following this, the sacrificed animals were prepared for baking in an earth-covered oval pit lined with hot stones. The sacrifice was evidently convivial; the worshipers would collectively feast on the nourishment consecrated to the gods. A sensible notion, Edin thought. While the thralls worked at this cooking, the Viking women caught up on their visiting, and their men played chess on the green outside the hall. Edin had never seen so many dice and board games and beautifully made chess sets.

The summer afternoon was long there at the northern rim of the world. The insects sang a drowsy verse as worn and comfortable as the knees of old breeches. Yet the weather began to bite with the coming of dusk. The gathering moved indoors, where the night's ritual feast and festivities filled the heated banquet hall.

Inga herself took around the first course of the meal, a thick cream of barley soup which she ladled from a magnificent silver cauldron carried by two thrall-men. Once this prettified gesture of hostessing was accomplished, she took a place near the jarl and let the thralls continue the more arduous serving. Edin, her shawl removed so that her arms were bare, moved among the glittering guests with trenchers of roasted sacrificial bull, mutton, and goat meat; Juliana served wooden platters of all kinds of fish; Dessa served honey bread and rye bread, pale cheese and sweet butter; and Olga helped Juliana with the wooden platters of fish, and several baskets of nuts. They toured and toured the abundant tables. The Vikings and their ladies drank, laughed, and ate — they ate like wolves.

Every time Edin raised her eyes, gold winked at her. She was nearly blinded by the beautifully worked gold brooches, the silver rings wound with sinuous Viking art, the arm rings and bracelets of gold, the strings of pearls and brilliant glass beads, the finely wrought silver chains, and the ornate belt buckles and pendants.

"See the combs that young lady with red hair is wearing?" said Dessa. "Are those really jewels?"

Edin glanced at a redheaded girl of about fourteen who was lacing into the food as eagerly as the rest.

"Is she not beautiful?" Dessa sighed.

"Yes," Edin said. She'd grown a little benumbed, what with the great fire burning, the noise of the feasting, and the clamor of the ale cups.

And over and above any other concern was her constant awareness of the jarl. Tonight he didn't look the pirate he was, sitting in his dragon chair like a king. She'd never seen him outfitted in such fine clothes, his fair hair held by a gold-encrusted band about his forehead, his strong light beard combed and trimmed. He was square-shouldered, powerful-bodied, with rings on his fingers and an unusual openness in his face. Everything about him was undeniably grand, and beside him, other men paled to insignificance.

Despite all that he'd done to her, all the excruciating intimacy they'd shared, she felt sure he wasn't even aware of her presence in this room, filled as it was with so many lovely women, free Viking women. But then a moment came that proved otherwise. A small moment. She was doing nothing but serving, but suddenly she felt his gaze on her. Across the width of the room. Through the crowd. She felt the strength of his look, despite the distance. Her palms went wet. Her knees got weak. Before she could help herself, she turned in his direction.

Then she could do nothing but stare back at him as blatantly as he was staring at her. She wondered what it meant, this strange response in her. It was like whirlwinds and flashes of lightning. The look in his eyes was approval mixed with a gauging uncertainty, as if in dressing her so gorgeously she now appeared more attractive than he'd ever intended or wished. That flicker of uncertainty in him made her feel instantly beautiful, as beautiful as any Viking woman present. Radiantly beautiful. She couldn't comprehend it. Mayhap she was only exhausted.

A small reluctant smile appeared about his mouth. Reluctant because she was a mere Saxon captive? Too lovely for a thrall? Was that his thought? It was she who broke the look and turned away.

Once the enormous feast was served and the prodigious appetites of the assemblage appeased, jollity took over. A group of clumsy, booted little girls danced for the crowd, grinning and holding wide their skirts. The Vikings cheered them effusively. They were growing merry with drink. The smith, Eric No-breeches, did a trick with a dagger. Already so drunk it seemed he was having trouble balancing himself on his two legs, he tipped his head back and tried to balance the deadly point of the dagger on his bearded chin. Somehow he managed that, but then, with a toss of his head, he flicked it up and opened his mouth beneath it. Edin gasped. But he caught the point neatly between his teeth. She watched him do it again, in fearful fascination until she realized she was being hailed by a man who wanted more of the wine she was now pouring.

She kept her eyes down as she approached him, knowing he'd been leering at her for some time. She hated to be looked at like that. After she'd filled his goblet, he suddenly hooked her with one unreasonably large arm and toppled her onto his lap. He laughed, as did the other Vikings at the table — though the women didn't seem to find it so amusing. The one across from the man snapped him an icy blue glance of disapproval, then lowered her eyelids until her lashes, lighter than her skin, touched her cheeks.

Edin only glimpsed this however, for her full attention was on him. He held her with such burly strength. His beard was bare in one place, marred by a large oblong welt that looked as if a patch of pink-colored clay had been fixed there haphazardly. He was gabbling at her in Norse as he held her against him with one hand, leaving the other free to rove. Slapping at him only seemed to make him bolder. He found the hem of her gown and rapidly skimmed his fingers up to her thighs.

She'd dropped her pitcher when he first toppled her, and so reached now for the only weapon at hand — his full goblet on the table. She emptied it over his head.

He stood, dumping her onto the rushes. She scrambled to her feet and ran unconscious fingers through her hair. He wiped his face with the fine fabric of his sleeves. His easy laughter was gone, replaced by a lurid glare with flame behind it. The hall began to quiet, and Edin knew she'd become a spectacle again. A slow flush crept up the Viking's scarred face. His right hand went to the hilt of the short, broad-bladed *scramasax* in his belt.

Out of the corner of her eye, Edin saw Sweyn lolling at the end of his bench with a smile that showed his yellowish teeth through his beard. She was surrounded by Vikings.

A furore Normannorum libera nos, Domine! From the fury of the Northman save —

The armed man made a lunge for her. Somehow she dodged back out of his reach, but how long could she keep that up? Where could she go? The jarl had earlier forbidden her to leave the hall without an escort, even to visit the privy.

The jarl! No sooner did she think of him — the thought was of an immense and implacable power — no sooner did she picture his face in her mind, than she turned. The Viking behind her made another lunge. She felt his hands catch and yank out a few strands of her hair. She ran — to the jarl.

She dared not step up on the dais of his chair, but took mindless shelter at his side. By now the hall was completely silent. Edin felt censure coming at her from all directions. The man came on.

Casually, the jarl reached for her elbow and drew her up to the arm of his chair. The man stopped a few feet away. He spoke in Norse, with that undercurrent of hot fury, jabbing his finger in Edin's direction. When he was finished, the jarl spoke, in a calm, slaying voice.

Not a man or a woman moved. All sat on their benches as if their limbs had turned to stone. Only their shadows swayed on the walls.

The man seemed taken aback. Slowly, he found a smile, a carefully courteous smile. He inclined his head to his chieftain, then turned stiffly and marched back to his place. The jarl looked around at all the faces staring at him. It was a challenge, clear and simple. One by one, people picked up their cups, turned to their neighbors, and gradually the celebration grew noisy once more.

He still held Edin's arm. He observed her now. His face was stony; she could feel his wrath.

"He took liberties," she said in her own defense. "Mayhap I should not have spilt the wine on him, but—"

"But you did. And just as well, since if his hand had traveled an inch higher up your skirts I would have had to kill him."

"Kill—! What did he say?"

He frowned. "When are you going to learn your new language? He said he found you desirable."

That explained nothing, and she waited for more.

He gave her a vexed look and began a surprisingly glib fabrication: "Aye, and so I said, 'Asmund Wartooth, this woman is truly a rounded morsel made for a man's fondling, but she is mine and I am a jealous owner.' 'Pardon me,' he answered, 'but I seem to have a serpent in my breeches that rears up most peculiarly whenever she passes. It is very hard to control.' So I asked him to try a little harder.

"Now come sit at my feet, Saxon; no one will tease you there, or find the serpents in their trousers rearing up."

Not for a moment did she believe this report. She was still thinking to understand what had really happened when his fingers tightened around her arm. "Do as I tell you."

She had no choice. She was as good as chained by his strength, and there was no one to free her from him. She was a captive, without defense or refuge. She sat as he wanted, on the dais between his feet, so that she felt his right leg up the length of her back and his inner thigh touched her shoulder. Mostly he seemed to ignore her, though now and then, as he drank and chatted, he toyed with her hair. No one chided him for it, for he was her master. And whatever he'd said to Asmund Wartooth had made clear his claim to the others. She was his and completely at his disposal.

Her sense of humiliation grew until she pulled away from his touch a little—and discovered that she had more of his attention than she'd thought. Putting one large hand on her bare shoulder, he said, most gently, "Be still."

Not long after, her eyes roamed past Inga—and something made them return. For a long moment she was held by a steady, icy look.

The evening went on, oblivious to her sufferings. At the tables, the guests conversed and cleaned their teeth with toothpicks. The noise was terrific. After a while the red-haired girl Dessa had admired earlier approached the jarl's chair. She bowed her head before him, then asked a question in Norse. Edin looked up to see him nod perfunctorily. The girl came forward and offered Edin her hand. "Come," she said in Saxon, "soon the skald will tell his tales. They say you still can't speak much Norse; I'll translate for you."

Edin cast the jarl a questioning look. Only his fingers moved on the wide arm of his chair, gesturing his permission.

The girl's place was one of the less desirable ones toward the end of a bench, which Edin found puzzling, for she'd arrived with a wealthy-looking family and seemed very sure of herself. She was called Red Jennie of Odinlund Steading. She was pretty, as Dessa said, with agreeable features and a tiny double chin.

"Why don't you sit with you family?" Edin asked.

The girl gave her coquettish, coy smile. "My master treats me well, but I am only a thrall like you." She spoke glowingly of her protector, pointing him out for Edin: "There—Ottar Magnusson's father,

200

Magnus Fair-hair. Isn't he handsome? Oh, I love him so!"

Edin looked again at the middle-aged man, who was tearing at a great hunk of meat at that moment.

"Everyone is talking about you," the girl said. "The jarl has never taken a thrall to his bed before. I would be afraid—doesn't he seem mysterious and frightening to you? And so big!" She giggled.

Edin tried to change the subject. "How long ago were you captured?"

"Three winters past. I was but a child. That probably made it easier for me than it must be for you."

"It is hard," Edin agreed.

"But now you have the jarl's interest." She said it with a sigh and a wave of her hand.

Her hand was not particularly delicate, Edin observed fleetingly, not so refined and well cared for as the hands of ladies she'd known. It was too broad, with stumpy fingers, and seemed a bit primitive and childish.

The girl went on. "No matter how frightening, I could never think a man anything but wonderful if he was a jarl."

"He is a Viking."

"Mayhap, but he desires you, and you can use that to gentle him—domesticate him—" she giggled—"and then make him love you."

"I don't want him to love me."

"Why not? Why shouldn't you sweeten your life as his is sweetened? He uses his weapons on you"—she winked—"why shouldn't you use your weapons on him?"

"I don't—"

"The difficulty will be the way his father died. . . ." Jennie went on, thinking aloud to herself. "Since Kirkyn was murdered in his bed by his own Saxon pleasure-thrall—oh, you didn't know that? Oh, aye, it's told all over—though mayhap not here on

Thórynsteading." She giggled again, then looked all around to be sure they weren't being listened to. "They say that Inga's love for the old jarl was obsessive, almost an insanity. Then Kirkyn captured Margaret in a raid and fell madly in love with her. One night, no one knows why, Margaret suddenly stabbed him with a kitchen knife—one so sharp you need only touch the edge and it would slice"—she made a gesture—"like cutting butter. She killed herself afterward. Inga claims Kirkyn had spoken to her about selling Margaret away—but who knows? A lovers' quarrel mayhap. Anyway, he was murdered, and Inga turned all that strange love onto her son."

Jennie lowered her voice to a whisper. "My master says Inga isn't always sure who Thoryn is, that sometimes she actually talks to him as if he were Kirkyn." She looked down the tables toward Inga. "I would watch out for her.

"But back to the jarl." She changed the subject with a turn of her head. "Whatever possessed you to run away from him? I heard Ottar telling Magnus that Inga wanted the jarl to use hunting dogs to track you down, but he refused, saying he wanted you to be very much alive when he got you back.

"The very day you left, he sent messengers to every steading on both sides of the fjord, and himself scoured the countryside from sunup to sundown. Most of us thought for sure when he found you—well, some of the younger men speculated they might find you staked out in the stables for them to use, well, as part of the evening's entertainment. They were disappointed, to say the least—" she giggled—"for there you were, seated at the jarl's feet with his hand petting your hair."

Edin felt her face pale. Staked out in the stables? She looked about at the Vikings washing down their captured wine and huge draughts of Inga's mead. If she had forgotten it, she was reminded anew that they were men who thought nothing of slaying hither and yon, and filling their longships to the gunwales with stolen treasure, including captured women.

"Everyone is quite put out with him now. They think that letting a thrall get away with what you did threatens them as masters and mistresses. Of course, they don't dare show too much disapproval. Asmund Wartooth tried, but the jarl shut him up easily enough, asking him so coolly, 'Just how important is this matter to you, neighbor?' But they feel safe in being as unsociable as they please toward you."

So that was it! The jarl wanted her badly enough to defy criticism, to risk censure. The realization gave Edin no sense of pride. Quite the opposite. She turned in anguish to her new friend. "How do you bear it—the shame?"

"Shame? You mean . . . oh." Her smile never faltered. "But the jarl has claimed you, and you must do as he commands. It's no shame on you. There are women who would give everything to have your chance—and your beauty."

"Life is so brutal and merciless here!"

Now the girl's face changed. All her irrepressible romanticism disappeared in an instant. "Life is brutal and merciless everywhere, in England no less than here. They say you were a lady. I was the daughter of serfs. When I was eleven, the earl's son—a bloodthirsty lad if I ever met one—did me. He was nigh a grown man, and I cried with the pain; but it was a thing of little import really, since in the hovel where I lived with my parents and married brothers I saw bluff couplings every night. I was more troubled by never having enough to eat, never being warm enough—or rested enough since I had to work in the fields from dawn to dusk. Before my new master bought me from the longship crew that captured me, I'd never had a bath in my life. The thralls he set on me scrubbed me so hard I nearly bled." She laughed again, her memories pleasant once more. "It was a year before I caught Magnus alone and coaxed him into taking me. Never will I forget that delicious afternoon. And now I know more ease than I'd ever dreamed of.

"Vikings are betimes brutal, and betimes sly, but if they make a pledge, they keep it; if they give their affection, they remain faithful; and—" she touched a fingertip to one of the jeweled combs in her hair, the movement causing her finger rings to flash—"now and then they're almost foolishly generous." She grinned. "I've learned to love every fair hair on my master's great fair head—as you should learn to love yours."

Edin looked at the jarl and remembered him looming above her on his naked, muscled arms, his masculine weight pressing her deeper into his bed, his eyes two fragments of evening, his mouth moving on her exposed throat. Her mind fluttered in a dozen directions, and she shivered. Love him? For a girl like Jennie it was different mayhap. She'd never known anything better. Edin's case was not the same.

She had no more chance to think about it then, for though the midnight was worn through, the skald hadn't yet been heard from. He now rose from his seat, a ragtag scarecrow of patched robes and tangled gestures as he took a place before the longfire. A hush fell over the gathering. Edin heard nothing but a rustling as the Vikings and their ladies made themselves comfortable. The skald's voice began to caress them.

Red Jennie was quietly translating when Juliana appeared behind Edin. She said sullenly, "If you want to go to the privy, you'd better come with me now while I have a minute."

Edin colored. The jarl had said she could leave the hall only if she had an escort. She excused herself from Jennie and followed Juliana out the door.

They were barely around the outside corner, when the door opened again. Juliana stopped in the shadows. Edin paused. "What's wrong?"

Juliana said, "You go on. You won't run away again—even you aren't that stupid."

And so Edin continued alone. On her way back to the longhouse, she heard voices in the shadows by the long outer wall. A man's voice: ". . . the sweetest little wooly-fringed notch. Lean back."

The laugh that followed was Juliana's.

A pale mist had drifted in on the night, but Edin's eyes picked out the two in the dark. She saw Juliana leaning against the longhouse with Jamsgar Copper-eye, that alarmingly handsome young man with the great burning eyes. He was holding her skirt up, and she had one leg twined around his waist.

Edin was sickened. How could Juliana invite ravishment?

She slipped back into the hall. No one seemed to notice she'd lost her escort—except the jarl, who'd been watching for her return. She quickly took her place beside Red Jennie again and pretended close attention to the girl's translation of the skald's tale. When next she stole a glimpse of the jarl, he seemed to be listening, too.

Chapter 14

Thoryn felt easier with the Saxon back in the hall. He wished the evening would end. The air seemed heavy with the odors of food, and the ale was beginning to go to people's heads.

The skald stood opposite his high-seat, beyond the longfire, and despite the warmth, the old man adjusted his patched cloak regally as he spoke. He was grey-bearded, one-eyed, baleful, and ugly, but there was the gleam of poetry on him, like moonlight on water. His voice had range and great vigor, conveying a sense of endless untold legends: mountains too far away to be climbed, distant seas never to be crossed, great heroes of lands utterly remote.

His first tale had been a saga, a long poem about the heroic activities of a mighty chief, demonstrating the theme that neither man nor god could fight his fate. Vikings liked legends full of storm and passion. Strong emotions were born into them by the fjords, the islands, the skerried waterways of their lands. Add isolation, cold, the intimidating darkness of January; add, too, dreams of domination and delusions of grandeur, and anyone could see that Norway could never be a nursery for a weak-natured people. The Norse were well-tempered to endure. They endured ice, they endured wolves, and, most important, they endured one another.

The next tale was one Thoryn hadn't heard before, about a big she-bear who'd made life a trial near Songefjord by standing in the middle of a road there and refusing to budge when travelers came along.

As the skald spoke, Thoryn observed Jamgar's return to the hall, and how he took his seat and stuck a toothpick between his lips in a self-pleased and relaxed way that was as telling as a shout.

"A man named Gudbrod Ibsnsson heard about this bear," the skald went on. "Gudbrod walked along the road to seek the beast out. After stumbling over the bodies of six men, suddenly, there was the bear. A truly *big* bear. She reared on her hind legs, and her lips pulled up in a sneer. But Gudbrod retained his strength of will and his mind for command, and he went right up to her.

" 'Do you realize you're nothing but a miserable, common animal?' he said in a firm voice. 'Why, how do you dare stand there and block travelers, knowing you're nothing but a miserable animal, a miserable *black* bear—not even a polar bear or anything honorable.'

"The bear's head began to droop, she lowered herself onto all fours . . ."

Thoryn lost the thread of the tale as Juliana came in through the outer door, trailing tendrils of fog, looking tousled and languorous: A few curls of her short hair drooped down over her eyes, and her round-necked dress hung off one shoulder.

When the tale was done, the skald was treated to laughter. The Saxon's fleeting smile seemed to light her corner of the hall like a touch of sunshine. Thoryn presented the old man with a broad-bladed dagger. And added a magnificent three-ringed collar, for the Saxon's smile.

Herjul the Stout, who, like many others, was getting to be full of beer, shouted, "Music! Have you no minstrels to treat us to a song, Thoryn Kirkynsson?"

He had cheerful crow's feet all the way from his narrow blue eyes to his ears. It was easy to see where his sons, Jamsgar and Starkad, got their good looks.

Elderly Finnier Forkbeard echoed: "A song!"

The answer came to Thoryn suddenly, a wizardly inspiration which he voiced immediately: "I have a new Saxon thrall who can sing like the breeze on a sweet spring morn."

He looked at her, saw that Red Jennie was translating his words and saw the Saxon pale; yet, without a flicker of apology, he said, "Come! Let us have a song, woman! Amuse my guests."

Everyone in the hall was staring at her again. She came forward hesitantly, until she stood before him, wrenching her hands in distress. *In front of all these people?* she seemed to ask as she looked up at him. She could feel, no doubt, the disapproval of the gathering. Did she realize what it was about—the favor he'd shown her, the mercy? And now he was going even so far as to parade her before them.

"I have no lute," she said in a small voice that carried in that ringing silence. "I can't sing—not *well*—without—"

"Who has a lute?" he called in Norse.

In a moment, Hauk Haakonsson was up and striding to his wall-chamber. Thoryn could see him with an iron key unlocking a cedar chest studded with copper nails. He pulled out a lute and brought it to the Saxon, his light eyes amused. She took it, looked at it, then looked at him strangely. Thoryn grasped that the instrument must be familiar to her, mayhap taken from her own chamber in England.

She stood holding it awkwardly. He said, "Give her a stool, Hauk."

An apple bucket was turned upside down for her beyond the fire, in the place the skald had recently held. She tested the instrument, her long white fingers rising and falling in a lovely pattern, and a new hush, this one born of curiosity, dropped over the hall. The first sweetly·plucked chords fell; then into the quiet her voice lifted sweetly, as gentling as Thoryn remembered it, music fair past all telling. Mayhap such was the music the Lorelei made in the famous river that flowed into Fresia, which caused pilots to drop into visions and shipmasters to stand dazed and rowers to pull their oars in madness toward their doom.

"O who will shoe my bonny foot,
And who will glove my hand,
And who will bind my middle slim
With a long, long linen band?
O who will comb my yellow hair
With a new-made silver comb?
And who will be my babe's father
Till Gregory comes home?"

There were more verses. Tears appeared on her cheeks. Then the last trembling notes died away. The surprised gathering sat silent, recovering from their unwilling enjoyment. The Saxon was flushed where before she'd been so pale. The firelight gleamed as yellow as afternoon light in her long, thick, amber hair. There was not a man there who was not hot, perspiring with the warmth in the hall, with the ale, and now with strong Norse lust.

Now at least the men understand why I spared her, Thoryn thought.

It unsettled him, however, to know they were thinking of her pretty mouth, her unusual green eyes, her fair flesh that looked as if it would feel quite cool. And her voice that had the color of the dawn. He felt a pang of possessiveness. That amber-yellow hair and that flower face belonged to *him*.

Suddenly a deep but slurred voice filled the hall. "She bewitches you all! The woman's a witch!"

Sweyn. Thoryn had noticed him drinking steadily all evening. Now he was shuddering a little, and putting on that daft, battle-mad look of a berserker. Once Thoryn had been moderately fond of that craggy-headed fool. Now he found himself avoiding the sight of him.

"That hair . . ." he slurred, "t'was fashioned by dwarves!" His pale blue eyes moped over the lip of his mead horn. "She's a Lapp spaewoman . . . c'n turn a tide. Beware! or you may end like me! She made Thoryn Kirkynsson attack his shipmate, and now . . . now I am as I am." He gestured to his maimed right arm with his drinking horn. In another moment he would start to foam at the mouth—and then who knew what kind of mayhem would break out?

Thoryn rose and strode to where the cripple was lolling on his bench end. Gently he took the horn away and gave it politely to another man. Sweyn stared up at him in a daze, with a young child's utterly shallow receptiveness—for the moment. Thoryn knew that look could change in an instant. He took the cripple by his neck and pulled him up. There was no resistance from Sweyn's once strong nature. His body merely swayed like a pine in the wind.

Thoryn led him to the throne poles of his own chair, and there tied him by his wrist—the good left wrist. There was no need to tie the right one, which was as useless as a broken axe. He said to Rolf, "See that no one unties him till morning."

Sweyn laughed—too loudly for any joke.

As Thoryn turned, he met Inga, who said quietly, "There is danger brewing here, my son. Mark my words, for I do not speak them lightly."

"What danger? I'm always anxious to learn of danger. It gives flavor to my meat."

A bright, brittle mocking expression contorted her face to ugliness. "This danger may not suit your taste. You are unwise to keep enemies in our house. You are unwise to take them to your bed."

His voice came out dry and rough. "Thunder threatens, but lightning may not strike."

At that moment lightning did strike, however, for Inga suddenly burst out, " 'Norseman' you call yourself! Yet you can find no better plaything that that—that slut! You dishonor yourself, Thoryn and you dishonor your father. And you dishonor *me!*"

He was aware of the multitude of ears listening, but he eyed Inga as narrowly as if there were no one else in the hall except the two of them. "Am I not a man yet, Mother? Do I still need to say 'yea' and 'nay' to my dame? Would you choose for me whom I may take to my bed?" He consciously lowered his voice, made it seem calm, cold: "There is no reason to worry. I'm not the man my father was, to become besotted by a mere thrall. But meanwhile—" he made himself smile a little, and shrug, for the sake of his audience—"the time passes pleasantly enough."

Smiles were restored, though at Inga's expense, which he liked little. Looking about, he saw that many of his guests were nigh to collapsing into drunkenness. He judged with relief that it was time to bring the night to an end. He crossed around the firepit to where the Saxon had risen and was watching his advance in fearful confusion. He knew he must look furious to her. And he *was* furious. In him was a storm of conflicting emotions—irresolution and obstinacy, exhilaration and anger. As he took her arm, she lifted her eyes to his. He saw they were still wet with her tears. What was she crying about?

He didn't ask; instead he said, "Come, I have need of you." She stiffened and tried to pull her arm from his grasp. Her long amber tresses moved on her shoulders, catching the light of the fire. He warned, "Would you prefer to take your leave slung over my shoulder again?"

"You—"

"—wouldn't? Is that what you think? Come, lead the way. I give you this chance to retain the regard you've just earned with that pretty song, *my lady.*"

As she started toward his chamber, Sweyn laughed loudly, a dreadful noise, and then began to hurl abuse at all the gods in turn: "Odin! You travesty! You dabble in bedevilment and award victory to cowards!"

Edin looked at him, then at Thoryn. Her eyes were wells of fresh water. He prodded her on.

"Freya! You whore of the gods—even your own brother!"

The cascade of bitterness was cut off as Thoryn drove the woman through the door of his bed chamber and slammed it behind them.

He lit the lamp in the corner. The room, its opulence of furnishings, leapt to life, strange and exquisite to Edin's eyes. He turned, and she met his look with one of pure hatred. He seemed—what was it that he seemed? Certainly something new for him. Dismayed?

"If I had my dagger back right now, I most certainly would try to kill you." Her voice was thin and high.

He fingered his beard beneath cloud-filled eyes. "Indeed. And what have I done to deserve such affection?"

She glared at him. "That lute—it was Cedric's."

"I'll buy it from Hauk for you," he said dismissively.

"Buy it? You think—are you stupid as well as savage?"

"You forget yourself, Saxon."

"I do not forget myself, Viking!"

He tilted his head and said softly, "Though it seems my generosity little affects you, you might at least consider my anger. There are those who think it

212

a thing to avoid at all costs. You are graceful and lovely, and for the time being I've decided to favor you; yet you should have a care."

"I *had* a care." Her voice became lower, huskier. "He is dead now, by your hand."

He reached for her, chewing Norse curses under his breath. She didn't try to move away from the hand that curved around her waist and yanked her toward him. Instead, she spat out an epithet so full of feeling that by rights it should have branded his flesh: *"Murderer!"*

It gave her great satisfaction to see the word penetrate him, to see him receive it like a knife in his heart, to watch it turn him to stone.

His hands dropped stiffly from her body. He seemed to brace himself, as though he were standing athwart a slanting deck. "I have never killed any man who did not show his arms to me."

"You invaded his home and threatened his bride-to-be." Her voice broke. "Did he deserve to die for trying to protect me?"

Would he have tried? She recalled that instant when it seemed he might not love her quite that much. Then her mind covered that crack with a flood of other images, recollections: wild screams . . . her dagger, its jeweled handle . . . her hands trying to cover Cedric's gushing death wound. . . .

"I am a Norseman," he said; his imperious tone bounced off the walls.

"You are a Viking." She turned her head away to hide her pain.

"Aye, if you will, a Viking. And there is nothing as cold as a Viking's heart. Remember that, Saxon. Now undress and get into bed."

She refused to move. He himself unfastened the brooches at her shoulders and unwrapped her gown. He bent to unloose the thongs that fastened the soft kid boots he'd given her.

When she was naked save for her mantle of hair and the torque around her throat, his eyes fastened on her breasts. They were trembling; she couldn't keep them from trembling. This was like a bad dream. His nearness was taking hold of her. His first caress made her nipples ache. She couldn't yield to him again! And yet there was no point in trying to resist. The things he might do to her. Memory had made her imagination very ripe of a sudden.

He scooped her up and tossed her onto the feather bed. She lay where she landed, unmoving, unrelenting. He studied her, and her hands closed unconsciously into fists; but she kept her eyes on the low ceiling.

He disrobed, pinched out the light, and joined her. When he reached for her, she refused to react; she lay limp in his arms. Angry, he seized the back of her head and ground his mouth against hers, forcing her lips apart so he could drive his tongue in. Her silver-collared throat arched back. His free hand found and used her breasts roughly.

And did he feel her racing heartbeat?

Despite that testimony, she continued to lay corpse-like, even when he touched her inner thighs, even when he placed himself over her.

He didn't enter her. Something in him seemed to fail. What had happened to that desire to outrage her? What had become of that boldly self-satisfied knowledge that nothing and no one could keep him from reveling in her whenever he pleased? He'd wanted her so much she knew he'd been ready to hurt her had she not lain there passively letting him do as he would. But all that was vanished suddenly. He fell beside her, shaking with fury, evidently filled with emotions so murky he could hardly contain them.

What would he do now? Would he strike her? One unmeasured blow from his mighty fist and. . . . But no, she was still a valuable piece of property. He needn't go so far as kill her. Not when there were so many other horrible ways for a woman to be degraded and destroyed.

Minutes passed. Her breath grew ragged with tension. She started when he said, "You loved him?"

It took her a moment to gather her wits enough to answer. "I loved my life, my home, my people and, yes" — her voice filled with anguish — "I loved him! He was brother to me, and friend, and . . . and. . . ."

She couldn't go on. And couldn't resist as he took her into his arms once more. Her mind was in no condition to fight him. She was alone; she'd lost even herself, Edin of Fair Hope Manor. Now she was merely a female body to be used, to be caressed to satisfy this man's urgings. She began to weep, for herself, for Cedric, for everything that had once been and was no more.

He pressed her wet face into his neck and held her as heartbreak wracked her body. "I wanted children," she cried, her voice aching and poignant, her fist mindlessly beating his shoulder. "I would have been a good mother. I would have done my best to make Cedric happy — I *would* have! But you . . . *why?* Why did you have to come? You're so ruthless and cruel. I *hate* you!"

She suddenly realized that even as she reviled him, she was pressed against him, he who was the cause of her misery, and her tears turned to venom.

"Let me go!" she hissed, scratching at his holding arms, trying to kick away from him.

He found her wrists and pushed them under her body, then lay over her, adding his weight to hers to keep them pinned.

"Let me go! *Murderer!*"

She heaved against him, moving beneath him like the sea surging against the headland. As his weight seemed to bear down all the more, she cursed him with more ferocity than she knew she owned.

But he was heavy and smothering, and gradually she exhausted herself and lay too spent to move. He lifted his weight guardedly. She continued to lay motionless, ignoring the power of his hand that stroked her hair so gently, that ran down her side to her thigh. Did he sense that anything might be done to her in that moment? If so, then why did he ask, "This Cedric, he was your friend—but not your lover."

She said spiritlessly, "He was my dearest friend."

"He went to Valhöll, you know. The defeated join the champions in death."

"He wasn't defeated, he was murdered."

"I murdered no one," he said with patience. "Think, Shieldmaiden. I was looking at you, at the salmon-pink tip of your breast, when suddenly I heard someone behind me. I turned and saw a man with a weapon at my back."

"You didn't have to stab him again once he'd fallen!"

"A belly wound makes for a bad death. He was screaming. I did him the service I would do any man faced with that agony. I pierced his heart to give him quick peace."

Her memory saw him lower his head, as if he were concentrating on the dying boy before him. His sword reached out and touched Cedric's chest as if to say, *I give you death, boy.* She wondered if it could possibly be true, if he'd acted with mercy, this man who had no mercy in him.

Or did he? He'd pulled her up out of the fjord when he could as easily have let her drown. He'd seen she was well-tended, even warmed her with his own body. He'd not killed her as his law said he should, hadn't even beaten her for running away. He'd taken her maidenhead, yes, but with a consideration that was akin to mercy. He'd even let her keep her hair. And dressed her finely. And now was explaining himself to her. Why? What did he see in her? Why did he go to such lengths to claim her?

She let him take her head between his big hands. "Shieldmaiden." He began to kiss her, kissed her endlessly, long narcotic kisses that inevitably penetrated her reserve and shook the core of her being, kisses that urged her to want more, until, mindlessly, she turned into his arms. The instant she did, she felt his muscles leap. His strong arms closed about her, and a moan of pleasure escaped his throat. He took her again, and again made her want something more, something she couldn't even name.

Thoryn woke fully aroused. The Saxon was sleeping softly in the crook of his arm. He calculatedly set about invading her dreams. He touched and caressed her gently, brushing the very tips of her breasts, touching her eyebrows with the tip of his tongue, and the corners of her lips. "Shieldmaiden." He felt her begin to drift awake. He let his breath rustle against her mouth. "I want you."

She drew in a long quivering breath, and realizing what he was about, sighed, "Not again, Viking."

He felt himself smile. For years it had been a rarity with him, but lately. . . . "You can't say no to me." His lips descended. He kissed her softly, continued to handle her gently, and whispered endearments to her in Norse, things like, "I don't know myself anymore; I almost believe I could be like this."

She was too drowsy to get up any resistance. She allowed herself to be touched and caressed, but kept her eyes closed. And she didn't respond, not by a single moan. That bothered him, but he wanted her and would have her regardless. When he parted her thighs in the darkness, she made a sound at last—a whimper of protest—but then with one surge he made his possession too deep to refute.

Only a few hours later, he woke once more uncomfortably and undeniably aroused. It felt as if his manhood had been hewn out of wood. He pulled off her blankets and took her again in the dawn light. She didn't resist this time, either, but only sighed plaintively. Because he thought she might be sore, and because there was enough light in the room for him to enjoy the sight of her now, he took more time with her, opened her like a flowerbud, and entered her slowly, savoring each surge of delight until his proprietorship was again beyond proof.

She fell asleep again as soon as he was finished, sprawled as he'd left her, her knees apart, her upper body slightly turned, her hands open, and her skin washed by the dawn light. He covered her against the chill. He dressed quietly so as not to wake her. He felt . . . purged. He felt . . . good, himself, Thoryn as Thoryn should be, as his youth had seemed to promise he would be, untainted, unbrutal.

For a moment, considering this and the implications of it, he stood motionless, looking at the Saxon's incredibly innocent beauty. Then he went out into the hall to set Sweyn free before the household stirred.

The cripple had chewed the painted wood of the high-seat pillar like a savage wolf. When he started awake now and looked into Thoryn's face, he bent his head as though shamed beyond bearing. And Thoryn felt ashamed — for causing this in another man.

He cut the thong that held Sweyn's good wrist, and the cripple rose — though not to his full height, which had once been a threat in itself. Once the man had been a champion; once he'd been as strong as a granite runestone. Now he was grey and flaccid and pitiable, half a man, a cripple.

Thoryn was unused to feeling shame and pity; he hardly knew how to handle such sentiments. To cover

218

them, he put on a severe look. "If I see you drinking like that again, I'll deliver peace to you suddenly, Sweyn Elendsson. Is that understood?"

"It's understood, *Jarl,* and I will abide by it, even if such treatment as you've given me is unmanly."

Thoryn reacted out of habit; he gave Sweyn a backhanded blow that nigh laid the man back down on the rushes. Sweyn regained his balance slowly. Thoryn said, "Jarl I am, and master of this steading, and I will not be criticized for any treatment I mete out to an oath-breaker. Now get you to your bed and snore off the rest of your drunkenness!"

Sweyn's eyes wavered ere they collide Thoryn's. He wiped his mouth on his wrist, but then he did as he was told.

Thoryn strode back toward his own chamber in a fume — yet, as soon as the door was closed behind him, he felt a mysterious sense of relief, of homecoming.

There she was, still sleeping, so peaceful, so beautiful, so *moving.* He sat carefully on the edge of the bed. And a thought that was violent in its unexpectedness rose in his mind: *If only she could learn to experience the pleasure I do; if only she could learn to feel safe with me.*

Safe? With him?

Her eyes opened to look at him directly, unflinchingly. He experienced a dizzy vertigo, a bottomless falling-away.

She let him take her hand and study her fingers, responding with nothing but that stare, completely unaware that she was tempting him profoundly, not to take her again, not exactly, but to try to regain that fleeting feeling he got whenever he was taking her — of having what he really needed at last, of having it in his embrace, of possessing it, of holding it and occupying it and *being* a part of it.

He said, for lack of knowing what else to say, "You

pleased me well last night, Saxon." He watched her eyes shift away. He felt dizzy again, with her innocence and the charm of knowing it and all else about her was his. It made his heart rise up; it made him want to laugh out loud. "Aye," he said, "you can sing a pretty song."

She looked back at him quickly her mouth forming a little *Oh!*

He pretended surprise. "You thought I meant something else?"

"I must arise."

He wanted to say her name; he had an unlikely urge to engage in physical endearments and gentlenesses. Suddenly his position and his responsibilities seemed heavy anchors, as did the daily round of herding, farming, and fishing. "Aye," he said, denying all his instincts, "we still have guests. I'm taking some of the men hawking this morning—else I would still be abed, too." He tried to look wicked.

Evidently he succeeded beyond his intention, for with a sudden slithering movement she was off the bed and winding her woolen gowns about her. He was left to pull at his mustache pensively as she combed her hair until it flowed down her back and arms like a cascade, glistening flexuously in the growing light from the window.

Though he had emptied himself into her no less than three times in the night, he felt his manhood stiffen and throb again. A tremor passed through him. He rose and reached for her and turned her around, and while she was busy avoiding his kiss, he pulled up her hems and placed his fingers between her thighs.

Chapter 15

At Thoryn's first intimate touch, the Saxon moaned, as if with great sorrow this time.

"Why do you arch away?"

"You make me ashamed. Why are you so sinful?"

"Let me, my Shieldmaiden — how soft and warm you feel." With his eyes closed, his fingers explored her.

"It isn't right."

"You're nothing the worse," he said, trying to be soothing yet knowing he sounded savage. "Let me kiss you."

Moving her head so that he couldn't capture her mouth, she murmured desperately, "What do you want from me?"

"What I want is very simple: merely that you be constantly and immediately accessible to me. Now kiss me!"

"You kissed me enough last night to serve for a year. Oh . . ." she moaned with his continued caress. Her head was hanging back on the stem of her silver-collared throat, her lips were slightly parted, and her breasts were rising and falling rapidly.

"By Odin, you're too beautiful!" Never had a woman evoked such fierce desires in him. He drew her toward the low chest at the foot of the bed, where he sat and opened his own clothes. "Don't," she said as he pulled her down onto him. At the same time he at last captured her mouth.

His tongue met hers. Fire filled his loins.

His palms went to her hipbones; his fingers splayed over her bottom, gripping; he rolled her hips. He'd never been so deep in her before; he gloried in the feeling of her shudder as he rolled her hips with his hands. And then she was moving of her own will. She pulled her mouth from his with a gasp, threw her head back, and undulated in his lap.

Given this sign of pleasure from her, the climax of his pleasure was not long in coming. The spasm took him so hard he could only hope his embrace wasn't hurting her. Behind his eyelids he saw nothing but thin, vibrating, golden light. When it faded, he found she'd fallen forward against him, limp, her head over his shoulder. He exposed her ear and planted a soft kiss there. "You please me, Saxon."

"You degrade me and make me ashamed." Her voice was full of unshed tears.

The hawking party was ready to set out on horseback. Thoryn's long green cloak was fashionably askew; his hands were coarsely jeweled. Upon his gauntleted wrist perched his fiercest, fastest hunting hawk, a frost-white falcon. The bird's head was covered with a little hood so it couldn't see. It was kept fast to his wrist by a silver chain attached to its leg.

From the midst of the restless horses and the pack of eager dogs, he looked back at the longhouse. Therein lay his treasure. Confident that from now on it would be there when he returned, he shrugged back his thick mane of hair and breathed the air deeply, hauling it in so his chest filled. The morning was so full of sound, so full of promise, it seemed to brim with unseen wild jubilance. He felt charged with the sheer fury of living as he set his heels to his stallion, and Dawnfire was glad to be off. Rolf and his mount started just behind them, then came Kol and his sons, and Leif the Tremendous. Their horses threw themselves into mighty gallops. The dogs followed with frenzied barking. The party left its prints in the dew as they rode up the slope toward the mountains, which were wrapped in wreaths of smokelike, summer-morning mist.

Thoryn was the first to spy a game bird. He quickly unhooded his hawk and turned it loose. The sharp-eyed bird soon saw its quarry. For an instant the air vibrated with excitement, then, with a swift spring, the hawk soared high, swooped over the bird, and brought it down. Thoryn blew into a little silver whistle. The hawk dropped the bird, then flew back to settle again upon his master's wrist. Its eyes held an excited glitter. The game bird was brought in by the dogs.

Later, at breakfast, Thoryn hardly tasted the goat's cheese and *fiskboller*, fishcakes. His thoughts took him off. He sipped his buttermilk, holding each sip in his mouth until it turned warm before remembering to swallow. When his guests would chat with him he cast off their comments as he would toss back small fish. He didn't want his mood tarnished by these men who clung to the grosser pleasures as greedily as sucklings to their mothers' teats.

He thought of the Saxon. She felt ashamed—because each time he took her, though she gave little, still it was more than she meant to give. And each time she gave a fraction more. He had no sympathy for her shame, for he meant to increase it until, like a bubble of brine foam, it burst and was no more. He formed a plan, and with it a new spaciousness invaded him. Why was it that with her he felt the possibility of a different way of life, a way that would take its time, that would stroll through whole sennights as if they were single days, that would allow

223

the world to approach him instead of he having endlessly to launch himself upon it, armed for combat?

He watched as she helped with the breakfast serving, then disappeared with Red Jennie. What could
she and that flame-haired minx be talking about?
What else besides their masters? What would the
Saxon say about him? He felt a bit uneasy — and a
bit proud. Could Magnus manage to take his little
redhead four times in one night? But would the
Saxon complain about that, and tell Jennie she was
being mistreated?

Whatever, at least he knew she was nearby. He
could leave her alone for now. His plan would provide him the time he needed to overtake her. All the
time in the world.

Inga sat next to the eldest man on the fjord, Finnier Forkbeard, whose head was heavy with grizzled
hair, and whose long, full whiskers formed two
points. She took no notice of him, however; instead,
she watched the spell that was overtaking Thoryn. He
was alight with that extraordinary, unreasoning happiness that only one who had suffered similarly could
recognize. Happiness like the flame of a lamp, which
burns down even as it glows, which is at its brightest
the instant before it gutters out.

Inga was afraid. The thrall-woman was a demon,
and what demons love they kill in the end. Her hand
came up out of a fold of her gown, clenched, as if
she meant to strike someone with her fist — or as if
she held something, a dagger mayhap.

Thoryn imagined the Saxon watching him all that
day, and he took the possibility into account wherever
he went and whatever he did. A feast like this was a
high-point in the life along the fjord. In the crowded

hall, the ale still flowed freely; love blossomed among the young; men reminisced—and sometimes came to blows; heroic stories and exploits were remembered and repeated. Thoryn however, found his mind hurrying on ahead to when it would be over, regarding it and the present moment as an obstruction. Finally the sun threw huge shadows across the valley. He hastened his exhausted guests on their way with host gifts, amulets in the form of Tiny Thor's hammers, which he'd kept Eric No-breeches busy making this past sennight.

As he was seeing Hagna off, he got word that Hrut Beornwoldsson had taken it into his mind to challenge Jamsgar Copper-eye over the thrall, Juliana. The widow Gunnhild could not afford to lose her only son, but as Snorri told it, the lad would not back down. And everyone knew that Jamsgar loved a fight as much as he loved a woman and would not pass any opportunity to pierce one or the other.

When Thoryn came upon the three of them, the girl was watching anxiously while the Viking circled around the boy, a gawky youth of fifteen winters. Thoryn said, "Put away your axe, Jamsgar; he's but an excited pup."

Jamsgar's eyes never left Hrut as he retaliated in a low, savage tone, "The pup boasts like a man, and thinks to fondle my woman like a man, so let him hold an axe like a man. Come on, puppy, let's test your mettle!"

"Put your axe down, Hrut."

The boy was growing tall and just starting his first beard and no doubt feeling very dangerous. He bunched his tough body and delivered a rolling, blustering, intolerably bombastic speech: "I know how a Norseman should die, and I mean to go like my father, who was as great a Norseman as ever lived." He added, more boyishly, "Besides, she's not his woman. She's a thrall, anybody's woman."

"She's *my* woman, my thrall and my mother's best loom-woman," Thoryn quietly reminded them both, and with those words he drew his own weapon. "Now put down your axes." The two suddenly seemed to regain their wits. Thoryn didn't relent an inch. "Either challenge *me* for her, Hrut, or go to where your good mother waits to take her leave."

The boy naturally did the reasonable thing.

Thoryn turned his head, impaling Juliana with his gaze. She had a new trinket, a slender bronze chain that banded her brow and head. "Thrall," he warned softly, "several things about you displease me, and we will talk of them in detail soon; but right now your presence is a gall to my eyes."

She took a backward step, then turned and fled.

Thoryn turned to Jamsgar, who had a look of amused chagrin. Thoryn said, "That girl is trouble."

The man's copper eyes were alive with light. He pulled his helmet farther down over his nose, as if that could hide his grin. "Aye, but such pleasant trouble, Jarl."

"I won't have you fighting over her. If you want her so badly, make me an offer for her."

"What would I do with her if I owned her?"

"The same thing you do with her now!"

"Aye, you get my point exactly."

Any other day Thoryn might have reacted differently, but his night with the Saxon had left him feeling magnanimous. All he could seem to manage in the way of discipline was an ominous voice. "If you're very lucky, Jamsgar Herjulsson, you'll be able to stay out of my sight the rest of this day."

An hour later, Thoryn and his stallion came across Rolf rescuing a frantically bleating goat kid from a hollow of the stream that watered the valley. The place grew thick with rich grass, which had lured the kid, but also with birch and willows, which had caught its hair and kept it from following its dame home for the night. The dusk was still; there was a sweet smell of fern, mud, and water reed here. The two men got the kid free, and Rolf tucked it under his arm and started back toward the longhouse on foot, traveling in the wheeltracks of the last carting of the harvest.

Thoryn, on Dawnfire, started off in a different direction, with the intention of inspecting a field soon to be planted with late rye. His land was farmed with care and hard work. The valley yielded grain and fragrant grass; sheep grazed the fells. This year it had not been necessary to take them up to the *saeter* for the summer, to fatten there till autumn.

At the thought of the unused *saeter*, Thoryn wheeled and cantored back. "Rolf," he said abruptly, "have you ever pleased a woman as well as you were pleased? What I mean is, well, had one, uh, erupt along with you?"

Rolf seemed thoughtful. "Aye—not often—but now and again. Mostly women are cold as the far northern ice, but, aye, there has been one now and again."

"So it has been with me." Thoryn's usual way with wenches was either a pretense of gallantry if she was Norse and freeborn, or a more honest disdain if she was not. Neither attitude seemed to make one female more pulsating than the other. Still, he'd considered himself pretty informed on the subject of beddings, but now he found his information inadequate. For the first time he considered that he might actually be ignorant. He said, "I wonder if a man can encourage such a thing. Coming home on *Blood Wing*, you said something about 'making a woman shudder . . .'?"

Rolf grunted. "Some do shudder prettily, don't they? Especially when you have the time to dally with them. Still, a man rarely knows the daylight desires of a woman, let alone her night desires. It's enough for a man to give his strength to protect his females. They can't expect more."

Thoryn felt his patience thinning. "Friend, you're ever-ready with advice when I'm not in need of it. Come, have you no thoughts at all on how a warrior can pleasure an untrained woman?"

"You're speaking of the Saxon, of course."

"Aye," he grated. "Whatever I do, I feel like an ogre. Though half my size, she struggles to be let go all the while I'm holding her. Or if she doesn't struggle, and only lies there and whimpers, I feel like an idiot. I know she thinks me a huge, tangle-haired savage, wild and rough and positively bloodthirsty—"

"It seems she knows you well enough then," Rolf put in, tilting his head teasingly to one side. "Why do you want to give her a false opinion?"

Thoryn's frustration reached an apex. "Odin, God of War! God of Guile in Action! I should have known better than come to you!"

Rolf chuckled. "I wish you luck, oath-brother, but I fear some things can't be captured: rainbows . . . reflections in water . . . women's pleasures. I doubt how much a man's will can accomplish along those lines."

Thoryn was sorry now that he'd ever brought the subject up. Yet he said grimly, "It remains to be seen what *my* will can accomplish, friend."

The fjord lay smooth and undisturbed, the steep fells were silent. Long, boney fingers of mist reached across the star-silvered sky. In the longhouse, the Viking gathered Edin into his arms. She trembled with sick anticipation. But he didn't take her. He pulled her onto her side facing him, so that her head was pillowed on his great shoulder and her palms lay open against his matted chest. His hands idled up and down her back. He seemed encompassed in the landscape of his own thoughts, hardly aware of her, until he said, "In the morning we're going away."

228

Her heart pounded. Into her head sprang the thought of a slave market. She'd never seen one, yet she could imagine it only too well. "Where?" she asked.

"My *saeter*. It's a hut on the upland plateau where we sometimes pasture sheep in the summer. Sometimes, when I was very young, my mother and father and I packed food and went up there for a few days. It made a break in the routine. Up there, in the Kolen, it's quiet and peaceful. I feel a need of quiet and peace just now. And there is something I want you to give me," he added cryptically, "a thing which needs all my attention, and yours, for a time."

"We're going alone?"

"Aye, but you will not complain of my company, I think." As he said this, his finger followed the rippling path of her spine down from her neck, making goosebumps rise. At the bottom his callused hand opened and stroked, idly again, with no particular purpose.

What could he want that needed so much solitude and attention? She had nothing more to give him than what he now took at his will. He'd made her an object, a thing for his use, not a person to be respected. She said, without much hope, "What about my work here?"

His answer was sharp. "It was never my intention in carrying you away from your precious England to set you to baking wheat cakes and to milking goats. The arrangements are already made. We leave before the first meal tomorrow, before anyone is up to see us off."

Which made Edin wonder if Inga knew of his plans.

"You'll ride Rushing One. She's the color of dandelions." His voice became drowsy; he spoke more casually than she'd ever heard him before. "The skald told me today of a king to the east who shods his

229

horse with gold and trims the hooves with gold filigree."

Edin spoke unguardedly, as well, as she would have spoken to anyone in the old days when she'd been free to be herself: "That undoubtedly makes a fine impression, but it can't be very practical, since gold is not a strong metal."

"Aye," he answered, tightening his hold on her fractionally, "iron is oft'times the better choice where strength is needed."

It seemed the middle of the night when next she heard his voice. "It's time, Shieldmaiden." She sighed in her sleep, but couldn't hold on to it, not with him patting her cheek so insistently. "We must be off." Not until he had her completely awake did he swing his long legs out of bed.

They were dressed and outside long before dawn. A thick, swirling mist covered the valley floor, as fresh as frost. Edin shivered in her purple shawl as the Viking himself quietly saddled their horses. Laag's head appeared briefly in the square opening of the loft above the stables. He was rubbing his eyes and yawning. "Is that you, Master?"

"Aye, go back to your sheepskin—but don't forget to give my mother my message as I told you."

"Aye, Master, at first meal. Good trip to you."

The Viking attached bundles of extra clothing and food to the horses' saddles. He helped Edin mount the smaller yellow horse, Rushing One. As he put his own foot in Dawnfire's intricately carved and inlaid stirrup, she arranged her blue skirts to cover her exposed legs.

He was dressed in full battle gear—metal war shirt and hammer-crested helmet, his sword in his scabbard and a knife in his belt. His shield hung from his saddle—a new one, emblazoned with a dragonship, since Sweyn had shattered his old one that night in Fair Hope's manorhouse.

They left the valley and the chilly arms of the summer mist by way of a damp path by the stream's side. The horses' hooves clopped softly along in the mud. It was so quiet Edin thought she could almost hear the worms wriggling their way through the liquified soil. Rushing One was clearly named for what she was not. She was a "fjording," docile, fat, and slow. The Viking claimed she could understand any language provided it was friendly.

The trail left the stream after a while and began to snake uphill. But then it came back to the water and disappeared beneath a falls. The Viking didn't pause, didn't even seem to give the action of heading his horse right under a waterfall a thought; he and Dawnfire slipped beneath as if this were an everyday occurrence.

Edin, however, hesitated, and in so doing, her little horse grew tense. The falling water seemed much more forceful than the gentle stream that irrigated the valley. It roared down and splashed and churned among rocks fifty feet below. The space behind it seemed misty and mysterious. Edin tried to look around the smoking fall, but somber evergreens spired and cut off her view of what lay beyond. The Viking was nowhere to be seen. The whole remote and lovely place was wrapped in the noise of the dashing water. Edin sat there trying to control her mount in that colorless, soulless, gloomy hour before the dawn.

At last the Viking reappeared afoot. Without speaking, he took hold of Rushing One's bridle and led the horse into the misty gap behind the water.

For a moment Edin was in a place of wonder. The sound of the racing falls echoed on the solid rock above her head and to her right, while to her left was a wall of unsolid silver, a sheet of moving glimmer. She came out on the other side, smiling with the marvel of it. "How beautiful!" she said, shouting a little over the noise of the water. "I was afraid—but really, it's beautiful, isn't it?"

The Viking looked up at her. His gaze was divided and made fierce-looking by the nosepiece of his helmet. His hand remained on Rushing One's bridle. "Aye," he said, as if he'd never voiced the thought before, "it is a pretty thing."

He remounted, and their journey continued. The trail wound ever upward. At one place it overlooked the fjord, and the Viking stopped to look down at the *Blood Wing* anchored in deep water.

Edin looked down as well. The fog had all but lifted, and in that silvering hour the valley was such a sight that she was moved to words again. "How green and deep the meadows look! And the water—it seems to glow!"

"Like a fire opal," the Viking murmured, a little reserved, as if trying out a thought to see how it sounded when given voice.

"Are there really jewels that glow like that?"

"There are."

"Fire opals," she murmured.

They didn't pause for long. Edin was glad he'd given her a pony with good legs and a stout heart, for up and up they went, following his own fast-stepping stallion. Sometimes they were surrounded by evergreen beauty. Sometimes Edin almost gasped with sheer amazement at the open views. The size and beauty of this great land! She'd never seen anything to compare with it. Once, from far below, a child's cries spiraled up, as featherlight as wood smoke. Could it be Arneld? She saw so little of him now. He'd learned to look out for himself here. Unlike her.

The dense forest thinned out and more and more gave place to bald rock and grassy slopes. When they rode above the timberline altogether, the path led them across an open sloping meadow. They stopped beside a stream for a drink of cold water, then went on.

At last, toward mid-morning, they climbed onto an undulating high plateau rich with heather, with wild flowers like glints of gold, and grass. Edin sat up in her saddle. The prevailing westerly wind stirred tendrils of her hair around her face as she gazed at peak upon peak disappearing into the distance.

"This plateau is called a *vidda,* and those mountains are the Kolen," said the Viking from his Dawnfire. "Kolen means 'keel.' The mountains range like a strong spine down the middle of the land, like the keel of an overturned ship."

Some of the peaks were snow-topped, but even where there was no snow, the highland was remarkably barren. It was a fierce yet exhilarating landscape. Great bare humps, polished and scored by glaciers, extended as far as Edin's eyes could see.

Closer to hand was a small, dream-lake ringed by reflections of those far-off mountains. The grass smelled sweet; the sun, golden now, invited them to sit in its warmth. Edin found the pack with their food and took out cheese, bread, sausage, smoked cod and herring, and a skin of buttermilk. She found a robe to spread and placed the meal for the Viking.

He stood a moment longer looking at the landscape, and she was impressed more than she could have anticipated by the majestic figure he struck, posed elegantly there against those distant, slatey-blue mountains.

At last he removed his sword, flung off his helmet and sat down. Edin pretended to be interested in the sights, being used to waiting for whatever was left after the men had eaten their fill in the longhouse. But then she heard "Come." She turned to see his hand held out to her. She drew near, took it, and let herself be drawn down onto the robe beside him.

She could tell he was in a generous mood; yet she

was always nervous in his presence, and the nearer he was the more nervous she felt. He was very near now, and naturally she had little appetite.

"Here," he said, offering her a slice of sausage from the blade of his belt knife, "make some use of your teeth."

She tried, but it was hard with him watching her.

"You must be homesick for your Saxon broths of horse hooves."

"We don't eat horse's hooves!"

There was a little quirk at one corner of his mouth. Was he teasing her again? She gestured to his sharp knife. "Does that have a name?"

"*Evil-doer.*" The quirk spread to the other corner of his mouth.

"Appropriate, no doubt," she muttered. She looked away, much as she wanted to see his smile. She was more than a little fascinated by the relaxed, teasing side of him, which she was beginning to glimpse now and again. It made her feel odd. She was glad her hair concealed her face. She plucked a tiny alpine flower growing near her hand and brought it close as if to study it.

"That's called Mountain Queen." His voice was close to her ear. She turned to find him leaning on his arm, his face bent to hers. He was going to kiss her, as she had known for some time.

He took her mouth gently, very gently. She didn't try to evade him, having learned there was no use in that, and she found herself lulled by that tantalizing gentleness. But as she'd known he meant to kiss her, she knew that now he meant to go on.

Chapter 16

The Viking opened Edin's dress and stripped the garment off her. She briefly saw herself naked, except for her laced footwear, in the full light of day; she saw her womanhood with its chevelure of delicate curls, her white breasts and thighs shining in the sunlight. His metal war shirt scraped her skin as he laid her back on the robe. He began to caress her, taking his time, taking care.

He cradled one breast with his hand. "Ripe as an apple," he murmured, and bent to taste it. Meanwhile, the fingers of his other hand were toying lower. She saw his big, strongly built, male shape bent over her, the only thing between her nakedness and the whole wide sky. He lifted his head, and she found herself staring straight into his eyes. He smiled and let his lips touch her forehead.

"Tell me, it seems that when I touch this little swollen knob, you like it." And he gently pinched a certain kernel of flesh between her thighs. Yes! it did seem there was craving accumulated there. Flustered, she closed her eyes and nipped her lower lip.

"Look at me. I want no modesty now. Tell me, do you like this, what I'm doing?"

She couldn't meet his eyes, but only stared at his corded neck, his broad shoulders. He was rolling the tender kernel between his thumb and forefinger. Her pulse deafened her. There was pressure in her ears, in her throat. She wanted to bury herself against his metal-clad chest, if for no other reason than to feel less exposed and vulnerable.

"Look at me, Shieldmaiden."

It seemed shock after shock was passing through her, gathering in a knot in her belly. She looked at him pleadingly—while he merely studied her with absorption and went on tormenting her. His eyes seemed grey to the core and revealed nothing; but his mouth was slightly open, his teeth showing perfectly white behind his lips. "Little plaything," he said in an underbreath, "talk to me. You know something that needs saying. I see it on your face."

Her mouth tried to speak, but only quivered and made no sound. She fisted her hands at her sides. What he was doing was like a dawn that threatened to blind her. Her eyes slid away—to two eagles that turned in patterns above them, their spread wings buoyed by the steady stream of the air currents.

"Do you want me to stop?"

"*Yes!*"

He did. She nearly cried out, did cry out: "Oh!"

"What?" He gave her a piercing frown.

She squirmed. Her breasts heaved softly. It seemed the air itself teased the ringlets between her legs. "I, oh, *please!*"

He seemed unsure, then opened his clothes quickly and moved between her thighs. But as he was opening her, his touch chanced upon that place again, and she moaned. He paused, looking at her—then suddenly embraced her between his thumb and forefinger once more.

"*Oh! Ohhh . . .*" Another soft shock of shameful pleasure. There was no way she could conceal it. She felt almost mad. She was throbbing, heaving. She looked at him: He was curiously pale, yet his eyes were keen as a hunting bird's. "Stop!" she cried, and

236

without realizing, stretched out her arms to him.

He spread her legs wide, quartered her, then covered her with his grand body and came down on her and, with a sudden downward plunge of his hips, entered her. His war shirt roughed her sensitive breasts exquisitely. He made strong thrusts, and she closed her eyes and let the sensations spear through her again and again.

When the muscles of his arms and back suddenly spasmed into stone and crushed her to him, when she heard the sound he made at the moment of his crisis, she knew he was nearly finished with her. And she was glad . . . yet not glad.

He rolled to her side and rested, then leaned up on his elbow to toy with her breasts again. "Did you feel pleasure?"

She turned her head away.

His hand on her far cheek turned it back again.

"You reached for me; you wanted me to take you. I think you felt pleasure."

She swallowed. "I felt . . . something. A wicked craving."

"Was it satisfied, this craving?"

She didn't know what he meant.

His eyes narrowed. "Do you feel it still?" His hand slid down her belly. His touch went through her like an impact. He saw. "Would you have me take you again, Shieldmaiden?"

"No!" She rolled away, sat up and reached for her clothes. In her spent state, this called for all the will she could muster, and if he'd made any effort to stop her, any effort at all, she would have been stopped. But he permitted her to dress.

He lay frowning at her, until, after a moment he sat up also. "Next time you'll tell me what I want to know."

Through the long, light, northern summer afternoon, following nothing but a thread of a path among tall grasses rippling in the breeze, he led her to his *saeter*. The hut he'd referred to was actually a good-sized cottage with a split-log facing on the outside and two rooms inside. The walls bore decorative carvings done by someone who understood the working of wood. The place was lifeless, however. It had an air of disuse. It was spider-scented, dusty, and damp, in need of a thorough cleaning after being used by only men for so long. Edin set about the chore immediately. The Viking seemed to approve. In fact, he took it upon himself to do similar work in the shed where he'd installed the horses.

He came in while she was finishing the cooking of their evening meal. She served him, and again he bade her to eat along with him. They sat at the table near the fire almost like husband and wife. He smeared a strip of dried fish with butter as if he were not a wealthy and powerful Viking jarl and she his captured slave, as if it were the most natural thing for them to share a meal. Yet it was hard for her to be at ease with him.

The log in the small firepit crackled and dispensed its scent. Hot coals glowed under it. The Viking reached for a hunk of flatbread. There was an inflexible authority in his every move, an arrogance. He gave her a sidelong look. "You haven't learned much of our language. The others are doing much better than you, though I know you aren't simple-minded. I think I converse with you too much in Saxon. I intend to remedy that while we're here."

The silence returned, as heavy as before, and expanded into a little forever. At last, when her nerves were on a knife edge, she asked, "How did you learn my language?"

He didn't look at her, but she saw his eyes flash with little dancing flames. "From my father's bedthrall. No doubt you've heard about her; I imagine thralls gossip among themselves no less than free women. She was cunning. Aye, she managed to seem a gentle creature—like you in many ways. A gentlewoman, not very tall, delicately fashioned. Her eyes were brown, not a glowing pale green as yours, and she wasn't allowed to keep her hair. She had a sleek blond head. But like you, she'd been brought into a hard country and a hard climate, and there was about her something that seemed to move even the stoniest heart."

Beneath his words she sensed a huge reservoir of emotion, restrained, but gathered, biding.

"How old were you when . . . when your father died?"

"Fourteen winters."

"Was she—"

"You ask too many questions, Saxon, on a subject that does not please me. You would do well to step as lightly around this topic as on the first ice of winter."

She got up quickly to clear the table. She washed the dishes in water from a hogshead he'd brought in earlier, while he sat tugging his beard. She thought he was thinking about his father's murder, and was surprised when he said, "I've decided not to sell you."

She stopped washing the ladle in her hand and stared at him. Relief flooded through her. Until that moment, she hadn't realized how the threat of being handed over to yet another strange man had weighted her. He met her eyes, and with a small smile he said, "Aye, I've decided to keep you for my own."

She missed the import of that smile, of the honor he felt he was bestowing on her, the honor of being his favorite. The lifting of dread seemed to make her light-headed, and with a dripping ladle in her hand, her frozen tongue unlocked foolishly. "Red Jennie says that sometimes a thrall can earn her freedom."

She saw her mistake too late, saw that in his mind

she'd just scorned his generosity once more and repaid it with indifference. She'd leapt over his proffered status to seek something else altogether. A serious tactical error. His look iced over; his voice was like thin ice breaking. "Fool woman," he muttered between clenched jaws. "Let me make clear your choices once again: You can stay with me and be my bed-thrall and learn all the terms and techniques of how to please me, or I can take you to Hedeby and stand you up among the market stalls and sell you to the highest bidder. Who knows what another master might teach you?"

The *saeter* had its own high-seat of sorts, a tall-backed, broad-armed chair placed at one side of the fire. The Viking sat there long after their evening meal was over. Edin sat on a bench at the table, staring like him into the flames. On the surface she probably looked calm, but she was swirling with subaqueous currents.

For the first time she was forced to consider the foolishness of her struggles against her situation. She'd fought stubbornly, as if she had some recourse to victory. Now she was forced to see what alternatives really stood within her reach:

She could make herself disagreeable to the Viking to the point that he lost patience and put her out of his feathered bed. Then she would sleep on straw again, and wear rags, and be put to lowly labor. And, since she was not a virgin anymore, and would have no barred door or strong man to protect her, she would be used casually by one man after another, night after night. And after a season of this, she would be sold to a stranger.

Her other choice was to try to please this Viking. That choice entailed deception. Yet no more deception than she'd been prepared to practice if she'd married Cedric, and for much the same reasons — stability, a place in the society in which she found herself, the comforts of a high status.

Children.

She slid away from that thought and rushed ahead with the consequences of falling in with the Viking's desires. If she pretended to welcome his lovemaking, would he not revel even more in that activity?

Well, wasn't letting him do as he wished with her better than being sold to a stranger, a man who might be much rougher, much coarser, much more violent? In the main, the Viking used her without causing her pain. He left her sore, but never had he injured her. In the main he was gentle. Gentle in the way of a man who was not accustomed to gentleness. In fact, the extent of his gentleness was a thing that confused her, because he was *not* a gentle man; he was a barbarian, a ravenous, rapacious Viking. He was big and often grim — but he'd never used her brutally. He'd taken her, ravished her, but if the truth be admitted, he might have done so far less gently.

What then would please him and insure that he would continue to want her for himself? He could already command her to submit without much more effort than a certain daunting tone of voice. He'd said in bringing her here that he wanted something from her. What more could he take? Earlier, by the lake, he'd said, "Talk to me, Shieldmaiden." She'd seldom seen anyone simply *talk* to him, except Rolf, and that not often. Mayhap — the idea seemed too outrageous — yet mayhap he was lonely. Mayhap he longed for companionship.

She stirred on her bench. The room she was sitting in seemed to snap back as though someone had lit it to life. She was aware of their solitude, of the night outside and the night sounds of this alpine country which were skeletal, like the veined framework of a leaf after the rest of it has crumbled. The room seemed full of stillness so profound a listener might hear the sentiments of her own secret mind. A mind that whispered, *I'm lonely, too.*

She'd been sitting there for a long while, and when now she moved, it was with a racing heart. She rose and went to him. She couldn't look at him, but instead kept her eyes down. She felt, rather than saw, the inquiry in his gaze, and answered it with "I . . . I would sit near you."

A fearful breath came and went before he reached for her hand and drew her down. She curled her knees and sat on the soft carpet of rushes between his booted feet. She felt his big hand on her hair, stroking. After a while he said, "It's too bad we have no skald to entertain us. It's a perfect night to hear about some hapless little gnome in the clutches of a big, wicked, and not very ingenious troll." Was there really a touch of self-consciousness in his tone, or did she imagine it?

Was he making light of the two of them? Surely not! She made herself rise above her nervousness and ask, "What's a troll?"

"What's a troll? Well now, trolls are gruesome creatures. They spend their time making life wretched for the unwary man of iron—and for any captured gnomes, of course. They're incredibly grumpy."

He was making a joke!

"And what are gnomes?" she asked.

"Gnomes are dwarfish beings, little, old wizened women who keep themselves hidden away in caves where they guard their precious treasure."

Dwarfish? Wizened? "Are there no men gnomes?"

"Oh, I suppose. But it's the women the trolls are interested in."

"Why, if they're so ugly?"

"As I said, trolls are not very bright. They take what they can get."

She felt him tug her hair and looked up to find him grinning.

"Evil as they are, big trolls sometimes meet their

242

match in these little creatures. Oft'times a troll finds himself with a captured gnome he wishes he'd never set eyes on."

"I would say he's got what he deserves."

"Mayhap. As I said, trolls are not known for their intelligence. They prowl at night and get into all manner of trouble. They sing, they weep, and they fight each other for the pleasure of it, then scurry home before the dawn comes."

"We didn't have trolls in England. They must be limited to this land, where it seems many untoward creatures have sprung up."

"Hm!"

She dared to continue: "You seem to know a lot about these nasty trolls. Where do you get your information? Have you ever spoken with one? Mayhap invited him to dine in your hall? Mayhap—"

"Mayhap my mother entertained one in her bed and gave birth to a trollish son?"

"Oh, no, surely not. Your mother has only one son, and that is you." She dared glance up at him again.

"Aye." His grin changed to something more rueful. Edin couldn't help laughing up at him. He seemed surprised. And pleased. He pressed his forefinger against the side of his nose as if to hide his pleasure, and said again, "Aye."

At length, making light of it, Thoryn led his "captured gnome" to the bed in the second room. Here the only light was what firelight fell through the open door. Her eyes were anxious, as they always were when she knew he was going to take her. Though she'd sat with him, and he'd made her laugh, now she was anxious again. She stood as if waiting for some signal from him or some order she must obey. He gestured to the bed; it was what she needed. She undressed quickly and slipped beneath the blankets.

He soon joined her, feeling a unique and voluptuous solace in so doing. In the dim light he caressed her face and ran his hand over her cheeks, her eyelids. The feel of her skin had a deeply soothing effect on him. He smoothed back her hair from her forehead. "I still terrify you." His big hand held her face and kept her from turning away.

"I-I'm trying not to be."

He looked down on her with pensive sympathy, then embraced her, seeing that she needed embracing. He stroked her hair, her shoulders, and kissed her. Tenderness unfolded in him, a sensation that was still as foreign to him as the voice of his conscience.

His next kiss was long and deep, and when at last he let her mouth go, she murmured, " 'From the fury of the Norseman, good Lord deliver us.' "

She was bantering with him again. About the fury of his kisses. Through the sweet fog of his anticipation, laughter welled up. Unable to restrain the urge entirely, he chuckled. "Aye, well may you pray to your god this night, for I mean to find new ways to wring entertainment from you."

He'd been in an aggravated state of desire for hours and was as erect as a tusk of ivory. His hand went down between her lovely thighs. She inhaled as he found the entrance into her. The cheerfulness went out of her face, and her lips quivered slightly. He let his finger rest within her for a long minute, until it seemed she began to melt around him; she became wetter and wetter.

"Do you like this?" he asked.

She wouldn't answer.

Have patience, he told himself. He meant to break through all her barriers, to wear down all her restraints, and his technique was going to be deliberate, meticulous patience. She would see how efficient it was. She would be totally open to him, and more profoundly enslaved than she'd ever thought herself capable of being.

He made his voice a whisper. "Saxon, you will tell me."

"I . . ." She seemed a little breathless. "It makes me feel .,.. truly I don't *know!*"

"Does it give you discomfort?"

"No, it-it makes me feel . . . *uneasy.* It makes me want . . ."

"What?"

"To move!"

He felt a leap of triumph. With a sliding motion, he pulled his finger out. She gasped. He found that her little knob of flesh was swollen as a flowerbud. As he took it between his fingers, he whispered, "This is very plump suddenly."

"Sweet *Jesu!*" She pressed her hands against his chest.

"Put your arms around me."

She did; she slid her arms up his chest and around his neck. Her breath was sweet. She was so young and fragile. Avoiding his eyes and looking shy, struggling to hide her reactions, she was at the pitch of her beauty. He knew that essentially he had not yet satisfied her, and without knowing indeed that such a thing was even possible, that was exactly what he meant to do. If she could be lifted to that surrendering pitch of depleted and ecstatic release that he knew so well, he felt then she would be his totally.

"Do you like this?"

Again she didn't answer.

"Saxon, I want you to heed me, and I am afraid you're doing a very poor job. Now answer me: Do you like this?"

"*Yes!*"

The fervency in her voice half-thrilled and half-frightened him. Anxious to see as well as feel her, he threw back the blankets. From the door, the firelight glowed on her thighs. His gaze touched her all over.

"Please . . . please . . ." she whimpered. There was

245

trouble in her face.

This was how he'd dreamed and imagined her, begging him to take her. Yet, though he was rampant, he didn't, not yet.

It was no small sacrifice. A sudden gleam of light showed him the pink, tender-looking, bud-centered flower of her open flesh—and an urge he'd never felt before made his mouth fill with desire. Impulsively, trembling at his own intention, his mouth descended.

And then even he was taken by surprise, ambushed by sudden revelation. The lush satin of her, the incredible taste and smell of her! He could think of nothing more. He felt her hands in his hair. He felt the unmistakable yield of her body. And after an unknown period of time, there came a limitless, endless sea of moment wherein he felt her convulse and cry out and convulse again and again and again.

Her fingers released his hair gradually. He kissed her white inner thighs, nipping them with his teeth. Then he touched her deeply again, possessively. She'd seemed asleep, but with his penetrating touch, she quickened once more. She looked at him with a gaze of mixed amazement and reproach, yet her knees naturally raised and spread. Now, he thought, now. He moved over her, but entered her no more than an inch. He gathered her in his arms. "Kiss me."

She kissed his forehead, his eyelids and his eyelashes. She kissed his cheeks above his beard, and then his open mouth. Only then did he stroke her. It went on just this side of forever, to a moment of total fulfillment and shuddering rapture.

Much later she asked, "Will this be all my life now?" Her voice quivered—with her unhappiness, with her disappointment that the security of her youth in another land was lost to her, with her recognition that fate had placed her in his hands, had made her his thrall.

"Listen to me." He felt solemn but not angry. She'd

been lying with her back curved into his chest. He rolled her so that he could lean over her and look down at her still-swollen breasts. He let her feel his hand between her thighs again. She grabbed his wrist, yet couldn't keep him from seizing her in an upward motion that caused her to twist with sensation. "You have pleasure at my touch, and when I have you in my arms, yes, this is all you will think about, all you will be."

He felt her dilemma: She was finding it important not to resist, yet finding the need to resist almost impossible to combat. Slowly yet very definitely he was probing her, creating in her exactly the sort of sensations he was trying for. "In some former life you were many things. Discard those memories, Shieldmaiden. You are mine now. Your body is mine."

She whispered, "It's not enough, Viking."

He felt a dull pain go through his heart. For an instant the room was filled by the echo of those words. "It will become familiar to you as the days pass," he said stubbornly. "I'll do whatever I can to teach you." Her look didn't forgive. "I pleased you," he said. "I pleased you very much."

She didn't deny it, and he couldn't resist the defeated look of her. It stimulated his desire, and he got to his knees over her.

He felt the curve of her waist, then placed his hands on her thighs and finally opened her. He saw their tangled shadows on the wall beyond the bed as he fell forward and took her again. She moaned in time with his movements—and when suddenly he pulled himself out, she gasped. Her arms came up to stay him.

"Do you belong to me, Saxon?"

She exhaled the words so low he almost didn't hear them. "If you want me."

Again that dull pain went through his heart. And he heard that echo: *It's not enough.* He felt his face harden to iron. He said, "I want you." To prove it, he sank back into her. She accepted him with a quivering, shuddering motion. "Aye, I want you." And he began another journey into delight.

Chapter 17

While the frost was yet merely moonlight and the still air outside the *saeter* had yet a shine of silver, the Viking rose to build up the fire in the first room. Edin watched through the door as he squatted to fuel the embers which were left from the log that had glowed through the night. New flames leapt along the dry kindling. When the fire was hissing and fluttering, he rose.

He lost none of his bearing when naked; he was such an astonishing figure.

He came back to bed. "True beauty is to wake looking like you do," he said, gazing down at her from his elbow with a well-satisfied smile. Immediately she started to rub at her eyes and mouth, trying to brush off the cobwebs of sleep. He stopped her, and continued his study. "Your eyes are as green as submerged ice."

But then he frowned. "It ill becomes a Viking to talk so much bark-language. This seems as good a time as any to further your instruction in *Norsk*."

She was willing, though uneasy. Now he would find out how basically stupid she was. Lying facing him, she luxuriated in the freedom to delay the day; nothing else seemed so precious. With the blankets up to their chins, he made her say words again and again before he went on. She surprised herself at her ability to learn. Many of the words were familiar to her already; it seemed that her sensitive mind had been too frightened, too constantly bullied at the steadying. Here, given this chance, she was able to put words together with their meanings quickly. Within an hour she was able to answer simple questions:

"What is the highest peak in Norway?" he asked in slow, clear Norse.

"Glittertinden is the highest peak in Norway," she answered, using the complete sentence form he demanded.

"What is the longest river in Norway?"

"The Glama is the longest river in Norway."

"Tell me about the glaciers."

"Joste . . . Joste . . ."

"Jostedal." He moved his hand from beneath the blankets to brush her hair back from her cheek. His eyes were as grey as armor.

"Jostedal is the largest glacier in Norway."

"Where are the highest mountains?"

"The highest mountains are in the south of Norway."

"How long is Sognefjord?"

"Sognefjord is over one . . ."

His hand had curved behind her nape, while his other hand had burrowed beneath her and was now sliding up and down her back, bringing her closer, tight against his full length.

". . . one hundred miles . . ."

What was this new bodily appetite he'd awakened in her? How could she desire a beast of prey? Yet last night . . . last night in the arms of this Viking her world had momentarily expanded, her life had briefly been suffused with spectacle. In truth, every time he'd ever taken her into his arms, the excitement, that combination of fear and pleasure, had transformed the mundane, crowded each second

250

with sensation, enraptured her. She felt that the truest, the most daring, the most alive part of her, was aroused in his arms.

Even so, it was wrong. It was wrong for him to enslave her. But in his society, as in most, privilege went hand in hand with power. She must accept it.

Yet to be nothing but a pleasure-thrall—it was not enough. She wanted more. She wanted to understand and be understood, to be seen as more than something "always and immediately accessible."

Still more poignant was her memory of another world: that lost, precarious, touching world of Fair Hope Manor, a world wherein she'd mattered to those about her. Thus what she wanted now, what so powerfully drew her—the urge to touch this Viking, stroke him, hold him—she pulled against, forestalled. Overnight she'd been abducted from her home, bereft of protection. This Viking had ruthlessly slain her bridegroom. And no matter how he explained it, he had not killed Cedric simply in self-defense. He'd killed for pride and because he was a Viking. How could she endure life as his concubine? How could she endure this hateful thralldom? How could she want to kiss him?

She tried to remember what she was supposed to be saying—"Sognefjord is one hundred—" but the sentence broke into fragments, the fragments shattered into unattached words "—miles long. In. Norway."

"Aye" came his wry response. "And it is even longer in Ireland. Kiss me," he whispered, his breath spilling vibrant warmth into her open mouth.

Despite her will to resist, a contentment came into her, a feeling of reckless sweetness. She looked into his heavy-lidded gaze and felt daring rise within her. "Kiss you?" she asked. "In *Norsk?*"

He grinned. It made her feel she'd achieved something whenever she made him smile or laugh. Too

251

often his face was threatening and thunderous; too often his eyes held a radiance as colorless and cold as starlight.

"Aye," he said, "in *Norsk,* in Norway, here in this bed. Now mind your tongue, Saxon, and kiss me."

Her daring rose, and she did kiss him. And as she did, he brought his hands up between them to cup her breasts. And that was the end of the geography portion of her lessons. After that he started to teach her the words for all the various parts of the human body, male and female, mingled with phrases of lovemaking:

"I feel the softness of your body against mine."

"I feel the softness —"

"Nay, I think it is the *hardness* of my body you feel."

"Oh, yes, the hardness." She felt herself blush.

"The smoothness of your shoulders is like warm ivory."

"The smoothness of your . . . *hardness* is like warm ivory."

He chuckled.

Sometimes she didn't learn the meaning of the words until after she repeated them, as when she parroted back, "I would like to be caressed. *Oh!*" He took her by surprise with that touch that was like a spear thrust of ravishment and that smile that held the oldest enchantment of time.

"Is Norse not an extraordinary language?" he murmured.

For a long moment she lay too dumbfounded to answer under that touch, under those pleasures that thrilled and spilled upon each other, measureless and long-drawn. He treated her with tenderness, stroked her, called her by his pet name, "Shieldmaiden." From there the lesson became increasingly pent and was voiced in increasingly breathless whispers, until at length he groaned wordlessly and she couldn't keep back a cry that meant the same in any language.

A quarter of an hour later, he sat with his back against the headboard, his lips pleasurably parted. Edin lay in his hold across his massive chest. Her hair hung in ripples over her arms and his. The blond of his hair resembled fine gold in the morning light. She'd bravely ventured to touch his beard, and he'd allowed it, seemed to like it, so she was toying with that strong blond growth of his cheeks and chin.

"I believe this is the superior way for you to learn Norse—abed."

She said at length, "But what I learn may be awkward to work into common, everyday conversation. Shall I say to Otarr Magnusson or Rolf Kali, 'I am delicately mossed,' or 'My breasts taste like bramble wine'?" She put the question with the gentlest courtesy—and was rewarded with a great grand squeeze. His arms turned her so that her breasts were flattened against his softly matted chest. His large hands soothed up and down her back lazily. She felt his heartbeat pounding dully, like a hammer muffled in cloth.

He said, "It seems to me it lightens your head to be up here in the mountains. But to answer your question: Should Ottar or Rolf ever broach the subject of your breasts, you will tell them this. . . ."

She repeated what he said, giggling, for she knew the meaning of most of the words. One or two she wasn't sure of, and so asked for a translation.

He tapped the tip of her nose with his finger. Her heart contracted beneath his look, contracted painfully. "It means, 'The fork of my thighs is a briar patch, and my breasts are wrinkled like potatoes in late March.'"

By noon, the sun had vanished behind amassing clouds, and it had grown chilly on the *vidda*. But

Edin's new cloak was warmly lined. Walking along the pebbly edge of a stream, she enjoyed the free feeling of the wind in her hair. When it got beneath her cloak, it molded her new butter-yellow dress against her body. After a while, she turned to find the Viking had stopped several paces back and was squatted down, watching her. He had an air of preoccupation; he seemed to be considering her beyond her immediate presence.

Viking. A word bathed in emotion. She never thought of him as other than the Viking. Or the jarl. What did he call her in his mind? The Saxon? When he was making love to her he murmured, "Shieldmaiden." She asked suddenly, "Do you know my name?"

"Of course," he said, "Edin. I've heard the thralls use it. Or they call you 'my lady.' "

She turned away to hide her hurt. "Except for Dessa, they only call me that to taunt me. They dislike me. I don't know why."

"Because you were a lady once." His sarcasm was gone.

"I'm not now." After a pause, she added, "You never call me by my name."

"You never call me by mine." His eyes were vigilant but soft in the overcast half-light.

"Because it would mean calling you Master Thoryn."

"I am your master."

The wind lifted her hair.

"Edin, wherever a man can rule he will. This law was made before me, and I am not the only one to act upon it; I did but inherit it, and I know that you, if you had my strength, would do as I do."

He was telling her nothing she didn't already know — that she'd been caught in the grip of currents that were too powerful for her.

"What would you have called your young Cedric?

When he took you to his chamber and laid you down on his bed, what would you have called him?"

"My lord."

"Call me that, then," he said casually, as though he were telling her to pass the salt at dinner.

She turned to face him suddenly, troubled. "But I would have been his wife; he would have called me 'my lady' in return. He wouldn't have taken me by piracy, in an orgy of killing and robbery."

His face was still calm. She'd triggered no anger. She saw no sign in him of the self-sufficient, coldly controlled conqueror which he seemed able to conjure at will. Yet before he answered, his chest swelled with a deep breath. "I can't call you my lady. The law of my people says that you are a thrall, and even I must abide by the law. Or find another people. As for how I gained possession of you, my ancestors have bred a love of battle into my bones and marrow. I am what I am." He added, "I am what I am, and your pretty manor farm was a sheep's dreamland."

Her eyes filled with tears. She waited in silence for the weakness to pass.

He held out his hand. After a while she went to him. He took her wrist, not her fingers, however, and squeezed. "You think I'm an ogre. But I will grant you this: No one, not even I—and I hold the greatest power over you that you're ever likely to feel—can take away from you the knowledge that you were born a lady. In your heart the Lady Edin may live on undemoted."

She couldn't hide her bitterness at this half-concession. "But elsewhere I am a thrall."

"*My* thrall. Under another master, you would have felt the whip's lash by now. Or worse. Another master wouldn't let you harbor even a secret memory of your former rank."

She stood with her wrist held tightly by him as he

squatted in the midst of all that austere, quiet beauty. Together they contemplated the view, which included, besides the rising distant mountains, two circling hawks. Lower down, a mixed flock of birds suddenly darted like one united family. One of the hawks plummeted earthward and vanished, then re-emerged beating heavenward with a small prey struggling in its claws.

Edin felt the hand clasping her wrist.

The Viking, his eyes on the hawk, said, "Tell me, the first time I took you, you whispered a thing: 'I'm so afraid of you,' you said. Even last night you were afraid—at first. Are you afraid of me today?"

"I—" she swallowed convulsively—"I'm not afraid to lay with you."

"And to walk with me?"

She wanted to swallow again but had no moisture in her mouth. "The man who walks with me is often a different man than the one who lies with me. You can change; you can become a warrior, a Viking with a relish for battle and a furious belief in belligerent gods. And I must remain wary."

He nodded. "I've threatened you. I've needed to, to impress upon you your true condition. But now—do you think I would harm you now?" His voice was even and serious.

How to explain to someone who had never experienced bondage? "I am your servant, your slave, you own me. My life is yours to direct forever. Or to take. Which means I can never completely trust you."

He said quickly, looking up at her, "But I would have your trust."

"That you can't command. And I couldn't give it, even if I wanted to. Because no matter how well you treat me, I am just a little white bone caught in the dragon's jaws."

"I prize you. You see how I provide for you." He

gestured to her clothing. "You know how I desire you."

"But," she whispered, "at any moment your desire could vanish, and then you could turn me out among that collection of unattached, brutish creatures, all self-worshipping, whom you call your oathmen. They would fall on me and breed without care or regard."

"I never will."

"You might! Because you don't love me."

"Love?" He seemed genuinely unfamiliar with the word. "What do we share in the dark then, if not love?" His color was gone, and his smile wasn't a smile. "What is love?"

She considered. "Mayhap we've shared love of a kind—in the dark. But true love is a thing of the light. It is a home for the spirit, a shelter of strong arms from the wind, a fire in the heart when the world without is cold."

There were lines in his face she hadn't seen before, two vertical lines between his eyes. "Huh! Sounds like bad poetry, and there are two sorts of people Vikings can't abide—fools and bad poets." He looked away from her dismissively, gazing up at the sky.

In a moment she too looked up, noting the way the clouds boiled and tumbled. She felt the wind on her face, sharper and stronger than before.

"We must go back," he said, rising.

He kept her wrist as they walked toward the *saeter.* At the door, he said, "You beset me with nettles and thorns, Shieldmaiden."

She gave him the look he deserved and said, "As you beset me with iron."

Inside, he went to freshen the fire. Squatting before it, the light in his face, he said, without looking at her, "You always look tragic, like you're on the verge of tears. Can't we be merry, you and I,

257

at least while we're here?"

His profile moved her to pity, an emotion she'd never thought to feel for him. He wore an amulet, a Thor's hammer, a potent emblem of his strength, his audacity, his effectiveness. He was a man without morality, who lived and would die brutally and carelessly, according to his people's heroic code. And yet he sought to be merry with her; such a simple request. She found she could not refuse him.

The next day at the *saeter* was full of rain and foul weather. The Viking kept the fire blazing, and all was warmth inside the two rooms. His weapons leaned close by the door: his helmet with its iron nosepiece, his round, wooden shield with its dragonship emblem. His most prized weapon, however, his sword so beautifully damascened, lay across his knees at this moment. Edin watched him clean and sharpen it, and couldn't refrain from saying in her new and halting Norse, "In some ways you Vikings are children."

His face was illuminated by the fire. He gave her a questionable look, a blank look she'd seen before, a look that could become cruel in an instant. But this time it became a smile. He said, "Very dangerous children." After another night and long morning abed with her, he seemed as near to full peace and careless contentment as she'd ever seen him.

She said, "You carry your swords and axes about constantly, like little boys playing conqueror."

"Every prudent man keeps his blades close at hand."

"You think you're a prudent man?" she said recklessly, slipping back into Saxon. "Is it prudent to burn and loot and kill? Why do you do it—really? That sword you handle so lovingly carries no virtue in its edge. It has drunk enough gore that even you must feel sated."

"Be wary," he said in Norse, in a voice of velvet, a

voice as soft as a lynx's paw with all the claws at the ready, "be wary, song-singer, what you say."

She too returned to Norse. "I only tell the truth: That sword has made much butchery in the world."

"Shieldmaiden, any moment now the dragon is going to snap his jaws shut—and that little white sylphlike bone caught between his teeth will be snapped in two."

He didn't want to talk about what he did during his raids. She absorbed this carefully, another piece of her growing intelligence of the man.

From where he was sitting in his chair by the fire, he said, "If you come here, I'll put my sword away. Come; truly I would rather fondle the hidden folds leading to your treasures than this sharp, cold metal."

He didn't want to talk about murder and mayhem—but it pleased him to talk of lovemaking. Oh, yes, that always seemed to make him glow with great good-feeling!

With her eyes on his sword, giving it a glare of acute distaste, she said softly, "It's my shame that I let you touch me as I have. You were a plague come from the edges of the world to murder my people. I myself saw Beornwold, the one you buried at sea, crack a helpless man's skull like a ripe apple."

He looked up from his work. "He did that? And you saw it?" He frowned. "And ever since, the sight has glowed quietly in your mind. You thought of it when I carried you to my chamber that first time—and many another time, no doubt." He shrugged. "Well, know that before we went into your village I gave the order for no senseless slaughter. And know that if I'd seen Beornwold disregard my word, I would have come down on him like the hounds of Odin. As I came down on Sweyn the Berserk, who is known as Sweyn the Cripple now."

She muttered, "He got his just reward."

"Aye, I suppose so. Not everyone does. Mostly it is a matter of odds. And when the odds are in your favor, you English treat captured Northmen as ruthlessly as we treat you. You flay us—skin us like deer—and nail our hides to your church doors; you fling us into adder pits; your women murder with pretty daggers hidden in their pretty bosoms—or abed in the dark of night. There are faults on both sides. No one is ever completely right. Not even you."

As usual, he'd chosen his ground with the accomplished eye of a fighting man. She fumed for lack of an answer, then exploded back with, "I wonder how you would manage in my place, feeling like a feather blown about on the whims of one rough, ill-natured man?"

"Ill-natured? I am that, I suppose. But rough?" He seemed to consider the words, his look harmless, mild as a spring lamb's. "Mayhap at times. But not lately that I recall. Come, you've made me wonder, and now I must check my work. Come, Shieldmaiden, let me see if I've bruised you anywhere." He gave her a great teasing grin.

She couldn't sustain her ill will when he was behaving so oddly, so very nigh amiably.

"Come! Don't look so hangdog, woman. You've been conquered, aye, but life is the thing!"

Another night had come blowing down. Thoryn propped himself on his elbow and studied his slave woman as she slept. She looked as innocent as a napping child—except that her mouth was swollen from the violence of his kisses, and the tips of her breasts were yet puffy with his suckling, and the nest of down between her thighs was moist with his spillings. The soft light of the dying fire cast a pink glow over her, and these signs of his use made him want her again—unreasonably, considering that not fifteen minutes had passed since he'd moaned and thrust himself throbbing into her warmth and released his passion.

What was this emotion she engendered in him that tore his insides like a captive eagle seeking exit?

He covered her carefully, trying not to wake her. She was exhausted. Her surrender had been absolute tonight. He'd coaxed her to a climax of pleasure three times. He loved to watch her tension build and then overflow from her like mead from a brimming horn. She was magnificent when she cried out, begging for mercy from his hands or his mouth, writhing and sighing and pleading for him to enter her and fill her.

Outside, it was now raining. He couldn't sleep. He'd spent much more time abed in these past few days than ever was his habit. He listened to the voices of the rain, the little torrents of running water falling from the eaves.

He'd brought her here to wring pleasure out of her. With nothing to go by but the heavens, he'd steered her into giving more of herself than she'd known how to give. His purpose had been to further enslave her. He'd never suspected that the moments in which he conquered her would be moments in which he was as much enthralled by her as she was enslaved by him. Mayhap it was just as well that this paradise of being alone with her was coming to an end. Tomorrow he would take her back.

He recalled the day she'd used the word *love,* and caused him to use it. Reflecting, he couldn't remember ever having formed that particular word in his mouth before, nor ever heard it from a stranger's.

She'd caused many changes in him. She'd caused him to look at his way of life from a different standpoint, and betimes to question it.

Was he bewitched, as Sweyn and his mother

warned? Could it be that a man who had seen just such a spell cast over his own father might have no judgement to free himself from the same magic when it fell over him?

Was what happened between them even real?

It was real. His body knew how real it was.

She was curled into a small mound. He pulled the cover back again, silent as a held breath. She was sleeping on her left side now, her legs slightly drawn up, so that the vision she offered him was her white flanks. She was only a woman, a small and helpless woman who happened to be rich in delights. He had nothing to fear from her. Only a coward would fear such a small, helpless female.

Only a coward would fear the word love, a word that suggested watered milk, something wan and insipid.

Only a coward would fear questions about his way of life. The Norse way could bear questioning. After all, didn't it gain him jewels, saddles of handsome and foreign workmanship, gold and silver, beautifully woven satins and silk in variegated scarlets and greens? Didn't he capture tender, youthful, bright, matchless girls and large, well-formed boys? True, he often felt like a man standing on a narrow ledge beside a precipice, but he was no coward.

Deep and close in his soul, however, he knew that something of him was conquered, and the knowledge caused him fear.

The code of Norse law was handed down verbally from generation to generation. The laws were many and varied. There were laws about boundary markings, about hunting rights, about the cutting of trees and the collection of wood, laws about the infringement of grazing, about libel, satire, and calumny, and light-headed young folk making love songs.

There were laws concerning sheep stealing, souring a woman's butter, and wooing her bees. There were laws about insulting the public morality, laws about hurting the community. Laws about severing a finger. Laws about severing a head.

Local *Things* were called periodically, during which any freeman could discuss a discontent or a problem. If a man was accused of some misdeed, he had the consolation of knowing his court was made up of his peers. Since there was no punishing authority, if a man was found guilty, the burden of punishment was left to the strength and intelligence of the offended party.

These courts were almost always called by the reigning jarl well in advance so that people could take advantage of the assembly to barter and trade. The event usually had the gala feeling of a fair. The beacon fire that blazed on the lookout point of Thorynsteading at sunrise today, however, had not been lit by Thoryn Kirkynsson. He was away, but according to the message he'd left his mother Inga, this was the day he would return.

He first saw the beacon leaping and smoking when he led Edin down off the *vidda*. After a moment's pause, he goaded Dawnfire and Rushing One to hurry.

Meanwhile, his neighbors began to collect in the open air on the lip of his valley where his father's runestone stood. This was the site where he traditionally met his people and exchanged oaths. The runestone was upright, carved with angular script. The letters were made of up-and-down and slanting scoremarks. There was a certain secrecy about runic writings. A runemaster was regarded almost as a magician. But the message carved on the late jarl's stone was really very simple: "Thoryn set this stone in remembrance of his father, Kirkyn."

Kirkyn Atlason had been discovered murdered on

a grey morning in late autumn. Thoryn recalled the gulls and the sea mews mocking him for crying—for boys of the North did not cry, no matter what. No matter what feelings a boy of only fourteen winters had to deal with: his mother's peculiar silence; his deep grief for his father—and for his father's murderer. And his fury at her betrayal.

Her name had been Margaret.

Hurrying beneath the waterfall in his rush to get home, Thoryn averted his head quickly as if by doing so he wouldn't see in his mind the appalling image of her. It did him no good. She was there in his memory, soft-voiced, always sweet and fresh-washed. He heard her laughter, bright as birds. She'd taught him Saxon at Kirkyn's order, because Kirkyn believed a man should speak the language of the thralls he owned. Thoryn had started the lessons badly, forewarned by Inga that the woman would try to poison his mind. But gentle Margaret soon won him over. He came to trust her as completely as his father did. And although Kirkyn ruled her, he was also enslaved by her.

As Thoryn feared he was now enslaved.

Emerging from beneath the falls, he drew in a deep draught of the here and now, which breathed so easily, which held no hint of death and betrayal. He brought his thoughts back to worrying about what business could be awaiting him with the summons of that beacon fire.

Entering his own valley at last, he went directly to the *Thing*-place, not even pausing to take Edin to the longhouse first. The gathering looked ready for battle. Each *bondi* carried his shield and axe or sword and wore his battle shirt. Around the Norsemen's shoulders were not the grey concealing cloaks worn into raids, however, but resplendent cloaks caught to their chests by gold and silver brooches. With their helmets polished to sheening brightness and their decorum stiffened for the occasion, the effect they made was of a great set of chessmen, stalwart and well-built, blond, ocean-eyed, and ornate, standing there against the sky.

"What is it?" Thoryn asked as he dismounted.

The sun had passed its zenith, yet the day remained bright. From the fjord, the breeze blew salt and fresh. Many of the men looked toward Harold Bluetooth, and as many others toward Leif the Tremendous.

Thoryn had little liking for Leif, a sullen man at best. It was rumored he beat his wife, Auor. For some time Thoryn had expected the woman to appear at a *Thing*-meet herself and demand a divorce.

He asked again, "What is this about?"

It seemed no one wanted to answer his question. He scanned the crowd. Finnier Forkbeard, the eldest and the honorary Old Man of the Council said, "Thoryn Kirkynsson, Harold Bluetooth's thrall Vred and Leif's thrall Amma together stole two of Harold's best horses, besides supplies, and have disappeared into the Kolen."

"When?"

"Five nights ago."

"You've searched?"

"We're not fools," Harold said. "And Vred is no barefoot girl. He's got horses and supplies and they're gone."

Leif burst out, "I told that bitch Amma it was time for her to breed. She wanted Vred and I told her no, but—"

"But it's your fault, Jarl!" Harold said. "You put it in their minds when you let that one there get away with breaking the law." He pointed his axehead at Edin.

"You should have laid her down on Thor's Stone and let the thralls see what happens to runaways!" Leif shouted.

Chapter 18

The *Thing* fell into a din of shouts. Every man had an opinion and was sensitive to his right to express it. Their voices got louder and louder. Edin's heart raced. She automatically sought to stay near the jarl. She even dared take a fold of his cloak between her fingers. He felt it, and turned and met her eyes—and she saw something in them; but quickly he seemed to staunch whatever it was. She almost felt him pulling away from her, felt the communion they had achieved in the *saeter* dissolving. His bearing became that of a man unaware of Edin's presence, a man leading a separate and independent existence from her, as if he'd not held her intimately only hours ago. Would he withdraw his promised protection in favor of his own interests? Of course he would! She dropped her foolish, feminine hold on his cloak and stiffened herself to stand alone. Frowning, his carriage suggested power; his helmet and his weapons made him seem unbelievably tall and deadly. Dread filled her soul.

She saw Inga coming up the slope with a cloth bundle under her arm. The jarl flung a cool and calculating look down at her as she arrived, puffing from her climb, her face alight with hectic excitement. He said, "This is a council of men, Mother."

"Yet *she* is here."

"Mother—"

She gave him a look that made Edin gasp. *"Traitor!"* Inga cried. She had the entire group's attention. Wrenching around, she spewed at Edin, "Witch!"

Edin looked at the jarl. His face was arranged to show nothing. Inga cried to the assembly now, "She killed Ragnarr—and was never punished. She caused my son to maim his berserker—dishonorably, I know some of you feel—and was never punished. She ran away and was never punished. She flaunts her hair as no thrall ever should be allowed to do. She wears gowns as fine as my own, and jewelry. She sleeps in your jarl's bed—and rules from there!"

The jarl suddenly grabbed her shoulder as if he meant to shake her. Edin's hand went to the breast brooch that closed her cloak. She felt all about her hard-living, hard-dying, forceful men, each one equipped with a magnificent sword or axe which could take her head off in one swing.

Despite the jarl's grip on her, Inga shouted, "She's escaped the law too often! She must die!'

Edin felt the color recede from her cheeks, felt cold perspiration break out on her arms. The wild beating of her heart stole her breath away.

Inga reached for the bundle under arm, but the jarl acted first. He dropped his hold on her and swiftly stepped before Edin. "These crimes, if they be crimes, are mine."

Edin swayed, giddy with sudden relief.

"Thoryn," said Kol Thurik, "why do you defend her?"

The jarl faced him down without answering. For once Edin was grateful for his ability to create terror with his eyes and his expression.

But then Finnier Forkbeard shouldered forward again. His face was seamed into a web of wrinkles; his stiff, parted whiskers moved with his jaw as he said, "You have shown contempt for the law, Thoryn Kirkynsson."

"The thrall!" Inga urged. "Kill the thrall!"

The men muttered. There was a growing excitement beneath their talk. Inga's little performance had much engaged them. They were like hounds who smelled blood. The jarl spoke into this muttering, each word falling from his lips individual and hard, like chips of stone: "No one will touch her."

Finnier Forkbeard said, "The law says, 'A master should take the life of any thrall who threatens his life, who harms him or his family, who is found stealing, *or who is overtaken in an escape.*'"

"He *should* take the thrall's life—which I interpret to mean that he may or he may not. I alone mete out justice on my steadying, and I am not in fear of my own chattel."

"Your fear is not the point. 'With law shall the land be brought up and with lawlessness shall it waste away.' It is not wise for any master to let his thralls do as you have let this woman do."

"She is my responsibility."

"Aye, in all ways. She is here through your venture; she is your subject. But when one thrall is allowed to mock her master, all thralls are tempted to mockery. More than once men of power have disregarded the sense of this, and they have paid a high price."

Nods of assent went around. Inga seemed calmer, more rational. She said, "I was a good and faithful wife. My husband Kirkyn was a brave fighting man and a good husband. Yet he was a fool in this way. He . . ." Her rationality seemed to fade; looking into her face, Edin had a sense of staring into something dark and sleeping. "He let himself become besotted by a Saxon thrall. . . ."

"They know the story, Mother." It seemed to Edin that since the jarl had stepped between her and her enemies he stood taller than ever before. It was as though his decision had physically enlarged him. All his arrogance, his pride of caste and birthright, was written on his face.

"Yes . . . yes." Inga seemed to come back to herself. "I know they do. We all know it—and it's ending." She turned to face the storm of pride in her son's face—which didn't seem to daunt her in the least. "I stood by while your father made a mistake that cost him his life, and now I'm supposed to stand by while you follow the same path? I'm supposed to watch you lust after a Saxon witch just as he did before you? I would think you'd rather cut the blood-eagle in her back in just revenge for him who was murdered so foully—but no, you favor her."

She turned back to the more sympathetic faces of the *Thing*-men. "Have I not suffered enough?" Now her voice sounded far away and forlorn. Edin saw that a flare for the dramatic must run in the family. "Must I live with another murdering harlot beneath my roof?" Her eyes filled and shone with the cool brightness of jewels.

"Enough!" The jarl's face had slowly gone dark. "I will hear no more of this."

There was silence. Edin wondered if she ought to say something in her own behalf—but what? After a moment, Finnier broke the silence with "Two men have lost valuable thralls, horses, and goods. What say you about that, Thoryn Kirkynsson?"

He answered, in a soft, a dangerous voice, "Thrall, go to my chamber."

Since he didn't look at her, Edin was a little behind time in realizing that it was her he was addressing.

"In my chest is a box of cedarwood, inside that a sack of coins. Bring—"

"No!" Inga exclaimed. She stared him in the eye without flinching. "You will *not* pay Harold and Lief and let the matter end at that. For the matter will not *be* ended with that!" Her eyes and mouth fisted and her nose twitched. "Here!" She unfurled the white bundle she'd brought under her arm. "Remember this,

Thoryn?"

Edin saw that it was a man's nightshirt, yellowed with age—and stained, particularly around a tear in the breast. It took Edin a moment to register what those brown stains were, what weapon could have made that small slit, and whose nightshirt it must have once been. She realized the truth all at once, and in the same instant felt a sharpening of her fear.

The *Thing*-men went stiff with shock. "Kirkyn's!" came a hiss. Another whisper said, "The very one he was found in!" They all stared unbelieving at the awful, blood-starched garment in which Inga's beloved had been murdered.

The jarl said softly, "You kept that, Mother? All these years? *Where* have you kept it? Among your gowns in your chest? Under your mattress?" His voice gained volume until at last it was like a rumble of thunder: "Have you kept it under your pillow, Mother?"

"Thoryn"—her voice was tearful and pathetic again, her tone soothing—"I kept it to remind me—and you. Your father was brave, but he could be obstinate, and in one matter he was a fool. Listen to me! A man you meet in battle is a plain warrior whose only strength is in the axe or the sword he swings. You overcome that weapon and the man is finished. But this woman is no axeman, no swordsman; she is too cunning to take up such simple arms. Her weapons are her thighs, plump and pear-shaped, and—"

"Mother."

"—and her mind, oh, yes, her woman's mind, the craftiest weapon of all. She will attack you unsuspected, with poison in your honeycakes and cream—"

"*Mother.*"

"—with a cord around your neck while you're sleeping—" she was all but clutching him with her words and her eyes, putting forth all she had to hold his attention—"or with a dagger slipped between your—"

270

"Mother!"

At last she was silent. She saw that he'd escaped her and was free. She kept looking at him, however, bent forward a little, fingering the cloth of that ghastly garment, her gaze so omnivorous Edin feared she would surely suck him back with her eyes. But then her breast wrenched out a sigh, for he turned away from her, dismissed her very presence.

His eyes were narrowed as they slid around the gathering of men. For a tense and hostile moment no one spoke, or even moved. Finally he said, "As you can see, my dame tends a small but pure flame of hatred deep within her heart—along with a keen sense of drama. It disturbs me when she takes me for a fool . . . but mayhap she does so with some justification."

Edin saw yet another change come over him; suddenly he was exuding a certain courtly manner. While the *Thing*-men were still stunned with confusion—many still stared at the stained shirt now crumpled in Inga's arms—while Edin herself still felt the echoes of that instant of awful realization, the jarl had already recovered enough to see how to proceed.

He moved to the standing stone that dominated the place, and put his hand upon it. From there he stared back at the gathering. "I appreciate the stability given to everyday affairs by *Thing*-law, and I have always confirmed its standing and authority. But when my new thrall ran away, she didn't even understand our language yet, let alone our laws. Considering her value, it seemed too much of a waste to see her bright lifeblood poured out for the crime of simple ignorance and fear.

"As for my gifts to her, that is my right. I will *not* drown her for having hair too lovely to crop, or for seeking to please me by ornamenting herself. By the High One, brothers, I've spent too much time coaxing her to please me to undo any of her learning along those lines!"

271

Laughter. Uneasy, but venting the unbearable pressure of tension that had built.

"I will do this much to make amends for any trouble the situation might have given my battle-brothers and fellow thrall-masters, Harold and Leif. I will pay them twice the value of all they have lost." He moved forward, placing a placating hand on Harold's shoulder. "Come. Come, Leif. Let us go down to the longhouse and settle this like men who have fought shoulder-to-shoulder and won."

Casually, he took Edin's arm and kept her close as the gathering made its way down the slope. He kept his hold as they entered the hall, and urged her to sit between his feet when he took his place in the high-seat. Though no words passed between them, nor even a look, it was clear to her that he didn't feel she would be safe anywhere else. There were still traces of bad feeling among the Vikings, mostly directed at her.

When she did not help with the serving, the house-thralls, Olga and especially Juliana, looked at her with bare tolerance. Did even they think she was trying to rule their jarl? If they only knew how much she wished she'd never caught his eye. Couldn't they see from where she was sitting that she was more a shackled slave than any of them?

The jarl did everything he could to make the gathering jovial. First he settled the matter with the injured men: In the eyes of Norse law, a thrall seemed to count as a superior sort of cow or horse. The jarl paid the worth of eight cows, one and one-half marks of silver, for each missing thrall.

Leif still grumbled. "Amma was due a hiding and would have got it if I'd seen her crying over that worthless Vred just one more time. If I ever catch up with those two, they can foresee no quarter from me. I'll as soon tolerate a wolf at the foldwall as a runaway. And their death will be a wolf's death, quick and bloody." He glared at Edin again.

The jarl turned the conversation smoothly and mentioned to Leif that he'd been thinking of improving the road through the difficult forest between Thorynsteading and Leif's *hof*, mayhap even placing a stone marker with both their names on it. That soothed the man's temper.

Soon after, the jarl announced, "I thought to ready my longship and make a trading voyage to Kaupang in a sennight or so. The *Blood Wing* will need a crew; I'll pay for rowing arms." He added, "Any man who can't travel with me yet wishes to send trade goods, I will gladly oblige and do business in Kaupang in his name."

A murmur of approval went around. Evidently this was a degree of generosity to which they weren't accustomed. Herjul the Stout raised his horn and said, "To our jarl, as openhanded with his neighbors as he is hard and cruel to his enemies!" The consensus of the raised drinking horns seemed to be that it was indeed a bighearted offer, big enough to make most of the men forgive him for his indiscretions concerning his Saxon bed-thrall.

Finnier Forkbear asked, "While you are in Kaupang, will you visit your father's brother, Olaf Haldanr?"

"Naturally."

"I journeyed with Olaf one season," Finnier mused. "A great warrior he was in his youth. I recall a time when he was insulted by a Swede." He smiled, looking around. "Olaf swung his axe over his head and attacked so fast the Swede was still putting on his helmet when down came the blow, clear to his gaping mouth."

Harold laughed. "Finnier, you have such a droll manner of telling a story."

The Forkbeard went on, casually, "Olaf has a daughter, does he not?"

"My cousin Hanne," the jarl said.

Finnier's voice rumbled. "A girl of noble birth,

descended from Vikings, no doubt with a nicely rounded swell of breasts and a pair of pouting lips by now."

"And a pair of knees meant to be slightly bent and widely parted!" called Jamsgar.

"It would do well for you to take such a woman to wife one of these days, Thoryn," Finnier went on as if he hadn't been interrupted. "It would set your mother's mind at rest."

"Somehow I doubt that," he muttered.

The ale flowed, and conversation became easier and easier, until at last the jarl bent a little so his lips were close to Edin's ear. "You may go to my chamber now. Don't tarry along your way."

She did as he said, but just before she reached the door, Inga loomed up before her. Edin felt the woman's boiling pride. "Soon," she warned, "I'll think of a way to get rid of you, but until that day I am content to wait."

A mild, moist dark came over the steadying. Fat spit from the meat roasting over the blazing logs in the long fire. Thoryn couldn't show his black mood. He'd paid out a lot of gold—and a lot of pride—this day. He'd been taken up like a boy before his own *Thing;* he'd had his manifest and passionate interest in a thrall discussed publicly; and his dame had shown her oddity yet again. All this he had to bear with a smile. Humility was not to his taste; in fact, his mouth was foul with it.

He glanced sidelong at Inga. She was waving away Olga's offered tray of wild apples and nuts. His eyes narrowed, as if by making his vision as slim as a knife blade he might see into her mind. What kind of woman would keep the bloody shirt in which her husband had been slain?

Don't!

Instinctively, he knew not to probe too deeply into the heart and the inner life of his mother Inga Thors-

274

daughter. There were some things in this world that could knock even a strapping Norse chieftain off his feet.

As the meal progressed, the longtables became spattered with spilled beer and milky curds of cheese. Ottar Magnusson and one of Kol Thurik's sons, a boy of eighteen winters with silky golden hair, were doing their best to make it hard for Juliana to clean up around them. So far it was only the usual play.

At last Inga rose from her place and went to her chamber. At the door she flung a look of misery and penitence at Thoryn, and made a placating gesture, then she went in.

The hour crept toward midnight. Thoryn lingered with his uninvited guests. Jamsgar and Starkad tried to coax him into talk. He saw the hard excitement in their faces; they were pleased by the news that he was taking the *Blood Wing* to Kaupang. Hauk, too. He toasted, "Here is to being off, to salt in the nostril!"

At the edge of Thoryn's attention he saw that the arch of young Juliana's eyebrows and the slant of her glances were suggesting that she was now available. It wasn't too long before she was "accidentally" tripped by Ottar. She fell to the rushes with a flurry of skirts— which Ottar and the silky-haired Thurik boy managed to lift even higher as they pretended to help her rise. Thoryn would ordinarily have said, "Find some other amusement," but tonight he said nothing. He felt mayhap it was time for Juliana to get what she was asking for. He even felt a sudden violent temptation to command it: Rape her! He'd never seen a woman rise after servicing several Norsemen in succession who seemed inclined to repeat the experience. Meanwhile, Juliana wriggled and giggled and showed her thighs— while nearer to Thoryn, Jamsgar's face flushed dark with blood. Against the pressure of his coppery glare, the girl finally straightened herself.

The gathering continued to toast one another and

275

share rough jokes until they got drunk enough not to notice when Thoryn's full attention receded. He stared at the flaming birch logs in the firepit. His anger was for all women—his mother, Juliana, the Saxon . . . aye, that one too.

The muscles in his jaw set. He felt a need for violence. Better for her if he had a raid to face tonight, or a sword fight with an enemy who would really like to kill him, or a storm at sea with his steering oar broken. Better for her if he had almost anything to face but her. For, he told himself, he preferred not to harm her. After all, she barely stood as high as his shoulder. Yet he was angry. He'd been humbled on her account. And secretly he feared there might be some truth in the notion that she was ruling him from his own bed. The wench was doing her best to make him a different man. She made him feel like a villain, a scavenger, a vulture who made his living off others' weaknesses. She spit the word *Viking* at him and made him feel uneasy with what he was. How dare she?

How dare she!

While the others drank on, he sat turning and turning his cup in his hands, glaring more and more blackly into the fire. Singing started up, then died down. At last men began to drift off to their beds or the sheepskins they'd brought. Thoryn decided he would *not* be the last one left at the board. Was he a coward, afraid to face a mere woman? By the gods, he would go to his bed and shape his bed-thrall in his arms and stable his steed in her as was his right! And just let her try to make him feel he'd ever done her or anyone else wrong! Just let her try. He'd teach her a pleasant lesson. She thought of him as a dragon; well, it was time, beyond time, for him to show her his red fangs!

He stood and fixed his gaze squarely on his chamber door. Stepping off the dais, he began to place each boot firmly as he walked toward the end of the hall.

Edin heard him come into the chamber. She lay very still, pretending sleep. She'd left the lamp burning and now heard him cross the rushes until he stood right over her. It took every ounce of will she possessed to keep her eyes closed, and for no reason she could fathom, she began to experience the acrid taste of fear.

Suddenly he ripped the covers from her. Her eyes opened to find him looming over her, his face a mask of fury. She flinched away. A sudden gust of temper seemed to overpower him, and he reached down, seizing her waist. She struck out at him in mindless self-defense.

It did less than no good: It hurt. It hurt her hands, for he was still wearing his battle shirt. Pulling against his grip was worse than useless, too, since it caused him to grasp her tighter.

The face and body he showed her belonged to a stranger, a warrior. The hands on her were not the firm-but-gentle hands that had in the past coaxed her to surrender. These hands had no intention of coaxing, and this stranger cared not at all if she surrendered. Here was the dragon that lived in him, a beast simply looking for a victim.

He fell on her. She glimpsed the glittering hardness in his eyes as she put her hands up to protect herself and locked her ankles. His mouth twisted caustically. He caught her beating fists and stretched her arms over her head. Holding her wrists hard against the headboard, he lay full-length on her, crushing her until she couldn't breathe. Finding her mouth, he took it, forced her teeth apart and thrust his tongue into her.

After an eternity, he lifted his head an inch to stare down into her face. Carefully, trying to keep her fear under control, she squeaked, "I can't breathe."

He lifted just enough for her to fill her lungs. Her breasts felt bruised by the metal mesh of his shirt. He said with cold purpose, "Open yourself."

Looking up at him, she was terrified, rapt.

"I said, open yourself! Woman, you'll either bend to my will or I'll break you with it; but either way you'll learn to obey me!"

"What have I done? Why—"

His head started down again. Once more the consolidated walls of his weight mashed her into the mattress. She squirmed in mindless panic, scraping her ribs and her belly against the metal of him. She shoved hard against his chest with her own chest and strained backward with her head, struggling to free her wrists. Now his legs forced hers apart. His boots scraped her shins as he wedged his foot, and then his whole leg, between hers. In another instant she was quartered. She tried to think of some way to stop him. He had no right to do this to her. He had no right!

Taking both her wrists into his right hand, he fumbled between his stomach and hers with his left. "Daughter of Loki," he muttered, nipping at her throat with his teeth.

Her head began to spin. "Barbarian," she whispered.

He raised his head enough to snarl down at her, "You attack with words. There are more merciful weapons, but as my mother says, you spurn to fight me with those."

"I would if I knew half the arts of violence you know."

He hunched his hips, and she discovered that he had opened his clothes. His manhood was brought to the mark. She cried out. It was dreadful. Suddenly, losing control, she sobbed, "Please, my lord, not in anger!"

Instantly his left palm covered her mouth. His shaggy blond head, his fine, bearded face, leaned over her almost casually. "Master—call me Master while you still can. Catch me now while I'm still in the mood

278

to strike cleanly."

Crying behind his hand, terrified, the sinews of her arms and thighs almost parted with his stretching, she nonetheless shook her head.

"You will! This is a Norse land. The sea round it is a Norse sea. *I* am a Norseman—and you are my thrall." Bitterness crept into his tone. "I made the mistake of treating you to a softer kind of life. I let you think I'd lost some of my toughness and fire. But I'm a Norseman, long accustomed to asserting my will by force, in my home as well as abroad."

She didn't understand. Why was he so furious?

"Why do you think I brought you to my chamber in the first place? For one reason." He nudged forward; she felt him slide into her an inch. "For one reason and one reason alone: because I'm sometimes in need of a female body."

She was helpless before the remorseless, bleak creed and history of the man. She came back to her first feeling that he and all his kind were benighted. In his eyes she was no more than a creature to be used.

But in the back of her mind, she wondered: What was this really about?

"You should never have been so beautiful," he sneered as if in answer. "It set me to craving you from the first."

Her eyes were fixed on his, his on hers.

"Will you call me Master?"

With her mouth covered by his big palm, she could only use her eyes to defy him.

"Who do you think you are! When you came here you didn't even have shoes!"

Now she tried to speak behind his hand. To her surprise, he lifted it. "How do you do it?" she asked, her voice suddenly calm. She saw him pause, and pressed on while she had the chance. "How do you change like this?"

He didn't answer.

279

Her heartbeat was strong and rapid. She hardly had breath enough to speak, yet speak she did. "How do you become this way? Who are you really, Thoryn Kirkynsson? I long for the powers of a witch they claim for me: I would become a swallow and dip beside you and study you when you think you're alone."

"At the moment you need only know I am a man who desires you and has you spread beneath him and in another moment will have you."

She grappled with her fear and, with a huge effort of will, shook her head. "It's no good, my lord; you've shown me too much of yourself. You're a Viking, yes, but you aren't a cruel man. You put on this cruelty in the same way you put on your war shirt. You decide what part is required of you, and then you play it."

"You think so?" he said in that voice of his that could be both so soft and so dangerous. An arch smile played over his lips.

Chapter 19

Edin was afraid, yet she forced herself to relax beneath the Viking. It was no easy thing. When one feared pain, it was no easy thing not to stiffen against it. Her body cried, *Clench! Strain!* But she didn't. She even tilted her thighs and hips, teasing him. "Come, come into me. You need me, and I'm here for you."

He kept her wrists pinched tightly in his hand as he sank into her abruptly. For a moment she regretted her foolishness. Alarm pounded in her throat and temples, behind her eyes. He was not a small man, not altogether nor in any of his parts. And she was not a large woman. Racked-out beneath him as she was, her body was utterly his. A fact he took full advantage of. She was the pool he plumbed to its farthest depths, the vessel into which he poured the wine of his desire. Yet after his first hard thrusts, after he saw that she was not straining away from him, his grip on her wrists slackened, and she found she could pull them free. She used that freedom to embrace him.

"Deeper," she said.

"Quiet!"

"I-I claim my due, Viking!"

"Keep quiet!"

"I won't let you cheat me of my due."

He went at her with his powerful springing muscles coiled and his feet braced against the footboard of the bed. He thrust deeply. He thrust and withdrew with such energy she had to wrap her legs around him to keep from being shoved upward in the bed. There was no longer any call to tell her to be quiet. How could she speak? Behind her eyelids she saw a swiftly winging shape. A mist seemed to fill the room, like the smokey exhalations of a mighty dragon. It wreathed her like veils, enveloped her in its flexures and cloaked all else beneath its diaphanous covering. She felt him pause, felt him quake. His arms dug beneath her to mash her even harder against him. His legs moved convulsively as if he would walk all the way into the heart of her. "Valkyrie!" he cried, his voice breaking.

"Yes," she murmured into his ear, "taking you to Asgard, the home of the gods."

He lay exhausted. After a moment she said faintly, "My lord, you're so heavy."

He groaned, but rolled, pulling her with him. She felt the blood rush back into her heart; it hammered violently.

He leaned away to inspect the imprints his shirt had left on her breasts. "Some of those will still be there come morning."

"No one will see them."

"I will."

"You need not look."

"I think I will."

His big hand, so superbly strong, came between them to cup a breast soothingly. "Did I take you, Shieldmaiden, or did you take me?" His eyes were still as bare as weather-washed stone.

She felt for the first time the elation of sexual triumph as a hectic flush flooded her cheeks. "Take you?" She smiled softly and with a tremulous hand smoothed his tumbled hair off his forehead. "When I am but a woman, a mere bed-thrall? How could I take a mighty Viking jarl?"

"Aye, that is the question."

Awakened in alarm from some dream, Thoryn turned for safety to richly recollected enjoyments. The bright half-moon outside threw a rectangle of light through the uncovered window. Edin was asleep, and he took the opportunity to study her, lying there naked, her hair to her waist. As he'd predicted, she was marked by the violence of his assault. Gently he began to cross her abused breasts with those fine tresses that gleamed in the moonlight on her marbled skin.

This is the most perfect moment of my life.

The thought slid into his mind with no accompanying warning. It came simply, the truth put into words. A delicious secret.

His idle play with her hair gradually awakened her, as he'd meant it to do. He fully expected her to recoil into the mattress. He'd used her sorely, caused her pain. She barely opened her eyes, just enough for him to be sure she knew it was him who was toying with her. And then a feeling he'd seldom — no, never — known swelled in him, for seeing him, she smiled sleepily and opened her arms.

He held his breath. The unanticipated shock was such that he froze, trying to cling to this exceptional moment. He could not remember ever feeling like weeping for gladness before. He moved into her embrace — and felt cleansed. Cleansed of self-contempt, of self-doubt. She moved herself under him, adjusted her position, and drew him into her. He slid in cautiously, ready to stop at her first wince. She didn't wince; she was uninjured. He wanted to weep again, with relief. Once he was totally encompassed by her silken flesh, he didn't move. He couldn't believe he hadn't hurt her; she was so tender, and he'd gone at her so brutally. Instead, he lay reveling in the sensations of knowing he was welcome within her . . . and in another sensation which he hardly knew how to define.

Holding himself well on his elbows, his big hands moved through her hair, stroking the silky strands. What was it, this emotion she radiated and surrounded him with? It formed a circle around them, containing them such as he'd never been contained before. It felt so . . . *safe*. This was the woman they said would trap him. Let her, if only she would hold him safe like this forever.

In the week that followed the jarl's announcement of a voyage, a spirit of adventure filled the air of the steadying, along with a frenzy of activity. He was busy most of each day victualling and outfitting his ship. Starkad Herjulson spent much of his time working in the water, tarring and testing the dragonship. Pots of boiling tar out-stank racks of drying salmon at the fjordside, women sailmakers sat day after day with crossed legs and plying fingers, and the backs of men bowed beneath heavy casks of butter, cheese, and duck eggs in brine.

With all that was going on, Edin seldom encountered the jarl during the day. When she did, always she lowered her head a little, out of deference — or was it a new shyness? He was in demand everywhere; everyone had a question for him, or something for him to inspect, but she had the satisfaction of knowing that a certain small, quick, crooked smile was hers alone.

Thus the days passed quickly. Then there were only two nights left, and then, in an eye's blink, just one.

The blue smoke from the longhouse fire rose into

284

the summer night. From the hall came the sound of rude laughter and the high wailing of a bone flute. In the jarl's chamber, Edin's cheek was pressed hard against her lord's bare chest, as if to partake of the very heat and life in him. His arms were around her, holding her gently and somewhat tenaciously. She felt a crushing need to weep, though the time for tears was long past for her. When pain was profound enough, nothing soothed it. And this man, with his muscled torso and strong loins, had brought her so much profound pain.

Earlier he'd called Inga to him in the crowded hall and said aloud so that the men and thralls should all hear, "Mark well: I go to Kaupang on the morrow. Since Inga Thorsdaughter is my mother, it is in her care that I leave the steadying. Her authority is absolute until I return."

"*When* will you return?" Edin asked him now, feeling that even to ask was in some way to plead.

"It's hard to say. I don't know how long my business will take me. And there's always the sea to consider, the possibility of storms — and pirates."

"I'll pray to Aegir for you."

"The God of the Sea? Why not to your own god?"

"I don't think he would stoop to help you, you're so wicked."

"He doesn't help the wolves that snuffle outside his sheep pens, eh?" She felt him laugh silently, felt his lips kiss the top of her head. "I'll bring you back a present. A mirror of burnished silver."

Things had changed between them. *He* had changed. Whenever they had a moment alone, even when he didn't seem to particularly desire her, he often took hold of her, her arm, or her shoulder, casually as it were. She sensed that he was as lonely and destitute inside as she often felt, and that he found some ease in touching her.

Just now he said, "It grows late; yet you are so

full of sweet mysteries, I feel I must explore you one last time before I leave."

She lifted her head and gave him a look of censure. "You are such a strange mixture of good and evil. I'm sure it's wrong, the things you do to me."

"You are, are you?"

"I used to imagine Vikings back in England."

"And what did you imagine, Shieldmaiden?"

"Roving scarecrows with scraggly fur strapped haphazardly around them."

"And what did you think when you first saw me?"

"Much worse, you were much worse. I thought: Here is a man of iron in whose judgement I count for absolutely nothing—at least nothing good. I was frightened, and rightfully so, for I believe the core of your conscience is missing."

He was silent for a moment, and she thought she'd offended him; but then he said, "But I was governed by desire in the end."

She smiled briefly, bitterly. "Not so. You desire me; but—I've been studying your people, and the classes are as carefully organized here as in England. And the number of classes is three. There are the unfree, the free, and the rulers. I am unfree; you are a ruler. And in the end, you are, as you warned me once, a man who sees what needs to be done and does it." Her eyes did not evade his.

His muscled arms caught her and turned her onto her back. His strength fired her. He said, "I swear that I'll never set you aside."

She wondered how far she should take her habit of frankness. "But someday, mayhap sooner than you think, you'll need to marry, to beget strong Viking sons and comely Viking daughters. Named children."

He drew himself up, let her go, turned onto his back, and stared up at the low ceiling. "As you say, I'll do what I must."

"I'm not blaming you," she whispered. "But I

would ask a boon." Her heart thudded. There was risk here. "When you bring home a wife—"

"*If* I bring home a wife."

"*If* you do, will you choose me a husband and let me make what home I can for him? I would like to have children. There are men along the fjord—"

He turned to her quickly. His harsh laugh rang. "Thrall-men? They are below you!"

She licked her lips and looked up at him unflinchingly. "I fear they are not."

His face went cold. He gave her a hard, humorless smile. "You have someone in mind—to plant the seeds of these children deep inside you?"

"Don't be angry. It's only that you're going away, and I have no way to know what my fate will be while you're gone, or even after you return. You may find you're indifferent to me."

He let the silence grow uncomfortable before saying, "You aren't without value, you know, even without your maidenhead. I could still sell you for a goodly profit in any market."

"I wouldn't dare ask you not to do that except I feel you harbor some affection for me; you've shown me some kindness."

"Some!" He looked cruel. "I've *favored* you. Given you gifts! Fed you tidbits and sweet yellow wine! And now I find I've nourished a snake."

"Please try to understand! It isn't that I'm ungrateful; it's only that I need to feel *safe*."

Inga had already made hints that if, in the jarl's absence, Edin presumed an inch above her place, she would feel the whip. She didn't tell him this, she still had some pride left. But her voice dropped to a mere breath. "I desperately need to feel safe."

His jaw visibly unclenched. "You're safe with me." His voice was almost tender. "I've sworn never to set you aside, haven't I? I will grant you a boon, not the one you asked, which is preposterous, but this:

287

The children I give you will be free. Your sons will grow up to use axes and shields, to practice sword-swinging and swimming, to sail the seas."

"Vikings?" she said, disbelieving. "No! I would rather they did dirty work, carried burdens, lugged firewood, dunged fields—anything rather than be Vikings!"

He eyed her narrowly. "They will be proud Norsemen, their father's sons. And your daughters will be the wives of Norsemen, with their own households to manage. They will carry keys and hold purse strings; they will provide food for their families, and clothing, while their men must be gone."

"No." She lay motionless, stupefied with astonishment and suffering, with an agony that was simple but deep.

"Aye." He drove the agony deeper still, speaking almost tenderly, as if he were granting her a great honor. "And as you see them grow, you'll know I was right to gift them with pride. But you, Shield-maiden"—his tone roughened—"you have too much pride already. Forget this foolish idea—marry you to a thrall! You'll always be mine. You'll lay with no man ever but me, and mother no children but mine."

The sun was just coming over the tops of the mountains, silvering the dew. Edin stood on the lookout bluff over the cobalt blue fjord. She reached outside her cloak to shade her face against the dawn's level rays.

Below her floated the *Blood Wing*, her gunwales deep in the water, for she was unnaturally laden with reindeer hides, bearskins, otterskins, wool, whalebone and whale oil, sea ivory, falcons and hawks, two sixty-ell marine cables, one made from walrus hide, the other from sealskin, herrings, salt, twelve rough-finished axe handles threaded on a stave of pine, ten measures of bird feathers for pillows, all for selling in the Kaupang market. Also aboard were dried meat, barley bread, casks of ale and cheese and fish and such for the crew.

Inga was standing on the dock as the jarl supervised the last minute preparations. She looked small beside her splendid son. Now and again she said something, made a suggestion or admonished him about this or that, as mothers will. Edin could almost imagine her words: *Have you got your woolen shirt on, son? The winds are bitter around the coast, and it would be too bad for you to take a cold.*

He answered her with the barest trace of a smile.

The air was full of noise and excitement. Tall, good-looking men with rugged features, dressed in brilliant-hued tunics, and women with pinched expressions lined the shore to say good-bye to their sons and lovers. Puckish boys, mostly knees and knuckles and scabs, raced about, too full of excitement to stay still. Young Hrut Beornwoldsson stood stiff, the down on his chin still not thick enough to cover the resentment and envy on his face. His look was so telling that even Edin could feel the pounding in his throat, the readiness of his body for action, for hurrying off. He wanted to be a man so badly.

Sweyn was there, too, his big blue eyes blazing in his wan face.

Even the thralls had dropped their work to see the *Blood Wing* off. Men and women, elders and children, vanquishers and vanquished, masters and slaves—all were gathered.

Those Vikings going with the jarl made a fine appearance in their polished and shining helmets and war shirts. From this distance Edin couldn't see that they were rather sullen: The night before had been drawn out with reminiscence; several barrels had been tapped to celebrate past vices. As they boarded the ship, the dragon bent her wooden, champing head. Studded weaponry gleamed everywhere—swords and axes, their wide slicing edges opulently etched. Even though this was not a plundering party, no Viking would ever set off without all the weapons he could carry. That would be a thing of shame. Consequently, the party looked formidable. It was necessary, mayhap, for as Edin understood it, a single longship heading for market made a vulnerable target, and the southwest coast of Norway swarmed with pirates. It seemed Vikings, given the chance, even attacked one another. Brute violence backed with arms lorded everywhere in this land. They had a saying: "Seek not to know your fate—but don't travel without your sword, either."

The jarl wore a fitted tunic of rich purple over his black trousers, which were cross-gartered to the knee. His cloak was black, lined with more purple. Truly Edin had never seen a more handsome man, none taller, blonder, more bronzed. Just to look at him caused a strand of delight to thread its way down her thighs.

He touched his mother's shoulder as she said something more, and this time he smiled and nodded gently. He answered her. Was it something prosaic as *Make sure Snorri gets the firewood stacked in cords;* or was it something more laden with affection? Inga's obvious pleasure gave witness to the latter; she seemed to light up like a burning lampwick.

Edin felt betrayed. While she stood drinking her fill of him with her eyes, he seemed to have all but forgotten his lowly bed-thrall, until suddenly—what was it? The gust of chill breeze that caused her cloak to billow and show her new royal blue dress? Or mayhap the sun catching on the wide silver torque around her throat, and the two new silver bands on her wrists? Whatever it was, suddenly something seemed to catch his eye; he seemed to wake up to her presence, like a hunting dog who suddenly smells a deer on the wind.

He lifted his head, and not for a single instant did his eyes sweep around the mountain summits which everywhere peered down; no, they came straight to her — and her heart stood still with an extravagant anguish the likes of which she'd never known before.

He didn't wave or shake an axe above his shoulder or by any other sign speak to her. He only looked his fill. Mayhap he was remembering her request again — or mayhap the last thing she'd said to him this morning. Either could be the cause of those thunderclouds on his forehead.

There was something else in his gaze, however. His grey eyes seemed to plunge deep into her very heart. It was a gaze that held her enthralled, held her immobile in the sparkling air, sustained.

Last night this barbarian had wrung everything he'd wanted from her. Yes, even after all he'd said, and the resolves she'd secretly made in response, she'd still given him whatever he wanted. And once more this morning she'd been awakened and brought to that transcendent moment when everything inside her turned to light, when time and thralldom didn't exist.

Afterward, he'd been amused when she forced herself to be a blank. "He rises early who wants to win another's wealth," he murmured with a wolf's smile.

"You ravish me and then make a joke of it."

"You like me to ravish you. It lets you pretend that you're not willing and yet still have what you want."

Was it true? Was there a paradox of freedom in slavery?

He'd then given her the new dress and the wrist bracelets and asked her if she had no word of farewell for him. That was when she'd said, "Only that you must not be surprised if I'm not here when you return."

He hadn't grown angry, but only answered, as if to a fretful child, "You'll be here till Odin decides to crush the world in his two strong hands."

Now for a moment more he stood like a salt pillar looking up at where she stood in the blue morning sky, mayhap waiting for her to give in and bid him the farewell he wanted. She braced herself not to do it, to withhold at least that much from him.

The men had noticed. Jamsgar's eyes glowed with a strange glare. His gold arm bracelet caught a fragment of sun and sent it flashing into Edin's face. Ottar Magnusson said something with dramatically mimed impatience: *Are you ready, Jarl? Will you keep the day waiting forever?* And so at last he turned and walked toward the *Blood Wing*.

She'd done it! She'd been strong enough to deny him. A bitter triumph unfurled like a flag in her heart.

He took his place high on the foredeck, where all the men could see him. He seemed unaware of the effect of his strong presence. He was still carrying his helmet; his tawny hair flew in the sharpening breeze. Big as he was, there was a grace and dignity about him.

Rolf stood just below him in a grey woollen tunic. He shouted so that even Edin could hear him loud and clear. "Loose the mooring lines!" Then, "Oars!"

For a moment, Edin hugged herself. They were going; they were actually going. The lean, low-hulled dragonship, manned by Vikings of reckless courage and invincible savagery, pulled away from the strand.

He was going, taking his desire, his fascination, with him. The movement of the ship disturbed a flock of sea birds that nested beneath the bluff. They fluttered up. Edin's heart raced. The birds repeated their cries over and over; the air around her seemed swollen with sound. And at the very last moment she lifted her hand.

She saw the slow, reluctant smile tugging at the corner of his mouth. Her triumph faded, to be replaced by something less proud.

They shoved off, a brilliant band venturing out from their hearths as Vikings always had, always in search of the unknown beyond the horizon. How far they were going, Edin could only try to guess. Distances seemed to be nothing to them. Aboard ship, they would be uncomfortable, wet, and close, with only the sea to look at and little to amuse them. But they were Vikings, to whom inconveniences were all part of a man's work, to whom being wet and cold were not worth mentioning. And as far as danger went — they enjoyed danger.

Edin swallowed back an aching lump in her throat as the oarsmen heaved strongly, slowly, pulling on the water, pushing the ship around the jetty, out into the fjord. The sail was hoisted. The *Blood Wing* was not a longship to wait about when she felt the breeze in her rigging. She began to skim the blue water as if blood pulsed in her tarry timbers, as if she meant to go on and on over the sea until she stabled under the golden walls of some distant, magic land. She sped past the waterfalls toward the mouth of the fjord, farther and farther, until Edin couldn't make out the jarl's face anymore. Soon the red-striped sail also blurred and then disappeared beyond the outer headlands.

And it was then, while the *Blood Wing* turned east into the *skjaegard* — the thousands upon thousands of islands that formed a sort of fence between the rocky, terraced strandflat and the sea — that Edin's love first struck her. Then, when the jarl had disappeared from her horizon and she faced the immediate future without him. Then, at that moment, she

293

finally understood.

She looked about her, and all she saw were gorges and plateaux and a fjord and clouds scudding across a sky speckled with sea birds. She seemed to hear the voice of the great mountains, the immense forests. Nothing she wanted mattered in this foreign world, and that was the way things would stay. But even worse, now she was alone here. More alone than she'd ever been. There was nothing anyone would do for her now except what she could do for herself. She hadn't realized how dependent upon the jarl's protection she'd become, or how deeply she'd fallen under the spell of his rough care.

She hadn't realized. She hadn't realized.

Tears spilled down her cheeks. She was at last out of the forced courage that had kept her dry-eyed. Now she wept, beyond the reach, beyond the power of her Viking's soothing iron hands. "Oh, God!" A pure bolt of love shot through her for that man who deserved much less.

Edin made her face a mask so that no one would know what she was feeling as she trudged down to the longhouse. She suspected that without the jarl's protection there would be changes in her station; yet even she was surprised at how immediately these came, for no sooner did she step inside than Inga confronted her. The hall was dark after the brilliance of the sunrise, but there was enough light for Edin to judge her mistress's mood. Hate hung about her like smoke from a fire.

Oozing bitter satisfaction, she said, "Take off that ridiculous finery and put on clothing suitable for thrall work. And do something about that hair, or I swear to the gods I'll cut it to within an inch of your scalp. Where are you going?"

"To change."

"You will *not* go into my son's chamber again! You'll sleep out here, as befits you, and hope that I

294

don't decide to put you out in the byre-loft with the thrall-men!"

Edin wisely kept her eyes down. The jarl had hinted that he'd left words with his mother to protect her in his absence. But as she'd feared, Inga would do as she pleased. Two Vikings had been left behind to watch over the steading, Fafnir Danrsson and Eric No-breeches. They looked at one another but did not interfere from where they sat at the tables. Neither man came to her aid. The message was clear that as far as they were concerned, the jarl had left his mother in charge.

From Olga and Juliana, Edin sensed a feeling against her, evident in whiffs and traces. Olga went on tending the fire for them, and Dessa, though she gave Edin a sympathetic look, went on pouring milk.

Something about Inga had always raised the fine hairs on Edin's arms. The woman seemed to have an edge in her mind, an edge that she stood back from most of the time, but occasionally she seemed to totter at the brink of . . . *what* Edin didn't know, and didn't want to know.

She said in a careful voice, "But my clothing is all in the jarl's chamber. If you will let me go in there but once more, just to leave this gown and jewelry and to change. . . ."

Her reasonableness did nothing to improve Inga's temper. Nevertheless, she was allowed to enter the Viking's chamber one last time. Not trusting Inga's patience, she didn't idle, but changed immediately. She folded the blue gown and put it in his clothes chest, and donned a much plainer dress he'd given her for work. She found his ornate comb on the washstand and wielded it quickly, then braided her hair like a man's into two long plaits that hung heavily over her shoulders to her waist. She went to the door, then paused, and looked back at the bed.

Impulsively, she crossed to it, lifted the Viking's pillow and buried her face in it, inhaling his scent. Inga burst in at that instant and found her in that purely personal attitude. She gave Edin a look that made her feel corrupt. "You . . . *Saxon!*" she hissed. "You're a lowly race, cunning and treacherous by nature!" She grabbed the pillow away. "You should be whipped, just to show you your place once and for all."

Edin stood very still, her neck prickling. Inga shoved her toward the door.

She put Edin to work immediately, not at cooking or cleaning or weaving, but outside the longhouse, in the fields, where Edin had never worked before in her life. Inga left her in Blackhair's care with the warning, "He has my permission to whale you black and blue if he ever once catches you sluffing."

Chapter 20

Blackhair stood contemplating Edin long after Inga left them alone. She told herself that at least by working outside she wouldn't be under Inga's constant, disapproving eye, nor subject to her jabbing wooden spoon.

But before the day was over, she knew that Blackhair was as determined to make her suffer as Inga was.

The hay in a steep pasture had grown tall, and she was taken up to help cut it. She was introduced to the boss of the job, Yngvarr, a broad-shouldered man with a low hairline. There was snickering among the other thralls. Edin stared straight ahead, solemn and withdrawn. Blackhair handed her a scythe. She hardly knew how to hold it. There was more laughter as she started to work. She felt awkward and knew she was creating amusement for the others. But by watching the men, she slowly taught herself how to swing the heavy tool.

It seemed she was a special case: No other woman was expected to cut hay. Their job was to gather it and drape it on racks to dry. Edin's hands soon blistered, and then the blisters broke. And her back screamed. And screamed.

During rest periods she was a target for thrall wit. She took a drink from the common skin, then she went off by herself, not wanting her weeping hands, which were so painful, to be discovered and laughed over. The men exchanged glances and nudged one another where they rested; the women tittered. She heard scraps of their wit, as she was meant to do:

"Looks like 'my lady' is a bit weary."

"Some women are more used to lying on their backs then standing on their own two feet."

"Aw now, be fair. I bet she can handle a man on her feet almost as well as on her back."

"I know what's making her tired. It's them heavy braids. Mistress ought to've lopped them ugly things off."

The hours seemed endless, and nearly were. She came down through the gloaming light with the other unmarried thralls who ate in the longhouse. She sat stooped over her meal, uninterested in eating it. The hall seemed unnaturally quiet with only two Vikings, and Sweyn the Cripple, in attendance. Fire flicker danced upon the posts, while deep shadows lay in the nooks and corners. The jarl's chair with its carved arms and back stood empty. Arneld tried to talk to Edin, but she answered him in monosyllables, and finally he went away. No one else spoke to her, and when she became aware that the other thralls had risen, she made a belated attempt to eat. She was having some trouble with the spoon, struggling not to show her hands, and had managed only one mouthful when Inga came to take her wooden bowl away.

A look of loathing passed across the woman's face. "Do you expect to be fed—in bed mayhap? My son isn't here now. You'd best learn to handle a spoon on your own." Edin said nothing. She wasn't particularly hungry, but she drank down her bowl of creamy milk before Inga could take that, too. She knew she was going to need her strength.

The next morning she showed up in the high field before dawn with her hands wrapped with rags Dessa had given her. The sun rose swiftly, hitting her eyes like a stab. The day was going to be hotter than usual.

By afternoon the rags wrapping her hands had become bloodied. She forgot to hide the fact, forgot everything but the rhythm of her swinging scythe. She didn't even notice that sometime during that day the field thralls had stopped taunting her.

The third day she arrived with hands so swollen she could hardly grasp the scythe handle. None of the thralls spoke, not to her, not to one another. The silence in the field felt thunderous. She worked as best she could, considering her back would hardly bend. She'd never been able to keep up with the men cutters, but now they got far, far ahead of her. At last, Yngvarr threw his scythe down and strode back to where she was swinging the shard of bright light that was the scythe's blade in short, awkward jerks, hardly cutting anything, yet maintaining a sort of awful, silent rhythm. He took hold of the tool. In a daze, she tried to keep it; he had to wrest it from her. She stood stooped, her head hanging, looking at his worn boots. Her sluggish mind asked, *What now?*

"Ingunn!" he called. His wife, a flaxon-haired young woman, hurried over. At a gesture from him, she unwrapped the stained rags around Edin's hands. The other thralls wordlessly gathered. For a long moment no one spoke. Then one of the men said, "I'll get that Blackhair up here."

Ingunn and the other women led Edin to the grassy place where they sat during their rest periods. Blackhair arrived, and there was an argument. Edin belatedly tried to follow it, and heard Yngvarr say, "The mistress won't always be in charge!" He had his low forehead ducked like a knuckled fighter about to give a punch. "Don't be a fool, you! When the master returns and finds her hands ruined, do you think it'll be the mistress who takes the blame?"

Blackhair glared down at her. Her palms lay open in her lap, a testament to his mismanagement. Even she was a little appalled by the sight of them. His tongue slid out from between his lips and in again with reptilian swiftness. "Put her to work gathering, then!" he said at last. "But work she will! No sluffing!" He waggled his finger and stomped off down the hill.

Ingunn produced a salve and clean rags from her cot, which was close by. The others went back to work. "Thank you," Edin murmured.

Ingunn said grudgingly, "Well, if you'd griped, we none of us would've cared how bad off you got. But I'd as soon see a weakling child put out to die as watch you try to swing that scythe another minute."

They joined the women in gathering. It was relatively easy on her hands to simply scoop the cut hay up into her arms, but it was hard on her back.

After a few days in the sun, the dried hay was loaded into wagons. The work was arduous and hot; even the strong thrall-men became exhausted, but everyone went on working. Edin never stopped a minute unless everyone stopped. There were no more taunts, but there was no friendly camaraderie, either. She was out of place there, and no one seemed able to forget it. Or forgive it.

When the last cartload of hay was sent down to the byre-loft, Yngvarr said, "Blackhair doesn't need to know we're done, not for an hour or so, anyway." He brought out a set of boxwood panpipes. Ingunn brought her little child up to the field. As her father piped, the child danced. Edin smiled. The little one toddled from person to person as they lay sprawled this way and that the grass, taking their ease and staring up at the bright, wind swept, blue sky.

300

When she came to Edin, she tottered, then fell. Her tiny face puckered to cry. Edin quickly caught her up and bounced her on her knee, and began to sing with Yngvarr's piping. The child grinned hugely, then plopped her fingers into her mouth and lay in Edin's arms, rapt.

Ingunn herself drew near, but didn't take the child away from her. "She's beautiful," Edin said, gazing down at the innocent face.

"She can be a handful."

"I wanted children," Edin said, in a moment of weary self-pity.

"You'll have them. The jarl . . ." Ingunn was clearly embarrassed. "Well."

"He says my children will be Vikings."

"Then, they'll be masters."

"They'll be marauders, savages. I couldn't bear that."

"But what can you do about it?"

Edin looked up at the mountains.

"No. They would kill you for sure."

"Vred and Amma made it."

Ingunn grew intense. "Listen, you, don't even think it. There's others besides yourself would suffer."

It began to seem to Edin that all her life before had not been so long as each day was now. Only a sennight had passed since the jarl had gone, yet it seemed a year. As if the changes in her circumstances and Inga's hatred and Blackhair's malice weren't enough for her to cope with, now Sweyn had begun to openly single her out with his disfocused gaze and his harping criticisms. He'd become a constantly drunk, ever-complaining presence in the hall, and nothing she did was beyond his vitriol, right down to the way she walked and sat and

301

looked.

This morning, outside the longhouse, the field thralls hung close together while Blackhair issued them their orders. As each was told what to do, he or she turned without comment and went to do it. The group got smaller and smaller, until only Edin was left. She felt a little queasy this morning and was hoping that her next task would be less arduous than the hay cutting. Just then, Sweyn came out. He leaned his good arm on a four-wheeled cart that was standing without its horse near the byre. Blackhair said to Edin, "This is bath day. You can fill the tubs, and keep them filled."

Smug, he went off to supervise the herring harvest. As Edin started for the bathhouse, Sweyn stepped away from the cart and blocked her path.

He'd lost weight, yet his body was still big-boned and imposing when it was leaning over someone much smaller. He stared down at Edin ominously. His battle-axe hung from his belt—on his right side where his useless arm was bound to his waist.

As he continued to stare down at her, irritation welled up in Edin. At last she tried to go around him. He stopped her with a rough blow with the butt of his left hand to her shoulder, which made her throw up her arms and reel backward.

He said, "How do you like being moved down the bench?" He smiled heartily; his yellow teeth showed in his beard.

Lately she'd been doing her best to make herself small, to become unnoticed, and all it had gotten her was abuse heaped atop abuse. She'd suddenly had enough of subservience. In a flash, she decided what her attitude must be in the future. She drew herself up and said, "I like it no more than you, Cripple."

He struck her face so quickly that she had no time to catch herself. She stumbled back, lost her

302

balance, and fell to the ground. His eyes were grim as a snake's. But even then, sprawled on her back looking up at him, a sense of calm and control increased in her. She was so angry she felt as if she could walk into spears. She pushed her temerity as far as it would go. "I do wish we bench-enders got more meat and less fish and cabbage. I never cared much for fish. Do you, Cripple?"

As soon as she had the words out, she saw the foam at the corners of his mouth and a new white-ness in his face. His lips spread in a mad grin. She rolled away and got to her knees, a movement that flooded her with nausea.

He loomed over her, and she realized he was murmuring. "What a spring it was," he said, "the byres burning and the churches flaring . . . folk running! The women trying to conceal the craving between their thighs! Aye, what a season—until a Saxon witch fell at my feet. . . ."

He straightened, became cunning, and even wag-gled his eyebrows. "So you're to carry water to the bathhouse today. I hope the work won't be too hard for you."

She started to get to her feet and, by dint of extraordinary effort, succeeded. She tried not to give any sign of the nausea she felt, and got away from him as quickly as she could, before she gave herself away and was further humiliated. But as soon as she was out of his sight, she dropped to her knees and wretched.

The work was too hard for her. Each Saturday was set aside for everyone on the steading to bathe. In a small hut was the bathhouse. The Vikings were a clean breed. They took care to wash before meals and to change their clothes often. Once a sennight a fire was built in the bathhouse, caul-drons of water were heated, and everybody, in order of rank, scrubbed from top to bottom. The tubs had to be filled and kept up to level all day.

Each bucket of water Edin drew was a trial. Her hands were hardly healed, and her back was still sore from the hay cutting. Bearing a heavy yoke with a full bucket swinging from either end did her no good.

The sun never shone that day, and at the spring where she drew her water, the gnats were out, those extremely small black gnats whose bite was so much larger than their bodies. By afternoon she welcomed a spitting rain that made them take cover. It didn't matter to her if she got wetter. Her skirts were already heavy with sloshed water from the buckets, and her feet were soaked. And her head ached from the blow Sweyn had delivered to her cheek.

She complained to no one, however, not even when Fafnir Danrsson stepped between her and the bathhouse door, directed his long nose and fixed his stare down at her face. She'd never been quite so close to him before, and now saw that his eyes were a grey-sapphire, or a sapphire-grey — an indefinite, ambiguous color, like the shade of distant mountains. He blinked them slowly and said, "What happened to you?"

The pride that had reared up in her earlier, and the anger, had not diminished. Somewhere during that day the love she'd been feeling so helplessly had become rage. She asked, *Was no word or sign at all left to protect me from being cast down into this position of drudge? I gave that Viking everything — and this is my return!*

"Nothing happened to me," she said to Fafnir. The rain kept up a slow-running tapping on the thatched roof of the bathhouse. The pale silky beard covering Fafnir's chest looked as soft as duck fluff. A few drops of rain jeweled it. Beneath it, his jaws chewed indecisively, until Edin went past him with her burden. She felt his grey-sapphire glance, but got the distinct feeling that he didn't really want to know the answer to his question.

All day she carried that wooden yoke from which hung those two big buckets, moving from stream to bathhouse in a ceaseless round. She closed herself up, shut herself against the world. Arneld was one of the last bathers. Though most of the thralls had seen the bruise on her face, only Arneld asked about it: "Who did that, my lady?"

She tried to center her gaze on him, and make it catch, but she was so exhausted her eyes couldn't seem to hold steady. She said in a monotone, "You mustn't call me that anymore. I'm just Edin now."

"There's white all around your mouth, and you winced when you set the buckets down."

Once more she tried to catch him with her gaze, and once more, curiously, she couldn't. "I'm weary."

"You aren't strong enough for that job."

His concern touched her. She dredged up a little smile and tugged his sleeve. "We must each do what we're told."

"Who hit you?"

She shook her head sadly. "I bumped into a door." She knew he wouldn't believe that, but she couldn't tell him the shameful truth. She'd had enough of shame. More than enough of shame.

Inga was ladling out the night's cabbage soup for the thralls when Edin went into the longhouse. She was last in line and so got mostly broth in her bowl. She sat bowed over it, too tired to eat, while Inga threatened Juliana with a beating: "He has no business here except that you encourage him. He's an idle, devilish boy—and you're a slut!"

They had to be discussing Hrut Beornwoldsson.

Juliana gave her mistress a meek answer and looked down humbly enough until she was dismissed, freeing Inga to turn her temper on Edin. She said in her hardest tone, "Come on, now, stop your pretending. Olga is waiting to clean up and there you sit, hanging your head as if you're half-dead."

Edin dipped her slice of dry black barley bread into the thin broth. It hurt her cheekbone to eat.

The night beside the brooding forested slopes of Dainjerfjord was damp and cold. Over Thoryn-steading a great silence had fallen. The hall was quiet. Scents of woodsmoke and roasted mutton hung heavily in the air. Edin walked toward her bed while the two Vikings sat finishing a chess game. Her movements were wooden, guarding against pain, but she kept her back straight and managed not to wince or grimace as she passed them.

In her sheepskin, she listened without hearing as Erik heckled Fafnir. She spread her hand over her bruised cheek. With luck, it would be less painful tomorrow. She was glad she had no mirror; she'd rather not see herself just now.

Exhausted as she was, sleep didn't come. She wondered if Sweyn was still sitting up over his ale cup as usual. She'd insulted him, knowing full well that a Viking wouldn't put up with cuts of any kind, especially not from a thrall. But he'd goaded her to it, hoping for an excuse to hurt her.

How could he blame her for his lameness? It was, as her captors would say, "a rune hard to read." Was it only that he was mean-minded and vicious? Or could it be that he felt as disoriented as she did, without any clear sense of himself anymore, and that he was frightened?

Sweyn the Berserk had probably thought of nothing but looting villages and possessing females. He'd no doubt regarded it as a most profitable, a most exciting, way of life. But now, what was it like to be Sweyn the Cripple? What did a man seemingly made out of pure pugnacity and love for glory—mingled with a more fundamental relish for plunder—do when he could no longer participate in the far and bloody raids of his comrades, when his jarl sailed off without him, when it seemed his very gods had turned against him? What did he feel when he was faced with his weaker and more cowardly side and found it soft and squeamish?

For the first time Edin considered Sweyn the Man—and discovered that she had much in common with him. For instance, both, in the despairing, heartless flicker of those few hours at Fairhope Manor, had lost their identities. She supposed that for a long time afterward his mind, like hers, had moved sluggishly. He must have been as dazed and shocked as she'd been. And now they were both trying to find a way to survive as people they had never thought to be.

And both of them were dependent in this upon the jarl, clinging to him as to an island in a stormy ocean, hoping he could in some way fulfill them, restore them, make them whole again. The same man who had cut them down was their only hope—that great blond barbarian!

He'd taken everything from Edin, yet her heart had somehow twisted itself to love him. The fact of her love kept splintering her picture of him like a rock thrown on a sheet of water. How could she love such a man? She didn't know. But the knowledge kept coming at her with an overwhelming jolt. She'd lost her heart to a Viking along with everything else. And she knew she would never fall back from that love, never try, never wish to, even though he kept her a slave all her days, even though he made her children into his own image, so that she would both love and despise them as much as she loved and despised him. And the conflict would continue to twist her heart until one day . . . might she too be capable of stabbing a man in his sleep?

Sweyn shook his long thick mane. He thought he was the last man up. He preferred it when he was alone in the hall. When the others were about, he took no part in their talk, but kept his head lowered, kept his eyes on his plate or his cup, kept his face blank.

Suddenly a voice came from behind him. "So, Sweyn, you fight daringly against a thrall-girl."

He turned to see Fafnir Danrsson. "The witch insulted me. I taught her a lesson."

"She belongs to the jarl, to whom I'm sworn. It would ill-befit a warrior to have to take a cripple into the woods and put him down like an old thrall not worth his keep. Don't teach the girl any more lessons, Sweyn."

Sweyn turned back to his ale cup, laughing. He took a draught and gained courage to answer Fafnir back, but when he turned, the man was gone. Sweyn turned back to his cup with an uprush of feeling, the misery of unexpected and unbroken loneliness. For an instant, a fraction of an instant, his stern expression cracked.

Another sennight and a day passed. Yesterday Blackhair had made Edin carry the water for the baths again. She was getting stronger, yet the work he and Inga put her to was hard. Today the recurring nausea was bothering her again, and she stirred her first-meal porridge listlessly. She studied the other thralls eating their oatmeal and wondered how soon it would be before she looked as hard and stringy as they did, before her face took on that beggared and inward expression so many of them wore?

Had the serfs of Fair Hope been so dispirited? Though that old life was growing more and more distant, she didn't think so. There had been laugh-

308

ter. As their mistress, she'd felt affection from them, not this fear Inga commanded.

She looked about her at the hall. Inga was strict and worked herself and everyone for long hours, yet as a housekeeper, she lacked a knack for creating comfort. For instance, the rushes on the floor had needed changing since Edin's arrival. Beneath the tables they were thin, and the underlayer of sand had been scuffed away so that often tired feet rested directly on the hard, cold underfloor of stone. The food they all ate was filling and nourishing, yet it was monotonous—cabbage soup, meat stew, porridge—and mostly tasteless, for Inga had no sense of the use of flavorsome herbs. And how much more satisfactory would things run if the thralls were made happier, given praise when their work was well done, rewarded with honest appreciation, and coaxed more with kindness than with threats?

She was the last to leave the table but for Sweyn and Fafnir Danrsson. Fafnir was carving a piece of wood into an animal head. He was respected as something of an artist with wood. As Edin got up wearily, Sweyn called her name. "Clear my bowl away," he said.

Inga had just gone to the dairy. The kitchen thralls were already clearing the table, but Sweyn wanted to humiliate her again. Taking into account her nausea and low spirits, she didn't consider refusing worthwhile.

She gathered his porridge bowl and milk cup and the scattered shells of his boiled egg. He lifted up his useless arm and thumped it on the board. She cleaned around it until he said, "Look at me!" Her eyes lighted on his yellow hair, avoiding his face. "I used to be a warrior, woman—you may remember. Shall I ever sail over the foam and shake an axe with this hand again, do you think?"

She studied the way his food and drink had

stained the untrimmed fringe of his mustache, and finally said, "If you ever lift a horn spoon with it, it will be a miracle. It looks to me, Cripple, as if your axe days are over."

The words fell into the high shadowy room as stones fall into a bottomless lake, sinking without a ripple. He seemed stunned; his smile shifted a few notches. Olga giggled nervously. The fire crackled. Sweyn's blue eyes burned dully with the reflected glow of the blaze. Edin turned away before he could gather his wits, before the muscles of his jaw could knot and he could decide to retaliate.

She grabbed her cloak and went out, giving a good margin to Eric, who was axe-throwing on the green. He'd set up a cord, tied it tight between two sticks, stepped back ten paces, and now was aiming his axe to try to sever the cord in the center.

Fafnir came out a moment after Edin and was hailed to compete with Eric. Edin soon realized that he was following her, however. He caught up with her in the byre-yard and seized her arm to stop her.

His long face was knotted like a club. He said hotly, "You have the gall of the gods themselves. That was no way to answer a warrior. First you put a dagger into Ragnarr's throat, and now a knitting needle into Sweyn's heart."

"Mayhap you should do the same!" she answered back—unwisely, for she didn't know Fafnir well and couldn't say how he would react. He always seemed friendly enough to others of his kind. She'd heard that he'd had a wife and children in his youth, but that they'd died in a fire. Nonetheless, he was a Viking, raised in the cruel North; she could see the bone handle of his little bright-edged carving knife protruding from his belt, and for all she knew, she could be doomed this instant.

Her answer to him—as unpremeditated as the one she'd given Sweyn—seemed to startle him, and she took advantage of his hesitation.

"You all treat him as if he can do nothing now." Her voice was so tight it broke. "He has another arm, does he not—and blood beating through his veins? He's not dead, is he? But none of you encourage him. You all make him feel he stopped living the night he lost his axe arm."

"He broke his oath to the jarl."

"For which the jarl punished him severely. But you take it upon yourselves to go on punishing him—and I don't for a minute believe it's for oath breaking. It's because he's become something you all know you could become, too. A cripple. You silently blame him for reminding you that next time it could be you who comes home with no arm or no hand or no foot. So you push him to the end of the bench, and—far worse than anything else—you show him contempt."

Fafnir's mouth dropped open. No doubt he was used to thralls replying to him with a mere nod or shake of the head. He seemed shocked to the point of stammering. "Well . . . what would you have us do, wench? Challenge him?"

"*Yes! Challenge* him! Make him use the good arm he has. I once knew of a boy who as a babe fell into a fire that withered his right arm, but by the turn of the next year he could use the left amazingly. He was a Saxon, however; there's every chance a mere Viking couldn't do as well."

"Have a caution, thrall."

She felt her heart give a quick beat, felt her whole body tense with a wish to be gone, yet she continued. "You Norse have a saying: 'Be a friend to your friends and a foe to your foes.' But sometimes it needs to look as if one is being a foe in order to be a friend."

He watched her from beneath lowered eyelids. "He has no place here anymore. He eats the jarl's meat, yet he can never be a warrior again."

"It looks that way; his strength seems to have deserted him, the way he walks around with his head down and his back sagging. His mind acts as though it's slept through a season and can't quite decide what's changed. But then, it's hard to say what a man can do. With so many warriors, does Dainjerfjord really need another? There must be other occupations of honor."

He looked skeptical. "For a cripple?"

"A lame man can sit a horse. A man without hands can herd goats. A deaf man can build a house. Only a corpse is completely useless." She could feel her anger tightening her throat again. "At the feast I saw a widow with a son on the brink of manhood, a son she can't manage. Every other day he's down here trying to lift Juliana's skirts. And Juliana's skirts being so easily lifted, the boy is bound to be in for trouble when Jamsgar Copper-eye returns. He thinks of the girl as his own, you know. There's already been thunder between them over her. A boy like that needs a man's guidance, and no doubt Gunnhild's steadying needs work."

"Beornwold's widow," he said thoughtfully, at the same time watching her from beneath the protection of those motionless, lowered eyelids. "Freyaholf is in disrepair. Hmmm. . . . It's good for a boy to have a man to guide him. So you think Sweyn should work for Gunnhild?"

Edin shrugged. "Her or someone like her. It seems you Vikings have an uncommon number of widows struggling to survive in your land." She stood with her hands quiet at her sides now. "Tell me, what was the Cripple doing when you came out here after me?"

"He'd thrown himself down on his sheepskin again and lay staring at the wall."

She nodded; this was Sweyn's usual way of passing his days, by slumbering off his drunkenness of the night before in his little cell of a chamber. "He needs to see more daylight," she said. "His skin is grave-pale. A friend would get him out of the hall—even if he had to infuriate him to do it."

The man turned his head half away, though his sapphire-grey eyes remained on her. There came and went a fleeting, almost imperceptible smile on his lips. "Do you manage the jarl this way?"

A cold fist clutched at her queasy stomach and squeezed it hard. "The jarl is managed by no one."

Chapter 21

Fafnir and Eric began to prick and goad the Cripple to do something about himself. Nothing changed until toward the end of the next sennight. There came a day of such heat that the two Vikings said they were going down to the fjord to swim. Fafnir asked Sweyn if he would join them. "You used to be able to swim across the fjord and back."

Sweyn's look was ugly. He watched his former companions leave the hall with eyes that seemed to promise retribution.

As Edin stepped out of the longhouse after the first meal, the heat closed like a sweaty palm around her. The light was brilliant. Squinting, she saw Sweyn directing Laag, the stable thrall, in setting a pine log into the ground in the stackyard. When Laag was finished, the log stump stood at man height.

At first Sweyn only looked at it, and wiped his nose on his sleeve, then he went into the longhouse. Edin was working nearby and so saw him reappear in a few minutes with his war shirt and battle-axe. He seemed to droop under the weight of his old trappings, and held his flashing axehead awkwardly in his left hand. In a desultory fashion, he began to take little chips out of the stump. Gradually he took more interest in what he was about, his swings becoming harder, until at last he was hacking the stump, aiming his strokes at this angle and that. Sometimes his weaker left wrist twisted, and the flat of his blade hit the stump. And being lopsided, sometimes he stumbled—and then his eyes glittered and he cursed.

After an hour he gave up in a fury and strode toward the longhouse.

But in another hour he was back.

Within a few days he was able to put some force in the arm that had played little with weapons before. Edin often watched him from some point out of sight.

When he finally seemed able to swing the heavy blade in a true arc, without losing his balance, he took Arneld away from his shepherding duties. Curious, Edin watched through a crack in the byre wall as he handed the boy a stout blackthorn staff like the one he himself was holding. "Swing it at me," he commanded the boy.

Arneld looked up at him with a trained smile. "Do it!"

Arneld swung, and Sweyn parried the blow. This went on until the boy began to stagger. Impatient, Sweyn pushed him so hard he fell. That night Arneld walked slowly, as if his body had become glassy and fragile.

Sweyn was weary as well. His eyes at the evening meal were filled with a dead sparkle, like that of a slaughtered bull's. Yet the next day, as dawn came stealing through a steady late summer rain, he drove Arneld out to the stackyard again, despite the weather.

At first, many of the boy's blows struck Sweyn's shoulders. The man's face became an insane scowl of effort and concentration. Edin was afraid; the Cripple was so red-tempered. But after a while, try as the boy would, he couldn't touch the Viking.

This lesson learned, Sweyn sent the thrall-boy back to his shepherding. That was when Edin learned her spying hadn't gone unnoticed. Sweyn caught her behind a corner of the longhouse and backed her against the wall ominously, so that her view of the valley was completely obstructed by his wide body. He said, "You're so interested in my doings, witch, it's time you took a part in them." He took her arm and pulled her to his exercise area. He handed her Arneld's blackthorn staff— while he took up his axe. "Strike me, up, down, anywhere. Well? Go on!"

She swallowed; her gaze caught on the silver inlays and the glinting edge of his huge battle-axe. "I dare not."

He grinned sourly. "Afraid? Of Sweyn the Cripple? Of Sweyn the Bench-ender?" The grin faded. "If you don't do as I say, I'll take off my belt and beat courage into your hide."

She thought he meant it. His heavy belt had an iron buckle. Lifting the staff, she took a half-hearted swing at him.

He moved away easily, with a calm that was almost serenity. She saw at once that he'd regained a certain grace in his movements. "Harder!" he growled.

She let the staff's end rest on the ground. "Why are you doing this?"

"To get the nimbleness back in my legs. I've lain around too long. Isn't that what you told Fafnir Longbeard?"

She should have known her words would come back to haunt her. She said, "No. I told him you ought to find useful work." He was glaring at her. "Very well—at least you've made up your mind not to drink yourself to death." And she swung the staff with all her might.

Blackhair had never spared her from the hardest labor in the fields, and she'd been growing stronger. The first crack she gave Sweyn caught him by surprise on the shin and made him wince and go to his knee. He clutched his axe handle with his good left hand and screwed up his face so horribly that she was terrified. She rushed in, hovered, stepped back, then cried, "You told me to do it! I was only doing what you told me!"

He schooled his face before he looked up. What she heard was not what she'd expected: "A good Viking leg-sweep, that one! But you won't get another one in on me."

"Please! I don't want to do this!"

"Why not? Because you bear me so much affection?"

"Because I don't like to see anyone hurt!"

He grinned unpleasantly. "Then, you were born into the wrong world, song-singer. Now stop squawking like a parrot. You've been told what to do—do it!"

The next day he had her at it again. And the next. Then came the day she swiped low for his knees, and he, judging his moment like a hawk, brought down his axe so fast it was only a sparkle in the sunlight. Her hands went numb with the shiver of the blow. Most of the stout blackthorn staff fell at her feet. She stared at the splintered end mutely: It was severed not more than five inches from her grip.

When she straightened, he put on an evil smile and gave his axe an idle swing, as if to admire the glimmer of its bright silver inlays. He said, "I believe I need a new partner. I'm not ready for Fafnir or Eric yet, but mayhap I'll ride over tomorrow and see if Beornwold's boy, Hrut, can swing a staff any better than you can."

"And mayhap you should ask Gunnhild if she

could use some firewood. That would be a better use for that axe."

He pulled the weapon in protectively. "You don't use a good war axe like this one on firewood."

"Then find another axe."

He lowered his head. "You're telling a Norseman what to do, thrall? Don't you have work?" He brandished the axe and shouted, "Be gone!"

That night, he was not in the hall for the last meal. When Edin finished her broth and her slice of coarse bread and left the board to make her way to her sheepskin, Fafnir, and then Eric, looked up at her from their chessboard. So direct were their gazes, she faltered and finally stopped. Fafnir raised his ale cup silently, tipped his head in approval, and then drank.

The sea was not the flat, monotonous plain it seemed from the shore. It was various and interesting, full of moving hills and veering, dimpled valleys. The light and color changed from green to purple to blue to silver and back again. Sounds filled Thoryn's ear: the low drone of the wind in the *Blood Wing*'s rigging, the crack and whisper of the sail, the whir of the water under the bow, the shrill, sweet mewing of the trailing seabirds. This was the sea Norsemen loved like a second home. And on this particular voyage no one was aboard the *Blood Wing* who didn't want to be there. They were all good mates sailing a fine, proud ship.

Thoryn felt the sheer physical quickening of it. He thrilled to the vibration of the oar strokes, the lines thrumming in the wind, the whole ship undulating like a serpent. By no means was it easy being a Norseman. Sometimes a Viking rowed till his shoulders cracked; sometimes sea spray froze his beard; sometimes the ship bucked and corkscrewed.

Yet always there was this physical quickening, this sense of being a master of the elements.

The trade route down the protected coast to the summer market had given Norway its name: the great North Way. It ran more than fifteen hundred miles from the White Sea in the northwest to Kaupang, the country's main market town, in the southeast. The journey from Dainjerfjord required one and a half sennights, more or less. To a mariner who knew the waters, it was mostly free of natural hazards.

Thoryn sailed the *Blood Wing* with confidence between the thousands of small skerries so thickly clustered they formed a breakwater, always keeping the jagged coast of the mainland in sight. The precipitous coastal cliffs were cleaved by scores of deep-water fjords which offered shelter from storm and concealment from pirates when necessary.

But this trip had been uneventful. With her sharp keel, the *Blood Wing* ploughed the foaming deep and sailed a swift course between the skerries and the headlands. For a few days they had traveled under a sky full of anvil-headed thunderclouds, but had felt very little rain. And of pirates they had seen nothing.

Now Thoryn could see Kaupang's turf-walled booths and larger buildings in the distance. The town was undefended, had no earthwork ramparts, nor even a wooden stockade. It looked solid and strong, however. Located in the Tjolling district, it stood adjacent to the prosperous region of Vestfold, where there were warm valleys of lush farmland, uplands carpeted in dew-drenched forests, and lakes that swelled fishermen's hearts. The port was small, with its own protected harbor on the shores of Viksfjord, which cut into the land off the larger Larviksfjord. It was densely inhabited and an extremely prosperous and busy place all through the summer months.

The weather here on the east coast was not so prone to clouds as it was on the west. Today was as clear as spring; the sky seemed swollen and aching with light.

Well before entering the harbor, Thoryn had ordered his men to hang their shields over the sides of the longship, alternating the colors, blue and red. For special occasions like this, he kept aboard a spare dress sail made of velvetlike *pell* lined with brilliant silk. It wasn't practical for the open sea, but it made a fine display. His banner flew from the mast, gaily colored and embroidered with his emblem, Thor's hammer.

He felt the *Blood Wing* made a fine sight going in, with her bright sail taut, her sides shedding smothers of white foam and green water, her taunting gilt dragonhead rearing proudly, flashing her ruby eyes.

Starkad Herjulson was soon beside himself with gawking at the glittering menagerie of longships anchored in the harbor. Most were caparisoned with wealth, rank, and might. Kaupang was not only a distribution center for all kinds of goods going in all directions, it was a point of assembly for merchants sailing south to Hedeby or proceeding by way of Oresund to the Baltic. Ships waited here to find others to sail with them as a safeguard against piracy.

Starkad rhapsodized over one vessel after another. This one had lions molded in gold, that one had a golden bird weathervane on the topmast to indicate the direction of the wind, and yet another one was covered with carvings close-clenched and complicated, as convoluted as the syntax of skaldic verse.

Hauk Haakonsson was more interested in the tented booths they could now see stretching along the shore. He swore he could smell "cauldron snakes," sausages spiced with herbs and garlic. Jamsgar claimed he could smell the local ale which was made chiefly from bog-myrtle with apples and cranberries.

It took the *Blood Wing* a while to find a place to nudge her prow up to a stone jetty along the seafront. In the presence of a small clutch of on-lookers, Thoryn gave thanks to the gods for their grace in granting the seapaths safe for their ocean journey.

He too was dressed for show. He had on his father's horned bronze ceremonial helmet and was bearing his new shield emblazoned with a dragon-ship. His cloak was held by a silver brooch deco-rated with a motif of twining tendrils.

The town swarmed with life. The bustle began at the water's edge as men waded or put out boats to load and unload ships. The packed settlement was composed of irregular clusters of buildings. The backbone of trade therein was iron processing, bronze casting, cloth, soapstone utensils, and the manufacture of jewelry from rock crystal, glass, and that marvelous substance amber, the transparent, fossilized resin of pines that had died eons before and were covered by water. The sea washed ashore big chunks that fetched premium prices. Men and women alike loved the golden play of candleflame on a string of amber drops. And when rubbed, the stones took on a seemingly magical magnetic charge.

None of the crew of the *Blood Wing* was to see much of the marketplace today. Thoryn required them to accompany him along the "streets" between the houses—actually exceptionally cramped path-ways, often no more than a yard wide. They tramped past merchants with fine-balanced scales, past handsome displays of Rhineland pottery and glassware, past high-quality woolen cloth from Frisia, and past several lofted, winged dwellings, to the steps leading up to the oaken door of his Uncle Olaf Haldanr's town house.

Once admitted, they entered the feast-hall with a clatter of trappings and mail shirts and marched across the floor strewn with rushes, around the stone-lined hearth, to where a man who had seen fifty or more winters sat on his great chair like a proper Norwegian sea-king. "Uncle," Thoryn said formally, "I come to deliver greetings from Dainjer-fjord, past the far sea's swell."

Olaf, all gold to his chin, where his short, wolf's-hair-grey beard began, rested his arms on the chair and smiled faintly. "How is your mother, nephew?"

"Well."

"Good, good."

There was a stir behind Throyn just then. He didn't turn until Olaf said, "It has been a year since your last visit, but you must remember my daughter Hanne? Eh?"

Thoryn didn't miss the craftiness in that last syllable.

The girl's step was gliding rather than springing; her round face was full of prettiness, but lacked animation. She wore a pink gown, and there were pink blossoms threaded in her long yellow hair. She couldn't be more than fifteen. Though her body showed new signs of curves beneath her costly gown, her hands were still the short, pudgy-fingered hands of a girl.

And she was not overbold. She summoned no more than a tremulous smile for her cousin Thoryn Kirkynsson. She didn't meet his eyes, didn't raise her chin or straighten her back or steady herself under his gaze. Instead, she toyed with her pink gown, stroked the skirt, and straightened the folds. Thoryn's eminently pragmatic mind wondered if she could rule a longhouse, if she could handle livestock, if she could sew, cook, milk, make butter, spin, weave? If she would survive as the wife of a ruler of unruly people? What he saw tended to make him think not.

"You must be my guests during your stay," Olaf was saying. "And a guest needs water, a towel, and the right sort of amusement: We shall feast tonight!"

Olaf's mead-hall was not as big as Thoryn's, but the house contained several other rooms. One wing, called the "fireroom," was where all the cooking was done. The women could chatter in private there while they did their sewing and weaving. Another wing held a row of bed-chambers.

Early on, there was an interchange of presents. Olaf received from Thoryn a silk tunic garnered from his spring raids, originally from the Orient.

"A gift for a gift, that is the law!" Olaf claimed as he reciprocated with a set of bronze scales complete with chains and pans brightly polished on the inside and a dozen handsomely molded weights with lead cores sculpted and ornamented with enamel and glass, all of which folded neatly into a bronze container no larger than Thoryn's palm.

He received this with pleasure. It required no conflict of personality for him to lay down his sword and pick up a pair of scales. Whereas to some it might seem a Norseman's only interest was to steal and destroy, the fact was that to realize a profit from his looting he must needs sell it.

At the meal, Olaf seated Hanne between his own somewhat compact body and Thoryn's larger presence. Thoryn knew full well that for years Olaf had nurtured a hope of seeing his nephew and his daughter wed. It would be an insult to treat the girl with the total indifference he felt. An insult Olaf would not overlook. Olaf Haldanr was a man of great violence, yet capable of deep and enduring loyalty, which made him the most dangerous kind of man. Therefore, Thoryn put himself out to be friendly to the girl.

A difficult thing to do considering her avoiding eyes. She'd disappeared after their earlier introduction and come to the table in a new costume, this one yellow and even costlier than the pink. It hung lower from its shoulder loops and humped oval brooches, showing not only her delicate collarbones but also the pale shimmer of the tops of her tender breasts. Being a man, Thoryn's eyes traced the delicate blue veins to where they disappeared beneath the gown's folds.

She'd refashioned her hair, as well; now the gleaming strands were held by a narrow band of tawny ribbon around her forehead. Thoryn found himself thinking he must find some ribbon like that in the markets to take home to Edin.

The wooden doors of the hall were closed against the night. Besides the firelight, candles, torches, and crude lamps, the gleam of metal spread a double radiance in the air. Thoryn's eyes studied Olaf's sworn-men. One stood out, a Black Dane with dark hair and eyes.

They dined well. A broidered cloth of white linen covered the head table. Servants carried in loaves of thin, feather-light bread made of wheat. Local boats, which ventured out at night, had returned that morning with catches of pink shrimp. Hanne served a course as a hospitable gesture. Olaf sat with his elbow on the arm of his chair and smiled at her. The dish she offered was slices of a side of sheep that had been dried, then smoked, and finally roasted. Behind her, servants brought other meats and vegetables in brimming trenchers plated with silver.

They drank well, too. There was iced red wine in earthenware jars and bright goblets. Thoryn drank more than was his wont, until the room was a blur of faces, and he became aware of a vague benevolent feeling, like a wispy ungathered mist in his mind.

In that mood, it seemed to him that Olaf was a fine man, and that little Hanne was quite pretty. She was a bit distant, mayhap, and tended to smile very thinly, very unsurely, but he decided he could unravel her should he so wish. Her father was rich, and she was of good Viking stock. She'd make a proper wife for a jarl.

Olaf, his voice beginning to slur, bragged a great deal about his courage in his youth, and exaggerated the difficult victories he and his two-handed broadsword, *Essupe*, Gulper, had achieved. Thoryn nodded and tried his best to look impressed.

"Hanne!" Olaf broke off his bragging to shout, "a song!"

Harp in hand, the girl had a nice voice, but no real dream-spinning quality. Her song was about the implacable power of fate. Listening to her, Thoryn felt a shadowy disappointment, for her singing didn't give a glimpse of that mysterious realm that hung shimmering behind all the busy doings of men. She didn't have the talent Edin did.

Nonetheless, the wine he'd drunk had built up a fire in his heart which felt like hunger. He noticed the girl had an enticing sway to her hips as she glided along. Very enticing. When she returned to her place beside him, he glanced slantwise down his beard at her.

Shall I marry you, little Hanne, and do with you as I please?

He took another draught of the blood-red wine and imagined how it would feel to place his hand on the back of her neck, to caress her, gather her hair back, to hold her tenderly as he engulfed himself in her young body. A thrill of voluptuous enthusiasm rushed through him.

But when he was finally given a bed and sank into it, he suddenly felt an unmanly urge to weep. From somewhere came a feeling of grief too keen to bear. "*If* I take a woman to wife," he muttered to his pillow, "she'll at least be full-grown and have a good straight look in her eyes."

Half waking, Thoryn realized that Edin was not in his arms as he'd been dreaming. But he wanted her there, the white innocence of her breasts against his chest, her slender back in his hands. He lay still, his eyes not yet open, loose, calm, happy, thinking he had merely to move his hand to find her warm thigh. The notion tingled through him, rushing to his nerve ends, his fingertips. He would reach for her, and she would turn to him and put her arms around his neck; he would push her hair aside and kiss her jaw, her throat, and in sterling silence they would come together.

He came a little more awake and reached out—and found nothing, no one. His mind turned over with a start—and there it was. This was his Uncle Olaf's house in Kaupang. That sense of loose, quiet happiness left him; all that pure sense of ease vanished. He opened his eyes to a strange bedchamber filled with the lavender twilight of pre-dawn. Over him loomed two sculptured animal heads, exciting little creatures with big, goggling eyes and bobbed noses carved into the headposts of the bed.

A thrall-girl knocked lightly, then came in, keeping her head of dusty-colored curls down and murmuring "Master" as she set a basin of steaming water on his washstand then disappeared again. He rose, still painfully aroused. He washed his face and hands. *Don't think of her!* he told himself. Yet her memory was destined to skim across his brain like a bird all day.

In contrast, every time he saw Hanne that day, she hid her face and hurried off to some other part of the house. His uncle kept him, on this pretext and that, pretending he placed great importance upon his duties as a host, meanwhile often calling for Hanne and obviously hoping to promote an interest in Thoryn.

The girl had just as obviously been told to make herself attractive. Today her violet gown fell straight from her breasts with bands of ornament. It was short enough to show her feet in the front; the back was longer, trailing and pleated. A little cape was drawn over her shoulders. Her hair was gathered at the nape, from which it fell loose down her back, mingled with blossoms. All Thoryn thought of this effort to enthuse him was that he must ask Edin to wear her hair like that sometime. Meanwhile Hanne managed to come and go so swiftly that Thoryn's most enduring impression became that enticing sway of her hips.

He noticed the Black Dane's eyes seemed to travel the same road as his in following the girl's swaying disappearances. He saw at the first meal how the Dane sat quite lost in mooning at the girl. He would turn away, speak to his fellows, but then twist back in her direction. Later he placed himself between her table and the exit so that she would have to pass by him. When she did, she seemed to give the poor fool no notice or thought, while he all but swallowed her at close range, and then followed her with a look full of sadness to the depths, his dark eyes gone velvet and natant with desire.

Thoryn's company went out to sell their wares that day. Rolf volunteered to do the business of those of Dainjerfjord who had sent items for Thoryn to sell, since Olaf seemed intent on keeping Thoryn at hand. Starkad prowled the harbor to learn all he could, and that evening brought Thoryn descriptions of warships, small traders, even ferry-boats.

Bored with being manipulated into a courtship that interested him so little, Thoryn decided to see some of the town himself the next day. He slipped away from Olaf and went with Rolf and Ottar. Each of them were properly accoutred with pointed conical helmets, weapons, and shields. Rolf had on a new woolen cloak, nearly as red as his beard. The day was cool enough for it, with nothing but streaks of sunlight coming down through high clouds.

The large conglomeration of sheds, stalls, tents, and wagons was thoroughly chaotic, all shrouded in the smoke of dozens of cookfires. There was a smell to the place, a mix of smoke and midden fumes and cooking and people all swirled by the bustle of mercantile activity. Buyers and sellers haggled in a dozen tongues and thronged and jostled in the dirt streets. Swedes and Danes and Norwegians, bumpkins from the surrounding countryside and warriors fresh from gory raids, hunters from the frozen north, Aland Islanders, Dniepir Slavs, Rhineland Germans, Englishmen, Franks, and Frisians, many of them mortal enemies in any other place, were here united with knowing nods above the shared coin of trade.

Sleek merchants in doorways waited casually for business with self-absorbed expressions. Itinerant craftsmen bargained enthusiastically. By small boat came *bondi* with barley, fish, meat, walnuts, hazelnuts, and acorns, which they bartered for German quernstones and household bowls and decorative brooches. Evident everywhere were adventurous and acquisitive instincts.

Shoppers fingered ornate combs, pins, knife handles, and sword mounts carved from valuable reindeer antlers. Walrus tusks became ivory chessmen as they watched. Gold was fashioned into bracelets and finger rings by the regular clang of hammers on jewelsmiths' anvils. Beads and ornaments were fashioned from amber; glass blowers contributed colored beads; wool was woven; and stonecutters chiseled with their pointed tools.

One transaction for a large quantity of down involved a simple trade for soapstone, this item for that. In another booth, a Muslim coin was sliced up like a pie to achieve the necessary value for a purchase of Rhenish pottery. Next door a man was breaking off part of his own jewelry in payment for an ivory box lined with silk. Rolf and Ottar were less interested than Thoryn in the sheer enormity of the exchanges going on and soon managed to insult a rough woman selling foods from a tray braced on her ample hip. Already the size of a buxom-breasted *knorr*, she now swelled to double her size with hostility. Rolf got a gleam in his eye, and Ottar's head took on a rakish tilt. The woman put her tray aside, uttered a growl, then flew at them, swinging both fists. Thoryn decided to continue his tour alone.

He threaded his way among the surge of people and animals, pushed himself between chesty men with dirty aprons and coarse men in mail, and passed young, well-to-do youths of the town in velvet tunics with their hands on their hips as they scanned things from a distance, unwilling to be jostled in the crowd. A pony cart trundled down a side-street carrying workers with wooden spades; two young women, lifting their hems daintily, looked over an exotic peacock pacing stately, majestic, sapphire, and emerald.

Outside one booth a dozen shaggy-headed farm-thralls sat fettered together, supporting their chins on their knees. All of them wore garments of rough grey frieze. Included among them was a Christian monk with eyebrows like tufts and a long-nosed, ugly boy with ears that stood forward like small sails. As Thoryn paused, he overheard a purposeful customer, a young Swede of brave proportions, say to the slave trader: "I'm anxious to buy a female, higher quality than these."

The slaver waved him inside and drew back a drab curtain behind which were no fewer than six women, varying in age from about twelve to twenty-four. Thoryn was familiar with slave trades, yet his interest was inexplicably caught.

Chapter 22

By the light of a stone lamp, the customer cursorily looked over each female. He came back to one, and began to examine her more closely. She was a mere girl, with a soft, sweet profile. Her face was very white. The Swede inspected her fingers, which were long and pale and delicate.

"You have taste, sir," said the slave trader. "That one was an Irish king's daughter—and she's a virgin."

Thoryn's heart suddenly felt like a cold stone in his chest.

The Swedish giant stood back. He put his upper teeth over his beard, drew some of it into his mouth and nibbled it. He scratched his tawny head. "How much?"

"Four and one-half marks of silver."

The customer grimaced in disgust. "I'm a businessman like you. Do you know how long it would take to get my money back out of her at that price?"

The slaver said, as smooth as honey and hemlock, "Four marks, then. She's a virgin, a king's daughter," he emphasized. "Look at those eyes . . . rare jewels."

"Aye, aye, but I paid three marks of silver once for a virgin Irish girl—thrice the cost of a common bed-thrall—and all she could do was get pregnant. She was always pregnant, and not many of my customers want to lay on a belly as big as squash, even if it belongs to a princess."

"Well, of course, if you're looking for a regular whore, choose another, one of these three. They're still young and little used yet."

Thoryn's eyes scanned the "little used" three. Two were dark, but one was fair, about eighteen years old. The customer seemed drawn by the fair one.

"She was just traded to me," the slaver said. "She's had only one master, an old man with a taste for virgins. He takes them, uses them for a season, then trades them back to me for fresher flesh. I took her to my own bed last night, and never have I experienced such rapture, such transport, such a surpass of—"

"And your father is Loki," the Swede said offhandedly, "the father of lies."

Again there was haggling. The girl was stripped a little at a time, until she was naked. This was the usual pattern any competent trader followed in selling a female thrall, but Thoryn felt the stirrings of an unease, as if it wasn't quite right for him to stand and watch like this.

And then, for an instant, he found himself looking straight into the girl's eyes, and so clear an understanding of her despair came to him that he felt the blood leave his face. He felt himself growing pale. He felt new emotions being honed out of him on the spot, leaving him focused and keen. He seemed to understand exactly how it was for her, what it meant to her to be stripped naked and revealed to unknown men, to be helpless. He could imagine too well Edin standing there, held at the attention of a stranger's scrutiny, knowing that the ordinary privileges—personal honor, dignity—were irretrievable. He could feel her horror, her hot frustration. His jaws knotted.

At one time he would have found himself swelling

and throbbing to see a man fondling a woman so intimately, but now only his blood throbbed in his ears.

More haggling. All three men's eyes were fastened on the girl, the Swede was touching her, causing her to moan in panic, and meantime other passersby were gathering to enjoy her misery, until at last the slaver said with a tone of finality, "Three half-marks, silver."

The customer threw back his powerful head and laughed. "Drink goat's piss, old man."

The slaver shrugged as if to say, *I've grown fat on slaves; take this one, or leave her, it makes no difference to me.*

The Swede realized that the haggling was at an end. He grumbled, "Well, for that much, I'd have to see what she can do first."

The trader shrugged again, now calibrated, calm, judging. He motioned to the slave, who seemed to brace herself as the Swede began to open his trousers and said, "Down on your knees, little whetstone. I've a sharpening job for you."

The slaver pulled the curtain, leaving the customer to take his free sample in the semi-private presence of the other females. He approached Thoryn. "You're interested in a bed-thrall? Mayhap a virgin to warm these cool nights?"

"I —" Thoryn found he had to swallow to wet his voice before it would work — "I have a bed-thrall."

The slaver laughed. "Then mayhap you would like to trade her and buy my Irish princess. There's nothing like a virgin — and nothing in the world like an Irish virgin."

"No." There were by now distinct noises coming from behind the curtain, willful and rhythmic masculine noises, base and exploitative and relentless, accompanied by little feminine noises that spoke of fear and shame and misery. Thoryn tried to remember what he'd been saying. "My woman is Saxon."

"Well, Saxon is good, but I always say Irish is better."

"Saxon suits me." Thoryn turned and strode out under the light-shot cumulus clouds of the day.

After that it seemed slave booths were everywhere along his path. They drew him like beacons. In one place there was a small clutch of a half dozen or so "princes" and "princesses," all naked or nearly so, loosely bound around a stake. They were newly captured, just taken off a longship, and not yet dispersed to the various booths. One of the younger girl's little breasts were quivering with her crying.

A swarthy Muslim with a small chin beard and wearing a costume of striped wool paused at the same time Thoryn did. Moving gracefully with the help of a blackthorn staff that was taller than he was, the Muslim went right up to the thralls. They automatically backed away, afraid of being poked or prodded. The Muslim studied them for a moment then stepped back to view the scene from Thoryn's distance.

"That one interests me," he said with a heavy accent, casually, idly, as one stranger will sometimes speak to another. "The one with red-copper hair." He gestured with his staff. "Notice the lovely peach-colored curls of her sex. Put her up on a block so the buyers have to look up at her, part her legs a little at the right moment. . . ."

When Thoryn didn't answer, the Muslim looked up at him, then moved off.

For the first time, Thoryn was conscious of the plight of the captured slave. For a thrall born and bred, existence must be hard. For a freeborn warrior captured in battle—or a well-brought-up girl ravished from her smoldering home—it must be Hell itself.

Suddenly he'd had enough of the market, the

teeming activity, the raucous jabber of foreign tongues, and the buying and drinking and brawling. He headed down a winding alley in search of a wine shop. He wandered near the harbor; the smell of the water rose around him comfortingly. Then he found what he wanted.

The room was hot and dusty. It was a strange place. Strange music played; strange drinks were handed at the tables; the spiced oil of the lamps put out a strange, sandalwood tang.

A dark-haired girl began to dance beside his table, making her own music with little cymbals tied to her fingertips. She was wearing a dress of pure green silk cut severely straight from shoulder to toe. Everything about her moved, her chains, her bracelets, the hammered golden rings in her ears, even her round breasts that were half-bared. The sable curls of her armpits glistened in the lamplight as she twirled her creamy arms and trailed a scarf of green silk near Thoryn's nostrils. Her dress clung to her like a mermaid's scales. Her face was full of animal life; even her mouth was in play as she showed white teeth in a laugh.

The lascivious motions of her dance incited him; he felt his manhood taking significant and formidable shape, until it felt ready to burst from the confinement of his trousers.

He wanted a woman; he'd wanted one for days. Any woman would do—this dancing girl in her cheap finery and her falling hair of deepest black. He was like a beast in rut who'd caught a whiff of female moisture. He grabbed her waist and pulled her onto his lap. She was startled, but schooled herself to laugh, still as unconscious of her peril as a spring lamb. "You want me, Master? There is a bed in the back room." More softly she murmured, "I have learned many curious arts of love."

"What is love?" he said, smiling his fury.

She laughed again. "Come." She was struggling to get off his knee. He let her rise, but held one of her hands with its blanched nails. "Come with me"—she laughed, her golden earrings swaying—"and I will show you love."

The room was small, the bed smaller, and the girl was not able to deliver what she'd promised. She undressed with seeming eagerness, and kissed and fondled him and let him do the same to her. But something happened. In the wine shop his manhood had been like an ice pick in his trousers, now it refused to rise.

He decided he must go more slowly, mayhap see if he could give her the pleasure he'd learned to give Edin. He admired her golden belly, her gleaming thighs, and her tight black triangle. He placed his hand on it and explored, while with his lips he excited the tip of one breast. His eyes carefully watched her half-open mouth and her neck, which was thrown back, showing the gold rings in her ears.

The girl dutifully approached her crisis; he watched the frantic writhings of her body with satisfaction. And afterward she was ridiculously grateful. She sat up and pressed her forehead to the back of his wrist, as if to say something that could not be said aloud. *I will be your thrall,* that gesture told him. But Thoryn could still not manage to take her.

He began to feel angry. What pleasure did Edin yield him that this dancing girl or any other woman couldn't? What was the matter with him that he could not stiffen for this embrace, that he could not quench his desire?

For a long while he simply refused to reconcile himself to this impotence. He struggled for the enjoyment he'd always gained from having a woman in his arms. His will continued to protest in pride and misery against the dictates of his wretched spirit. The girl encouraged him, stroked him with most skillful inspiration, called him *Leantri*-Seether, and *Aifur*—Ferocious. But it seemed the dark, safe deeps he'd found in Edin had spoiled him. Finally, worn out and disgusted he pushed the girl away, threw down a coin, and went back into the wine shop.

The scraggly occupants of the low room didn't seem half so exotic now. The place was simply dark and dusty, the gloom hardly decreased by the dozen oil lamps emitting clouds of smoke where they hung from overhead beams. The low, splintery tables were littered with pools of wine. Slumped over his wine bowl again, he felt despairing and ashamed. This raging, mad preoccupation with a mere thrall! He had an almost physical longing for reassurance—but the only one who could give him that was the very one who was causing it, and—lucky for her!—she was too far away.

Someone came in and took the stool across from him. Thoryn looked up to see the Muslim with the little chin beard. The man was just leaning his blackthorn staff against the wall beside him.

Thoryn said nothing. The Muslim smiled and said abruptly, "Shall I tell you the four things I dislike most about your land, Viking? First, children born here are thrown into the sea to save the trouble of bringing them up. Second, your wives have the right to declare themselves divorced whenever it suits them. Third, I have seldom heard more horrible singing—it is like a growl coming from your throats, like the barking of wolves, only much more beastly. And last, I have never been fed so much fish."

Thoryn's hand had gone to his sword haft. To insult a Norseman was always a dangerous thing, and at that moment this particular Norseman was like a man with a bear at his throat and a wasp in his hair.

Mayhap, in the end, it was the very audacity of it that saved the dark-eyed little man. Thoryn was amazed — and intrigued. He took a deep breath and said, "Arab, it's true we serve a lot of fish, because we have a lot of it; but you'll notice many pigs and goats in the market, for, despite the haughty remarks made by some, we eat pork and mutton, too. Exposure of sickly or crippled infants is allowed because there is no place in the North for physical weaklings. As far as Norse women enjoying a little independence, it is necessary when their men roam so much; what man wants a wife who despises him looking after his holdings? On the subject of our throat for song, and the Arab ear for music, it is not for me to comment."

The Muslim laughed. "Well said, Viking!" He introduced himself: "Jakub Tartushi Muqqadasi. I have come a long way and am not over-impressed with this market. It seems to me you Vikings love every sort of bauble, going to foolish lengths to get hold of mere colored beads. Frankly, I am homesick for the elegance of my native Constantinople."

"Then mayhap you should return to it with all speed."

The Muslim laughed again. "You think me ill-bred. Indeed, travelers show vulgarity when they jeer at the habits and standards of their hosts, for there are no scales to weigh honor."

"What I think, Arab, is that you're lucky not to look down at the floor and see your body lying there without your head."

"Am I? I confess I was testing. You seemed different from most of your kind. A little more sensitive, which is a ray of sunshine in this cold northern place." He smiled hugely, showing white teeth. "Actually it is a great bronze dahlia of light! I saw you looking at those poor slaves, and there was sympathy in your face. Unusual for a Norseman."

"For a barbarian, you mean. A mindless barbarian thug."

The Muslim blinked his heavy, slow eyes. "Indeed."

With deceptive leisure, he gestured to the shop owner, and two fresh bowls brimming with golden wine were placed before them. He paid with a Muslim gold dinar. He was as loquacious as Thoryn was taciturn: "I have dealt with Rus Vikings at Bulgar on the Volga bend. I have seldom seen a more perfect physical species. Positive Goliaths, as tall as date palms! And fair and ruddy and strong as camels. But they are also crude and uncouth—and the filthiest of Allah's beasts. They do not even wear clothes, neither tunics nor caftans, but merely use skins to cover their bodies on one side, leaving their hands free to seize their axes."

Despite himself, Thoryn was interested.

"When they anchor in the great river, they build big longhouses on the shore, each holding ten to twenty persons. Every man has a sea chest to sit on. With them are pretty girls destined for sale.

"A Rus will have sexual intercourse with a slave girl while his fellows look on. Sometimes whole bands come together in that fashion, one seeming to make the others wild with lust. A merchant such as myself trying to buy a particular slave may need to wait and look on as the Rus completes his act with her."

Thoryn recalled the sounds coming from behind the curtain in the slave trader's booth. "Things aren't much different here."

For once the Arab refrained from comment. His dark eyes were slumberous. A lazy, thoughtful smile hovered about his lips and about his prominent cheekbones.

Thoryn felt moved to defend his kind. "But you Arabs are like grandmothers; you tremble at the facts of life. And you seem to set yourself above us, yet you're nothing but a slave trader yourself."

"That I am. Slavery is one fact of life I am not

prone to run from, especially not if I can profit from it. But I pride myself on being civilized about it."

Thoryn grunted. The man made him feel naive, provincial. For a moment he was lost in that feeling of impotence again. He gestured to the wine seller and raised his refreshed bowl to the Muslim. "May your heart keep youth and your Muslim mouth grow full of good Norse music."

Muqqadasi laughed.

"Tell me about your precious Constantinople, which we Norsemen call *Miklagardur,* the Great City."

The Muslim's gaze seemed to wander away in the immensity of the task. "The Great City. But that is an understatement. It is the *greatest* city.

"Its original name was Byzantium, the most magic of names, until in 300 A.D. the Emperor Constantine moved the capital of the Roman Empire there and renamed it in his own honor." He shrugged. "Whatever you call it, it is memorably beautiful, with its domes and basilicas and pinnacles and towers gleaming in the sun. And also memorably shocking, for power and religion sit on twin thrones; courtesy and cruelty stroll hand in hand. There is wealth to be got there past the dreams of peasant Viking greed. Constantinople is the mecca for every merchant and mercenary from every known corner of the world. It teems with half a million people. It is not hard to imagine the effect it would have on a sea voyager accustomed to rough living—that heady blend of opulence and corruption, of bartering and brawling, of West and East."

What Thoryn heard seemed a legend for the saga-sayers. It ill compared with the rugged life on an isolated steading where men wrestled their livings from stingy earth that was rock-sown and frequently frost-bound.

They ranged through many subjects in the course of the next few hours. The clever Muslim drew Thoryn out about himself, until he admitted he was not married.

"And yet it is clear to me that you are a man smitten with love."

Thoryn bristled. "I know nothing of love, Arab."

Muqqadasi chuckled into his wine bowl.

"You find that amusing?"

"I find you amusing, Viking. Vastly amusing. You are a walking example of the platitude that great love makes wise men become fools. You suffer, Viking, you are distraught. Your mind is full of sharp impulses. Who could help but mark it? And the only attitude I can take toward suffering of that sort is sympathy and boundless patience."

Thoryn's hand went a second time to his sword haft.

"To change the subject," the Muslim said smoothly, "do you realize that you Norse have a natural resource that could bring you wealth beyond measure in my land? You have access to pine and birch forests where many a warm-coated animal scuttles and burrows and swims—and I know whole markets that would buy as many as you could deliver."

Thoryn's hand relaxed.

"There are men the world over who can never get enough furs to flaunt their wealth and magnificence." He shook his head in mock sorrow. "Even the high clergy of the holy Christian church clamor for furs. Such a deadly poison of pride. To their shame they hanker after a lynx-skin robe as much as for eternal salvation. And they care not whether they gain either by means fair or foul." He sighed. "An able man could get rich satisfying such unsated and insatiable appetites."

Thoryn lingered, listening, until the moon had risen, pale and full. It was Rolf who came to find him, Rolf, whose fine red cloak was torn. Thoryn refrained from asking who had won the argument between the Norsemen and the market woman. Unlike the Muslim, he knew when to keep his thoughts to himself.

Thoryn was not sleeping well in his guest bed. Olaf was unhappy with him for staying away the whole day, for letting Hanne slip away to her bower instead of demanding her attention. Thoryn was hard pressed not to tell the man outright: *Your daughter is not the wife for me; I would have so little trouble mastering her, young as she is, shy as she is, that soon I would make her my thrall. I need a stronger woman, a woman who will stand up to the dragon in me, a woman like . . .*

Edin.

That made no sense! How could a woman who already was a thrall be stronger, more independent, less slavish than a woman who was free?

And how could he, a free Norseman, be so mastered by his own slave? Frustration flamed out of him into the dark. He was like an ox wearing an iron ring, his tonnage tamed to the pull of a frail Saxon female. All he could see in his mind day and night was Edin. Edin's silky hair spread over his bed pillows, a lush coverlet; Edin's shoulders and breasts; Edin's voluptuous body.

Enough! He had to school his thoughts. By force of will he imagined Hanne in his bed, sweet-smelling, virginal. She was small, she was female . . .

But she wasn't Edin.

"Sheepsdung!"

His curse sounded loud in the silence of his chamber. He groaned as luxuriant images of Edin crowded out the chaste little Hanne. Edin, who was beautiful where Hanne was only pretty; Edin, who challenged him even while she feared him, who ever made him feel he should be a better man, who had given him more, much more, than mere pleasure, who had given him *hope*.

Thus he fought with himself. He'd just re-plumped his pillow and thrown himself into a new position when he heard his door quietly open. He saw a feminine shape standing there, half in and half out of the narrow opening. His eyes made out a white nightshift, a lock of yellow hair lying over a shoulder.

If this was more of Olaf's doing, he thought grimly, he'd chosen the moment poorly, for in an instant Thoryn was out of bed and catching Hanne's arm. She gasped as he yanked her into the room. He shut the door quickly and pulled her off her feet, up into his arms.

"Thoryn!" she whispered.

He took her to the bed and tossed her down, irritated beyond words by her cloying sweetness and her girlish bashfulness and her father's relentless pushing.

"Oh!" She turned her head away quickly. Her hands fluttered with an air of not knowing what she was to do or where to go. "You're naked."

What had she expected? What was her game? He climbed onto the bed with her and pulled her half beneath him.

Still she kept her protests to sibilant whispers. "Let me go!"

But he was not about to let her go. "You were sent here for this," he growled. "You were sent to act the whore, as if your honor was not a thing some women would give their very lives for." In his rakish mood, he willfully placed his hands over her breasts.

They were small and maidenly, and beneath them her heart was fluttering like a captured bird's. She was hardly more than a little girl. He found his anger and frustration vanishing, though he tried hard to keep both hot.

"Lie still now. I'm not going to take you—I'm not the fool your father thinks I am. But I don't mind toying awhile." One hand he placed beneath her nightshift's wide neckline, on the upper mound of one little breast. "Be still. This is new to you. Let me show you how it's done."

"Thoryn—"

"Stop squirming! You think you want to be my wife—this is part of what being a wife means."

Suddenly she began to cry. "I *don't* want to be your wife! I don't! That's what I came to tell you!"

That put him up on his elbows. He eased off her and sat up, finding enough blanket to cover the important parts of himself. She curled beside him, still weeping softly.

"You don't want to marry me?" He smoothed his beard. "Well, I must admit I wasn't expecting that."

A pin and a comb were falling out of her hair. He plucked them free and fingered them idly. At his touch, she got onto her knees and quickly put the length of the bed between them. Kneeling at the footboard, she faced him—almost. She was so shy, and embarrassed of course, and thoroughly afraid of him now. "Cousin," she said.

"*Cousin*, is it?"

She made a miserable sound. "This was a mistake. Please accept my apology. I'll go."

He tossed the comb and pin aside and caught her hand. It had that slightly sticky-damp bonelessness of an infant's. He put a warning in his voice: "You will go nowhere—cousin—until you explain this visit to me."

She stopped, checked the determination in his eyes, and sat on her heels again. She didn't fight his hold on her hand; she was as submissive as he'd known she would be.

"Now," he began, "you don't want to marry me?"

Her head made faint movements, as if the monosyllables *no! no! no!* were making a lie out of what she said: "Marrying you would be very nice, I suppose." She dared to peep at him. "It is just that, well, I'd rather marry someone else."

"Anyone in particular? Or just anyone rather than me?"

She looked close to tears again.

"Who is he?"

She shook her head helplessly. "My father is very determined that I should marry you."

Thoryn was thinking. So the girl was infatuated with someone else. He should have read the signs, but he'd been blinded by his own appeal—and assumed Hanne found him as acceptable as he found himself.

She was gently twisting her hand, trying to free herself. When he dropped his hold, she whispered, "Thoryn, are you very determined to marry me?"

He said roughly, "I'm not a bit interested in taking a little slaughter lamb to wife."

She bowed her head and sniffed.

"Go. If you're to be another man's, it better not look as if you've already been mine."

She climbed down off the bed. "You won't tell anyone I was here?"

"I owe you no promises."

Another sniff.

"By the gods, girl, get out of here before I—"

No need to finish the threat; she was already gone.

Chapter 23

Thoryn borrowed a mount from Olaf to go riding the next day. Several men from the *Blood Wing* and from Olaf's hall rode out with him into an eye-whipping wind. Once away from the town, they rode through an avenue of walnut trees, which formed a shady tunnel of moving light and shadow. The men talked of battles and falcons. Ottar launched into a tale of wenching that soon had everyone laughing.

Thoryn asked the Black Dane, whose name was Far Reginn, about the tide of Christianity lapping at the Danevirke on Denmark's edges. The man shrugged and told how he'd cheerfully submitted to provisional baptism as a condition for being allowed to work as a mercenary in a Christian community. "It is a common custom, yet a Norseman keeps whatever faith is most pleasant to him."

Without thought, Jamsgar said to Thoryn, "And how goes it with fair Cousin Hanne?"

Thoryn put on a little smile. "The girl understands me now."

It took no more than that to draw the Black Dane out. "What do you mean?" he asked.

Thoryn let his eyelids close and open again lazily. "I was growing tired of her hesitancy. She smelled vulnerable last night, and I took the chance I had."

Far's black brows knotted, and he seemed to chew

the inside of his cheek. His confident manner had deserted him. "What are you saying?"

"I thought it was plain enough, Far Reginn."

"And I say it wasn't, Thoryn Kirkynsson."

Thoryn shrugged and scratched his fingernails through his beard. The Dane's eyes darkened as his anger grew. He was strung so tight he would draw his sword any moment. Thoryn said, "She strayed a little too near my chamber door and I . . . invited her in."

Far laughed uncomfortably. "Of course you did — we're all great tellers of stories."

Casually Thoryn drew out from his belt a hairpin and a comb. He showed them with a little smile.

The man went white. Stopping his horse, he said in a shocked voice, "You dishonored her?"

Thoryn halted his own mount. "You seem to feel an unnatural amount of interest for a man who is unconcerned in the matter. Or who *should* be unconcerned."

Far's glare threatened to catch Thoryn's tunic afire.

"Mayhap," he added, "she has wandered too close to your door in the past?"

Far drew his sword.

Thoryn's hand went to his own sword; he loosened it in its scabbard as he slid off his horse. "A challenge, Far? One can only wonder why?"

The Dane's black eyes gleamed. "You took her — no doubt hurt her!" He swallowed his rising emotions and said more quietly, "For that I will send you out on the long voyage that ends in Valhöll, Thoryn Kirkynsson."

The wind took his words off, leaving a breezy, but nonetheless dangerous, silence. Thoryn said, "If you want a fight, a fight you shall have. But I would know exactly what we are fighting for."

"For Hanne Olafsdaughter's honor."

"I think not. I've suspected for several days that she had a fondness for another. I told the truth in that I did pull her into my bed chamber last night, and even into my bed. I know well how her breasts feel—but I didn't take her. She struggled a little too desperately, and wept, until I was half inclined to be angered. I want no wife who weeps for another when she should only be thinking of me. So I decided to find out who might be scenting after her—and now it seems I know. Olaf's hard-eyed mercenary has an odd romantic fleck."

The man stood stiff with pride, saying nothing. The wind billowed under his cloak. One day he would be formidable; the arched staves of his rib cage were like the frames of a longship. But for now he was still young enough that his body was mainly hulking bones and nerves with little meat to hide them. Still, he already had a certain reputation as a fighter. Thoryn glowered at him. "You are poor, Far Reginn, forced to eat another man's meat. Such a thing is not above the ability of a man to set right— but let's see if you have any real skill with that sword you're so quick to draw. This I swear: If you can best me here today, I'll sail home on the first east wind—without Hanne Olafsdaughter."

He signaled to Rolf, who spread his rather tattered, square red cloak on the ground and said formally: "He who steps off the cloak loses."

Those from the fjord ranged about Thoryn, their eyes on him trustingly. Drawing *Raunija,* he said, "Aye now, see that each stroke meets its mark, Far Reginn, and none of that silly flailing of the sword you Danish men are given to. Every thrust must bite if you expect to father the children of my tender-breasted little cousin."

Far gave a little jogging dance, as though to work up his boldness.

An over eager puggy! Thoryn thought. For his part,

he stood still, with his longsword poised before him, until at last Far struck.

Sparks rained from the length of their longswords. Thoryn pressed to the reaches of the Dane's strength and skill—but did not press beyond. Far sustained a cut to his neck—but did not lose his head. He snarled a curse and tried to surge forward, hammering for Thoryn's skull. Thoryn was defter, however; his longsword leaped, caught Far's blow, and turned it.

It was a thing that went against the grain to hold back, yet hold back he did. The Dane hacked at him from the left and then the right. Thoryn took each blow with *Raunija;* sparks spat over his forearms. And then came a moment that seemed right. He let his longsword be caught. *Raunija* held the light; she glowed evilly as Far's blade struck more fire off her. Then Thoryn let his heel step back off the spread cloak.

There was an unbelieving silence among the men. Without speaking, without giving any hint of how much this forfeit cost him, Thoryn swung onto his horse and rode for town.

By nightfall, word of the event was sown all through Olaf's house. Olaf himself was in a fury when he came to Thoryn's chamber. "Far Reginn has asked for Hanne."

Thoryn knew what was not being said. His uncle wanted a landed jarl for a son-in-law, but there was a matter of honor involved now, Thoryn's and Far's—and Hanne's as well, since her visit to Thoryn's bed, however unwilling, was whispered about everywhere. Thoryn's open admission of that placed Olaf in a cleft stick. And Olaf was not a man who liked cleft sticks. Just now he was radiating a barely tethered, ruthless power. There was something primary and dangerous about him, a hint of what he must have been in his youth.

"Thoryn, by Odin, they say that raw boy bested you! What is the truth?"

Thoryn had to unclench his jaw to speak. He forced the words out against vast aversion: "Far struck, and I stepped off the cloak."

Olaf raged silently. "I don't believe it! There's more to this than meets the eye and ear. But if I don't give her to one of you now, there will be thunder."

"Aye." Thoryn felt his pride stinging. "Well, the oath I made was that if Far won the challenge I would sail home alone."

Olaf's rage went cold. "I could demand that you wed her—you told one and all that you took her to your bed."

"It was the impulse of the moment, Uncle. You have my word that as far as I know the girl is still a maiden. The Dane believes that or he wouldn't have asked for her."

"Aye. But I swear I would not give her to him if . . . I can't believe he bested you, Thoryn! Is this the man they say makes the earth shake, the one they call the Hammer of Dainjerfjord? The Dane is a fine swordsman, mayhap my best, but he doesn't have your lack of mercy."

Thoryn avoided seeing anyone else until the *Blood Wing* was ready to sail. Then, as he was packing the last of his belongings into his sea chest, a knock came at his door. It was Hanne. When he said nothing, she came in and shut the door behind her.

"This is not wise," he said shortly.

"I know. But I had to tell you—thank you, Thoryn Kirkynsson."

She was fairer than ever he'd seen her. She was radiant. He squinted down at her a moment and couldn't help giving her a faint smile.

Her responding smile was brilliant. Suddenly she went up on her tiptoes and pecked his lips with her own. "Cousin, you must find someone to love you."

He backed away to look at her down his bearded cheeks.

She hesitated, then said all in a rush, "You should, Thoryn! But first you must learn to be less fierce! If I weren't half-frightened of you most of the time, I would have liked to speak with you. I've oft thought I would like to be your friend."

He said nothing. He saw her eyes searching his, as if for some sign.

It was a day of swift clouds when Inga drove her horse-drawn cart along the cunning zigzag of indented sheep paths to Soren Gudbrodsson's hut. Soren had once sailed with Kirkyn on his raiding expeditions, until the old man received an injury to his head. That was long ago. Now he lived alone. He often sat for hours beside the fjord, stroking his old dented helmet with his gnarled hands. Thoryn let him stay on a corner of the steadying, knowing he had nowhere else to go.

When Inga knocked on the door of his one-room hut, he opened it with a really dreadful expression on his face. For an instant she was alarmed, but then said, "It is Inga Thorsdaughter, Kirkyn's wife."

"Kirkyn's . . . ? *Inga!* Come in, come in!" He bowed as low as his stiff old frame would allow as he backed into the hut. He was of large build, even in his old age, and still strong and muscular; but he seemed more befuddled than Inga had expected. His voice was gruff, and his beard was threaded with grey and in need of care. His eyes were as colorless as a blindman's. But really, none of that mattered; indeed, it all served Inga's purpose well.

"I am honored," he was muttering, "honored."

351

He offered her a stool near the little fire. From there she took in the dark room. It smelled of dung, for a cow lowed at the back end. The hut had been built with his own hands, out of rocks and turf and driftwood. Brown swamp reeds made the thatch for the roof. It was a rough home, with drafts coming up beneath the door. A weak fire burned in the stone-lined pit, and a thin broth bubbled beneath the lid of an iron pot. She saw he'd been greasing a pair of ancient leather leggings by the hearth.

"How do you fare, Soren?" She was aware of a little pulse in her cheek, ticking.

He smiled doggishly and shrugged. "I have no longship, no crewmates—but I have a home and a fire and food. I do well enough."

"Well enough to refuse to embark on one last adventure for your jarl? I grasp your sadness and your burden, Soren. Your talents have not given you the patience or the experience for niggling country life. You must die a hero or else die unsung."

He straightened his old back as if to say, *I may be a feeble-minded old man, ignored by my kin, scolded by cooks and thrall-girls, but Norse fires still burn in Soren Gudbrodsson!*

"Here is the thing, then," Inga said. "The jarl has a cold foreign witch working spells beneath his roof . . ."

He listened attentively, his eyes unmoving. When she was done, he was silent for a moment. The fire made soft, taffetalike sounds; the broth bubbled. He said, "And this is what the jarl wants done?"

"He sent me to ask it of you. The ties of kinship impose fearful demands, even on a woman."

"Aye. Well then, what else can I do? If I have to kill, I will kill, and if I have to die, I will die well, laughing at death. After all, I owe the jarl. He's a good man. Once we swept through a place, there was little left, not enough for a mouse to eat. It was

352

he himself who carried me out of that burning Christ-church in the Orkney's when I got that head wound. You should have seen the stains on his arms that day, as if he'd been picking blackberries!"

"That was Kirkyn," Inga said. A draft seemed to creep under the door and chill her back. "Kirkyn is dead. I am a widow woman and my son Thoryn is jarl now."

"Thoryn? Oh, aye, young Thoryn!"

"Are you sure you understand what is to be done?"

"Aye." Clasping his big hands together and resting his elbows on his knees, he repeated it back to her.

"You feel you're strong enough?" she asked.

He seemed to look at his hands. "I used to be the best wild-horse trainer on the fjord. And quick as a cat with a broad-axe." His eyes opened, bright with incipient tears. His poor mouth quivered.

"I remember," she said.

"Then you know what this means to me. One last deed." He suddenly threw back his rough head and guffawed. "Ha! An adventure!" His bravado vanished under her stare and stony silence, and he finished more soberly, "I will do as the jarl says, Inga Thorsdaughter."

That burst of laughter more than anything else satisfied her that she'd chosen well. Dazed and grey as this man had become, there was still enough iron in him for her purposes. She left him some cheeses and cold smoked trout to build up his strength a little, then went out into the grey, dry afternoon. The fjord was as slate as the clouds. Lightning flickered low on the horizon, as though armies were locked in battle far to the east. She would have to hurry her cart horse if she wanted to get back to the longhouse before nightfall.

Standing at the single, huge rudder-oar to the right of the *Blood Wing*'s raised stern *lypting*, Thoryn wore a thick frieze cloak and a catskin cap. His dandy clothes were put away in his sea chest. If it hadn't been for his sword's golden handle, no one could have told he was a sea lord.

He looked at the water, which rippled like the back of a dusky, slowly swimming serpent, but his mind saw something else entirely: hair like a sheaf of amber wheat stirred by the wind. He felt a yearning to caress that wheaten spill. . . .

He shook himself and came awake to the sea again. The dream was sweet, but he had to mind his steering. They were sailing along a serrated stretch of coastline where there were known to be nests of marauders. Every fjord was the private principality of some self-styled sea king, living well by preying on the lucrative trade that tried to sail past his lair.

Nonetheless, only a moment later his mind was off dreaming again: When she saw him coming home, would she pick up her skirts and rush down the sea path to meet him? No. And that was all right. Much of her charm was her reserve, because it challenged him to break it down. He had in his chest the promised bronze mirror, and also a new pouch filled with large beads of amber, which he planned to use to weaken that reserve of hers, granting her no mercy or quarter, as soon as he had her alone. The thought made the blood sparkle in his veins.

A drifting gull screamed. The *Blood Wing* loped along through the inner leads between the shielding *skjaegard* and the coast, her prow-head snarling as always on her carved hull. Rolf came to sit on the *lypting* near Thoryn's feet. His rusty beard swayed as the sea breeze toyed with it. At length he said, "We've had an uncommonly good run so far."

"The winds have been good, right out of the wide mouth of Freya, praise her."

Rolf inhaled deeply. "A true Norseman can live a week on one breath of salt air."

Hauk Haakonsson called from his sea chest, "Then a true Norseman is a fool, for there is nothing so desirable as a good pork stew, and barley bread spread with butter, and a flagon of well-brewed beer to wash it down. By the gods, this dried fish tastes like gritty driftwood." They had as a matter of course eaten their fill of their fresh supplies as soon as they'd left Kaupang, and were now down to their preserved rations.

Across from Hauk, Jamsgar Copper-eye lolled on his sea chest and pretended to polish his gold arm ring as he said, "You're both as simple as Lapplanders. A real Norseman knows the most desirable thing on earth is a warm woman undressing in haste. Did I tell you about the one who invited me into her chamber in Kaupang? Swanhilde was her name. She lived in Coopersgate, the street of the woodworkers, where her husband had a little business. She had enormous pale eyes and a forlorn smile. Aye, now there was one who undressed in haste, brothers, and no sooner had she done so than I seized her and tossed her onto her bed."

He looked around him, eyes agleam, to see if he'd captured everyone's attention yet. He had, and so went on. "Aye, she lay there, not daring to look me in the face, but watching my hands undoing my belt."

The massy necklace that Hauk was wearing glimmered as he stirred restlessly. "And then?"

"And then I got over her and rubbed my naked chest on her splendid breasts."

"And then—?" Hauk half-moaned, half-laughed, wrinkling the bridge of his high, hooked nose. They had all been aboard ship, without women, for well over a sennight.

"Her face turned up to mine, I lowered my lips to hers."

More moans and laughter, from others besides Hauk now. Lief the Tremendous shouted from the other end of the ship, "You're a bawdy devil, Copper-eye! Get to it and tell us the good parts!"

"The good parts, hmm, let me see—this was no smash-and-grab assault, you know." He frowned like a man trying to seize the tail of a memory to drag it into the open. "Well, eventually she did dare to take a cautious hold of *Victory Giver.*"

"*Victory Giver!* What's that?"

"My stiff-stander, of course."

A shout of laughter. "You can't name that!"

"Brothers, do you want to hear the story or not?"

"Tell the story," Leif grumbled, impatiently waving the others to silence. " 'She took hold of *Victory Giver . . .* ' "

"Aye, she did, and gave a strange half-cry, a sort of overwrought laugh, you know, naturally fearing its great size. Don't laugh, brothers, I actually felt the fear flash through her; I felt it make her weak. It terrified her into silence. And not being one to waste my chances, I rapidly spread her knees, opening the road to the earthly paradise of men.

"She knew this was not a Norseman to refuse or argue with. She was utterly silent as my fingers opened the way for my entry. Friends—" he paused—"she was ready, luscious, oozing the soft moisture of a woman with voluptuous wants and urgings. A glow of excitement was in her face. I was now pushing forward, touching the entrance to her. At that first contact, she quivered with fear even as she campaigned to relax her body for me.

"Then suddenly she flinched away. If I were a smaller man, and if my fierce desires hadn't been so fiercely goaded, she may well have flung me off.

356

Startled, I looked up to see her husband. He gave out a yell from the doorway that would shrink a cedar pole to the length of a rye sprout!"

The groans were painful to hear. Even Thoryn smiled, though he kept his eyes fixed on the distant horizon.

"Brothers, he had a massive form — a Norway elk wouldn't go up against a man that size! Being a cooper, he was all covered with wood shavings and chips, and he had a lathe-turned bowl in one hand and the spoon-gouge he'd been using to make it in his other hand — a nasty-looking tool that."

Asmund Wartooth hooted, "What did you do, Copper-eye, roll onto your back and bare your breast to the stroke of Chance?"

Harold Rignivaler cried, "I know! You told him you were her long-lost brother just escaped from captivity by the Christians."

"I considered that, Harold, but didn't think he would believe it, not with her full sex gaping, with its rosy folds throbbing and clasping, and my organ erect, its tip already glossy with her moisture. So, thinking fast, I asked him if I might buy that pretty little bowl. For a moment, his face remained colored with rage, but then — you know how these town-bred Norse are — the man asked me how much I was thinking of offering. Let me tell you I bargained brilliantly; silver-tongued Loki could do no more than I did."

Hauk moaned painfully. When the hoots of disappointment died down, Kol Thurik shook his long head so that his grey plaits moved on his chest. He said, "All you young beards can think about is women, and when you win one, you burst with pride, like a cock on a dung heap. But women are dangerous. Their hearts are tailored on a turning wheel. They can melt a tough Norseman's spirit, make him into a charcoal chewer, a half-man who

357

stays at home like a good little boy. And that is not the way to get to Asgard."

Thoryn felt pricklings across his neck.

Kol waved his hand at Jamsgar. "Don't waste our time with any more of that babble."

"Babble? You make light of a solemn matter, Kol Thurik. Personally, I have a prejudice against being caught with my trousers down by a man with a spoon-gouge in his hand. It was not a moment to wave aside lightly. When I have an hour to spare, I think I'll challenge you for that insult."

From above them, still keeping watch on the surrounding sea, Thoryn said, "If you featherheads start anything now, I'll toss you both overboard and let you swim home."

Jamsgar replied flippantly, "Didn't you hear? I can walk and breathe under water. As can Starkad. Both of us visited a school in Kaupang run by a Finalnd witch fresh out of her cave. We paid good silver to learn the trick."

Was Thoryn only imagining it, or was the Copper-eye showing disrespect? Thoryn couldn't tell anymore. His "defeat" by the Black Dane had left him with a mantle of gall so weighty that he was having trouble gauging others' reactions to the thing.

Jamsgar turned back to Kol. "I'm not a fool you know."

"You should be more cautious."

"But not overly cautious."

"But above all cautious with another man's wife."

Hauk put in, "Don't argue with a fool, Kol."

"Are you calling me a fool, Hauk Haakonsson?" Jamsgar asked.

Norsemen could keep this sort of exchange going for hours at a stretch. They could get drunk on words—or burst into anger at any moment. It all depended upon their mood.

But what was their mood? For once Thoryn

couldn't tell. The trip had been successful, but their jarl had been bested by a man many of them felt they might have shortened by a head's height themselves.

Thoryn did upon occasion lose a game or contest, of course. But never before had he *let* an opponent triumph over him. He felt their rankling, unspoken questions: Did he step off the cloak—or was he forced off it? Is he losing his might? Is he still the best man to lead us?

While his mind was thus occupied, he saw, without first comprehending, the enemy. A pirate ship came rowing forth from where it had been lying in wait behind an island. It swooped out of the sea haze now, full of marauders.

"Ship ahead!"

The *Blood Wing* came instantly alive.

The pirate ship was already dropping sail to row into battle. Thoryn hastily maneuvered the *Blood Wing*, fighting against the powerful currents of the inner leads. While Ottar Magnusson and Rolf made to unstep the mast and clear the deck for action, Lief the Tremendous yelled in great alarm, "No, Thoryn, turn us about! We can outrun them!"

"Strike that sail!" Thoryn's voice sliced out. "Never shall men traveling with me think of flight."

"Do you realize how much silver I have? We *all* have profits. We can't risk a brush with so great a ship!"

Those words had the impact of another public defeat on Thoryn. The pirate vessel was indeed larger, but the *Blood Wing* was a thoroughbred warship, a ship for heroes, for warriors, not cowards. He said, "My father never fled from a battle, and until the gods dispose of my life, I shall never flee from one either! Rolf!" he snapped out, "if Lief opens his mouth once more, stick a blade through his teeth."

Hot vigor thrilled his veins. He was almost glad for this opportunity, almost drunk with it. He was thirsty for honor. Now he could release his pent and frustrated fury; he could slash off this shame he carried in the eyes of his men.

Chapter 24

As the Norsemen cleared the deck for combat, suddenly the enemy released a crosshatch of arrows. At once the air was cut through with a furious hissing. Jamsgar went down with a scream. There was another low *thung* of strings being loosed and the waspish hum of a dozen shafts hissing. A shaft struck only a yard before Thoryn and scuttered on, like a stone skimming over water, past his legs, before it stopped against a sea chest. The oarsmen lost their rhythm. Before they could pick it up again, the attacking longship veered, its oars beating powerfully, bringing it straight into the *Blood Wing*'s ribs. She was rammed amidships; her stout oars snapped off like kindling with the impact.

The pirates' selected champions stood in the prow of their dragonship and delivered the first fury of the impact. If one prowman fell, another stepped forward to take his place, while the men aft in the ship rained spears and even stones on the defending ranks. The invaders pressed forward, a few of them managing to leap aboard the *Blood Wing*, using their shields to ward off the blows of the defenders. This bold handful included a screaming, bare-headed chieftain wielding a stupendous battle-axe.

Thoryn leaped down from his platform. He heard

a grumbling. "We'll have a hard grind of it here," said Ottar Magnusson. Furious, Thoryn drew back his fist. But Ottar shouted, "Strike another way, Jarl." He gestured with the axe in his muscled hand. "It's more needful in that direction."

The pirates heaved a four-pronged grappling hook, binding their vessel fast to the *Blood Wing*. The Norsemen of Dainjerfjord settled to the work of defending their lives.

Thoryn had never fought so savagely. He was hard-pressed from every angle as he maneuvered his way through the fracas to engage the big chieftain. The man was a great figure, a towering crag of a man, larger than life and twice as ugly. He shouted, "I bear an invitation to a party! Let us dance together!"

For a long while Thoryn knew nothing except that he must keep hacking and hewing. At last he saw blood running from the chieftain's arm. The man was wounded, but Thoryn couldn't tell where, and had no inclination to ask.

"You seek a glorious death, Norseman!" the chief screamed.

"I seek *your* death, dog-dung!" Thoryn muttered grimly.

"Come to me, my beloved." The chieftain laughed.

The clutch of men in the pirate ship had been thinned by their attempts to cross over. Seeing a gap in the invasion, the chieftain suddenly leaped back across onto his own vessel. Thoryn leaped across right behind him.

For a moment he was alone, working a deadly way along the line of the attackers. But then others of his crew came aboard behind him. There were few niceties of strategy; it was a grim process of wearing down, hammering away, until exhaustion or numbers swung the balance. A Norse sea battle was no place for the faint-hearted.

Outnumbered and weakened at last, panic seemed to bite into the enemy ranks. As their numbers grew fewer, they retreated. Sharp was the clang of axe blades, and shrill the ring of swords. Blades flashed everywhere.

The toughest men were fighting in the stern, up on the high steering platform. The deck was wet with blood. Only a small band was left about the chieftain. More of Thoryn's men climbed aboard and closed on the platform, chopping with their broad-axes and swords. Rolf appeared beside Thoryn. "I see you can use a hand here."

"Aye," Thoryn said laconically.

They fought side by side, their arms red, their faces streaked with blood and sweat.

The chieftain began to grit his teeth so savagely that pieces broke off. He began to gnaw his lips with such abandon that his blood ran down his long beard, turning it red. He swung his iron axe perilously, beyond speech and reasoning. When he saw they were surrounded and clearly doomed, he screamed, "Norseman, this ship is called the *Surf Dragon;* treat her honorably!" and he jumped into the sea.

His last men, wide-eyed with surprise and hysteria, one-by-one paused, and then followed him overboard—all with their armor, shields, swords, and axes. Thoryn, still in the haze of his battle fury, leaned out frantically, trying to seize the leader before he went down. But the chieftain pulled his shield over his upward floating hair and vanished beneath the waters.

Thoryn would have gone in after him, but hands gripped his legs. He turned, his sword raised to slice off the fetters that kept him from his rightful kill.

Hauk Haakonsson and Kol Thurik backed off quickly. "Easy, Jarl, easy."

Thoryn lowered *Raunija*, whose blade was blunted. For a moment there was silence, and he thought he heard the Valkyries singing.

The victors took possession of their spoils—the pirate's gear, including booty taken from other raids; and their ship, which became Thoryn's. Many a man lay on the deck, spread-eagled by death. Their bodies were pitched unceremoniously into the cold water.

On the *Blood Wing*, Jamsgar was on his knees, groping at a shaft high in the back of his thigh. Thoryn stopped to help him pull the arrow out, saying, "Lucky your back was turned, or *Victory Giver* might have been damaged."

The Copper-eye grinned. "Jarl, *Victory Giver* always seems to have a following breeze and good luck."

The *Blood Wing* had not been so lucky. She was filling quickly with brackish water from a gap in her oaken bones. "We're holed—and soon will be swamped! Starkad!"

Using the *Surf Dragon*, they made for the nearest land, towing the *Blood Wing* behind. Beneath a flat-topped mountain, they found a sheltered cove, full of shoals. The Norsemen waded ashore, pulling the battered ship as far up the strand as they could. Her oaken keel scraped noisily up the shelving sandy beach. For two days she lay half settled in the cove while Starkad filled the hole in her with rope strands and patiently tarred them over. The men cursed "the dark ones who spin our web," but did so with self-satisfied smiles.

Many of these smiles were bestowed on their jarl. As they sat around their driftwood fire, Kol Thurik said, "Did you see him? With every fall of his longsword, a man went sprawling."

"Makes a person wonder how a bony Dane could force him off a cloak," Rolf said, one rusty eyebrow raised.

Thoryn said nothing.

At last, when the sun was lowering on the second day and her tarred side seemed to keep out water, the *Blood Wing* set out again. Thoryn stood, feet well apart, upon the steering deck, bracing his weight against the ever-moving currents of the leads. The pirate ship moved in tow behind.

The sun dipped down toward its rest. In the well of Thoryn's ship most of the men were sleeping, their fair hair gemmed with spray. A few casually wiped and cleaned their weapons or buffed the edges back into their axes.

Thoryn was eager to return to Dainjerfjord now. Already summer was at the verge of autumn. He had an uneasy and unreasonable feeling that he should never have gone to Kaupang, that he should never have left his longhouse, that he should never have left his thrall-woman.

Soren Gudbrodsson left his hut just after midnight. He stood for a moment with his legs wide apart and sniffed the dewy air like a man grown young again. He was off on an adventure!

The sky was cloudy, but there was no fog. This was all to the good as he traveled on foot toward Thorynsteading. He wore his old shirt of mail. It had long sleeves and came to a point above his knees. On his back he carried his round wooden shield, sheathed with hide and centered with a metal boss. His armor had cost him dearly back when he was newly bearded and trying to outfit himself for his first summer raids. He'd paid eleven cows for his helmet, which was made of interlaced strips of iron. He remembered his impatience over his battle shirt, but even the best armorer could only weld two hundred and fifty or so rings a day.

His axe, of course, was his pride. The armorer

had lavished much care and decoration on it. The blade-sides were etched with intricate designs inset with copper.

It took him several hours to make his way to the jarl's jetty. There he chose a small mast-equipped fishing boat lying half-ashore, surrounded by scuds of foam. He hadn't brought his sea chest; there wasn't room for that, but he did have a sack containing a few things he thought he might need. He stowed this and prepared to wait.

"Wake up."

Edin heard the voice and understood that it came from beyond the wall of her dreams. She started up when a hand shook her. She always slept with her face to the hall and now opened her eyes to see Inga standing over her, holding a small stone lamp. The flame danced before her eyes.

"Get up, girl. I have an errand for you," she said in a tone Edin had never heard before, a tone of unnatural calm. She seemed to see someone or something that existed through or beyond Edin.

It took another moment for Edin to gather her wits. Yesterday she'd gathered driftwood from the fjord-side, and had come to her bed to sleep the sleep of exhaustion. It must be very late now — or very early. The hall was full of a silence that seemed to press jagged edges against her sleep-clouded mind. She measured Inga with unfocused, mistrustful eyes. And Inga returned this look with that strange, calm dispassion.

"Get dressed. And bring your cloak."

She led Edin down the mead hall to her own chamber. Inside the rich, cluttered room, she sat in her high-backed chair, carefully putting her feet up on a carved footstool, leaving Edin to sway sleepily in the middle of the floor. "I want you to take that bundle down to the dock. Old Soren Gudbrodsson is traveling to the next fjord today. I want him to take something to a friend of mine." As she said this, her gaze seemed to be focused through the opposite wall.

Blowzy with her sudden waking and hasty dressing, Edin's eyes fixed on a small bundle on the floor near the door.

"Well?" Inga said. "Pick it up. And be quiet, people . . . people are . . . sleeping. . . ." She broke off the words as if they were thin twigs snapped from a tree.

Sweyn left Gunnhild's farmstead, *Freyahof,* rather late. He'd made another excuse to pass by there this afternoon and had stopped to help Hrut with the sheep again. Once the chores were done, he'd showed Hrut how to grasp an axe handle and how to stand. He challenged the boy to cut him with the blade, and as the boy swung, and swung again, Sweyn dodged away. Gunnhild came out with the sound of their blade play and invited Sweyn to stay and share their late meal.

Gunnhild. Why had he never realized before what a handsome-oared vessel that one was? There were still a few young men, tall and yellow-headed, to be got out of her womb. And *Freyahof*—there was plenty of rich grass for the sheep there.

Hrut pestered him for stories of his summer's activities. The boy was anxious to go a'viking, to stand at the stern post of a dragonship and hew down some foemen.

With all their talk, Sweyn had left the farmstead rather late and was getting back to the longhouse in the desolate middle of the night. He looked forward to his sheepskin.

Not so long ago night had seemed to stretch before him like a dark tunnel at each day's end.

Now he slept through that darkness, as a man should.

He crept into the hall quietly, noting the smell of stale cabbage that persisted from meal to meal. Inga's cooking was not getting any better. He made his way through the shadows, but then stopped and stood with his left hand resting on his axe head. He saw the Song-singer, which was what he privately called Edin, following Inga to her chamber.

Busy with gathering up his life again, he'd seen little enough of the thrall lately. Her hair was loosely snarled over her shoulders, and dirty. The sleeve of her threadbare dress had torn and hung unstitched and flapping. She had her cloak thrown over her arm. Unfamiliar with the emotion of pity, Sweyn felt immediate anger instead. When the girl disappeared behind Inga's door, he stood on, his face in shadow, concentrating, listening.

But he heard nothing and soon turned for his bed. Lying alone in the dark he raised his left hand to run his fingers through his blond chest hair. He ran it over his hard muscled shoulder. He flexed his fingers. He'd shown Hrut quite a few tricks today. The boy admired him. Gunnhild needed a man, and he was a man again. The thought was like a cool pebble for his thirst. Once he'd been a great warrior, but there was no sense in weeping for days that would not happen again. Meanwhile, Gunnhild. . . . Edin and Inga were forgotten as he drifted into a pleasant dream.

Inga accompanied Edin to the door of the dark hall. But there Edin hesitated. Her disorientation at being wakened in the middle of the night was lifting. Suddenly she had so many questions; suddenly she saw how many ways Inga could be working against her. This could merely be a means to catch her in a seeming escape and call for her death. And death it would be, for that was the law and not even the jarl could protect her if he wasn't here.

Inga didn't notice her hesitation immediately; she'd gone away again. Her eyes held nothing but two tiny flames, two reflections of the stone lamp she held cupped in her hands. At last she gave a small start and fixed Edin with a look. "What are you still doing here?"

The realization clearly surfaced in Edin's mind: *Inga Thorsdaughter is not right.*

At that moment the ever-lingering smell of cabbage almost made her gorge rise. But she mustn't wretch. For several days now she'd been struggling not to draw any attention to her morning attacks of nausea. She had a secret inside a secret, something she hadn't divulged to anyone. She compressed her lips against the churning urge.

"Go!" Inga said.

Edin needed to get outside. It was too late to ask questions. She had no choice but to do what she was told anyway. After all, she didn't own herself anymore.

Outside, it was dark as midnight. Clouds hung over the bowl of the valley like woodsmoke in a closed room. Her poor cloak hardly protected her from the chill, even with the hood pulled low over her head. But the fresh air checked her need to wretch. She breathed it deeply. Out on the green, the lush wet grass soaked her footwear. Briefly the tree's branches made a web against the night sky over her head. She skirted a small byre from which came a sheepy smell, sharp and proclamatory of its usual occupants. Passing close by it, she thought she heard a voice and stopped in a renewal of suspicion.

"Here now, give me a kiss, pretty lass. Mmm . . . you got nice legs — and what is this?"

Another voice answered, a feminine murmur, a

voice Edin recognized: "You know what that is—oh! Blackhair!"

Blackhair! The worm! Edin looked at the byre wall wide-eyed. How could Juliana . . . ?

"Come on, you know you want it again" came Blackhair's muffled chiding. "You got to go back inside in a while."

"But—oh! don't you do it so hard!"

Then came whimpers and the sound of bodies in harsh motion. Edin continued on.

She couldn't blame Juliana for falling so low. The girl only wanted more from life than serving endless horns of buttermilk and ale. They all wanted more than this existence they had, this never-ending labor which gained them no reward, no single moment of satisfaction or happiness, and they were all driven to desperate measures.

She hurried the short distance to the path leading down to the water's edge. Near the dock, she felt a large, immovable hand on her shoulder and turned with a gasp. An old Viking stared down at her fiercely, with grey eyes so colorless she thought at first he must be blind. Her heart vaulted into her throat.

"You're late, girl!"

She pulled tentatively at her shoulder, and after a moment he released her. He had in his free hand a very fine axe, its head decorated with copper in the image of a creature like a bird. Mutely, she held out the bundle Inga had sent her to deliver. He grunted and motioned toward the boat he had ready to go. Edin looked at this slantwise, and the thoughts that went through her head in that instant were multitudinous, and by the end of the instant, she felt the center of her heart harden.

He took everything from me and left me to this end. So be it.

Slowly, fatalistically, she turned, presenting her

back to the old Viking. She was not surprised when he struck her. What surprised her was the strength of the blow and suddenness of its effect on her.

The *Blood Wing*, with the *Surf Dragon* in tow, entered the mouth of the Dainjerfjord under a cross-grain of wind. The sea birds gave voice to their homecoming. Thoryn had had more time than he'd wanted to think on this trip, and it was Edin who'd filled those thoughts. She'd seemed so distant for so long. But now he was home and Edin was here. A straight road ran ahead of him.

The land on either side of the fjord glittered under the glare of the overcast day. He had to squint to spy the small figure on the look-out point, a dark-headed thrall-child who turned and disappeared, no doubt to spread the word that the longship was home.

The welcoming party was not large. From Thorynsteading there were only thralls to greet the ship. And there was Sweyn, who said, looking at the *Surf Dragon*, "I see the trip was fruitful."

Before Thoryn could comment, Inga came huffing down the path. His eyes scanned behind her, looking for a particularly bright head of hair, amber hair that flashed and hung down nearly to the knees. She wasn't among the welcomers, however. He wondered, but couldn't bring himself to ask his mother outright.

Inga was saying about the *Surf Dragon*, "What do I take for the explanation of this?"

"You will get your explanation, Mother—but where is everyone?" This seemed an ominously uneasy arrival. No one was saying much; there were none of the usual little knots of welcoming conversation.

Sweyn stepped forward. "There's been some trouble." Thoryn sensed a change in him, but he didn't have time to identify it, for Sweyn was saying, "Your Song-singer, Edin, is missing."

Thoryn's whole heaven collapsed. He turned deaf, as surely as if a whole fugue of sound had hit his ears at once.

. . . missing . . . missing . . . missing . . .

A voice in his mind quietly promised: "I may not be here when you return, Viking."

She had deserted him.

Snorri bumped into him under the load of a standing whale-oil lamp of iron and a brass-bound wooden bucket, booty from the *Surf Dragon* which he was carrying up to the longhouse. His nudge seemed to bring Thoryn's emotions suddenly and violently to the surface. He turned on the man and cursed him harshly, too charged with emotion to hold it in.

He swung back to Inga and braced himself, but it was useless. She was looking at him with an expression both stern and maternal. Though he had oft suffered that look, he didn't like it. Not at all. She said, "I sent Fafnir and Eric into the mountains to look for her."

Thoryn's heart was still stopped.

"She ran away again."

Sweyn started to speak, but she cut in, "There is no other way to account for it." She looked at Thoryn with faint censure fused with affection. It was so maternal, that look. "It isn't the first attempt she's made at running away, is it? She was lucky last time. Most likely this time she'll be wolf meat before the sun rises again. She might as well have jumped in the sea and tried to swim home to England."

Sweyn said, "Jarl—"

Thoryn's urge was to shrug him off, but there was an urgency in the Cripple's tone. "Speak!" he said against the searing anguish that clutched his throat.

Sweyn glanced at Inga. There was something in

his manner that suggested he wished to exclude her. Thoryn said, "Walk with me up the path."

As soon as they were alone, Sweyn said, "Jarl, I suspect foul play. I have little to base my suspicions on, but—"

"Foul play? I would say so! I would say Loki, malignant Loki, has been at play here."

"I don't think she ran away. I think Inga had her taken away."

Thoryn's eyes narrowed. Sweyn had become taut. The slack was gone, his eyes were clear, the timbre was back in his voice, and twenty years had left his face. "Explain!"

Sweyn told him of seeing Inga lead Edin into her chamber so late last night. Thoryn remembered what he'd called her earlier, "Song-singer," not "the Saxon thrall," not "the witch." After listening, he said to Sweyn, "That may have a perfectly acceptable explanation."

Sweyn's eyes glittered. "Mayhap, since Inga has tried her best to break the girl. She's been put to tasks . . . hay cutting, carrying water for baths— men's work. I myself used her as an axe target, and not a word was said against it."

He went on quickly, "A few days ago, Inga made a trip to visit old Soren. Who knows why? And today, when one of the fishing-thralls reported at the first meal that a boat was missing, Inga quickly shut him up. I talked to the man myself later and sent him around by rowboat to see if Soren was about his place. He got back just a while before you—and Soren is not to be found. His hearthfire is cold. Jarl, it takes less than the ability to read runes to make out that Inga arranged with Soren to seize your woman and take her away. If I were you, and owned a woman like that, I would look into this."

Thoryn stared at him for several heartbeats before he said with massive sarcasm, "I can't help but wonder why you tell me this, Sweyn, or why I should believe any of it. I find it easier to believe you of slander-bearing than concern for the woman you blame for your crippling. You used her for an axe target?"

"It's a long story, Jarl. Let the skalds tell it later; there's no time now. Only know that your Edin challenged me to become a man again, and so I have. And it would be sorry of me now to let her be taken out to sea and drowned by the likes of old Soren Gudbrodsson."

Thoryn paused in indecision only a moment more, then turned and went down the path to where Inga was watching the unloading of the ships. He took her arm, and she turned to him with a look of such sweet, tolerant unhappiness that he almost cried out for mercy. Her eyes were as blue as the sky. She said, "Son, you look hungry. I have just what you need up in the longhouse—bread, honey, yellow butter—"

"Did Soren take her?" His voice was low; he felt icy; he was holding on to his patience and his temper and his sanity for dear life.

Inga didn't dissemble. In fact, a sort of mask came over her face. She'd always been extremely fickle in manner, but this was different. Her blue eyes seemed to fill with the old cumulus of nightmares. "Aye," she said simply, "he's taken her to Hell."

Thoryn was stunned, doubly stunned. It was all true, what Sweyn had said.

Drowned!

It was not until that moment that he knew exactly what Edin meant to him. When he spoke, the words came out slowly: "Then the curse of Hell shall you bear, woman. Your only son curses you forever. I swear this, and swear I will never forsake it."

Inga's face went black, and then . . . she laughed. It was a sound he'd never heard; it was something

374

new beneath the northern sun.

"Let her go," she cackled, "and thank Odin for it! She was a demon. She unmanned you, made you feckless and cowardly. She was slow poison, wanton death. I was duty-bound to get rid of her, just as I—" A wretched pause, as if she were trembling on the edge of saying something far more consequential, and then, again, that laugh.

A bolt of horror ripped through Thoryn. The corners of his jaws bunched against it.

All day Soren sat at the tiller bar of the little craft, never saying a word, not even when Edin regained consciousness and picked herself up from the bottom of the boat where he'd tossed her. Not even when she asked him quietly what he meant to do with her.

Like a flying bird, the boat sped on, a bloating wind in its small sail, past shining cliffs, past towering hills, past ranging headlands. She grew tired of sitting on the hard bench. Her head hurt badly from being struck by the hammer of his axe, and now and then she kneaded the sides of her skull to try to pacify its contents. Her stomach felt most delicate and doubtful. Eventually the slip and slide of the horizon sent her to the gunwales. But after that one time, she wretched no more. The hours passed with nothing but the pervasive sound of the sea. She tried not to think about dying; her thoughts along that line were not brave.

At last, as the winterlike sun withered toward the western horizon, Soren nosed the boat into a little cove just inside the mouth of a small, uninhabited fjord. The narrow beach was backed by cliffs of black rock which leaned out into the sea on each end. The old man pulled the boat onto the beach and gestured Edin out. She didn't move far and never took her eyes off him. He reached for his sack of belongings and tossed it on the sand, then was quite open about taking his axe from his belt. As he raised it ready to swing at the level of her neck, her very life quivered within her.

Chapter 25

Edin would have lost her head in the next instant except that her young reflexes were faster than the aging Viking's. She ducked to one side, hearing the whisper of the blade just above her ear.

That made Soren angry, to swing and miss like that. His breath made a snorting sound in his nose. He charged her, axe up and swinging, fully expecting to connect with his victim this time. But she escaped the swing again. Her hours with Sweyn repaid her now.

A third swing came. Her hands were by now circling the reed of her neck, as if she could protect it. Meanwhile, she wasn't simply standing and waiting to be cut down. She danced fast away from the swinging axe. Soren staggered. He was out of control with rage now, but he was large and strong and his axe was a monster thing; if he ever connected it with any part of her, it would be all over.

Before he could regain his balance, Edin ran — but there was nowhere to go! The beach was walled on all sides by rock, except for the side bounded by the sea. Soren caught her by her hair, which streamed out behind her. She screamed as she went down. He panted and puffed above her, rabid with rage. His insane passion seemed the only thing keeping him upright. She watched as he raised his axe again, gripped the weapon two-handed and lifted it high to his right. He screamed, to gather every ounce of strength left to him. He had every intention of cutting her in two.

Not until the giant axe started down did she move, rolling to his left at the last instant. He'd already committed himself; he couldn't stop the swing. His axe buried itself completely in the sand.

"One moment, I beg you!"

The old man, pulling his axe free, seemed surprised at the sound of her voice. She went on frantically, "I know Inga has put you up to this, but—"

"It's the jarl's orders I carry out."

"The jarl is gone! It's Inga who wants me dead."

"You're a witch, and the jarl doesn't want you around anymore." He lifted the axe again.

"He may not want me around, but he wouldn't order this murder. It's Inga, I tell you!"

"Bah! You would say anything to stay alive."

Truly she was saying anything that came to mind: "Thoryn Kirkynsson is no fool. And no coward. If he wanted me dead, he would do it himself. He wouldn't have me killed by an old man. But why should he want me dead at all? I have value. Men like girls . . . concubines . . . bed-thralls, and-and those who can afford them frequently acquire them. In fact, I have double value now, for I carry a child—the jarl's own child."

She saw Soren's hold loosen on his axe. Reluctantly, he lowered the blade.

"You saw me wretch. That is why—I have the morning sickness women get."

She could see his mind wrestling. The more he thought, the more addled he seemed to become. He took to pacing. As soon as he turned his back on her, she rose and started to back down the beach. Soren turned to see how she'd lengthened the distance between them, and an angry growl came from his throat.

She ran wildly for the boat. He couldn't catch her, yet he managed to shove her, destroying her balance and making her fall. He landed on top of her with a yell of exultation. Now her heart was wild, pounding at an incredible rate, as if to compensate for the eternity of stillness ahead.

But he didn't use his axe again. Instead, he dragged her sobbing and stumbling to where he'd dropped his sack. Holding her with one hand — he was so strong, despite his age! — he found a length of rope. He locked her hands mercilessly behind her back and tied her ankles. He wrapped her cloak about her body next, encasing and trussing her like a sausage.

At length, he lifted her and carried her under one arm. At one end of the beach the black rock formations made a pool. The tide was out for now, and the water was shallow; yet what was there was cold as Soren laid her down in it, and it seeped through her clothes.

"I leave it to the gods to decide your fate, woman. If you can manage to escape before the tide comes in, then you will live." He stood to turn away.

"Please don't do this!"

He looked at her once more, with those frosty, ungenerous eyes. "I leave you to the gods. Your fate is not mine anymore."

Thoryn had sailed home from the south, and although there were fjords and coves and innumerable islands where they might have passed by a small boat without seeing it, Thoryn felt old Soren would not have taken that chance unnecessarily. The old man must have taken Edin northward.

When they set out, it was into an opalescent world

of dusk. Too soon night fell. The Thunder God showed some mercy, however; the clouds cleared and the stars shone at their full. Thoryn had the *Blood Wing*'s sail lowered, and he ordered his men to row—slowly, for they were near the shore and had nothing but the stars to light their way. Their voices toned away to mere whisperings, for this was wicked water studded with bald-rock skerries.

He'd brought the *Blood Wing*, despite her fractured ribs and strakes, because he wanted a ship he knew, a ship that followed his will as well as a familiar horse. He maintained a tight-lipped silence while his thoughts ate at him. Thoughts that all had the same center: Edin. Why hadn't he seen his mother's unsoundness before? He'd so long ago lost patience with her that he'd learned to mostly ignore her, and thus he'd left Edin unprotected in her care.

Standing at the steeringboard of his dragonship, with its sail stowed and oars out, half of him thought, *It is silly not to hope,* and the other half felt a dark and brooding pessimism.

Edin lay in the rock pool like a sickly infant left for the sea to smother. She'd quickly become cold, and colder. Now the touch of the sea water was as painful as nails piercing her flesh. Her body shook in spasms, stirring up swirling, muddy sediment in the shallow pool. She stuttered, half in rage, half to keep herself sane, "I want to live . . . I want to live . . . I want to live!"

But gradually her voice got far away as her battered head grew buoyant and strange. The very bones in her skull seemed to swell with fear. Her flesh ran with terror. Screams rose in her, but she wouldn't let them out.

She heard the spray of the rising ocean as breakers cascaded against the stand of offshore black rock.

Little by little, steamlets of rising water began to make their way into the pool. She felt the tide creep ever higher about her. How long until the regular rhythm of waves broke over the short seaward wall and covered her face?

Looking up, the sky seemed so close that the stars were like some infeasibly bright light straining to break through a pitted black dome. They sparkled, sparkled. . . .

The water in the pool lapped her chin, and Edin twitched to wakefulness. Something within her had cried a warning, bringing her out of the shocked daze she'd slipped into. The water level had risen considerably. It covered her mouth so that she had to lift her chin to breathe. Soon it would quench her. She'd stopped shivering; her muscles and nerves were too numb to react anymore.

She wondered if she could maneuver onto her knees — but what if she fell forward? She would lay facedown in the water as totally helpless as a turtle on his back. She decided against trying, and anyway, it didn't seem terribly important anymore. Everything seemed far away now. Was this the end? It wasn't so bad. It was like standing on the threshold of a dream. She even felt warmer, felt a sensation of warmth like a fine embering fire. A silly smile took hold of her and wouldn't let go. She imagined the air smelled of summer, of English roses, warm, sweet, drowsy. . . .

The sea broke over the pool's wall, and fear called Edin back yet again, stark and vivid and primordial. Even now there was something in her that refused defeat. The water churned; the great wave tossed her. She was powerless to fight it. For a moment she was submerged, in a place of almost pure darkness; then, as the wave subsided, she was left lying on her side, her hip wedged against a rock so that her face was above the water. Now all her in-held screams gathered into one scream. She cried out in a voice deep and guttural, unfeminine but determined: *"Vi-i-kinng!"*

Before she could catch her breath, the high tide brought in another dashing wall of sea water. It hit the rocks with splitting force, seethed, and washed over them into the pool.

The *Blood Wing* found Soren's small craft floating bottom-up near a rock-fanged skerry. Its bow was staved in, and it was clear what had happened: In the dark, the boat had been tossed against the rocks. There was no sign of the old warrior. Nor of Edin. The crew was silent, waiting for Thoryn to say something. Finally Rolf asked him if they should turn for home. Thoryn's mind was occupied with a vision: Edin's face blank and waxen, her hair floating about her like seaweed, his hand reaching and not quite catching it as she sank away from him.

When Rolf touched him, he came back to life abruptly. "We will proceed."

"Oath-brother, be reasonable."

Thoryn's answer was as cold as the waters of Dainjerfjord in deepest winter: "We proceed, Norsemen."

And so they did, for no man aboard was willing to argue against him, though he heard a word muttered: "Witch!"

They were just passing the mouth of an insignificant fjord when they heard her call, one word in Saxon, hoarse and throaty, then . . . nothing. No man said a word; their oars had stopped motionless in the water. They sat silent, waiting. Thoryn held the steering-oar in a grip that could have broken a man's back. But no other sound came to help them locate her. The sea crashed loudly up the shortened beach of a nearby cove. Thoryn watched it, his eyes straining for a welcome shape, then suddenly he said, "Take her in! Hauk—up on the prow platform! Watch for hidden rocks!"

Hauk leapt forward as ordered, to hang on the neck of the dragon and study their passage intently. It would be unwise to race in and tear their bottom open and so end like Soren Gudbrodsson.

Meanwhile Thoryn waited until the others completed their row, then shouted, "Oars up!" He steered the coasting *Blood Wing* toward the sloping beach.

There was a crunch as the prow landed. He instantly hoisted the rudder. A wave came in with them, and the ship ran in farther; then, as the wave fell back, the *Blood Wing* settled into the sand, listing slightly to the left. The men shipped their oars and stacked them in a pile. Then . . . a deep hush. Every man turned to watch their jarl still standing alone at the stern.

He tried to pierce the darkness with his eyes. The beach was nearly gone, nearly swamped by the tide. The sand ended in a rock tangle at the base of the nearest bluff. Those splintered fangs of stone probably formed a pool.

"By the gods—!"

He raced the length of the longship, barely touched the prow platform with his feet, and leapt ashore. A breaker burst against his thighs, and he had to wade through its thick foam. He felt as if he were in a boyhood dream, the kind in which he tried to run but his legs seemed weighted. The heavy sea held him pitilessly; he could only move in slow motion, no matter how he wanted to hurry, *hurry!*

Out of the blackness, Edin caught a glimpse of a ghastly pale face distorted by the water over her eyes. Hands reached for her; she was lifted. She sucked in breath. She was being carried. Arms had her. She was handed up into another pair of arms, then laid down upon a bed of wood. Again that pale face was over her. Death. Death had come for her. He was like a figure of fog. This must be the ship the Vikings believed to be the ferry to the netherworld.

Gradually her vision cleared, and with a shock she found the jarl bending over her, standing between her and that vision of menacing Death. Already he'd unwrapped her sodden cloak; now he was bent to untie her ankles. She thought she felt his hands chaffing her feet; but it was hard to tell, for she was completely numb.

There was nothing wrong with her sense of smell, however, and when his hands went beneath her to free her wrists, he was so close that she could smell the familiar and intimate fragrance of him, so extremely lush and alive; he seemed a miracle of life.

"Viking," she whispered. She could speak barely above her breath. He had to lean his ear near her mouth to hear. "You came home."

"Aye," he said, his voice nearly as soft as hers. He was leaning over her, speaking for her ears alone. "I had to come home when I started to hear your name inside my head. But when I arrived, you were not there to greet me. I won't punish you too severely for that, under the circumstances. Just a small beating. Never say I'm ungenerous." His voice was odd; it didn't seem to belong to him.

He brushed the water from her face, and at the chill feel of her skin, she heard his chest fill with breath. "Shieldmaiden, I will have this dress off you and put you in my sheepskin." While talking, he was busy with a knife, though truly the garment she was wearing was so threadbare as to hardly need a blade to rend it from neck to hem.

He braced her so that she was half-sitting, to pull the garment from beneath her. It was then that she realized she was in the longship that had brought her away from Fair Hope. She was lying on the platform beneath the dragon's head. And more than a dozen Vikings stood looking at her. The jarl had cut open her sodden dress, and she was mercilessly exposed. She flinched back, thinking to cover herself—but her numb arms hung like empty sleeves at her sides.

He commanded, "Oarsmen, face aft!"

For a moment the atmosphere fairly quivered with taut nerves; but then one moved, and next they all obediently turned their backs. Swiftly he stripped her of the soaking gown. She didn't feel the cold night air before he helped her into the sheepskin sleeping bag; she hardly even felt the sleeping bag. She was numb through and through, so numb she could hardly move, and certainly could not shiver.

Once he had her safely stowed, the jarl shouted a staccato of orders. The next wave broke with a roar on the beach and simultaneously the men dug their oars into the sand so that as the surf receded, they backed the *Blood Wing* down the slope. Thus the dragon slithered back into the sea.

When the jarl bent over her again, she asked, "How did you find me?" Her voice was failing; it was no more than wind whispering to his ear.

"We were out harpooning seals, sailing along the coast and leisurely picking our targets. Then we heard a funny sound, something like 'Viking,' in Saxon—a dog's tongue if ever there was one. I wanted to go on, but some of my brothers begged to investigate."

She accepted that without a murmur. She had no more strength to murmur. The long wait for death, the fear, and now this sudden release. Soren . . . seals . . . she couldn't sort it out anymore. Her eyes refused to focus, the lids closed, and she drifted. It seemed a dragon had her in his talons and was carrying her high above the star-sparkled sea. The thought of resisting didn't so much as cross her mind; resistance was impossible, and she knew it. He carried her clutched in his claws while his powerful wings beat and beat and beat.

Thoryn raised his voice until echoes of it reverberated off the high cliffs. "If she lives, in honor of you, Odin, I will sacrifice in thanks. This I swear—*if she lives.*"

As soon as Hagna, the medicine woman, arrived at the longhouse, she expelled Thoryn from his chamber. That was when he discovered that though everyone else had long ago found their beds, Inga was still up. He'd almost forgotten about her. He wished he could forget about her.

He made his weary way to his high-seat and sprawled in it. Inga crept close—but not too close. "Son . . ."

He didn't raise his voice, didn't bother to make it hard, but said quietly, "Let me tell you, Inga Thorsdaughter, I am not your son, so do not use that name to me again."

"Oh!" Her hand went to her mouth as if he'd struck her.

He steeled himself with what he'd learned in the last hour, from Dessa and from the evidence of Edin's body—the calluses on her hands, the snarled filth of her hair, the pitiful thinness of her. "In the morning," he said, "you will leave my longhouse forever."

"Where—Thoyrn, where will I go!"

He thought for a moment. "You will go to Soren Gudbrodsson's hut." It seemed a fitting exile for her.

"Alone?" The word came out of her with a shiver.

"No, you can't be trusted to be alone. I'll send that troublemaker Juliana with you."

She stared at him without answer. Tears filled her eyes. She turned away.

"You will never come here again. You are banished. Do you understand?"

"But . . . who will cook your meals, make your clothes, take care of you?"

"I have a thrall," he said dryly, "who was bred to manage a manor house." His tired mind took him back briefly to England, the large hall, tapestried and bannered for a wedding that never took place.

Inga had moved to her kitchen area, and her hand was idly moving over objects, as if to say good-bye to them. He could hardly bear to watch her, and so turned his eyes away—therefore not seeing her grasp the knife handle.

Inga stood very still in the shadowy darkness. Her mouth tasted of copper. The Saxon had taken Kirkyn from her, had taken her home from her, had taken her place from her. How dare she? Her with that hair as pale as barley beneath a white spring sun! Those eyes as blue and clear as the best sky of summer! How dare she when . . . when she was supposed to be dead? Inga remembered . . . or had she only dreamed that? The dark chamber, the knife, the lovers lying abed, Kirkyn snoring a little, the Saxon's head on his shoulder? It must have been a dream, since the thrall was still alive.

Well then, Inga had to take care of that. She felt a gathering in the air, a racing current that made it difficult to stand still. Aye, she would take care of it this minute.

It wasn't until she started for his chamber that Thoryn was alerted. By the time he stood, she was holding the kitchen knife up, dagger fashion, and was rushing toward his door. He rose and raced after her. She was already half inside before he caught her arm and spun her about. Even then she tugged to get away. Her eyes . . . she was mad!

Loathe to touch her, he shoved her away from the open chamber door. She fell, and when she lifted her head, she was grinning and making a sound, a hiss, like frying oil, like rain. "I'll kill her. You can send me to the ends of the world, but somehow I'll get back." She looked past him toward his bed. "Do you hear me, Margaret? He can't stop me! If he tries . . ." She lifted the knife. For Thoryn, the night fell away from any pattern and shattered.

"Odin, save us!"

"By the gods!"

The hall was awake; there were witnesses to this scene of shame. Edin lay unmoving in his bed. Thoryn told Hagna, "Close the door!" Now Inga was crying in low broken sobs, hugging the knife to her breast, appealing to Thoryn, "I love you. My beloved! And you loved me until she came between us. I have to free you, somehow I have to—"

"I am not my father!" he shouted, feeling with horror a start of tears in his own eyes.

Her tears stopped flowing; she started laughing. "Thoryn! He told me he was going to free her, that she would never be easy with him until he did. *Easy!* He wanted *her* to be easy! He said that she would always think of herself as somehow his thrall, his property."

There was a froth of foam on her lips. And those eyes!

She got to her feet, lifting the knife again. "But she is a thrall! She has no right to more. She has no right to my place, my bed, my husband . . . my son!"

Thoryn stood unmoving. It was Rolf who appeared behind her and disarmed her, and Eric who helped him drag her to her chamber.

The two sennights following her rescue were vague in Edin's mind. Every moment had a plausible meaning; but none of them seemed connected, for she had not survived unscathed her time in the North Sea.

There were hours when she thought she must be still caught in that taloned dragon's grip, which seemed to choke off her breath and make her cough painfully. There were hours when she shivered, suffering one spasm after another, until it seemed as though she would never be warm again. There were hours when she feared she'd drowned after all, for her lungs seemed full of sea water.

As she struggled to sit up, to rise above the water and draw air, unknown hands braced her. When she was hot and fretful and ached for coolness, hands bathed her face with cool cloths and provided her with little spoonsful of water to partially quench her great thirst. The feel of these hands varied, from a young woman's, to an old woman's, to a man's. They too were blurred in her mind, for all were equally gentle; all equally served her as lifebuoys in that vast sea that threatened to swamp her.

Another thing: Sometimes weak sunlight came through a window; other times lamps burned about her. It seemed to make no sense, unless time had spun out of control so that the days and nights were revolving minute by minute.

Within that crazy spin of time she lived an almost inaudible life of heartbeats and recurring dreams, a life of fever and privacy, a delicate yet laborious life which weakened her, which wore her down finally to simple coma.

Then came a day when she awakened. It didn't happen all at once. First she was only aware — of her mind and her thoughts, of being a person who was called Edin. She roused slowly, realizing she hadn't been fully conscious for a long while. She remained at that level of torpor for what seemed forever, but then eventually noticed her body, how it lay nestled into — not a dragon's underbelly — but a feather mattress. She felt pillows behind her head. She forced her unwilling senses to take stock: Where were her

389

hands?

There, yes, lying along her sides above the blankets. The instant she located them she felt the pulse in her palms leap like a trout in a brook.

And where were her feet?

There, somewhat weighted by quilts.

Her tongue . . . lay in her mouth like a dry wad of wool.

The chamber in which she lay was quiet, but through the window she heard shouts and dogs barking and the pounding of hoofs. Life was going on without her. She heard the door open, heard quiet footsteps on the rushes. She forced her eyes to open, which they did only narrowly. She saw a girl in a chair with a high carved back and arms. Her head nodded drowsily. *I know that girl, who is she?* The girl leapt up as though stung by a bee when she saw the figure of the person who had just come in, a large, familiar figure. A big enough man, with a sword slung on his hip, partially concealed by his cloak. He looked exceedingly strong. *I know him, too.* Edin couldn't remember exactly who he was, yet the sight of him made her heart behave peculiarly.

The girl said, "Her hair's been made tidy, Master."

His face was set like flint. Edin heard him say over the wordless blows of her heart, "Aye, you've done your day's work. Go now and get you some food and rest. Tomorrow Hagna will come again and—"

Edin listened to the words and tried to follow them. But it was hard going, and she gave up before long.

The girl—*Dessa! that is her name*—had meanwhile crossed the room. Paused at the door, she said, with something like sympathy for the man, "There's so much we can do and no more, Master."

When she'd closed the door behind her, he unfastened the brooches holding his cloak to his shoulders and tossed it aside. He came to the bed. He stood

390

looking down at Edin, then reached to adjust her blankets. Through the slits of her eyelids, she watched him, the father of her unborn babe, her owner, the man she loved — and hated.

He said, "Your eyes are open again. What do you see, Shieldmaiden? I would give Odin my best lamb bearer to know."

Exerting a terrible effort — no one would ever know what effort it cost her — she forced her woolly tongue to move, made her dry lips part, forced her jaw-hinge to unlock, and she murmured, "I . . . see . . . you . . . Viking."

There was a pause full of silence, then, without warning, he reached out with both hands and gathered her to his chest. It was a fierce and muscular hug.

"Your best lamb-bearer?" she struggled to say into his ear. "What terrible men you Norse are for making bargains. You would bargain with Christ himself."

"I would have if I'd thought of it. But it was Odin to whom I spoke, who doesn't mind if a man is wicked or not but only whether he is known to keep his word."

Chapter 26

The next morning was cool with an overcast sky out the bedchamber's high window. Dessa was helping Edin to some warm wine and a dish of boiled mutton mashed into shreds so that she might swallow it without too much chewing. Even so, she lay back wearily before much of the food was taken.

The Viking came in. She moved her head on her pillow to see him. At a gesture from him, Dessa hurried out. "You have color in your cheeks," he said when they were alone.

She blinked slowly. This was the man who had saved her from being washed overboard by the monster storm on the open sea coming from England, the man who had pulled her out of the depths of Dainjerfjord, the man who had kept her from death punishment when she'd broken the *Thing*-law, who had lifted her from the flooded tide pool. He was also the man who had killed her Cedric, burned her Fair Hope, stripped her of her *self* and made her an object of property; he was the man who had ravished her, and impregnated her, and then left her to be persecuted and almost murdered. He was a Viking, a man who could be gentle one moment and savage the next. He followed no rules but those he made himself, and was therefor never to be trusted, no matter how much she might love him.

He stood with one shoulder negligently leaned against the bedpost, at home against the frieze of coiled serpents and taloned beasts carved into it. He crossed his arms loosely over his broad chest. Something flickered in his stone-colored eyes; a smile played at the corners of his mouth. He moved to sit beside her on the edge of the bed, and she slid over, as if to accommodate him, but really because she had no wish to be any closer to him than was necessary. By the way he fixed those close-lidded eyes on her, she had the feeling he knew everything she was thinking.

It took her a long time to speak, and it took courage. "I wasn't running away," she said in a husky voice. "Your mother sent me down to the fjord—"

"I know." He paused. "Soren drowned. We found the boat smashed by a skerry."

She bit her lower lip.

"Was it my mother's plan that you be left to die slowly, or was that Soren's own idea? I cannot but wonder, since he had an axe, why he didn't simply take off your head."

Visions rose up. She closed her eyes against them, swallowed hard, then said only, "I reasoned with him."

The Viking raised his brows inquiringly, but she said no more. She would not tell him she was carrying his child. Let her keep that much from him as long as she could. Something had happened to her in that instant when she'd realized Soren was going to knock her unconscious and take her away from the fjord to kill her. Her heart had hardened. There was now a case of stone around its soft core. The Viking would have this child eventually, and no doubt he would have her passion again, and he would have her love in moments when she was weak and weary; but never would she give the smallest part of these things to him without a struggle.

His look was inscrutable. At last he said, in a voice that was chilled and charged, "I've sent Inga from the longhouse. There are those who say I should kill her. Not for what she did to you—"

No, of course not; she was but a thrall.

"—but because . . . she confessed to my father's murder. It was Inga all along. Not Margaret. They say I should avenge my father . . . but I seem unable to do the deed, and so she is alive yet."

Edin said, "She is not right in her mind. You can't kill her for what she can't help."

"Aye. So I thought you would say. Kindness is ever a habit of yours."

How strange that he should say that, the very thing Uncle Edward used to say to her, which she always wished were true! Now she hoped fervently it was not, for kindness would doom her in this place. These Vikings showed no mercy to those who were kind.

He took her hand in his and turned the palm up. She was conscious of the calluses that had not been there when he went away. He muttered in a much quieter voice, "I never dreamed so many labors would be laid on you. I didn't realize my mother was . . . mad."

She was tempted unbearably to comfort the pain he was trying to keep hidden.

"I found changes on the steadying after my return—when I was sufficiently sure you would live so that I could look about me. Sweyn, for instance, is changed."

She lowered her gaze to his big hand still holding hers.

"I am told you played shieldmaiden in earnest and gave him many a good wallop with a blackthorn staff, risking his temper with a nerve as steady as my own shadow."

"It wasn't nerve so much as fear. He told me to swing at him, and one doesn't argue with a Viking holding an axe."

"That defiant pride of yours has more than once

argued with my sword, as I recall. And you say you 'reasoned' with old Soren's axe. It seems to me you know not how to cringe any better now than the first time I ever set eyes on you. And because of it, Sweyn is a man again, and seemingly bent on wooing Beornwold's widow."

Her interest was piqued. "Do you think he will make a farmer? Will he treat Gunnhild well? I wonder if I did the right thing there."

"You are late in wondering," he said with severity.

She fluttered her eyelids to cover her returned resentment. "But you were absent so long, and the matter could not wait."

"And you have been ill so long . . . you've slept so many days and nights that there is a matter with me that cannot wait." He cradled her face between his two hands and leaned to kiss her. He took her mouth as he would take a first long drink, thirstily, looking into the bowl as a child would. It was a gentle kiss, full of consideration.

Afterward, he toyed with a strand of her hair. He said, so softly she wasn't sure she'd heard right, "Sometimes I fear I'll never master you, Edin, and that I couldn't endure."

She felt gulping and tremulous. She wanted him to kiss her again. She saw how it was going to be, how desperately hard the battle between her love for him and her hate for all that he was.

"I see you haven't finished your wine."

The change in subject was hardly subtle, and he gave her no choice but to drink deeply from the bowl he held for her. But as he caught a drop from her lower lip with his thumb, she couldn't keep herself from whispering, "I missed you."

His smile was sudden, a full dawn in the low-vaulted chamber. This time his kiss was long and hungry and thorough, and it drained her mind of all thought, so that when he lifted his head, she was caught unprepared for his question: "What did you think about when you were alone; did you daydream?"

What a strange question! But he seemed very serious. "Did you think of your life before, and long to be free?"

"Not really," she said slowly. "I-I thought rather of what might happen to me next."

"And did you think of me? Did you ever think of me?"

"I . . ." She closed her eyes. "I thought of you. Constantly." She looked at him again and saw he was beginning to smile. "I thought of you when my hands stained the scythe with blood, and when I couldn't eat or sleep for weariness, and when Soren's axe swung toward my throat — I thought of you then especially, and wondered if it was really the wisest thing to duck."

The sun rimmed the western horizon, sending out its last slender shafts of radiance. They seemed to vibrate slightly, with a soundless music, like harpstrings playing a song that was great and deep and fair but mingled with a yearning sorrow. When they were gone, silenced, there was only a razor-edged blueness everywhere. In the far distance was a hint of knife-edged, blue peaks capped with adamantine snow. A cold blue country was Norway.

Up on a little hummock above Dainjerfjord, under the storm-writhen hawthorne tree, Thoryn Kirkynsson hunkered down and let the blue twilight wrap him. Before him was the *hogre,* the sacred pile of stones. There was a peculiar stillness under that tree where blood sacrifices were made to the gods.

Thoryn was dressed simply, with nothing except a torque of twisted gold strands to pronounce him a man of wealth and strength. He sat alone, with only the curlews crying and the sheep's melancholy bleating in his ears. And he thought about all that had passed since he'd taken the *Blood Wing* a'viking last spring.

After a while a shaggy grey and white sheep dog came to sit with the jarl of Thorynsteading. The animal was one the thrall-boy Arneld had been making a pet of. Thoryn had spied the boy talking to it in that special dog-doting voice.

Eventually he took out his sword. His father's armorer had written upon it: "May the Tester spare no one."

In Thoryn's youth, Kirkyn had let the steading fall into poor times while he went raiding year after year. He'd shown no interest in his homefields or his longhouse. It was only when he brought Margaret home that he seemed to notice his holdings and grow interested in being a steading owner. Thoryn had accepted the change in him without considering what it had to do with Inga and Margaret. It seemed to him now that he'd accepted a lot of things without thought.

Margaret, a captive thrall, had won his father's favor. His *love*. And Thoryn's. He could admit that now — now that he too loved a thrall. As a boy, he'd loved Margaret more than his own mother.

He felt a strong, hurtful instant of guilt, like a fast deep stab wound. Inga had wanted his love so desperately, and Kirkyn's. She would stare at Kirkyn endlessly. Her gaze had frightened that young Thoryn who would turn away and shiver, seeing for an instant a shameful and obscure side of human existence, seeing, as he knew now, an evil as far from the sun as the depths of the utmost dark places. That tender, melting look of Inga's — he'd come to feel repulsed when she looked like that. And so in the end it was Margaret who had earned his affection. Which had made her seeming treachery all the more painful.

Oh, these ceaseless, obsessional thoughts! The past was dead. Kirkyn and Margaret were dead. And Inga was past help. He had to think of the future. Of Edin. She was all that was left to be glad for. And she was enough.

Edin. Her very name made gladness roar through him. He felt a giddy uplift of his heart. He loved her—and his love was *proud* of itself. He was afraid it seeped out of him even with his tightest security. Even now—just look at him, sitting here like a fool atop an imaginary ocean heave of happiness, atop a glistening wave of hope! He had to restrain himself, because the wall had been breached, the wall that had sealed off his childhood, his best self, his early aspirations. Since the framing of that wall, his shape had become harsh, brutal, and . . . somehow wrong. But now the air flowed in, air from a springtime he'd forgotten. The imprisoned energy of those young and wasted seasons was blowing into his limbs and his spirit.

He still didn't understand exactly what Edin did to him, but her effect was so unfailingly powerful that he believed he'd been born to love her—her face, her throat, her shoulders, her form full and perfect, her body of velvet, her cool, soft voice—born to feel this heat and spaciousness that no single word could begin to express. She made the blood hammer like a prayer through his veins. He had to stop himself from shouting aloud with joy. And her remoteness, her suspicion, and even her resentment were part of his youth regained. It was only right that he should have to overcome these obstacles. Nothing of value was easily gained. He felt confident, however, that there would come a time when her struggle against him could not be sustained.

He sighed and threw his head back. The great timeless tree above him held intricate patterns against the motionless sky. Was it only a season ago he'd still tried to maintain a distance between himself and his new thrall? He'd wanted her to be an unknown Saxon female so he could put her on the auction block without feeling. It was better not to feel anything for people you sold. And impossible to sell one whose every touch drew reaction.

He reached to touch the dog and found it willing to be scratched behind the ears. The animal's big head hung over its breast. The two of them sat in companionable silence. Then, when it was full dark, Thoryn rose and found the sheep, and he put his sword edge to the gentle pulsing throat of his best lamb-bearer offering it to Odin, the Lord of the Gods, as he had sworn he would do.

Early in the afternoon, two days later, Edin ignored Dessa's protests and left her bed. As she dressed, though she'd been surfeited with whole-meal breads, a great deal of fish, goat meat, eggs, wild greens, and whey drinks sweetened with honey, she found that she was still remarkably weak. Nonetheless, she went out into the hall, determined to take a turn around the tables.

Olga, who had been trained by Inga, was in charge of the kitchen in her mistress's absence. The place smelled of the same horrid mutton and cabbage of previous days. Luckily it was afternoon or the odors might have made Edin sick. If she ever had a kitchen of her own again, she vowed there would never be a scrap of cabbage allowed into it.

She felt shaky as she started on the last stretch back toward the bedchamber. Icy perspiration drenched her body, and she felt as white as a linen apron. Her heart was going all ways, now just a thread of a pulse, now pounding. At the halfway point, she had to lean against one of the jarl's high-seat pillars.

Dessa had disappeared or Edin would have asked for her arm. Olga was there, but she was busy with a long-handled pancake griddle making *lefse*, thin cakes spread with butter and honey. It was a job that couldn't be easily interrupted.

Ottar was there also, but being a mere thrall, Edin could claim no right to request a favor of him; indeed, she didn't even think of it. Besides, he was busy in his own way—almost as quickly as Olga could cook the hot and smoking *lefse,* he stole the folded cakes from her and wolfed them down.

Edin eventually stood away from the pillars and started on, lurching a little like an old woman. Before she got too far, she learned where Dessa had hied off to: The girl had gone to tattle on her.

The jarl's voice boomed curses all the way from the door. It had the sobering effect of sudden intense light. Edin turned her head—and there he was, tall, forthright, and angry. He advanced on her so aggressively that she held out her hands and stumbled back. As he reached for her, she tried to catch his thick wrists. Neither tactic kept him from sweeping her into his arms and lifting her as effortlessly as if she were a sack of feathers. She was left stunned by the terrible deadly elegance of his swiftness and his strength as he carted her back to bed.

He stood scowling over her, his muscles knotted, while she stared at the handmade silver buttons of his tunic. He said, "I may have to beat you after all. Take care, Saxon." His eyes glistened with steely pinpoints.

She was briefly afraid; after all he was an immensely powerful man, and there were still ways in which she regarded him as a mystery, even dangerous. And she was more vulnerable than usual just now.

Yet the very next day she did the same thing. Twice.

The first time was when Dessa left her alone for half an hour to tend to some chore or other. Edin was so successful in getting up and walking around the hall tables that she decided to try it again that afternoon. But Dessa came back sooner than expected, and caught her. Still, Edin managed to get back to bed on her own before the girl's tale-bearing brought the Viking barging into the chamber like a longship under full sail.

He was cool today, where yesterday he'd been hot. He said—coolly, "You see the posts at the foot of this bed, and at the head there? I count four. And you have four limbs."

"I'm sorry that—"

"It surprises me to hear you say so," he continued quietly, "for truly you seem not a whit sorry, Saxon. But I can make you sorry. Shall I?" He blinked slowly, in a way that made her feel as low as a fly in a bowl of milk. Briefly a seasick misery ebbed through her. She felt the weight of his eyes as he continued to watch her in such an unwavering manner.

She said, "How can I get my strength back if I don't work at it? A Viking doesn't pamper himself this way. I want to go out, to breathe clean air, to see the sky again."

She watched his mercurial mood make an obvious, abrupt, bewildering reversal. He smiled! It was a lazy, intimate smile that made her catch her breath. Everything washed out of her mind when he smiled like that. He was so . . . *beautiful*. His limbs and features seemed to be formed as exactly and wonderfully as if some colossal woodcarver had made him. He said, full of relaxed amusement suddenly, "You want to be treated like a Norsewoman? I find that a good sign. All right. You may walk outside a little tomorrow— but not until I can attend you myself."

He started to go, but paused at the door. The smile was gone again, as suddenly as it had appeared. "You will *not* walk about without me. And I will *not* be called in like this again. Think carefully before you defy me another time, or—" he added with shrewd sarcasm—"I shall have to risk becoming the object of all your anxiety and hatred."

She lay back in her pillows, stiff with refusal, yet helpless to disobey, atremble with conflicting need and fear. She felt as if she'd just done battle with an army of giants—and lost.

In the late afternoon of the next day, she brushed her hair and parted it in the center so that it fell in waves that framed her face and spilled onto her shoulders and down her back. She put on a grey-blue gown and a black cloak fastened with two brooches joined by a chain across her breast, all gifts from the jarl brought home from his trip to Kaupang, and she strolled beside him out of the bedchamber.

He somehow tamed his long-legged pace to accommodate her slower one as they stepped up into the day. After more than two sennights indoors, the sunlight felt like a pour of golden nectar. He told her she could take one slow turn around the longhouse, but this was done all too soon. They paused to watch Laag saddle four horses for men who intended an evening deer hunt. When the men came to claim their mounts, Rolf asked, "You aren't going with us, Jarl?"

"Not this time."

"He's too busy walking his amber-haired pet," Hauk said.

"Better to ride than to walk, Jarl," Ottar jested.

"That depends. If you have a thorough-bred, there's her care and her temperament to think about."

"Aye," said Fafnir, "if you've got a filly with some pluck to her, you don't want to ride her into the ground."

On their horses, they saluted him—and grinned and nodded to Edin—before they galloped off. She was a little surprised by that farewell nod. Seldom had any of them ever acknowledged her presence except as an article of service, an object. That nod had said she was a person. What did it mean? Would the jarl comment on it?

He didn't. He stood beside her, not touching her,

watching his men ride away. The sun-drenched afternoon seemed to contain a quiet, easy domesticity that she was loathe to interrupt. At last he turned a little toward her—a minor movement of his body, yet it spoke of power, reminding her of how easily he'd lifted her the day before, and also reminding her that he was a man of raid and conquest. She sensed he was about to order her back to her dreary bed, so she said quickly, "Can we not go up the path to the lookout point? I would so like to see a clear view. My landscapes have been barriered for many a day." She stood hoping, under those imminent and unclosing eyes that were watching her with such terrible, unrelenting *tenderness*. "Really, I'm not at all tired."

The path, however, seemed steeper than she recalled. He noticed her lagging steps and gave her his hand. She couldn't quite look at him as she took it, but by the last few paces she was gripping it with all her strength. The climb done, he pointed out a boulder near the very edge of the point. "Sit," he said.

"I'm fine."

He gave her an exasperated look. "Simply remaining on your feet costs you an effort. Sit."

"I'd rather—"

"By my sword, *sit!* As far as I know, I am jarl here yet, and you will do as I say!"

She sat.

For a moment more he stood with his arms folded over his chest, staring at her as if his glare were a spike he meant to drive through her. Meanwhile she was miserably aware of growing weak and will-less.

But eventually he turned away. The sky above the valley was a profound autumnal blue, and the pastures, with the sheep tracks intersecting and intersecting, were still a jade color. From the rugged slopes came the notes of a cowbell, a peaceful *clank-clank* that floated through the quiet, thin, empty afternoon.

The Viking seemed oddly restless. She watched him

from the corners of her eyes, thinking him so bronzed and sleek, so difficult and bright in the level sun, so insolent and inaccessible. Suddenly his shoulders bunched, his hands clenched, and he turned to her, saying, "Freya's belly!" She was startled by his sudden fierceness, by the lightning flare in his eyes. "I need a woman to run my longhouse. I need a wife to give me named sons. I've decided to wed you, Saxon."

Just like that. For a long moment she ached to run to him. A wave of dizzying temptation swept over her, and she bent her head. *Yes!* The word came to the tip of her tongue—but there paused in a half-sweet, half-agonizing balance, like the rainbow on a waterfall, like the flame on a candle. She wanted to be everything to him, wanted to have everything she couldn't have. . . .

He'd come near and bent over her; his big hand closed on her shoulder. "What have you to say?" His ferocity was as awesome as fire. His bent figure reminded her of a dark dragon flying toward her with his talons forward, ready to catch up his prey. She couldn't seem to make her mouth move. He said, now in a completely contrasting tone, in a voice strong and formal—and strangely suppliant, "Edin, will you wed me?"

Her tongue loosed at last. "Wed the glittering serpent who ravished and ruined my life?"

His hand dropped away. It took a breath for all the suppliance to drain from his expression. It became stony. There was about him a warning.

"Why do you want me?" she asked bitterly. "Why should you marry a thrall you already take at will?"

He turned his back on her. His voice was suddenly throaty. "I . . . I seem to need you."

What was he saying? She struggled against a stupid, credulous feeling that mayhap she meant something to him, that she'd succeeded in melting that iron in him, that mayhap she'd somewhat softened and gentled this barbaric Viking.

He came to take her arms in his hands and pull her up. Her heart fluttered, sorely affrighted by what he intended. She felt so terribly, terribly slight in the circle of his powerful arms. Her head didn't even reach his chin.

"We know each other so little in some ways, but there are other ways in which we know each other full well." His eyes were shining; they were demanding her very heart; they were shifting the ground beneath her feet. His look was blatantly sensual, and she hid her face from it against his chest. Just that look from him, and she felt a bottomless, insatiable need to be weighted by his body and kissed savagely, to belong to him entirely.

"You believe you face a terrible fate. I admit I've been graceless in the past. I am, after all, the man I am. But you won't find me a cruel husband. I will prove to be less terrible than pleasant." He spoke with hypnotic sincerity. "I will try to make you like me, Edin. I . . . I love you." He seemed overcome by feeling as he gathered her and kissed her thoroughly.

After a while he held her head against his shoulder and stroked her hair. She lay against him in a kind of lethargic torpor. She had to struggle. She had to think of Fair Hope, which in her mind was always a place where clouds threw no shadows but were ever fleecy white, where the grass grew greener and taller, the strawberries big and plentiful, where the garden and woods and people never changed.

He lifted her chin and tapped her on the nose. "Are you getting used to the idea, Shieldmaiden?"

She swallowed hard. "Will you swear to me never to use your sword again, never to sail away to raid and kill, never to worship your warrior gods? Will you swear that my children will be reared as a peaceful farmer's sons and daughters? If you will then swear this to me, I will wed you, willingly."

His hold on her loosened. His lips parted.

"I thought not," she whispered. "You are a Viking and ever will be a Viking. Unflinching, wrathful, purely pagan, more skilled in making battle than love. And rather than wed myself to you, I would be a thrall all my life."

His shout had a horrifying ring. "You obstinate, wicked creature!" He was abruptly glowing with monstrous anger. She hadn't seen him so ferocious since the night he'd killed Cedric and burned her home and made her a slave. "You are my thrall," he said, "despite the fact that you own a sharp, ready, cool, never-shrinking, brazen tongue! My power over you is the mightiest you are ever likely to feel. And if I tell you to dress yourself in scarlet and become my wife, by the gods, *that is what you will do!*"

Chapter 27

The jarl had slept in the hall during Edin's illness and recovery. That night he moved back into his own bed. He didn't touch her, but she was aware of him all through the night. He rose early and left without speaking to her. She fell back into a troubled sleep. Dessa woke her later, saying he'd left orders for her to dress and take her first meal in the hall with the others.

He was in his high-seat when she came out. She avoided looking at him and started for her usual position at the end of the table. Hauk Haakonsson intercepted her. She'd never received much attention from this hooked-nosed, violent-eyed Viking, and was confused when he took her elbow now, muttering, "This way." His grip was firm, and she had no choice but to go where he led her, which was to the head of the table nearest the jarl's right hand. There was a stir among the blond, bronzed, blue-eyed men there, but Hauk said to them, "Make room—the jarl's orders." Edin sat without looking at anyone, her face hot with embarrassment, her heart pounding with anxious anticipation.

The meal proceeded. The jarl was near enough to speak to her, but he didn't. No one else did either. She fought back her terror with the useless fantasy that really nothing terribly serious was happening.

When the men finished eating, the jarl stood. The

hall quieted, and he announced casually, "In two sennights I am going to spread a great banquet and take a wife. Messengers will be sent out today to invite everyone on both sides of the fjord." He didn't mention her name, and for a moment there was a waiting silence in which Edin heard the crackle of wood in the longfire. Everyone seemed nailed to their benches in astonishment, her among them. When it became clear he was not going to say more, faint toasts to his news rose up.

Olga came to Edin as soon as the men went out. "The jarl says I should ask you what to do about the cooking for the feast." It was clear she felt awkward. Technically Edin was still a thrall. It was clear the jarl was not going to free her before the wedding. Whether they guessed the reason — that as a freed woman she would refuse him — she didn't know.

While her heart held on to the possibility that this disaster would suddenly stop, turn around, and vanish, her practical mind told her she'd be wise to make the best of things in case it didn't. She said tentatively to Olga, "Mayhap we should go through the stores together and see what we have." Without ceremony, Olga relinquished to her the keys that made her the factual, if not yet recognized, mistress of the steadying. It was no great transition for her. She was experienced in running a home; she'd even planned her own wedding once — before that night that had divided her life.

Once she saw that Olga was going to accept her word as law, she grew more confident. She decided what dishes would be served at the feast — excluding cabbage from the menu — then encouraged Olga to plan the cooking herself. Edin's ways were very different from Inga's. It was her wont to point out to servants what needed to be done and then step back and let them get on with it in their own best way. Olga seemed unsure at first, and kept hesitating, as if waiting for Edin to direct her every idea, but Edin refrained from giving more than reassurance.

Later she spoke to Dessa about changing the old floor rushes for much-needed new ones. Dessa said, "I could ask Blackhair for some field thralls to help us."

"Ask Yngvarr," Edin said.

"But Blackhair is the one—"

"Yngvarr is the one to ask from now on," she said with more satisfaction than any Christian woman ought to feel in an act of revenge.

When she tucked her hair into an apron belt, intending to get down to some real work herself, Ottar Magnusson, who had been loitering about the hall, suddenly claimed he had no partner to play chess with him. "Edin!" he said, "come out on the green and learn the game."

How could she refuse? She was still a thrall, and he wasn't asking but rather firmly assuming that she would do as he wanted.

They sat beneath the great, wide-spreading tree where Ottar proceeded with a slow instruction. Yngvarr, who was already organizing the cutting of the new rushes for the hall, came to her with several questions. Unlike Blackhair, no sarcasm salted his comments. He seemed eager to please, and grateful for the chance to better his position. Ottar patiently waited while Edin spoke to him, using the same technique of encouragement and reassurance. Next Dessa came with a message from Olga, and again Ottar waited. When Dessa was gone, he went back to holding up one walrus-ivory chess piece after another, laconically explaining its use in the play of the game. Edin interrupted him with, "Did the jarl order you to teach me chess specifically, or simply to keep me from doing anything useful?"

Ottar grinned. "He suggested, casuallike, that you shouldn't be doing anything too strenuous yet, and that if you were to learn to play chess it might help you

409

pass the hours and keep you out of trouble — and then he looked at me. You know how he can look at you until you realize you've always longed to do what he's just said?"

"I know that look, yes." She'd often enough stood within the sweep of his personal aura.

There was more to the jarl's plan than just keeping her from overwork, however. It was clear to Edin that he was insuring her presence at their wedding by maintaining a rotation of Viking guards over her. Rolf would appear and politely pull her away from the foaming busyness in the hall to take her for a maddeningly pointless morning stroll in the harvested fields. Sweyn, who was becoming known as the One-armed, was learning to manage a horse again and insisted he needed her help. And so she took an afternoon ride with that awkward man through the moist, earthy, scent-laden woods. There was one whole day with Starkad Herjulson, in which he taught her to fish for *seith,* "the best fish in the fjord." This required going out in a boat. At first she was nervous, but the craft he'd chosen — or had the jarl chosen it? — was very steady. And because the cliffs of the fjord were so high, breezes rarely got down to ruffle the surface of the water much. Starkad told her as he rowed them slowly along, "You need to learn to swim. People who live on the shore must learn to get along with the sea. You can't always depend on the jarl to save you from drowning."

Though her heart beat with a feeling of audacity, she said, "Actually, I've decided that the sea doesn't want me. It's had three chances at me, and tossed me back each time. I've all but lost my fear of it."

"Aye. Well then. That's good."

She felt ridiculously pleased to have gained this young Viking's approval.

And so it went, nights of intimate silence beside the man who intended to make her his wife, and days of

410

clumsy companionship with men from whom she'd once shrunk. And meanwhile a grand preparation going on for her own wedding, despite her racing heart, her queasy stomach, her frantic sense of opposition and disbelief.

She shuddered at random instants and told herself it wouldn't really happen, right up until the day before.

She woke feeling wonderfully well, completely recovered, ripe for the world once more. When she sat up, she found on the footboard of the bed a pile of garments left offhandedly, a lady's wardrobe such as would serve a king's wife, let alone a remote Viking chieftain's. There was a gown made of red brocade from the Byzantine Empire; another of woolen fabric dyed blue with woad from Fresia; one ornamented with meticulous English embroidery; and one of shimmering patterned Chinese silk.

She found the jarl supervising the digging of the oval pit and the building of the cooking fires and great spits for the ritual roasting of the sacrificial animals. His blond hair gleamed in the silvery light, for the morning was cool and cloudy. A trailing mist lay motionless across the valley, while great clouds, grey and white, hung down over the distant peaks. Edin hung about until he grudgingly took note of her presence. There was no caress, no sentiment in his greeting. He simply said, "Did you want something?"

"I . . . the clothes. . . ."

His mouth thinned. "I didn't gain them by plunder. They were Margaret's, bought for her by my father."

"I didn't come to accuse you, but to say thank you."

He nodded. "You'll wear the scarlet tomorrow. It's the traditional color for brides here."

"All right."

"You agree, then? You won't make me bind and gag you to get you through it?"

She realized that he must have been worrying about that. She saw that his eyes seemed a little bloodshot, as

411

if he hadn't been sleeping well. She said, "I have no wish to humiliate you. And I have no taste for being made a spectacle. If you say you mean to make me marry you, then, according to all I know about you, that is what you will do." She could have stopped there, but in full obedience to her heart's most urgent commands, she dared to reach out and touch his sleeve. "Can't we talk?"

His fair brows furrowed into a deep crease. "I have something I must do today."

"Of course." She started to turn away.

His hand on her arm stayed her. "Edin." When she looked, she found his expression open. "We'll talk tonight."

Relief flooded through her. She hadn't realized how painful had been the silence between them. She nodded, even smiled a little.

The low hut, once Soren Gudbrodsson's, to which Inga was exiled, was to be visited regularly by supply bearers who would also see that the place was kept in good repair. Thoryn had decided to visit the place himself that day. His honor seemed to insist that he see the place and know it, but he intended this to be his first and last visit.

It was a warm autumn day, that day before his wedding. Evidently Juliana had let the fire go out in the hut, for no smoke came up through the roof hole. As Thoryn stepped off Dawnfire, he heard the two women's voices arguing about it through the low, open door. Inga tended to get frantic if anything kept her home from running smoothly. The slightest mishap bound her up into a tight-smiling fury.

Thoryn saw that the two women were facing one another like fighting cocks. Juliana's raven hair, cut short according to the custom, was in dramatic contrast to the blond head beyond her. He stood watching them, his arms folded across his chest. The thrall looked harried. She was going to suffer, no doubt, being away from the men. By spring, mayhap she would be ready to behave herself back at the long-house. And by then, mayhap Jamsgar would have found another wench.

He'd given as little thought as possible to his mother since the night the egg of her madness had cracked open. Now the sight of her stabbed his smugness to the core. She looked diminished, hardly dangerous.

He ducked his head and stepped down through the low door, prepared to have to judge the right or wrong of their quarrel. To his surprise, he wasn't asked to take sides, however. When Inga saw him, she seemed to forget Juliana altogether. She put on that sweet, repulsive smile and said, "My son." Juliana slipped past him and disappeared outside. Inga said, "Come to the table, son, and drink your broth. I thickened it with oatmeal just the way you like it. And I have a dried onion for you; I save it especially for you."

He managed not to shudder as he sat down at the small table, momentarily amazed by the rush of mixed emotion he felt, and the force with which it wrenched up from some hidden pocket inside him. But then she smiled again and served him, and he said, "This is not broth and onions, woman; it's meat and honey ale."

"Oh . . . so it is." She sat and poured herself a cup of the ale. A mercurial shadow passed across her brow. She leaned over the board and said, "You may not want to call me mother, yet you can't stop me from knowing you as my son, Thoryn. I know the sadness in your heart at what you're doing to me, though you try to hide it." She shaped her mouth into pathos. It was soft, pale coral, atremble.

He avoided making an answer. Instead he took a deep swallow of the ale. He said, "I came only to satisfy myself that you will fare the winter satisfactorily."

"The worst thing is the bed. I'm unused to a pallet."

Guilt ripped through him.

She looked down into her cup, as if she were staring into the cup of her own brain. At last she said, in the same dulcet and winsome fashion, "You will have a son of your own come spring." She presented him a face that seemed never to have known malevolence. "The girl is with child, you know."

He said nothing, thinking this was more nonsense.

"Oh, aye, that is why I had to act when I did. She was sick each morning. Her breasts were beginning to strain at her dress. It was clear to me, to any woman who has born a child." She showed no bitterness; in fact, she said, "When he is born, bring him to see me. Bring my first grandson to me—please, Thoryn!"

The pleading in her voice touched him. His heart turned in pity and guilt to behold this formerly brisk, sturdy woman looking like a ghost of herself and pleading with him. Her face was chalky, and her pale eyes were glazed and sunken into dark hollows. They were the eyes of a farm dog not well treated. Her hair, going white now, fell from a careless topknot. Her gown was wrinkled with a spot or two down the front. There was only a trace of pride left in her: He saw it as her will to keep her stinging sense of shame hidden from his sight.

He quickly finished the rest of his ale, which tasted mawkish and dishwatery now, and rose to leave. Outside, he met Juliana again and took her arm to speak with her: "You have little to do here but care for your mistress. Can you not keep her dress clean and see that her hair is combed?"

"Master, I try." There was something new in the girl's manner. When before she'd projected an aura of boredom and sullen muteness toward him, now there was anxiety. "She orders me off and—and sometimes she makes threats."

"What sort of threats?"

She glanced nervously at her charge, who was waiting near his horse. "She says that she will kill me in my sleep, Master, and then return to the longhouse where she says she left something undone. And then she laughs—not the way a human being laughs. Master, it's the most indecent, ghastly laughing I've ever heard."

He felt a sudden sympathy for this poor girl who all alone cooked and cleaned and chopped and nursed a tyrannical mistress while he was living far from her concerns. He said, "She is mad. She will say things . . . but give her no chance to handle a knife. Do you hear me?"

She nodded dispiritedly.

"Last out this winter and—" he searched for some reward suitable for such a service—"and I will let you choose a husband come spring."

Her expression lightened immediately. "Truly? Any man I choose?"

He couldn't help a rueful chuckle. "Any man who will consent to take you on."

He left and crossed to Inga and his horse. As he settled into the saddle, she said, "I know you won't bring the babe. You must forgive my asking. I think it was the honey ale talking, not Inga Thorsdaughter." Her features were now fixed in solemnity, courage, and sorrow. She was a picture of unquenched mother-love. It made a special impression on him, distinctive and strong. It said: *Beware!*

Though Edin had wanted to talk that night, it seemed she sensed his mood and was astute enough not to break their silence, even though he made sure he got to the bedchamber early—in plenty of time to observe her undressing. And aye, it did seem her breasts were fuller; the tips were definitely pinker. He looked back. He'd first taken her to his bed in early summer; it was now autumn, and in that time, almost a full season, she'd never once held him off with the

415

normal feminine apology. She must have conceived during their first nights together. He felt a leap of emotion, a mix of pride and anticipation and pain and anger.

When she joined him in bed, he lay rigid and mute. She knew she was carrying his child and still didn't want to marry him. Didn't even want him to know.

When she slept, he got up to stare out the window. There would be rain within a day or two. Already clouds were gathering under the mountains, leaving only one pitiless star in all the black night.

Gradually the edges of his emotions blunted. To-morrow he would make her his wife. She would be the recognized mistress of the steadying. He was giving her back all that he'd taken from her. Surely the barriers between them would come down then. And long before spring, long before she mothered his child, she would open her cautious heart and let him in.

Bring my first grandson to me!

She says that she will return to the longhouse where she left something undone.

He shuddered and saw in his mind the hut where Inga was kept. He saw the door opening. He watched it open again and again, but what emerged from behind it he wouldn't let himself envision. When he returned to bed, however, he positioned himself pro-tectively around Edin and slept lightly, his ears seem-ing to strain for the least furtive noise at the chamber door.

Edin wrapped the two layers of the fine pleated gown of brilliant red Byzantine brocade about her, clipping the loop-straps at each shoulder with small golden brooches. The gown reached the sweet carpet of new rushes and had a three-foot train. Over it she wore a knee-length cape made of more of the beauti-fully woven cloth which when thrown back showed her bare arms.

From inside the jarl's bedchamber, she heard the guests arriving. Her nerves tightened with each new hailing. At last there came a knock on the door, and a man's imperious voice: "It's time."

It was time. She thought she would faint if her heart beat any faster. The door opened, and Kol Thurik and Magnus Fairhair stood waiting. She tried to move toward them — and found she couldn't. Her pulse was heavy in her throat. She whispered, "I-I don't think I can do this."

Kol came forward, a powerful middle-aged man. As long as he didn't smile, one couldn't see the tooth he'd broken during the stormy voyage from England, and he wasn't smiling now. He was wearing a magnificent helmet decorated with molded bronze plates; in his belt was a costly double-edged sword with ivory embedded in the hilt. He glanced down at her, at her gown, at the rich scarlet fabric against her skin. What orders had the jarl given him in case she seemed reluctant? Would he bind her? Throw her over his shoulder?

He merely took her elbow, firmly, and led her to the door, tugging her out of the panic in which she'd been anchored. Magnus, Red Jennie's doting master and Ottar's fair-haired father, took hold of her other arm.

It was all right then. She walked between them without resistance. Gliding down the length of the hall at the insistence of two elder and unquestionably mighty Vikings, her gown flowing behind her, her throat and wrists adorned with necklaces and jewels and her forehead banded with a gold fillet sprigged with wild flowers, her hair loose in spiral curls and waves to her thighs, she felt that it was all right, it was only *reasonable,* to accept what was about to take place, to yield to it, to surrender.

The new carpet of rushes lent the hall a delicious fragrance. Gay banners hung from the timbered rafters, the walls were tapestry-hung, and the tables glittered with gold and silver plate. It was Sweyn who had tramped through the woods at dawn to collect the golden-leafed beech boughs that Dessa had used to adorn the roof posts. Lamps threw mellow light over all, including the strikingly colorful costumes of the Vikings and their families.

These men of relentless vigor and savagery who had once intimidated Edin with their stares now deferred to her as she passed. Their women even bowed. Edin's stomach quaked.

Kol and Magnus took her behind the jarl's high-seat, down the length of the hall, around the end tables, and brought her back along the opposite side, past all the fjord folk, people of all manner and years, until the procession stopped between the firepit and the jarl.

Kol and Magnus stepped aside. Edin stood alone before her master.

Slowly he rose with gorgeous ease and came toward her. From head to foot his tall proud body was outfitted as only a great chieftain's could be. On his head was his horned helmet, carefully polished; his tunic was encrusted with gold thread; in his belt, where other men carried their axes, he carried Thor's sacred hammer. Power was in his whole figure. But she couldn't read his face as he looked down at her. What was he thinking? Nothing showed in those piercing eyes. Intimidated, she let her own gaze fall away.

"Give me your hand," he said.

She lifted her right hand. He placed his big palm beneath it.

"Look at me."

When she did, she was dazed by the sudden ferocity in his face. Her breath caught. He was frightening, arrogant, forceful, this man who was to be her husband.

"We walk hand-in-hand from this day on." He

turned, raising her right hand with his left, and presenting her to his people.

The celebration was a rich, pagan affair. Vikings seemed to love a wedding better than anything—the marriage procession, the ritual sacrifice made to Frey for the bridegroom's potency, the traditional consecration wherein Thor's hammer was laid on Edin's lap. "You are a Norsewoman now," the jarl said.

And it was at that point that he murmured vows to her in a voice for her ears alone, "I make you my wife." He held a gold wedding band at the tip of her third finger. "I vow to defend your life, to share with you my victories, to give you no unnecessary sadness. I also vow," he added grimly, "to kill anyone who tries to take you from me."

The post-ceremony festivities included drinking and dancing—colorful, intricate dances performed to folk ballads. The occasion warranted the use of an incredibly ancient *lur*, a long, hornlike instrument that had been set up on the point overlooking the fjord. The cliffs and water echoed with its dark, rich resonance as it told the very mountains that the jarl had taken himself a bride.

The fact that the bride was the foreign thrall he'd staunchly vowed to sell in Hedeby brought him a great deal of jesting and chiding now. He bore it well, assuming a bluff, downright attitude. This was his fine and splendid side; it was the side of him that Edin loved.

When the sun began to set in a russet flush along the horizon, the wedding feast began. Dishes of smoking viands were duly presented to everyone in order of their importance, from the wedding couple in their finery to the oldest thrall, bent and toothless, his dark clothes reeking of manure. The tables groaned, and the guests ate hugely of piled venison and mutton, beef hearts and tongue, succulent backstrap, stewed seal meat, and the inescapable fish. They drank ale until it seemed impossible they could hold more.

Magnus Fairhair proposed a toast: "To Thoryn Kirkynsson. Sweet and pleasant may be his days with his goodwife Edin, and stirring his tales of his nights."

Men, their faces swollen and scarlet with food and ale, shouted, "Drink, bridegroom!"

Edin was asked to sing and, with Hauk's lute in her hand, gave them a graceful little poem sung to music:

"I love the gay summer weather,
When the rose trees all do flower,
When a hundred larks together,
Make music outside my bower . . ."

Simple as the tune was, the people shouted and clapped their hands. When she tried to give the lute back to Hauk, he wouldn't take it. His expression, which was hard, pitched her off balance, for what he said, looking down the length of his thin nose, was "My bride-gift to you, Song-singer."

She returned to her place beside her husband's high-seat blushing and flustered. He signaled Arneld, who came rushing to him with a fur-wrapped bundle he'd been entrusted to guard. "From your husband, my la-
. . . er, Mistress," the boy piped, holding the bundle out with both hands. She glanced at the jarl, then folded back the furs to discover a silver-gilt beaker on a stem, decorated with ribbonlike animals intricately entwined. He leaned to fill the cup with sweet mead and set to her lips. His nearness caused the blood in her veins to rush through her body.

Another rich-hued hour passed. A skald rose to entertain the gathering, a tall man with a slight stoop. He stood with his head thrust forward; his long face had a nose that tilted upward at the very end. Gradually he took the power of words into his hands and began to build a bridge of bleak beauty with them, reciting a poem about the Valkyries, the Choosers of the Slain, who exulted in blood and in weaving the mesh of war:

"Blood rains
From the cloudy web
On the broad loom of slaughter.
The web of man,
Grey as armor,
Is now being woven;
The Valkyries
Will cross it
With a crimson weft—"

The jarl interrupted, "Skald! give us something more beguiling, something fit to amuse a bride at her wedding."

The skald nodded regally. "I will tell you then about Hastien, who with his companion Bjorn Ironside sacked Paris 'til, of all the great buildings of that city, nothing but four kirks were left standing."

The jarl seemed ready to protest again—Edin was stirred by his motive—but the Vikings cheered. Edin reached for his arm, making her expression say, *Thank you for thinking of me, but it's all right.* He made a sound of grudging acquiescence, and the tale began.

Chapter 28

"Now, Hastien was a flamboyant man, dissatisfied with his triumph in the land of the Franks," quoth the skald. "He sailed on with his men across the green, cold sea until he came to a city so big, so white, so splendid and columned that what else could it be but Rome? Its defenses were strong and impervious to assault; thus the Norseman devised a crafty ruse. Messengers went to the city with the story that Hastien and his following were honest men expelled from Norway by an overbearing king. They were weary and hungry and needed provisions — and their sick chieftain was knocking at Death's door.

"Later they came to town again, to report that Death's door had opened. All they now required was a Christian grave for Hastien. The townsmen agreed. A long procession of sorrowing Norsemen accompanied the coffin. Wailing was heard, and mourning. The bishop was so moved he summoned the people. The bells of the cathedral tolled in such a way that the citizens knew a great funeral was taking place. The clergy came dressed in their vestments. The chief men came. Women came. Scholars holding their candles and crosses came, and all followed the procession right into the cathedral.

"The Norsemen took the coffin up to the golden altar and set it down. The priests began their prayers. Suddenly the dead Hastien rose from his bier with a mighty roar and drove his axe through the officiating bishop. The Norsemen erupted into a frenzy of slaughter, a merry lark of rape and pillage.

"Hastien's exultation had no bounds—until he discovered that the ravished community was not Rome at all, but a place called Luna, hundreds of miles north of Rome. All that ingenuity squandered! He gave orders to fire the town and massacre the men.

"The women were shown more mercy," the skald ended with a wink and a grin.

The jarl, despite his initial hesitancy, laughed with the others. His mirth was strong and clean. Rape and murder were his way of life, so much so that he even found humor in it. Edin knew she would never adjust to this love of the bloody tale—the gory joke—not when she'd been the victim of such an "adventure." While the skald bowed to the approval of the crowd, her mind leapt from memory to memory. Her courage faltered; her throat tightened. An inner voice cried: *Edin of Fair Hope, is this your wedding? Will these Vikings now be your people, and shall you never escape from here? What have you agreed to? What have you wedded yourself to? Your children—tall they will be, and fair-skinned and pale-eyed— but they will be Vikings!*

A ditty started up among three of the older men. Hands tugging at their stubbly whiskers, they sang deep and strong a tune that had a repeating admonishment: "Hungry wolves take big bites!"

The valley had long since fallen into shadow, and Edin was weary, worn out by the bearded kisses of the Vikings and the good cheer of their ladies—and by this relentless questioning of her future. She hardly noticed that the jarl was on his feet, commanding the attention of all, until she heard his voice: "Friends, to my goodwife, Edin!"

They drank to her, accepted her, unthinkingly surrendered whatever reservations they might have about her to his domination, his charisma.

"And now, since she has recently been ill, I beg you to excuse us. She needs her rest." His glance rained down on her upturned face.

"Oh, aye!" came the first of a quick chorus of jests, "rest indeed! Mayhap they would have believed that tale when the world hadn't yet grown its beard."

A woman called, "The Song-singer will get more rest out here than pressed flat between you and the mattress, Jarl!"

"Have mercy, Thoryn Kirkynsson, let the girl stay with us awhile longer! After all, she's been ill!"

At that point Rolf started the story of how the jarl had thrown her over his shoulder the first time he'd taken her to his chamber. She stood quickly, interrupting him. Anger had been rising in her, and finally she couldn't hold it back. She said, "Forgive me, but since this tale is not so pleasing to me as it might be to you, I think I will retire."

The Vikings made a lane along which she and the jarl passed. The procession took several minutes, what with more jesting, more kisses of congratulation for her and slaps on the back for him. Udith and her husband Lothere had been allowed to come with Kol Thurik, their master. The head cook of Fair Hope darted forward to curtsey before her former lady.

"Udith! Do you do well?"

"Aye, my lady."

"I'm so glad." Indeed, the two resembled very little the shivering slaves Edin had stepped forward to save from separation her very first night in this hall. Udith looked plumper than ever, and even the lank Lothere had a belly that spoke of eating largely and drinking well.

Udith was slightly elevated with all the ale that had flowed into her cup. "You look like a lady in a tapestry," she chattered. "I've watched you all this time—there you sat, sparkling as a queen above them all!"

Edin felt the squeeze of her husband's hard fingers on her elbow, a reminder that he was waiting, so she said good night. She let herself be gently pulled along through the well-wishing crowd, let herself be inexorably led to their chamber.

There was a single lamp burning, but most of the room was heavy with shadow. Even with the door closed, the sound of the revelry penetrated. She recognized Jamsgar Copper-eye's voice chanting a feast-hall ditty about a man who threw his arms around a bear in the dark thinking it was his darling.

Edin turned and faced her husband, who was leaning with his back against the door, watching her. She suddenly felt very small and lonely.

The Viking in Jamsgar's song "had pride and prestige and battle honor" and persisted in trying to claim his kiss.

"Are you afraid?" the jarl asked.

She looked down at her twisting hands. "I suppose I am." She looked up again and saw that he was not pleased. "You are a fierce man to take for a husband."

"A barbarian, brutal and murderous." He crossed his arms over his chest, unconsciously emphasizing the great standing veins in his forearms. His eyes were startlingly colorless. Bravely, she held his look, until it proved more than she could bear.

"You have my ring and my vow to shield and harbor you," he said. "You know by now that I'll never purposely hurt you, abed or elsewhere."

"Yes"—her voice was a whisper—"I know that."

"Then what do you fear?"

She paused, searching for the words. "You," she said finally, "what you are."

He seemed harder than ever, broader, more massive. His unreasonable size was straightened to the full. "I am your husband. And you are my wife, the

425

woman I have always sought. I have confessed my love like a puling boy. Can't you even now trust me?"

"Yes. No. Oh, I can't explain!"

Abruptly he was several feet closer. He took her arm and led her to the chair. He sat, pulling her onto his lap. "Try," he said.

Mayhap because she'd expected rumbles of thunder and flashes of lightning, that one softly spoken word compelled her to tell him everything that was in her heart. "I fear . . . to have your sons."

"No need. You'll have Hagna."

"Not birthing them, *having* them, *loving* them, and watching them grow to manhood, only to watch them take up swords and axes and step into a dragonship and go off to kill and ravage—all in order to prove they aren't cowards!"

He said unsympathetically, "There is no question of any son of mine proving he's not a coward. No man of the North is a coward. Yet a boy wants to find out just how brave he is. Every boy hopes to perform outstanding feats and be recognized as a champion."

She looked up at him with tears in her eyes. "You will lead them, won't you? They will follow their father, the Hammer of Dainjerfjord, who will go voyaging, beating about in his boat, killing—or mayhap getting killed. My sons will prefer burning churches to visiting them. I can't bear to think of it. You—*all* of you!—seem to look forward to dying. Oh, why can't you simply stay at home and live in peace? Why must you go ranting out into the world with your swords and your helmets?"

She would have wrenched away from him during this, but he held her closely. When she stopped struggling, she saw he seemed troubled by his inability to comfort her. She said, more calmly, "Let me go now," and stood away from him. "Our guests wouldn't believe this scene—the bridal couple so glum."

"There would be many an expressions of horror at

things that have taken place in this chamber."

He rose, and her heart drummed. She had learned well what it meant when his eyes turned to silver seas and his voice became low and husky.

For a moment, he just stood and gazed at her in silence, evidently enjoying what he saw: her timid look, the fall of her hair against the scarlet of her dress. He reached for the square brooches holding the straps of her gown. "I have wondered all day what would happen if I unclasped these—ah, now I see." His hands came up, lifting her breasts. "How lovely these look. What is it that gives them such unwonted roundness and fullness?"

She was bemused by this delicious preliminary in spite of herself, until he swooped down and lifted her off her feet. She made a valiant attempt to prevent him, but he held her and turned to the bed. There she struggled a little more—for the sheer pleasure of it, really—then let her body collapse into softness beneath his iron-hard weight.

He grunted his satisfaction and rose off her to remove her footwear, then to see to his own disrobing. His eyes were heavy-lidded and deep and strange. When he joined her again some minutes later, and reached for her, she tried to hold him off once more.

"Brave," he murmured. "But brave is not always wise, my Shieldmaiden, flesh of my flesh, mother of my sons."

The phrase was not lost on her. And he'd asked about the change in her breasts. Could he suspect?

With a gasp she felt his strong arms gather her. She was pressed to him full-length, every inch of her molded to his hard body, his chest, his flat hard stomach, his thighs. It seemed like forever since he'd held her so. Meanwhile, she'd learned to relish any little pleasure, which made this truest pleasure almost excruciating. Her mouth open, her eyes half closed, she realized that she wanted this Viking with a yearning pain she couldn't stand against.

As his mouth lowered and his soft tongue searched for hers, she felt they must be beautiful, two people beautifully, flawlessly making a single whole. As their mouths fit together, so did all of them seem the right size and shape—the angle of each arm, the curve of her thigh against the agreement of his, the mound of her breast against the muscle of his chest. His iron, her silk. There had never been a thing of such goodness and beauty in all the world and never would be again.

His kisses grew fierce; his hands caressed her everywhere. Like a shipwright, he worked entirely by instinct, by eye, by feel, until it was impossible to deny him anything he desired.

Finally he put her beneath him and entered her as was his right, not as her master, but as her husband. She went up in flames. Such a savage delight! Hips thrusting, he stroked deeply to satisfy them both. And for the time being what was bestial in him was calmed.

Dainjerfjord's surface was ruffled by waves no bigger than a woman's hand and stippled by rain in the first pearly grey light of the new dawn. Within the longhouse on Thorynsteading, the jarl's marriage celebration went on regardless of the gentle storm without. Vikings, being fond of noisy games, early on began matches of a sort of wrestling. Two of the men would clasp hands, brace elbows, and try to force one another to the ground. These contests didn't need much space; the game was tailored to be played aboard a ship.

Edin made her appearance with her hair put up and studded with flowers. She found a place by Red Jennie to watch the wrestlers. Jennie was as cheerful as always, gaily attired and redheaded and lovely, exclaiming over Edin's bride ring.

A moment of doubt fell when Sweyn stepped up to Thoryn and challenged him to a left-handed wrestling match. "It's undignified for me to take on a puny fellow like you, but if you would, Jarl . . . ?"

Thoryn blinked slowly, then nodded. They drew off their tunics, positioned themselves, braced their legs, clasped one another's hands, and began. The muscles in their arms stood out like ropes and cables, sweat sprang up and glistened on their faces and backs. Sweyn warned the jarl in a voice clenched to save breath, "Don't put on any airs; I won't tolerate any bragging from you."

This had the effect of doubling their efforts. Their backs and shoulders revealed every superficial and buried muscle, every sinew and tendon. Their faces tightened like fists; the skin went red behind their beards. Beneath the simple rules of the contest lurked all sorts of opportunities for subtle, ruthless, and cunning strategies. And beneath Sweyn's challenge lurked subtle meaning. Edin's nails bit into her palms. Why must they do this—behave like heaving stupid beasts?

It seemed to go on forever, but at last Sweyn grunted mightily and gave a sideways shove. The jarl missed his footing, his stance broke, and he was forced to one knee. He cursed himself. Sweyn leaned down and stroked his face gently, like a mother. "There, sweeting," he mocked, "no tantrums now."

The jarl tossed his head. He stared up at Sweyn with flinty eyes, a magnificent chief in the pride of his manhood bested by a cripple! Suddenly he laughed. Edin's hands relaxed; her pent breath escaped in a sigh. As Thoryn stood, he pulled a fine gold ring from his finger and placed it on Sweyn's strong left hand. There was applause, for it was an honor when a chief gave a ring to a warrior. Edin felt proud of him.

A wandering fortune teller appeared at the door. Having heard of the merriment, she'd come to make her quota of coins. The jarl beckoned her in. "Welcome!" The woman looked as old as motherhood. She never smiled or even seemed pleasant. She made herself at home in a corner and began to entertain one and then another of the gathering. Starkad Herjulson was among the very first.

Mead and ale were all this time flowing freely. Ottar, his eyes a little wild, stood up on a bench and raised his cup as if to make a toast. He'd dressed for the celebration in his best war shirt and had his hair in multiple braids over his shoulders, with a leather thong around his bronzed forehead. He was too drunk to be prudent in his words, and said, "Jarl, your lady is beautiful, with a wonderful, er, succulence—" he was openly staring at Edin's bosom—"aye, and . . . and . . . but she seems somewhat slender, I think. She would look fine with more of a belly. What say you?"

What *would* he say? From what Edin knew, a Viking expected his legitimate wife to be esteemed and respected, for in his absence she must serve as his representative. Evidently others wondered as well. The gathering was so ablaze with light and finery that Ottar's folly was like a sudden gust of wind fluttering the leaves of a sunlit autumn birch. He stood shifting from one foot to the other on his bench, as if only now realizing the possible offense of his words. His face changed, colored oddly; an ashyness glimmered through the weathering.

Edin took a pitcher from Olga as the thrall passed by her, and moved toward Thoryn, as if to top his cup. She murmured, "He meant no harm, my lord. He is merely over-merry with drink."

Thoryn accepted the refill of his cup from her, raised it, and took a slow, deep draught. At last he said, "What say I, Ottar Magnusson? This: I wager you a half-mark of silver against that chess set of yours, the one carved out of walrus ivory, that my lady's belly will be round as a cabbage by the time the Yule season arrives."

Edin stirred uncomfortably.

"Careful, Ottar," Rolf called, "our jarl is called the Hammer, not the Drooper!"

This occasioned a new round of boisterous jest and laughter and, of course, refreshment. Food was served again. Thoryn shouted, "Come! I challenge all comers to an eating competition!" No more need be said. The gathering swarmed to the tables where they began to eat like mastodons, some laughing and conversing as they ate, others silently absorbing themselves in dedicated gluttony.

Juliana sighed yet again. Inga snapped at her, "What is wrong with you, girl! You've been doing that for two days!"

Juliana looked at her mistress with sudden spite. "It's just that they're all having a grand time at the longhouse."

Inga's blue eyes focused on her with new attention. "What do you mean?"

Juliana wanted to smile. She was learning how to goad her hateful mistress. "Well . . ."

"What?"

"I only know what Fafnir said when he brought the supplies."

"*What?*"

"He said the jarl was taking a wife."

Inga's voice was low. "Who . . . who would he . . . ?"

Juliana swallowed. The woman's look was more than she'd bargained for. "Edin," she said a little timorously.

Inga stood in the sudden dead silence, stood so quietly it was as if Juliana were dreaming it. And then she laughed, an insane giggle. Fear became a living thing, feeding on Juliana from inside, pushing mewling sounds out of her throat.

Edin was passing among the banqueting guests. She still felt shy of these Vikings, yet she could not shirk her duty as hostess. She asked Starkad, "What did the fortune teller say to you?"

Beside him, Jamsgar grumbled, "No man may see his future or mark his fate. His life is in ghostly hands beyond his reach."

"Why, Jamsgar," Edin chided, "how morbid you are."

"Don't pay any attention to him," Starkad said. "He can't find anyone to take that little Juliana's place." He laughed at his brother's grimace. Wiping down his red beard with the back of his hand before he looked back up at Edin, he said, "The crowbones said I would earn the nickname *Scafhogg*, Smoothing Stroke, whatever that means."

"I can tell you what it means, little brother," snorted Jamsgar beside him. Both of them grinned as Edin turned away with a blush.

By the time the meal was over, the weather had cleared, and Hauk Haakonsson offered to take on Eric No-breeches at foot-racing. Eric said he would prefer a drinking contest, but finally consented to the race instead. The jarl went out with the others, but shortly came back. Edin had slipped into their chamber to tidy her hair, and that was where he found her. She turned, arms raised to her head, eyebrows lifted in question.

"I only came for a bracing drink."

"I'll get—"

He stopped her as she started around him. "You have what I came for." He took her into his arms and with his hands held the back of her head, tipping it to his mouth.

When he raised his lips from hers, it was to say, "Ottar prizes his ivory chess set. When he has to give it to me, he will remember not to let his eyes wander where they shouldn't, or to speak of my wife's 'succulence.' "

Edin found herself vaguely delighted with the jealousy she heard in his voice. But then realized what the bet had been about. He knew. She should say something, but didn't, couldn't. He seemed to wait. Gradually his face changed, and he looked at her as though she'd betrayed him. He said cruelly, "You know you have no other home than this one now."

"Not since you Vikings made a visitation with fire on the home I knew before."

"If you were a man, I would take out *Raunija* and hold a blade discussion with you to settle this dispute."

"But I'm not a man, so you must find another method, Viking."

"Aye, Saxon!"

It was late that afternoon when every pot and tray was finally emptied, every bone gnawed and the marrow sucked, and the Vikings, their ladies and children, their favorites and folk, at last wiped their chins and cleaned their greasy fingers and went home. The jarl was down at the dock seeing the last boat off while Edin stood waving from the look-out point above. The fjord glittered like molten silver in the fading light. It was cool, and she'd worn a new dark-green cloak edged with white fur. As she turned it rustled.

The steadying was crowded with sunset shadows. Arneld was calling the dogs to gather the sheep. The jarl was right; this was her home now. She looked over her shoulder at him. His profile was dark against the fjord which glimmered like elf silver behind him. He was her husband.

Out in the water bided the two dragon ships, the *Blood Wing* and the captured *Surf Dragon*. These were her enemies.

Upon her pillow that moonlit night was yet another fur-wrapped package. "My lord," she said, a little mutinously, for she still remembered he'd forced this marriage on me, "you must stop showering gifts on me or I shall own all your wealth."

"And by your hurry to unwrap that I see you are foolishly unwilling to impoverish me. You're still more Saxon than Norse."

Inside the fur she found such a thing as to take all mutiny from her mind, however, for there were eleven beautifully wrought amber beads.

He took her into his arms with that sense of power and ease he could exude with every movement. "What was that prayer you used to offer up in your Wessex kirks against me?"

Even as she tipped her head back for his kiss, she murmured, "I still offer it. 'Deliver me,' I pray, 'from this Norseman.'"

His lips lowered to hers, and his tongue passed into her mouth and probed profoundly. When he lifted his mouth away, he said smoothly, "I think you lie. Do you want me to let you go just now? If you say yes, I will— I swear it."

She looked up at him helplessly. His eyes were like mothy clouds, with hardly more color than smoke in a sunny noon. He'd made her his wife, a freed woman, yet her body and her heart were still held in bondage to him. "You are a demon, Viking. I wish I could make you my thrall for just one day."

He smiled down at her and laughed softly. "I grant you your wish—but for a night, not a day. Tonight I will be your bed-thrall."

At first she thought to demur, but then the idea caught her. She would take him at his word.

She began to undress him, a thing she'd never done before. He watched her hands unbuckle his sword belt, unbutton his tunic, unwind his leggings, and unlace his trousers. When he was naked, she stood back a step. Slowly she raised her hand, letting it reach toward him almost as though it had its own purpose, its own intent. He stood motionless. Her hand hovered. The sensitive tip of her middle finger touched his

434

upper arm. His muscles clenched. She murmured, both hands now going high to caress his chest and shoulders in one smoothing stroke. "Get onto the bed, thrall, and wait for me there."

He stretched out on the bed to smooth his beard and watch her undress herself. She did so slowly, though she felt a rush of fire through her whole body, something more violent than anything she'd felt before. It was the essence of power replacing the blood in her veins. She couldn't help trembling as she loosed the long and thick rope of her hair which had been wound about her head. His eyes narrowed as she let the heavy waves spread around her.

When she joined him, she unleashed a long-denied desire to touch him at her own pace, to trail her fingers over him languorously, to hold him as she would. She was aware of a certain dominion over him which she'd never used. She used it now, to run her palms over his mighty shoulders, to smooth them over his broad chest, stopping to lightly pinch his flat nipples into tiny points. She lay half over him, reveling in the feel of his hard body beneath her.

"Strands like rays of amber sunlight." He'd taken a piece of her hair between his fingers. "What is your name, Mistress?" In his voice was an amused pretense of meekness. "I've never met such as you before, and I would know who takes me."

"My name is Edin. You will remember me before I'm through with you, thrall." As she spoke, she sat up and tangled her fingers in the short crisp hair of his loins. "Do you like this?" she asked softly.

"Aye." His hands came up, but did no more than bracket her breasts. His touch was like mead. Her hair dangled over his shoulders and amused face. "As you can see, I am ready to serve you."

She looked down. "Well then." She put her hand on him intimately, possessively. All amusement faded from his expression as she leaned above him, inclined into him, and bent her head over him. "Shall I be the dragon now?" she murmured, her lips so close to him she could feel the heat of his flesh. "Shall I?"

Chapter 29

Now the sea birds, the ducks, grouse, puffins, and warblers began to leave for warmer places. All along the fjord, drying racks became familiar sights, where cod was cured for several weeks. The window hole in the bedchamber was covered with a thin hide to keep the new chill out. One night, after loving Edin, Thoryn told her, "I sent Hauk out today to invite a few men to the hall tomorrow."

"Why?" she murmured, almost asleep in his arms.

"There are some matters that need discussing."

She accepted that. He was the jarl; she supposed it must be usual for him to meet with his people.

The men arrived in time for the first meal the next day. There was the normal gossip over the food, but as Edin rose to help clear the tables, Kol Thurik said, "What did you have on your mind, Jarl?"

Edin tried to seem as if she weren't taking much notice, yet when she saw her husband unconsciously take on that stature of heroism and powerful deeds that seemed to make him the kind of man other men were eager to die for, her attention was caught. "I have many things on my mind, friend," he said. "Adventure, danger—"

Herjul the Stout hooted, "Thank the gods!"

"The first thing I have in mind is to build a new ship, the best, most commanding ship ever made in the

North. A *knorr*. And Herjul's son Starkad will be my shipwright."

"Why do we need a new ship, Jarl?" Jamsgar asked.

Starkad's irritation was immediate and waxed as erubescent as his beard. "Are you trying to axe me out of a job, brother?"

"Of course not—but we already have the *Blood Wing* and the *Surf Dragon.*"

"For what I have in mind," Thoryn said, "we will need a third ship, a cargo vessel."

"Where do you want to go, then, to need a full fleet?" Kol prompted.

"Everywhere there is to go, to dare everything there is to dare. I have a yen to see Muslim minarets rising high, to visit cities wherein every exotic vice men know is nurtured. It's said that the orb of the world is riven by many fjords. Well, I propose to visit one far from Dainjerfjord."

Edin stood stricken, her housework forgotten. The men gathered closer around Thoryn. Taking a quick consensus of their faces, Edin saw in each an insatiable wanderlust and felt in herself the sting of panic.

"There are markets in the East that can be spectacularly exploited if I read the thing correctly. Furs are wanted, as well as hides, cables, sea-ivory, and down, and these we possess, or can obtain, in abundance."

"Are you saying we should take to the seas in search of *Miklagardur?*" Leif the Tremendous scoffed. "Bah! Mayhap it's time for Thoyrn Kirkynsson to trim his hair and take his ease."

Ignoring him, Fafnir Danrsson asked, "How do we get there?"

Elaborately casual, Thoryn said, "We need only set a course across the Baltic to the Gulf of Finland. From there, the twisting Neva River will carry our ships forty-three miles through reefs and rapids to Lake Ladoga in north Russia. Some seventy streams feed the lake, but by far the most distinguished is the Volkhov

River, leading south to Lake Ilmen and to the fortified trading market of Novgorod.

"From there, we row. The waterway is too swift and too cramped to maneuver by sail. Farther south, up the River Lovat, we'll arrive at a point where we drag our vessels on logs a short distance overland. Thus we'll reach the source of the great Dnieper River, winding fourteen hundred miles to the Black Sea, along the coast of which we'll make our way to Constantinople— *Miklagardur,* the Great City."

Gasps had been heard through this; faces grew open-mouthed. Edin swayed on her feet.

"The journey will be desperately difficult, make no mistake," he continued calmly, "especially below Kiev, where the Dnieper turns south through granite ravines and a series of brutal cataracts. In the middle are sheer high rocks. The river, dashing against them, causes a loud and terrifying tumult." He scanned the faces watching him so attentively, and added dryly, "Any Norseman afraid of loud noises had best stay behind."

"How do you know all this, Jarl?" asked Magnus Fairhair.

"I met a merchant in Kaupang, a traveler from far places, a man of great inquisitiveness of the doings and dwellings of strange folk in strange lands—a Muslim who had many dinars and dirhims. He told me all this and much more."

Edin felt faint. Her heart was throbbing. Such a journey would take years, mayhap a lifetime.

Thoryn was speaking on: "For some time I've considered the Middle Sea—in the light of glory as well as profit."

And what of his wife, sea-tossed from her homeland to this far coast where she had no one but him? Had she been considered?

"I for one am a man whose heart is that of an explorer—"

"As is mine!" Hrut Beornwoldsson, who had just

439

arrived to visit Sweyn, stepped forward. "I'll go with you, Jarl. I'm fifteen winters now and should be reckoned a full man. I'm sick of staying up at night to help gravid cows drop their calves!"

The older Norsemen hid their smiles at this boy who was wearing his father's outsized war shirt and helmet. But Jamsgar said, "You're just a puppy too witless to keep silent in the presence of your betters."

Hrut's hand fell to is axe haft, and at the same time he surged forward. He was stopped by Magnus and his son Ottar. Thoryn said, "Hrut, you think you are man enough?"

Deflected from his thoughts of challenge, he answered in a voice vibrant with daring and adventure. "I'll prove my valor as soon as I get the chance."

The older men's smiles were not so well hidden now. In fact, Jamsgar was staring with open derision. "The boy thinks because he can get his hand up a thrall-girl's skirt he can get his spear in a pirate's heart."

Hrut's prominent cheekbones flushed angrily. "You mock me, Copper-eye?" Magnus and Ottar renewed their hold on him.

"What? Would I mock Hrut the Juicehead?"

Thoryn said to Jamsgar, "A crime in words is the worst crime. The tongue injures more than a blade." To Hrut he said, "I will be watching you this winter. What I see will influence whether or not I think you are as manly as you say." It was not a promise, but not a rejection either.

Jamsgar would have said more, but Leif shouted, "By Odin, God of the Winds, Rider of the Eight-hoofed Horse, God of Battle—this is crazy! You're getting excited about a tale told by a greasy merchant, whose knowledge of ships probably goes no farther than the price of rope and sails. What have we to do with some Muslim heathen?"

Ottar Magnusson, forgetting Hrut, shouted back, "Mayhap you'd best stay behind then, Leif, with those afraid of loud noises."

The big man flushed and glowered. "What he's pro- posing—" He swung his heavy face back to Thoryn. "You're asking us to become mere traders."

"The man who is a trader has to challenge many perils," Thoryn answered, "sometimes at sea and some- times in alien lands, and nearly always among heathen races."

Rolf, scratching his rusty bearded chin thoughtfully, said, "I've always wondered why the good gods made the world so strange and diverse if it was not to be seen."

Leif adjusted his big paunch like a sackful of apples. "Bah! You talk like boys with moonlight in your eyes."

Thoryn's patience came to an end. "Better than to talk like a droning old man. I am not the sort to tackle an enterprise like this lightly. But to each his own earn- ing of fame. If you choose not to go, I will hold no grudge—but if you try to undermine me in this, Leif, you will see how resolved I am . . . and may find your- self sorry."

By the time the discussion was over, the longhouse was covered with a quilted pearl fog. The visiting Vi- kings went out into it like men disappearing into a magic realm. Edin turned from the heavy carven door, leaving Thoryn to shut it as she made her way quickly to their chamber. There were some things that couldn't be borne in public.

She was not able to grieve alone for long, however, for he soon followed after her. "Edin!" he hissed like a blaze.

She'd thrown herself on the bed and raised her head slowly.

"You're angry! Why? You want me to stop raiding. My only alternative is to become a trader."

She searched the urgent emotion in his eyes. And even as she did so, abruptly he took hold of himself with an almost visible clench of will. The look of self-doubt vanished, and with it vanished her hope. She said quietly, "I think we are doomed, you and I."

He crossed to the bed and caught her in his arms. He felt her belly with his hard hands. "How can you say that, mother of my sons."

She tried to wrench away. "I hate you," she cried. "You're going away—who knows when you'll be back, if ever? I hate you, do you hear me!"

His head reared back. He went stiff and dropped his arms from her. Taking her chance, she slipped away, to the opposite side of the bed, where she sat with her back to him him. She felt him rise off the mattress. A moment passed, another, and another. All at once she turned to him, all her love ready to make itself plain. "Thoryn, I didn't mean—!"

But he was gone.

Thoryn slept poorly. He couldn't forget that his mother was alive and ranting about "something left undone." He should have killed her. The man he'd been before he'd sailed to England last spring, before he'd been captured by his own thrall, would have killed his father's murderess without hesitation. Such a crime demanded revenge. Even if it meant a son raising his sword against his mother. But what would gentle Edin think of him then? If she thought she hated him now, what kind of revulsion would he see in her eyes if she knew he'd killed his own mother? And so the days marched on, and he took no action except to keep Inga in exile.

The autumn passed, and the world took one last deep breath before the dive, and then, as it must, winter came on. Bitter was the wind that for three days came from the south, giving no quarter, scrubbing until the mountain peaks looked near and stark. Clouds came up and were driven eastward. It rained heavily. Then the rainfall turned whitish as snowflakes mingled with it. Soon it was just snow. The wind stilled. There was silence, the intense, frigid silence of the north. The temperature fell, so that the snow couldn't quite dissolve but lay covering the valley like a threadbare, white garment.

The next day a pale grey sky hung overhead; by noon it decayed into flakes and began to fall soundlessly, continuously, that day and the next and the next. The pines showed black on the mountainsides; the snow rounded over and built up; a reflected brightness came from it, a milky gleam.

Edin, a southernwoman and unused to such weather, seemed apprehensive. It was Thoryn's instinct to comfort her, but the chill outside the longhouse was no fiercer than that inside. For a sennight he forbore to touch her—then he woke from a pleasant dream one night to find it was no dream, that he really was caressing her, and she, in her sleep, was responding.

"Shieldmaiden," he murmured. She woke and rose into his arms in the dark, mutely, passionately. He saw that she'd been waiting for him to take her, that she wanted him to open her and move into her and make her cry out.

And yet in the morning he took the precaution to reinstate the winter between them. He was not a man to take unnecessary risks. Though he'd married her to assure himself of the happiness of her, that summery shore seemed far away now, a mere line, a thin lavender bruise dividing the water and the air of his life.

The snow became a nuisance. Trails had to be shoveled, and the shoveled snow formed frozen barriers creating snow-halls so narrow that people had to walk in single file, and if you encountered any one. . . .

Every pillar and post wore its white cap. The heights lay suffocated. Thoryn's sworn-men grew red and lusty. They donned gay-colored winter caps to shovel the longhouse roof or to drag logs down from the forest in sleds. Their blue eyes shone in the snowlight like ice.

The nights became intensely cold. The thralls lay

quietly in their beds. In Thoryn's bedchamber, soft jerking movements began to pulse in Edin's belly. She had yet to speak one word of the child to him. Though he willfully placed his hand over her swelling abdomen, he felt as outcast as Inga did from her rightful place; he felt as forcibly removed as Edin did from her Fair Hope; he felt the exile's choking ardor for *home*.

It was clear to him that though Edin persisted in her silence, the baby was overwhelmingly important to her. She often stopped as she walked, to check her body's feel of it, and only when reassured, walked on. That kept his hope alive, even if her internal absorption made him feel further excluded. He wondered what was going on within her, how it felt to have a living being in her belly. Was she frightened? He felt curiously ignorant and innocent — and shut out. But surely when the babe was born, before he had to leave her. . . .

His notice of her now was more intense than ever. He saw how she began to chide his men — men whose lives were fraught with incident and exploit, who drained each day like a cup to its dregs — how she gently scolded them to curb their voices and leave certain coarse words out of their talk, and to treat the thralls better. "After all, Rolf Kali, you are so strong, I would think you'd have no need to taunt someone as unoffending and defenseless as poor Snorri. The more superior the man, the less need he has to wound those lower than him." Her eyes, which were very green, stayed on Rolf a little longer before she gave him a smile. And amazingly that subtle flattery worked: Rolf stopped.

When the pelts came into their prime, Thoryn encouraged every man along the fjord to harvest as many as he could for the coming journey. They went out on their long skis, taking with them sledges which they brought back bale-heaped and full of gorgeousness.

He also reminded them in their outings to keep a lookout for an oak tree tall and straight enough to become the keel of the new ship. The keel had to be carved from one piece of wood, and the size of the *knorr* would depend on the size of the oak available.

Hrut Beornwoldsson came one day along the narrow, high-walled paths of snow to the door of the longhouse. With ice on his shoulders and frost on his eyelids and his face all chapped and blue, he claimed, "Jarl, I've found the perfect tree for your longship."

Thoryn gave the boy a hard-boiled stare. "I'll have to have a look at it."

Edin had looked pale lately, and it occurred to him as he went for his heaviest fur cloak that she might like a day in the open air. When he invited her, however, she said stingingly, "I won't have anything to do with the making of that ship."

Frustrated, he said, "Woman, get yourself a warm cloak and mittens. You're coming!" In the back of his mind was the idea that if he could get her involved somehow, she would learn to resign herself, as a good Norse wife should.

She sat unspeaking beside him as they traveled in a sleigh, an elaborately chiseled box with an undercarriage fitted with wooden runners. Beside them rode Fafnir Danrsson and Hauk Haakonsson. Hrut proudly led the way on his skis. The brothers, Jamsgar and Starkad, skied along behind.

The tree was gigantic all right, an oak eighty feet tall. Thoryn stood peering up at it. Starkad did the same, utterly absorbed. Thoryn at last nodded to Hrut. "I think you've just earned your oar to *Miklagardur.*"

The boy's red face twisted into an expression of huge pride. Edin sat looking straight ahead.

The keel tree was felled and brought home two days later. Thoryn's private army was then sent out to find other trees for the planking of the new ship. Then the men were sent out to find naturally formed oak and spruce elbows and arches for the vessel's ribs and struts. In the longhouse, they turned spruce roots into strong, naturally fibrous ropes to bind the ship's shell and frame together. Eric No-breeches was set to fashioning kegs full of metal rivets and nails, while other men handcarved wooden pegs called tree-nails, and made walrus-hide thongs.

Mists, half snow, enclosed the longhouse as the men carved or twisted lengths of rope around the evening fire. They told tales in which axes danced and sword metal pealed and blood ran free. Names for the new ship began to be proposed: *Deer of the Surf, Stallion of the Gull's Track, Lynx of the Waves, Sea Dragon's Sleigh.*

Edin's belly grew high and round, and her beauty bloomed. Thoryn occasionally chafed at her obstinacy in refusing to accept what had to be accepted.

One morning, he stopped to observe an unusual sight: Jamsgar and the auburn-headed thrall boy, Arneld, with their heads bent so near they were all but touching. Edin was close by, watching what they were doing. The Copper-eye was smoothing down one side of a horse's haunch-bone, making a pair of *isleggr,* ice skates. Arneld saw Thoryn and held up a bone which had already been shaped. His excitement was bursting. "For me, master!"

Jamsgar didn't look up. He cut the remaining bone to the size of the boy's foot and attached thongs at the heel and toe. When he was done, all he said was a bluff "There!"

As the boy ran out to try them, Edin placed her hand on the Copper-eye's shoulder. Thoryn experienced a lance of hot jealousy. His heart hammered, and his arms went weak with rage—until he heard her words: "That was very kind, Jamsgar. Thank you."

"Huh! Well, he's a good enough puppy."

Thoryn stood amazed. He'd seen Jamsgar Copper-eye cuff a thrall across the head and send him flying for no reason except the man mayhap had not called him master. What manner of woman was this Saxon wife of his that she could tame men born to live briefly and die violently with words like "kind," and "thank you." And "please"?

Most of the men went out skating that afternoon. Edin pronounced a half-holiday for all the thralls. Thoryn had never heard of such a thing being done before, but the thralls didn't question it. They eagerly followed the Norsemen out to their rink, spreading the word of their good luck to their fellows as they went.

It occurred to Thoryn that Edin was proving an excellent housekeeper. The meals were tastier, there was a sense of quiet order in the hall, and yet the thralls seemed less weary and worn. Indeed, there was more laughter all around.

He suddenly had an urge to take advantage of this opportunity to have an hour alone with his wife, to mayhap coax her to their bedchamber. Her ungainly shape hardly made her less appealing to him, and the thought of taking her in the middle of the day, in the light again, ignited a fire in his loins he'd nearly forgotten.

His raid was not carefully planned; he simply crossed the hall and caught her hand.

"What is it?" she asked.

"Come and see."

She was letting him lead her. "Where?"

"To our chamber."

She pulled back, giving him a look. He gave her a look in return, and when he tugged her hand again, she followed.

He shut the door behind them and lifted her and swung her onto the bed. She laughed—laughed! after so many sennights of sobriety!—and fell back. "My lord, anyone could come back at anytime."

"Aye, but if they have a pebble of sense, they'll stay away from this door." He joined her on the bed, prepared to take full advantage of this mood she was in, to kiss and toy the entire afternoon away if possible. He unpinned the brooches holding her gown and pushed it down off her breasts. They were very full now. He could bury his face between them. He suckled one and then the other while she held his head and made little sounds and arched her back to better offer herself.

"Mistress!" The call, though muffled by the door, was unmistakable. "Mistress, I beg your help!"

Edin started to rise. Thoryn pressed her back down. "I'll see who it is."

It was the thrall she'd chosen to raise to a position of stewardship over the field workers in place of Blackhair. Yngvarr was his name. He told Thoryn a frantic tale of an infant daughter who was sick and hadn't eaten for two days. Edin came out before the man was finished, her gown properly fastened, her look properly cooled. The man's eyes immediately veered from Thoryn to her. "Mistress—"

"Yes, I heard."

Thoryn felt left out again, by his own thrall, who obviously preferred to take his troubles to his mistress!

". . . come and cheer her with one of your songs?" Yngvarr was saying.

"Of course, if it will help. I'll get my cloak."

Thoryn followed her back into their chamber. "The child may pass the sickness to you, Edin. You have another child to think of."

She said, "What choice do I have?"

He blocked her way out the door.

She stood facing him, her cloak over her shoulders. "Yngvarr and his wife were kind to me once. Is it the Norse way to repay deeds with neglect?" Her green eyes met his with a shrewd fire. He knew he was being manipulated; he knew that she understood his desire to see her become more Norse in her outlook.

In the end he insisted on accompanying her. It wasn't far to Yngvarr's cottage, and the snow was hard now and provided footing; but once in a while a man broke through the crust, and scrambling out and regaining the surface took great effort. Thoryn led the way, obdurate about at least furnishing a safe path for her.

She greeted Yngvarr's wife, Ingunn, as if they were friends, not mistress and thrall. And she took up the fretful child without a qualm and began to sing softly. Her voice had its usual effect.

Thoryn resisted it enough to motion Yngvarr outside to have the story of his "kindness" to Edin. He'd been told that she'd been overworked, and he'd seen the calluses on her hands. What struck him was Yngvarr's impression of her: a woman able to rise above all degradation. It was clear that the thrall saw her as a heroine, as brave as any warrior.

When the women came out, Ingunn said, "Master, my little one smiled—and even ate a spoon of porridge for your goodwife."

Thoryn eyed Edin and said, "Aye, she has a way with her that neither babes nor Norsemen can seem to stand against."

By the Yule season, the days were very brief and often grey. The mornings didn't lighten until late, and it was night again by mid-afternoon. Ottar Magnusson gracefully gave up his ivory chess set in front of all, but still no word of the coming child passed Edin's lips.

The year was inevitably taken from its loom and folded away on the pile of other years. The new ship proceeded. Starkad, though young, was proving his worth in deploying men. The *knorr*'s plan was in his head, and as it was built he gauged each piece by his eye. A frame had been set up in the shipyard, and the great keel fashioned. Starkad brilliantly bowed it amidships so that, if need be, it could be wheeled about virtually on its axis. Construction went on in some form daily. During bad weather there was the indoor work of making sixteen pairs of long, slim-bladed oars cut in graduated lengths so that the rowers' strokes would hit the water simultaneously whether they sat in the relatively high bow or lower amidships. The task of carving the curved, monster-jawed prow and identically curved and fiendish tail was entrusted to Fafnir Danrsson's skill. The hall smelled always of resin.

Edin continued to side-step anything to do with the ship. Especially she avoided the corner of the hall wherein Fafnir did his carving.

Meanwhile more names were put forth: *Crane, Bison, Reindeer, Long Serpent*.

No man, drunk or steady, right-about of backward-on, could say that it was anything but a wolf's winter. Snow filled the bowl of the valley. The hint of night never seemed to leave the sky. Great piles of precious furs grew in the outbuildings, however, beaver and sable past counting, bales of ermine so large it was impossible to tell how many furs they contained, shiny Siberian squirrel, ruby-colored fox, dark lynx skins scattered with yellow.

Feeling helpless to make Edin happy, Thoryn's mind centered on the *knorr*. It was going to be the most beautiful ship ever conceived, a means of transport, a way of life, something to love—and to fear. Fascinated, he watched it take shape from the keel upward. Once the carved stempost and sternpost were in place, the body began to swell gracefully with the first overlapping strakes riveted together and caulked with tarred animal hair. Just as this planking got under way, however, Starkad and Jamsgar were called to their father's steadying. Herjul was ill; his death seemed imminent. A day passed, then two. No word of the older Norseman's death came, nor any sign of the man's sons. Thoryn, impatient, ordered the planking tó proceed. After all, it seemed a simple enough process, and he was eager to see the ship take on her skin.

The workmen sought to do their best in the shipwright's absence. They even thought to make the ship stronger by cutting the planks a bit thicker than the first ones Starkad had ordered.

Edin meanwhile finished swelling. The babe huddled in her womb, ready to be born. Winter was throwing a last fit the night she woke Thoryn to say, "My lord, do you think Hagna can make it thought such a storm?"

"What is it?" he asked, awake yet not immediately clear in his thoughts. Automatically his hand went to her belly, which at that moment hardened and bunched alarmingly beneath his palm. Edin gasped, hit with the pain. Her face contorted as she endured it. In an instant his heart was full of large love. "Shieldmaiden."

He sent Ottar for the midwife, then came back to lay with Edin, hold her, and murmur encouragement through the hours it took for Hagna's cottage to be reached and the old woman routed out and brought back by sled. Then Thoryn in turn was routed out of his bed, out of his very chamber. "Here, leave off fondling that poor woman and dress yourself, Jarl! By the Thunder God's red beard, your wife has work to do—and surely you have ale to drink? And, please, Freya, if the babe's a girl, don't let her have her father's huge hands and nose and ears!"

Hagna had arrived.

Chapter 30

Thoryn built up the fire before his high-seat, but he couldn't sit still there, couldn't find rest anywhere. He felt as if he were being towed by a harpooned whale. Edin was fighting a battle, a woman's battle, which had often been known to be mortal.

It gave him pause to consider that seldom did men do battle alone as women did. The courage of it, to face sure pain and possible death without so much as a shield or sword, without axe or helmet. He thought humbly that the strong quality to stand fast in the face of hardship and danger was his only at great moments, while for Edin it had become a part of daily life.

Rolf got up to keep him company. And soon Dessa and Olga joined them. Then Fafnir, Hauk, and Sweyn. They listened to the sound of Hagna's muffled voice, which was by turns comforting and frightening. When Edin's labor pangs finally grew to the point of causing her to cry out — in her native language, to her own god — the block-jawed warriors stood facing the chamber door shoulder to shoulder, motionless as statues.

The hour of dawn approached. The wind began to lose its power. Thoryn went to the heavily carved outer door and cracked it open to see that, aye, the clouds were spent; the wild weather was stilled. Nothing moved within the range of his eyes. The land was dead and white in the intense pre-dawn. Winterkill was everywhere. But then a vague glow showed over the ridgetops, then grew, and just as the night broke to a sparkling sunrise, he heard the squawl of his first-born.

The babe was a boy, still glistening with the fluids of his mother's womb when Thoryn broke into the bedchamber. Thoryn didn't know what to think. He was helplessly silent, trembling; his entire body seemed weak. Seeing his expression, Edin smiled, wearily to be sure, yet the sight of her was like something remembered from a paradise he'd visited ages ago. "You look as if you've been on an all-night revel, my lord."

He inhaled mightily. This woman, who had lived through all catastrophe and fear and loneliness, who had lately been wrung like a skein of wool by birth pains, still she had courage in her eyes — and a tart barb on the tip of her tongue!

"Look at him! A more vain father would be hard to find. You're as big a goose as they make them, Jarl," Hagna said, giving Edin the child, now cleaned and swaddled. Thoryn watched her smile down at her son and kiss the amazingly tiny hands. After a moment, he said, "Let me see him." She didn't move, and when he reached for the small bundle, it hurt him to see how reluctantly she gave it over to him. Still, he was the babe's father.

He took the child to the door, to show those in the hall and say formally, "This is my son. His name will be Bodvar Thorynsson. As my sworn men, I expect you to protect him as you do my wife."

Both parents lay abed late the next day, Edin nursing the child, Thoryn holding them both in his huge embrace and watching them indulgently. The babe fed lustily, with little grunts of pleasure. The softness of his downy fair head against Edin's breast, the tantalizing scent they together exuded, and the feel of their bodies stirring gently in his arms made Thoryn feel as if his cup of happiness was filled to overflowing. For a moment he wondered if his own father had held his mother this way — but then he sliced the thought of Inga in two. These two were all his family now; they were his home. And he felt like a king in cherishing them.

He knew there was a waiting time to be got through after a babe's birth, yet he wanted Edin more than he ever had before. Just watching her walk across the chamber could make his breath leave his body. And when she bared a breast and shaped it in her fine-fingered hand for the child's mouth . . . such an innocent thing, yet it drove him wild with desire. It seemed his manhood never lost its stiffness. He grew testy.

The world seemed to be going through a waiting time as well. The snows melted. The mornings were made up of frozen mud, the afternoons of slippery muck, which helped Thoryn's mood not at all. It was while this cloak of irritation was daily growing heavier that Starkad and Jamsgar returned, their father thankfully recovered. Starkad couldn't wait to get down to the shipyard, muddy paths or no. Once there, however, once he saw that the planking was nearly completed, he stopped and stood quite still.

Thoryn, misinterpreting his silence, stood admiring the sleek, towering *knorr* that stood in the stocks. Jamsgar said obligingly, "Never was there so large and beautiful a ship, Jarl."

Starkad said nothing.

The next morning, Thoryn took another inspection of the masterpiece — and immediately went rigid with a fuming rage. He stormed back to the longhouse, threw back the heavy door, and charged inside. All sound and activity ceased with the sight of him. The words he had to say fell from his lips slowly, one at a time: "The man who ruined my ship will die, and I will reward whoever finds him out for me."

Starkad hesitated — mayhap his mortal life flashed by his eyes in that brief span — but then he spoke up: "I'll tell you who did it, Jarl. I did it myself."

"You!" Fury surged through Thoryn, a wrath like

thunder. Only the barest thread of curiosity kept his hand from his sword. "*Why?*"

"You *lapstraked* her with boards so thick the vessel would be much too ungainly in the water; the whole undertaking would have been a disaster."

"*You* have made it a disaster," Thoryn countered in his quietest voice. Now his hand went to his sword and drew it.

"Jarl, give me a sennight, and I promise you a ship that will skim the very tips of the waves."

Jamsgar appeared at his brother's side, his war axe in his hand. Silence reigned as they faced the man they'd sworn to serve, who now felt ready to kill them both. Thoryn's expression didn't flicker; the sight of his ship as he'd seen her kept passing through his mind, and somehow he felt more violent with every passing second.

Edin burst out of her bedchamber, wearing naught but a thin nightshift and a hastily donned cape. Barefooted, she crossed straight to the brothers and shouldered between them to stand a little before them. Both Norsemen were clearly incensed. They were not much older than she in years, but knew themselves to be much her elder in experience and the ways of the world. Yet she stood straight and slim as a sword before them, snowy of skin, with her amber fair hair gleaming to her fingertips. "What is this about, my lord?"

"Starkad Herjulson, whom I trusted, has gone up and down one side of the *knorr,* cutting deep notches in every plank. And for that he's going to die."

"And Jamsgar as well, I suppose," she said, "considering his honor will insist that he stand by his brother against such a threat."

Thoryn's eyes flicked to the Copper-eye's. "I bear him no ill-will, but if he stands between me and his brother—"

"Did I not hear Starkad ask for a sennight? That seems a small amount of time to allow him. You can always kill the two of them after a sennight. After all, you are the champion, the Hammer of Dainjerfjord. I myself watched you cut down Sweyn, who as I understand was deemed among the deadliest of warriors. If you could fell him, surely these two younger men, who have their prime yet before them, will go down before your *Raunija*. And it will cut as deep seven days from now as today. Their blood—the blood of two valiants who have always served you well and truly—will flow as red—"

"Get back to your bed, woman."

She took a step toward him so that no one but he could see her expression. "Gladly, my lord, if you will come with me." Her face was white, but her green sea-foam eyes were pure invitation.

He knew she wasn't ready to resume their marital life, and he knew with a sweet despair that the craving she was inducing would not for a long while leave him. Yet she was teasing him blatantly. He stepped forward and clutched her waist with his free hand and jerked her toward him.

How slim she was again! How sweet she smelled, all warm and milky!

His anger, in spite of his will, began to melt. Still, he managed to glare at Starkad over her upturned face. "A sennight," he growled. "And if at the end of that time that ship fails to look as I have dreamed it to look . . . do you know the arts of sorcery, Starkad Herjulson? You'd better, for only such as that will save you. It's certain my wife will not do so again."

He thrust *raunija* back into his scabbard, and bent and caught Edin's legs up and lifted her to his chest. He heard the shipwright say just one word—"Sheepdung!"

He himself had something to mutter as he carried his goodwife back to her bed. "You'll be remarked far and wide, Saxon, as the handsomest female to be put on the market."

"You can't sell me now," she said complaisantly, her slender white arms twined about his neck. "You made me marry you, and now you must keep me."

"You can scream that at the top of your lungs. The slave traders won't listen—but it will afford me pleasure to hear it as I walk away with my gold in my hand."

He dropped her on the bed as roughly as he dared—he didn't really want to hurt her—and placed a hand on either side of her as he leaned over her. "I'll tell the slaver all your good points—how you might struggle at first, but your woman's strength is soon exhausted and at last a man can get you on a bed and have all he wants from you. I'll strip you of your gown and show him all your assets, your pretty breasts, the cheeks of your rosy bottom. He'll want to try everything before he buys, of course. And when I leave him with you to do his sampling, I'll tell him that if he keeps his place, the second finish is usually even better than the first—"

"Thoryn! How can you make up such things!"

"I make up nothing. You know naught of the workings of my barbaric world, beloved, and therefore should not take incautious risks."

He left her without another word.

He forbore to walk down the path to the shipyard during the days that followed. He was unable to know for sure that he wouldn't strike down the stiff-bearded Starkad if he were to again gaze upon the ruin of his great ship.

But then Starkad himself summoned him.

Edin, who was on her feet again, wanted to accompany him, but he said, "I forbid you to leave this hall. Do you understand me?"

At the shipyard, he walked down the once-scarred side of the ship. Starkad had painstakingly trimmed the planks down even with the deepest of the notches. Thoryn walked up the other side, which had not been changed since its planking. He came to stand beside the shipwright. Both of them looked at the adjusted side. He said at last, "You've proven your skill with a tool-axe."

There was more to it than that; Thoryn saw the improvement clearly. Before him was a large and sturdy but

457

very light shell, a craft that would flex in the ocean like a slim leaf. The keel could bend up and down now, and the gunwales could twist out of true without damaging the ship. This would enable the hull to bend with the waves and slip through them, making the big ship fast and yet stable. These were matters of life and death.

"Well done, shipwright."

From behind him came a feminine voice, a voice to stab his heart: "His name was foretold at our wedding, my lord. He is Starkard Smoothing Stroke."

Juliana watched Inga surreptitiously. The woman sat outside the hut, staring in the direction of the steadying valley as if she could see the longhouse and all its doings clearly, despite the fact that it was miles away through the forest. Whatever she saw in her twisted mind seemed to have her in a silent rage. She made fists of her hands, digging her fingernails into her palms until they bled. Eventually she looked down and was for a long moment preoccupied by the sight of the blood. Foam flecked her lips.

Juliana vowed that no matter what, she was going back to the longhouse with the next supply bringer. No matter if the master withdrew his promise of a husband — no matter if he had her whipped! — she wasn't going to stay here another sennight.

At last true spring arrived, with a brilliant sun, no breeze, and the ocean murmuring gently in the distance. The cliffs of Dainjerfjord filled with the first birds, chattering and swooping for fish. Great meetings were held upon the high ledges. In those pleasant days, many things that had lain torpid through the winter started to stretch themselves. Edin's mind was one of these.

She knew that her Viking husband was doing everything he could to ignore the fact that no one ever gets everything he wants, or if he does, can never keep it, not for long. For instance, he refused to speak his mother's name, as if by pretending she didn't exist he could forget her. And he was doing his best to ignore the deep sadness within Edin. She couldn't blame him, really. Who, being happy, didn't want to keep his happiness whole?

But her misery surfaced and was clarified one evening. The sun's last gold had ebbed through the budding leaves of the tree on the green and slipped into the forest to sleep till dawn. Thin mist clouds blew, causing the stars to fade and brighten, fade and brighten. In the bedchamber, Thoryn sat with his offspring on his knee, making dreadful faces at the poor babe. He glared and looked at the child angrily — and Bodvar looked back at him as fiercely. Thoryn touseled the babe's downy hair — and Bodvar's tiny hands grabbed his sire's beard and ruffled his mustache. It could have been an hour of homey peace, but then Thoryn said, "Hm! He is brash and eager and has much to learn, but you are raising a future hero here, little mother."

Edin's shell of control then simply burst. Sudden tears flooded her vision. "I want no hero for a son!" She hurried to snatch her child from him. "There is no lack of heroes in this land. I have a hero for a husband, and what good does it do me? As soon as the planting's done, he's off for *Miklagardur!* Life is already brief enough without such a journey to shorten the time we have together. You — !" She sobered and went on in a lower, more passionate voice: "You pretend to love me, and all the while you build your ship, your big beautiful ship, so it can carry you away—" her voice faltered—"away for who knows how long? Mayhap forever."

She felt her heart in her throat like a fist, knocking there quicker and quicker. She clutched her child to her breast as he stood slowly, looking like fury itself. Yet his voice was gruff when he said, "Norse women don't weep for their men. It's not our way. Men travel—sometimes to trade, sometimes to fight—and women stay behind to care for the home. There is no more to the matter than that."

Such a flat and callous denial of all her pain! His eyes were like the sharp reflection of stars shimmering on water. She felt very young, too young to be a wife to such a man.

He went on, "I don't *want* to leave you, you know. But I'm a Norseman. A seafarer. And my people's jarl. You don't want me to raid, so I have proposed another occupation. I don't know what more I can do to satisfy you."

What more could he do? Why, nothing more than to share his life with her, his every day and night, to be always available to her. Why couldn't she have that?

A door seemed to open. A light slowly sifted through the gloom in her thinking. Why *couldn't* she have that? The answer flooded her like sudden sun. A wild, impossible answer — but when had her life not been filled with wild and impossible things?

In an instant her mind accepted it and turned to the problem of how to convince him of its rightness. She looked at him. Fear of a new kind made her sight acute, immediate, as if no distance separated them; each line of him was definite. *I love you, I love you!* her heart shouted. He would never agree. A hand clenched inside her, stopping her breath. He *had* to agree! She had to *make* him agree.

No, a small voice whispered, *he has to believe it is his own notion.*

But she had so little time for so convoluted a method!
Then you must start immediately.

She laid down her babe, very gently, and turned and advanced on her husband, her head dropped to one side. Her anger was gone, replaced by something infinitely more feminine and wily. "You could satisfy me — if you would only look in more than one direction." She went up on her toes to kiss his lips, and went on softly, "I do recall you once told me that you are master here, that your word is law."

He took hold of her waist. "What . . . ?"

But she knew she must not say more. She knew his obstinate nature. Instead, she took his bearded face between her hands. "Lean down, Viking. You are too tall for a small Saxon to kiss well on her tiptoes."

His eyes narrowed. "Why do you look so foxy-faced of a sudden? If you're asking me to give up the sea, woman, to be what I'm not, have a caution, for it will destroy everything we have together."

"I'm not asking you to give up anything. Indeed, that is my point. Give up nothing, Viking, not me, not Bodvar, not even your precious *Miklagardur.*"

He frowned as his hands tightened about her, drawing her close against him. But now she pushed away from him, and as he watched, removed her clothing, a layer at a time, slowly. She reclined on the bed, not even trying to conceal her stiff little pink nipples with her arms. She arched her back, posed like a wanton. "Come to me," she said. "It has been far too long and I need you so."

He stood looking at her, then began to remove his swordbelt. His eyes were mingled frost and fire. Keeping his gaze on her, he put his clothes aside, less slowly than she had. In less than a minute he was beside her, firmly taking her provocative breasts in his hands.

It *had* been a long while, however, and she'd sensed his pent passion. He seemed ready to ravish her, this large and formidable Viking. The knuckles of his hands on her sensitive breasts were covered with scars and cuts; the palms were smooth and bone-hard from hefting death-dealing weapons. He could be a violent spirit, a kind of fury. Her will faltered; her hands went to his chest.

Her momentary misgiving must have shown on her face, for he paused, and then smiled down at her. His fingers, thick and strong, closed around hers and slid her hands from his chest to the back of his neck. "Are you frightened of me again, Shieldmaiden?" he murmured, feeding on her trembling lips. "I know you've had a babe and must be taken tenderly for a while. Hagna drummed

461

as much into my head. Mmm, your breath is so sweet."
His hands went around her, felt the smooth flesh of her
back, then her breasts again. "Look at your white shoulders, burnished and succulent as fruit. And your stomach, all flat again." In another moment she was surging
toward him as his fingers stroked the moisture of the
softest and most intimate part of her.

She'd always loved the anticipation, and he drew it out
until it was the thinnest, tightest thread, until her want
was almost like pain, until she was in an agony of delight.
Even then he went on teasing her desire and spinning out
his own. She called his name until she was one calling
cry. She felt like a Messalina. Wildly, she pulled his head
to hers and kissed him, her eyes closed.

Then suddenly he was over her and nudging himself
into her, hard but not violent. Once buried, he held her
firmly and moved slowly, languorously, like water lapping the hull of a ship. It built, and built, to pure ecstasy,
pure bliss.

Afterward they slept, side by side and face to face.
Please God, she prayed, *let us always sleep so.*

Inga opened her eyes. It was time. She'd been saving
herself, feeling her hatred and bitterness swell within her,
but now, without mistake, her hate was ready. She knew
it, opened her eyes knowing it.

The thrallgirl was cooking their first meal. Her back
was to Inga, who sat up quietly in her pallet bed, lifting
the covers off without a sound. The girl cooked on, stirring a small iron cauldron of smoking porridge, oblivious.

But then she heard something and turned. "Oh! You
startled—"

Inga took three quick steps around her to the firepit
and lifted the iron cauldron from its hook. All the fetters
that had held her back snapped. Smiling hugely, she
swung the cauldron, at the same time giving an awful

462

scream.

The first swing broke the thrall's forearm; her white face went open-mouthed with pain. The second swing caught the side of her head. She fell back, unconscious. Inside Inga was a cyclone. She shielded her eyes, as if from a great light, and swung the cauldron away. It slammed into the wall; porridge splattered everywhere as she turned for the door.

She had nothing to eat all that day, and she had a long way to walk, first through pines and great soars of spruce that stood silently knifing the rainy spring sky, then through a meadow, and finally through ploughed fields ready for planting. The air meanwhile had grown heavy, oppressive, purple. Occasionally she turned and gave a full, strict look behind her, as if she suspected Juliana of getting up off the stamped dirt floor of the hut and following her. But mostly she walked and walked, with nothing to eat. Oddly, though she was hungry, she felt strong, felt she had the strength and energy of ten men.

All this miserable dark day Thoryn had been moody. Something was afoot with his wife, and he didn't understand it. Out on the open sea he could draw meaning from cloud formations, from wind and wave patterns, from ocean currents and ground swells, from sea fogs and the water's color. He could read the movements of the sea birds and certain land birds and the activity of the fish. But he couldn't seem to read his own wife.

The day after he'd resumed their married life, she came down to the shipyard, which she'd done only once before — the time she'd come to make sure he didn't punish Starkad. Suspicious, he left it to the shipwright to show her the *knorr*. And she praised it! "I see it will be a neat, uncluttered ship." Starkad was flattered. Seeing her there with the young man, Thoryn thought that no male lived who could resist the green and moving waters of her eyes. She asked the shipwright questions about every aspect of it, particularly about the little box of a room in the bow that Thoryn would exchange for his bedchamber in the longhouse. "Could you not make it just a bit larger?" she told Starkad. "I would like to think my husband is comfortable while he is away from me. And he will be away so long."

That was two days ago. Tonight, as she fed Bodvar, Thoryn waited in the bed for her. He was even suspicious of her newly aggressive desire for him, the way she turned into his slightest touch with eagerness and drew him into her embrace that was like distilled desire. The way she'd uncovered him this morning and rested her lips against the burning sword his passionate dreams of her had built. His suspicion didn't make him want her less, yet he was rankled to think she was up to some sort of manipulation.

Knowing he was waiting to examine her beauties and make love to her, she seemed purposely to linger and cluck and sing songs to the babe. At last she put him in his cradle, saying just loud enough for Thoryn to hear, "Good night, my gentle Christian son."

She took off her gown and for a moment stood in all her revealed beauty, then blew out the lamp and found her side of the bed. She settled, quiet as embers, and lay with her back to him. For a moment he considered ignoring her. But her sexual pull was so large it conquered him. He moved behind her; his mouth nuzzled the tip of her bare shoulder. "Gentle Christian son?"

"Why not?" she answered. "Why shouldn't I raise him to be Christian, and gentle? As I see it, you'll be gone throughout much of his youth. If Thoryn Kirkynsson says something is to be, there are few men to oppose him — but when he is away, it is his wife's word that will be law. Why shouldn't I teach my son of the Christ child and the Madonna? I'll make him into a man with an open, generous nature, a man imbued with mercy and kindness, a man steady and fair and even-tempered."

"In other words, a man not like his father." He pulled

her onto her back. "You'll not start putting up your crosses in this land, or have my folk praying all the time. Whenever a fold takes the priests to be their law-givers, they get to be so gentle it's almost a shame. Even the men are like women then, fainting off every time you shake an axe at them."

"Have I ever fainted at having an axe shaken at —" She stopped speaking to grab his wandering hands. "I think not, my lord, not after the way you've been grumbling at me."

The words had absolutely the opposite effect she intended — assuming he knew what she intended. He pulled her into the center of the bed, exactly where he preferred her, and his hands went exactly where they wanted.

"*No,*" she said more firmly, brushing him away.

"No?" He reared back. "You say no to me? By Odin the Evil-doer, how soon the wife forgets she was once caught and made a thrall! How soon her face becomes saucy and she forgets! Mayhap a reminder of that is in store."

Chapter 31

Edin struggled in earnest now, trying to keep Thoryn from capturing her wrists. As he caught one, she punched at him with the other hand, hitting the solid meat of his upper arm. He could tell the blow hurt her, much more than it hurt him. And then, in spite of her struggle, he had that wrist anyway and forced both her arms over her head to be held in his left hand.

He felt raw and ferocious. In vain did she resist him as he opened her legs with one of his knees, and opened her further with his free hand.

"You have the manners of an untamed animal!"

"I *am* an untamed animal."

But then, within minutes, she was moving to the urging of his fingers.

He was not content. He tormented her, touching her with one fingertip until she seemed as agitated as he was. She tried to move closer to him, tried to encourage him to give better than the scant touch he was permitting her. He could almost see the flames rising in her, forcing her to writhe, to moan.

"You appear to be excited, my lovely thrall-wife," he muttered, his tongue making a broad upward sweep between her breasts. "Can it mean that you wish to serve me again as you used to?" He ran his tongue around one breast, then the other. "I think I will taste the milk of

466

your kindness. Mayhap it will make me a gentle Christian, too." He sucked her yielding flesh into his avid mouth. She pressed herself up into his lips.

"Ah, what a lovely, obedient thrall, to think only of the service due her master. I would have you at once, but your wriggling is giving me so much satisfaction I think I'll wait a while longer."

His fingertip touched her again, and again. He watched her fruitless struggles, listened to her moans swell into cries. If only his hands could get to her soul as easily!

"Thoryn!"

"Have you suffered enough?" He moved over her, releasing her wrists.

"You're a monster."

"You think I'm treating you badly? Well then, let me wind about you and drink all the bad memories from your body's goblet."

He surged into her. She cried out as she welcomed all she could of him into her, saying, "I am a fool come to her senses; I obey you in all matters, I am your thrall."

He kissed her, and kissed her again. "Edin, you drive me crazy. You make me want to ravish you."

She leaned up, her mouth seeking his. "Ravish me, take me, Viking, never release me!"

The longhall was dark when Inga entered it, darker than the night without, where the low sky was finally giving way. Raindrops, like glass beads, had fastened to her clothes.

As she moved along the endmost table, she was brought to perfect attention several times by this or that sound of Kirkyn's hand-picked warriors moving in their beds. Each time she stood for agonizing minutes, her heart stalled. But then she gathered her shreds of courage about her and dared to move forward again.

Long familiarity guided her to the kitchen area.

Wood smoke hung in the air. She reached for her favorite knife — and found that someone had moved another knife to that easily-reached position. Someone had been reorganizing her tools, her knives, her kitchen! Let that one feel the blade in her heart, then!

The knife she found was thinner bladed than her old favorite. It was not the right one, not *her* knife, which was hilted with ancient walrus-ivory, lustrous black from ages in the deep sea, such as sometimes washed up on the beaches. Well, this one would have to do. With it in her hand, she walked silently over the rushes toward Kirkyn's chamber.

She held back, feeling for a brief sane moment all her desolation and emptiness and terror, then the madness shut down over her once again. The taste of copper filled her mouth. She remembered this all so clearly, this thing she'd dreamed, remembered it as vividly as if she'd actually gone through these motions before.

She slipped the blade between the door and its frame and, slowly, a fraction of an inch at a time, lifted the heavy bar. Then, just as slowly, holding up what she'd raised, she pushed the door open.

The room was dark. She heard something moving. It was Kirkyn, her Kirkyn, surging over the demon. She gazed in dismay — they were coupling! This was not the way it had been in her dream. Heart-frozen, she stole toward them. Her eyes could just make them out, Kirkyn's broad shoulders above the thrall's smaller frame, his hands sliding from her ribs to her breasts. *Oh, beloved, there is no help for you now.* Inga had tried to warn him that she was a witch, but she had her magic cord wrapped all about him. Inga could see that he was struggling to get free, but the more he strained and struggled, the tighter his fetters became. No, there was no help for him now. She'd have to kill him first, as in the dream, so he couldn't help the Saxon.

The heat of their coupling ignited her own passions. She hesitated a moment only, a dim figure in the dark

468

doorway, then stepped forward and raised the knife high over her husband's moving back.

Edin cried out with Thoryn's next thrust, and in that same instant, to the north of the longhouse, platinum forks of lightning leapt from the sky. In the sudden flash, Edin's eyes flew open, and she saw the shadow of an upraised arm holding a knife over Thoryn's shoulder. As the sound of the great electrical crunch boomed, the knife glinted downward. She reacted at a deeper level than mere thought. With strength she had no idea she owned, she rolled, taking Thoryn with her. The knife plunged into the feather mattress a scant inch from her own back.

"Mother!"

Inga began to scream wildly, shattering the deep silence of the sleeping hall. Her hair was white and wild as she pulled the knife back to drive it down again.

Rolf was there suddenly, behind her. He caught her shoulder. In an instant she turned, and her knife sank into his heart.

She laughed, releasing her hold on the knife handle and stepping back. Rolf stood staring at her. Slowly he sank to his knees. Thoryn caught him before he fell forward and eased him to his side.

"Avenge me, brother," Rolf said, and then he was dead.

Inga had flattened herself against the wall. Thoryn scrambled to light a lamp and pull on his trousers. At the door crowded a clutch of unbelieving Vikings. Edin crouched where she was, clutching the bedcovers to her naked breasts, shaking from having witnessed things so alien as murder and madness. She stared from Rolf to Inga, whose chin was flecked with froth. Another thunderbolt broke nearby, and Edin started in the flash of its uncanny white light. Thoryn bent over his friend again as the long roll of thunder sounded.

Inga's eyes were open wider than any sane woman's eyes ought to be. Her hands kept clenching and unclenching. "Thoryn?" she said. Then said his name again, more matter-of-factly, as if only now recognizing him. "How I loved your father. But he never loved me." Her fingers looked like roots knotted in agony as they fretted in her hair, at her mouth, over her breasts. Her face grimaced. "He never cared. Even you loved her more than me."

"Aye," he said in a voice Edin had never heard before, "I did." He took the hilt of the blade in Rolf's chest in his palm, his knuckles growing white around it; then quickly he pulled it out. He stood, paused for no more than a heartbeat, then stepped forward. "Let us finish this matter as it should be finished." And with an underhanded jab, he plunged the knife into his mother's breast.

"I did love Margaret better," he repeated, so that that was the last thing she heard.

Everything about her drooped—her long white hair, her eyelids, her cheeks, her shoulders, her loose gown. As she sank to the floor, an expression of acceptance fell over her face.

On Thoryn's face was no such look.

The sea gulls were crying, and Edin could hear the mumble of the ocean as six fierce-bearded shieldmen carried Rolf's body down to the fjord and laid it aboard the longship *Blood Wing*. In the middle of the ship the Vikings had fashioned a pavilion of four posts covered with fabric beneath which was Rolf's couch. His rusty head was pillowed; his hands rested on his chest. In repose, his scarred face had none of the mindless, fanatical ferocity of the Vikings who had burst into Fair Hope Manor so long ago.

The dead man was given everything to make his afterlife comfortable and honorable: utensils, personal articles, adornments, even food. Women went aboard to place around him different kinds of blossoms and fragrant plants. Men piled resinous wood high over all. Thoryn was last aboard. Yellow-bearded, massive of build, he hoisted the sail with his enormously strong hands and, before he leapt onto the dock, laid on the pyre a gold arm ring.

The sun was sinking. Jamsgar, Starkad, and Ottar, three golden chessmen in their swords, helmets, and battle harness, took up tarry torches which they lit at a fire on the strand. They flung these among the dry wood as the lines holding the longship were cast off. The *Blood Wing* had her anchor aboard, ready to be dropped at the end of Rolf's voyage. The wind of the rising heat ballooned her sail. The sight affected Edin profoundly.

Flames ungulfed the wood, the pavilion, Rolf's body, everything aboard. A breeze began to blow, and the flames grew fiercer. Someone muttered, "Odin has sent a wind to carry him away." The fire raged skyward. The Vikings began to beat their swords and axes upon their shields. The *Blood Wing* sailed blazing toward the savage sea.

She was twenty bowshots away when the red flames leapt the length of her mast and ate up the wool and leather sail; she was thirty bowshots away when the flames licked greedily at the fanged figurehead.

As the burning timbers hissed and sparked into the waters of the fjord, Edin stood with Thoryn. He was dressed in a black sable tunic with his cloak swagged from gilt-silver brooches at his shoulders. His horned helmet was on his head, and Thor's sacred hammer was in his belt. He was the Hammer of Dainjerfjord. Yet he appeared diminished. Some of the aura of largeness was gone out of him.

The dragonship moved on, the fire now ravening down to her waterline. The warrior aboard her was nothing but cinders and ashes, yet the *Blood Wing* still flared like a stupendous furnace. She had seen wars and wounds, hard deeds and death; she seemed to scream, *I was not made for defeat!* Even so, she began to wallow, a welter of fire and smoke and sizzling steam. And at last she slipped below the surface, just as the distant sun slipped from sight. The charred, embering sea dragon swooped down into her true domain with Rolf Kali's corpse in the scales of her wings.

The falls cascaded along the sides of the fjord. The men in their conical helmets, and the women in their finery listened and were silent. Finally someone coughed, mayhap feeling the smoke from the longship hanging bitterly in his throat. That sound seemed to set the others free. For a while there would be nothing worth saying; they knew that well enough, yet they came to Thoryn and said what it was suitable to say, in voices deferentially subdued. Then one by one, they drifted away, until only Thoryn and Edin stood on the dock in the purple dusk.

When it was full dark, she turned to her husband. He was shadow-edged, his beard stroked by the silver of the new-risen moon. He was without sleep, which gave his face an edge of roughened grief. She knew in that moment what he would look like in old age. And she loved him unbearably. She said, "My lord, you have done the duty of friendship. Now you must go inside and eat and rest."

A heavy shudder shook him. The breeze that smelled of ashes and salt lifted his hair. He said at last, "Had I done my duty sooner, my ship-brother would be alive." He stood quite still, like a big cat listening, then went on. "Had I acted as I should have from the beginning, I would have killed my mother when first I learned she was my father's murderess. That heinous crime cried for revenge. But I had a thrall, a gentle creature who wanted me to be a gentler man." He glanced down at her; his eyes looked at her as though from a great distance inside his head. "I was in love with her, and wanted her to love me in return. So I changed myself, I questioned my ways, and ignored my duty. And because of it my friend, who was only trying to serve me as he was sworn to do, will not travel to *Miklagardur* at my side."

Edin saw that he'd worked out what had taken place, and none of it was in his, or her, favor.

"What have you wrought in me, wife? Am I a Norseman anymore? A Norseman doesn't question when he should act. His courage doesn't hesitate to do what must be done."

"Then a Norseman must be more than mortal."

He turned away abruptly. "He must be more than what you would have me be — you who have tried to teach me naught but southern gentleness and Christian passivity and good conscience."

"And love."

"It was love that killed my father and Margaret, and Rolf — and even my mother."

"That was madness and mayhem, not love. The habit of love cuts through confusion and somehow, *somehow*, contrives a way out of every difficulty."

He said scornfully, "Even now trying to teach me, Saxon?"

"He who will not be taught can never learn."

He shrugged dismissively. "I am a barbarian. You surely cannot expect much from me along those lines."

She stiffened herself. "You can be barbaric. I myself have seen such bloody-mindedness in you that I have been appalled. Yet there is strength, determination, and pride among your basic traits. And these are things to build upon. There is hope for you."

"Hope," he said scornfully. "Hope."

There are moments in a man's life when he welcomes folk about him, so that they may comfort him. But there are other moments when he wants no one but himself. Thoryn was such a man come up against such a moment. He stood quite alone for many days after Rolf's

473

fiery funeral. For the first time since he'd become a man, he went without a sword, without any sign that he'd ever been a fighting man.

Mostly he walked the edges of the fjord that late spring, the warm sun beating down on him. He stayed near the water, the same water upon which, in a cockleshell of a longship, he'd often ventured out. He wondered now where he'd ever found the courage. He certainly felt no courage anymore. Rolf's death seemed to have opened a curtain behind which he now saw that he too could die. The knowledge filled him with more fear than he'd ever known.

One afternoon, as he stood looking at his new ship yet in its stocks, Sweyn came down to the shipyard. Thoryn didn't greet him. Sweyn spoke anyway. "Jarl, I ask you to relieve me of my oath I made to you once."

Thoryn still said nothing.

"I've decided to give up the salt life. I'm going to wed the widow Gunnhild and settle down to be a farmer." At the mention of the woman's name, Sweyn's eyes took on a warm carnal light. "What do you think?"

Thoryn answered slowly, "I think you aren't as daft as you've sometimes seemed."

"Aye, well, a man loses his good right arm and it looks to be the end. But the seasons go by, and there is no stopping them; they are wheels on a wagon, always rolling while there is a horse to draw them; they are trees that stretch toward the sky, fall, and rot. They mix with the soil, and new trees rise — and that's how it is."

Thoryn still didn't answer, and eventually Sweyn turned to go. At the foot of the path, he looked back. "I'll tell you something, Jarl, that I've never told another. The courage of your berserker was always but a blade's width away from being stark terror." He shrugged. "But that too is just how it is."

Thoryn's lips parted in surprise. Sweyn started to climb the path. Thoryn called, "One-arm!" Sweyn stopped and looked back at him. "For whatever its value in the world, go to your Gunnhild with Thoryn Kirkyn-sson's blessing."

Sweyn nodded.

That evening, Edin came out from Juliana's cubicle, where the girl lay with her head wrapped and her arm splinted, looking pitifully abused, yet in reality full of chatter over which thrallman she was going to wed. Surprisingly, Laag the stable thrall, was at the top of her choices. More surprising, the man seemed willing enough, if a bit shy.

Edin took her place at the tables. Thoryn's highseat was empty, as it had often been lately. The meal began without him.

Suddenly the heavy oaken door was flung open, and Thoryn stepped down into the hall. The effect was like still water shattering, like the emergence of something that was half beast and half god. He strode to the center of the hall and, looking from face to face, said, "I have been lost in a spell of grief, but now I am back."

Somehow, between the time he'd left their chamber early this morning and this moment, he had settled into his old manner. Edin could hardly follow the change as he went on concisely. "We have lost one of our fleet. The *Blood Wing* is gone forever. It was only right that such a ship should carry our brother Rolf to Vallhöll. But that is in the past. There is the future to be considered now. With the two ships we have, I say we leave this sheltered valley at the roots of the great ice-caps. I say that in two days we set sail for *Miklagardur*."

A cheer went up.

A shiver ran down Edin's spine.

Edin watched the slow birth of the day trailing its mist. Even the tiniest twigs were spangled over with sparkling, shimmering diamonds of dew. Everyone from the steadying was down at the shipyard. Thoryn had brought her with him to the lookout point. He'd positioned her in a proprietary way beside him, and she caught herself drawing closer, as though for safety. He noticed; his hand went around her back and found its natural place there.

Below them the *knorr* lay propped in her stocks. As they watched, Hauk, Jamsgar and Starkad put their shoulders to the tail of the dragon vessel and shoved.

The formidable monster budged. She budged again. And all at once she slithered into the fjord with a splash. She bobbed, seemed to flick her curving tail, then came around to face the strand with her beak. Starkad stood triumphant with her tether in his hand.

The loud gust of admiration rose to the cliff-top. Thoryn raised his hand in salute to his shipwright. He stood regally in his trousers, boots, and a brocade tunic with gold buttons.

Don't leave me!

Edin, looking up at him, felt the sheer strength of her yearning must be enough to gain its demand.

"What's her name?" she asked, and despite her will to remain calm, her voice had a quaver.

He looked down at her, and answered slowly, "She is the *Fair Hope.*"

For a moment Edin was more rapt with the changes she saw in him than with his words. He'd regained himself, and yet was different. Or was it that he seemed unafraid to *be* different? Then, abruptly, she realized what he'd said. "Why?" she whispered, thinking only of the gentle home she'd lost. "I would think you'd want a fierce name, something strong and invincible."

He smiled, a little sadly. "What could be fiercer or more invincible than hope? I have found that it is the only thing a man cannot conquer and his blade cannot kill and his fire cannot burn. There is always hope."

"And love?" she asked timorously.

His gaze wavered, then went out to the fjord. "I am

476

not so sure about love."

Her whole being trembled, yet she knew that now was the time to speak. "I am sure. I . . . I have not said it before, but . . . I love you. I love you unto death, Thoryn Kirkynsson."

His arm around her tightened.

"I love you —" she had to catch her breath in order to go on — "too much to let you go away without me. I have decided . . . I—I have decided to travel with you to *Miklagardur.*"

For a heartbeat, the sun in the heaven seemed to stop. She expected an immediate, firm refusal, and feared even more a slow, considered, reasonable one.

He said, in as dreadfully a reasonable tone as could be, "You are a true shieldmaiden, as brave as any Norseman. You've had courage enough to challenge me again and again, a thing others tread softly about. You stood up to Ragnarr, and Sweyn and Soren Gudbrodsson. All *Vikingar* are to be feared. You stood between my rage and Starkad. You've faced slavery and fear, near-drowning and childbirth, and I who know you best cannot say you've grown one whit less bold. Indeed" — he shook his head a little — "just listen to what you're asking."

Her head was swimming. Was he saying no? It seemed a strange way to come up on it.

A mock-sorrowful look played about his lips. "Not one whit less bold, I'm afraid. So I doubt that a simple matter like a journey across the world should trouble you. If you will travel with me, then you won't find me trying to keep you back.

"Of course, there will be arguments from others." He nodded toward the Vikings still admiring the ship. "But I think I'll just step aside and let the man among them who would bar your way try his best. It will be an interesting thing to watch."

Gladness was dawning in her, and relief, and *hope.* She said, still not quite sure, "Where I go my son goes."

"The babe is the son of a Norseman. He will live a

Norseman's life."

She couldn't believe this. "Who will run the steading?" she asked breathlessly.

"I think Sweyn Elendsson may do that—when I have a moment to ask him. I had best do that soon since we sail on the next dawn."

She went up on tiptoe and threw her arms around him. "I love you!" A brief kiss on his lips, then she was starting down the path.

"Where are you going?" he called after her.

"I have packing to do, Viking!"

That night, Thoryn tore her from her feverish preparations and firmly led her to their chamber. There he gave her a gift, a knife. From its sculptured pommel to the etchings in its blade, it was an extraordinary thing, wrought of tempered steel, bright with gold and silver and set with rubies as blood. When she gripped it in her hands, she felt an adventurous daring. She looked up from it, and her heart throbbed to see the expression on her husband's face.

"You will carry it? Though it be a Norse weapon?"

"I've nothing against weapons, my lord, only against the wanton desire to strike first with them."

He said thoughtfully, "You must still learn to swim."

"You can teach me along our way."

He took her into his arms. "Then let us sail to *Miklagardur*, Saxon. Let us fare out after gold, though mayhap we will give the eagles food, though mayhap we will die in Saracenland. Aye, let us always face the perils of the voyage together—but just now . . . I would hear you say it again."

Her desire became fluid. She knew exactly what he wanted to hear: "I love you, Thoryn Kirkynsson."

He looked like a man unleashed. She almost felt the torrents of dammed feeling flowing from him, a lifetime of withheld emotion. "And I love you, Shieldmaiden,

Song-singer, beloved," he whispered back, and repeated, and repeated. It seemed he couldn't stop whispering it. His eyes shone like Arabic silver. "I have things to say, things I meant to tell you when we were old."

"They won't wait?" she said with a secret smile.

"No." And his lips came down to her ear. She just made out the breath-soft words.

And what her Viking said to her, and what he promised . . . who needs to be told?

Author's Note

In trying to create an illuminated context through which a modern reader might understand the Norse experience, I have included in Edin's Embrace quotes and tales from the Icelandic sagas. Written long after the events they report, these have been for centuries a major documentary source for the history of the Vikings and their age. Snorri Sturluson is one saga writer whose name we know. Other collections were compiled anonymously. The roots of these sagas and mythological and heroic songs go deep into the pre-Norse world of Germanic legend and rank with the finest achievements of medieval literature.